HI-TE[C]
THE WO[R]
A WO[RLD OF]
MAGIC IS RISING

JOHN REDDY: He commits the crime of dreaming—and finds the path that leads beyond his wildest dreams.

KING ARTOS: When the Lord of Camelot becomes Prince of the Streets, will he trade his sword for a semi-automatic?

FAYE: An imaginary friend can be your only real, and only true, friend.

NYM: She's a punk with *real* bad luck—or an elf with *real* bad attitude.

TRASHCAN HARRY: A big-hearted goblin with a broom to push, he has an ax to grind.

BENNETT, SORLI, HOLGER AND SPAE: They're spies, they're rivals, they're deadly—but are they working for the Feds, the corps, the dwarves or the elves?

PAMELA MARTINEZ: Elven magic *must* be stopped—unless she can leverage a controlling interest in the otherworld.

A PRINCE AMONG MEN

ALSO BY ROBERT N. CHARRETTE

Never Deal with a Dragon
Choose Your Enemies Carefully
Find Your Own Truth
Never Trust an Elf

The story begun in
A Prince Among Men
will continue with
A King Beneath the Mountain,
on sale in April 1995 from Warner Aspect

ROBERT N. CHARRETTE

A PRINCE AMONG MEN

WARNER BOOKS

A Time Warner Company

Enjoy lively book discussions online with Compuserve. To become a member of Compuserve call 1-800-848-8199 and ask for the Time Warner Trade Publishing forum. (Current members GO:TWEP.)

WARNER BOOKS EDITION

Aspect is a trademark of Warner Books, Inc.

Cover design by Don Puckey
Cover illustration by Keith Birdsong

Warner Books, Inc.
1271 Avenue of the Americas
New York, NY 10020

 A Time Warner Company

Printed in the United States of America

First Printing: September, 1994

10 9 8 7 6 5 4 3 2 1

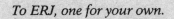

To ERJ, one for your own.

PROLOGUE

The sky was full of heavy gray clouds, a fuzzy blanket making premature twilight of the late afternoon. Al Churdy had been watching those clouds muscle their way to dominance in the sky since sometime around noon. Sky had been clear when he'd set out, but that had been hours and hundreds of klicks ago. He thought about turning on the Toyota's lights. The tint of the windshield made the clouds look darker, more likely to fulfill their promise of rain. Or worse, snow.

Snow would ruin everything. More rain might not be so bad; with what they'd already had there'd be mud. Mud he could deal with. The bike would be a bitch to clean afterward, but she'd get him through. She had before. Dirt runners like him learned how to deal with mud. Came with the territory. No covered tracks for guys like *him*. Yeah, mud he could deal with.

Buzz Tadasuke would hate it, though—and that was something Al could deal with, too. The thought of Tadasuke and his sleek Mitsutomo Serpent all covered in a thick, gloppy coat of Maine mud brought a smile to Al's face. Tadasuke's sponsors could put the latest crotch rocket under the Jap's butt and dress him up like a poster boy, but they couldn't order the mud to stay off him. Old Buzz would have to get dirty just like the lower classes. Al pictured doing a kick spin out of the pits and spraying Tadasuke's whole team with a spray of rich, brown, gluey mud. He grinned wider.

"Better even than making 'em eat my dust," he said aloud.

As if in comment, a small red sports job with a Connecticut plate buzzed past him, doing about one-sixty. Al shook his head. That guy was pushing too hard. No way to run in these mountains, especially with the weather closing in. The higher the road went, the closer to the clouds they got—and that meant the roads would be wet, slick. Al knew how to handle it, but he doubted the sprawl scut behind the wheel understood mountain roads.

Thinking about the road conditions made him think about the bike strapped down in the cargo bed. When he'd pulled out this morning the weather had been fine. Eager to let the world see his beautiful toy, he hadn't covered the Suzuki. Now he looked up at the clouds. They were closer now, shrouding the peaks. He pulled over and got the tarp out of the bin, rooting around until he found enough elastic cords to hold it down. Hiding the Suzuki was a crime. She was just too beautiful, all polished for the race. They didn't make 'em like her anymore. He flipped the tarp over her and tied it down. She'd be dirty soon enough; country rallies meant dirt. But if ya didn't start shiny, ya just didn't have pride.

And pride was all a guy without corp sponsors had to run on.

Satisfied that the cover was secure, he climbed back into the cab. He didn't pull out right away, waiting until the semi laboring up the grade got a good lead on him. He hated not being able to get up to speed at his own pace. When he returned to the road, he was thinking about tomorrow's race.

Tadasuke would be there. So would all the other sponsored riders. No reason for *them* to miss. They didn't have jobs that they had to skip in order to race. They didn't have to cut corners to cadge enough credit to keep their bikes running. They never had to drop out for lack of parts. They had it easy. Maybe that was why it felt so good when ya beat one of them. Not that it happened very often. Home rebuilds were no match for race-built specials with a corp factory's tech behind them.

At least this was an outdoor rally and not one of those indoor extravaganzas. The corp riders always had trouble out in the real world. Not that the course would be real challenging. How could it be? Too much of the States was developed now, especially on the East Coast, even Maine. Office buildings, rezcom fusions, strip malls, tenements, industrial parks, enterprise zones, commerce clusters, enclosed malls, and more office buildings. Plow under the trees and throw up the 'crete. More money in tenants than in farmers. Damn foolish way of living, but the way Yanks did business. They didn't seem comfortable if they couldn't see something they'd built everywhere they looked. Just couldn't leave well enough alone. They'd carved up whole mountains that hadn't done them any harm. Loons. Made a man glad he wasn't American.

Used to be saying you were Canadian separated you from all that. At least it did before the politicians down in Ottawa went off their nuts and signed up in the NACC. Economic necessities, my ass. Too bad the rest of the provinces hadn't the sense of the Québecois, and, God, was that saying something.

Thinking about all that stuff just made him mad. He'd grown up in Toronto before the big sprawl, before they'd dropped the border and the mess had merged with the blight that had been called Detroit. Pictures on the newscasts were all he'd ever seen of that and all he ever wanted to see. Life in Newfie was so much better. A man could breathe, live, out there. If it weren't for racing, he'd never leave the island, but there was racing, and hell, racing was living.

He'd taken a particularly tight corner and was just shifting back up when he saw the walker on the side of the road.

As he got closer, he could see that she had a knapsack slung over one shoulder. It disturbed the lie of her hair as it shifted. And what hair! It shone almost like old bronze and hung down past her waist, the ends twitching in a way that drew attention to the movement of her butt against the rubbed denim of her jeans. Not bad.

He hit the clutch and downshifted, not wanting to pass by too fast. He glanced into the rearview mirror; the road behind was empty as far as he could see. Nobody to make a fuss while he checked out the bird.

What was she doing out here? He hadn't seen any broken-down cars. She was walking at a steady clip, as though she had somewhere to be. Maybe she'd had a fight with her boyfriend and he'd dumped her out here. If so, she wouldn't be in a good mood. On the other hand, she might be interested in showing the putz she didn't need him. This could be an opportunity.

Her head tilted to one side. Checking out what's coming? She put out her thumb.

Oh, yeah. Al slid his foot onto the brakes and nosed the Toyota over. Maybe the trip won't be so bad after all. Gravel grated under the tires as he slowed to a stop. In the side mirror he could see her hurrying forward. She stopped at the door and looked in the window.

Her face was oval, a broad brow tapering to a pointed chin, and her features were sharp, kind of hawkish. Too sharp for Al's taste. Her startlingly clear green eyes were sunken in dark pits that could be exhaustion or makeup. Her face didn't match her body too well; it was too plain to go with those curves. Kind of spoiled the picture. Still, only a real dirtbag would pull out on her now. He leaned over and tugged on the door handle. As the door opened he gave her a smile.

"Need a ride?"

Her pupils widened and the tip of a pink tongue appeared between her lips. She might have been a deer caught in sudden headlamps. Her eyes left him, darting about the cab and, once, down the road the way he'd come. She nodded.

"Well, hop in."

She slid in, moving with a grace that promised all sorts of things under the right circumstances. She snapped the door closed behind her. Tucking her knapsack between her feet, she settled back in the seat and sighed.

"Been walking long?"

She shrugged.

Ooo-kay. Al put the truck in gear and pulled back into the traffic lane. He drove for a while, giving her a chance to get settled in, and waiting to see if she would start the conversation. A thank-you was in order, at the very least. He could think of several ways a hitcher could thank him for a ride, but she seemed to have her mind on other things. She might as well not be in the cab with him. Feeling stupid about driving along with two people in the cab and nothing but road noise for sound, he tried again.

"Not much traffic today." She was watching the side mirror. Leave something behind? "Going to be a lot less soon."

She gave him a sidelong glance, then twisted around in the seat to look out the back window. Al checked the mirror; nothing back there. She settled back, leaning her head against the rest and closing her eyes.

"I meant the weather. When it closes in, ain't too many people gonna be driving along here, you know. Guess you're lucky I came along when I did."

She made a noise that might have been agreement, thanks, or something else entirely.

"Name's Al," he tried.

No reply. She was a real friendly type. With manners like that she must be sprawl spawn. Maybe a direct question.

"What's your name?"

"Nym."

Odd name. Fit her, though. She was an odd girl. Still, now that she'd relaxed a little, her face looked a little less harsh. She was prettier than he had thought at first. He wrote his first impression off as a trick of the light. Maybe there was some hope for a warm bed tonight after all.

The road climbed as the clouds dropped, cutting visibility until Al had to turn on the fog lights. Their beams cut twin cones into the wispy white. The soup grew thicker, and Al slowed. Never a good idea to overpace your visibility.

Further attempts at starting a conversation weren't very successful, but he got the impression she was getting used to him. Her replies stayed little more than single words, but she did seem interested when he started telling her about his racing. That was good. Girls who had an interest in speed were often fast themselves. Unfortunately, the visibility dropped further, and he soon found himself spending too much time concentrating on the road and too little making moves. That was frustrating. Every time he snatched a look at her, he realized that his first impression had been off base. She was much prettier than he first thought.

"Can't you go faster?"

Her question caught him off guard. "Not unless you want to take up flying."

She looked at him, brows furrowed and lips slightly open. One corner of her mouth quirked up and she gave a small laugh. It was brief and hesitant, but it made him want to hear her really laugh.

"We'll be fine," he said.

She flashed that mercurial smile again and turned back to staring out the windshield. The fingers of her right hand danced in an irregular rhythm.

"Be careful," she said.

"Hey, babe. Not to worry. I'm ace on the roads."

No look. No smile. She didn't seem convinced. Ten minutes later he got the chance to prove his skill as a dark shape humped up in the roadway. Al turned the wheel, swerving to the right. Whatever it was moved too, scampering right into their path. Al cut the wheel hard the other way, felt the back of the truck start to fishtail. *Damn!* The bike tugged at its ties, rocking the truck up on its springs. The Toyota threatened to roll. He eased off on the wheel, throwing himself against the door to try to counterbalance the load. The truck settled back into something like control. He fought the skid down, pumping the brakes and bringing them to a stop with front tires in the gravel on the wrong side of the road.

Geez! That was close.

"What the hell was that?"

"Did you hit it?" She sounded eager, as though she wanted him to say he had.

"I don't think so. Didn't feel like it." They'd have felt an impact with something that big. "What do you think it was? Too big for a raccoon."

"I didn't see it very well. A deer, maybe?"

"Not a deer." He'd hit enough of them to know. It hadn't been the right shape.

She shrugged and turned her eyes to the side mirror. "Let's go."

He checked the mirror. Nothing out there but fog. They might have been alone in all of existence, nothing real but them and the truck. On the one hand, that was not too bad an idea. He ran his eyes down her shape. She was tense, frozen like a rabbit surprised by a hound. The tautness of her muscles promised real energy. Her breasts quivered a little with every breath.

"Let's go," she repeated.

The edge in her voice cut him, urging him to action. He put the Toyota into gear, cutting across the road until the fog lamps picked up the road lines. He followed them back to the right side of the highway. Damn, if he'd been thinking with more than his balls he wouldn't have left them sitting in the opposite lane. In this fog . . .

Something big went past them in the other lane, moving the other way. Or maybe they had passed it. That made more sense, since there had been no lights. Only an idiot would be driving without lights in this soup. An idiot who might have rammed into them while they sat worrying about some damn critter they had almost hit. A smart person would be sitting out the fog. That big shape must've been some trucker pulled over to wait out the fog. Had to be.

Didn't it?

He found himself checking the rearview mirror a lot as they crawled along. A ghostly sentinel of a sign drifted into view. Al read it aloud: "Skowhegan. One mile."

"Skowhegan," she repeated.

"Might be a good idea to get off the road." A warm bed sounded real good.

"Off the road."

Her voice seemed detached, as if she wasn't really listening. This was one strange chippie. A guy would have to be a little crazy himself to get involved with her. What was he thinking about? A glance at her boobs reminded him. The way her hair fell over them just accented their round firmness. What the hell; one night wasn't a lifelong commitment. How crazy could she be?

A shock vibrated forward from the rear, accompanied by a muffled thump. The left rear quarter sagged in a familiar way. "Aw, shit," he said. Tire blown. That last skid must have taken off too much rubber, then a sharp pebble, or a nail, and blooey. Damned cheap Malaysian work. So much for saving money. Al nosed the limping truck over to the side of the road. He pulled over as far as he could; no sense making it easy for some bozo to plow into the truck and smear them all over the highway.

"I'll check it out," he said as he reached over and popped open the glove box. He grabbed the flashlight before it rolled into her lap. Not that he wouldn't mind putting something long and hard between those legs. But this wasn't the place to do it. The fog made the Toyota more private than a cheap motel room, but it wouldn't be as comfortable. An airhorn sounded somewhere in the fog, telling Al that there was at least one trucker still traveling the mountain; one too stupid to know better or too far gone on his wide-awakes to think straight. The sudden appearance of a parked pickup might be too much for drug-reduced reflexes to deal with, and Al had no desire to be smeared over the side of the mountain. Later, he promised himself. Even walking, they could make Skowhegan before midnight.

The fog made the night darker than it should be, danker too. Al tugged his jacket closed across his chest to cut out the clammy chill. This weather was enough to dampen anyone's enthusiasm. Gravel crunched under his boots, crackling loudly in the silence. Somewhere down the mountain the airhorn moaned mournfully.

He flashed his light on the wheel. Flat, all right. He crouched down to see how bad, hoping that a patch kit might take care of it. The shredded rubber blew away any thought of repairs. Damn cheap workmanship. A decent tire would have just popped. Blown a sidewall at worst. But no, this thing had to go and disintegrate. The damn thing looked as if a dog had been chewing on it for a year. And the rim was bent, too.

He could leave the truck here and take the bike down into Skowhegan, but that would mean leaving her, since the Suzuki wouldn't ride two. He'd have to pull out the spare. Not the sort of physical effort he'd had in mind. Then he remembered what shape the spare was in; it wouldn't get him a hundred klicks. He'd have to replace it, and it'd be morning before there'd be any shops open in Skowhegan. And morning was a whole night away. But Nym had been so edgy, she might not want to stay. Maybe if he offered to pay for her room at the motel? He could tell her he'd take his own room. Money's no object for the gallant knight of the road. Like hell it wasn't, but she wouldn't know that. Yeah, why not? She'd agree to that plan because it would be better than spending a night like this outside. He could talk her out of it over dinner, talk her into his room. That warm bed was looking better and better. One room he could afford.

He walked around to her side of the cab.

She was gone.

Just great. Just fucking great.

Maybe she just stepped out to take a leak? He called her name and listened to his voice echo hollowly in the fog.

No answer.

Not from her, anyway. Something went skittering off in the brush beyond the guardrail, but it was too small to be a person. Al jumped at the sound, and cursed himself for it. He flashed the light in that direction, but the fog ate the beam. He couldn't see anything but mist. What was he worried about? It was just a rabbit or something.

He was wasting time. There was no point in waiting in the truck. He wasn't gonna get any help out here tonight. Not in this fog.

He turned to the Toyota. Unhooking the tarp, he threw it clear of the Suzuki.

"Come on, baby, at least you still love me," he said aloud as he dropped the back gate and climbed in. Unfastening the tie-downs, he freed the Suzuki. He filled the tank before running out the ramp and rolling her to the roadway. He patted the bike. At least he'd be riding to Skowhegan. She'd have to walk.

Hope you get lost, you ungrateful cow.

He set his helmet on the tank and went to the cab to get his bag. He'd need a change of clothes for the morning, especially after riding around in this soup. As he pulled the bag from behind the seat, someone grabbed him by the collar of his jacket and yanked him backwards into the air.

He landed hard on his rump and skidded a foot or so. He felt the gravel dig into and through his jeans. *Shit!* He looked around for his assailant and found him, a hulking silhouette against the wan light from the interior of the truck's cab.

Where had this gorilla come from? And gorilla seemed a reasonable description; the guy was huge. A dark wool cap made his head look even more pointy than it undoubtedly was, and it looked as if his arms might actually hang past his knees, though Al couldn't see for sure since the gorilla was wearing some kind of heavy overcoat, something like a navy greatcoat that hung almost to the ground. A sailor? They didn't like people messing with their chippies. The guy took a step forward and something clanked under the coat. Weapons?

What have I done to deserve this?

Could this be the boyfriend?

The guy took another step forward, planting his foot in the small patch of light illuminated by Al's dropped flashlight. The foot was bare and broad, with splayed toes tipped in grungy nails. Sailors ain't gone barefoot for more than a century. If this was the boyfriend, the chippie was weirder than he'd thought.

"Now look, sailor. I just gave her a ride, okay? Nothing happened, okay?"

The guy growled. He actually *growled*. Weird. Too weird for Al. He groped for the light. The flash was heavy, useful as a club, and he'd need something against this ape. His hand closed on the barrel. Feeling a little more in control, he scrambled to a crouch. He held the light before him, its beam thrusting up, a forlorn beacon vanishing into the night after only a few feet.

Too bad it wasn't one of those sci-fi laser weapons. You should never have come back, big man. Still, it was weapon enough; Al had done fine with less in bars. He pointed the light at the gorilla, figuring he'd club the guy while he was light-blinded.

The gorilla turned his head away, snarling, but not before Al saw his face. No, *its* face. This was no sailor. This thing was not even human.

Al stood openmouthed in shock.

A paw swept out, hitting his arm and numbing it. The flashlight fell from his grip. The paw closed on his arm, squeezing with bone-crushing strength. A second paw wrapped his shoulder and he was lifted bodily from the ground. When the flashlight hit the ground, it went out. Al hit the ground almost immediately after. He felt something snap, lots of somethings. Pain shot through him, lighting the night with false stars.

The thing bent over him and picked him up again. He might have been a child for all the burden he was to this monster. It shook him and something, something inside him, lanced through his chest. He choked as he flew through the air again. Something hard hit his back, and his face slammed into the gritty surface of the road. He smelled burned rubber.

Shit, he'd never make the race now.

The monster leaned over him, grinning to display yellowed teeth. It might have been Buzz Tadasuke bending over him, but for the foul breath. Couldn't be Buzz; sponsored types always had flower breath. Al tried to spit in his eye, but his mouth was full of something that tasted metallic. Like blood.

No race tomorrow.

No race. No tomorrow.

No . . .

The monster hunched over the body, prodding it with a meaty, taloned finger. It grunted satisfaction. The monster rolled the man over on his back, tilting the head to one side and baring the neck. A deft slash of its claws opened the throat. Blood oozed up. Humming, the monster tugged its cap from its head, thrust the wool into the gore, and kneaded the fabric until it was thoroughly soaked. When the cap was fully impregnated with the man's blood, the monster held it up and croaked, "Be it so."

It stood up, pulling on the cap. For a moment it just stood there, twisting its head back and forth and snuffling. Undecided. Nym made herself very small. The monster shuffled off down the road. Nym waited until it was out of sight.

Then she waited some more.

At last she slipped both her arms into the straps of her knapsack and trotted to the bike. Mounting it, she tapped the instrument panel on. Everything showed ready. She put on the helmet. Kicking the engine to life, she throttled up and roared off.

An hour later, free of the fog, she turned on the headlamp.

Part 1

———

WE COME TO THE CRUX

CHAPTER
1

John tapped in the entry code and mashed his thumb against the recognition plate. Nothing happened, so he wiped the plate with his sleeve and tried again. This time the sensor registered his thumbprint and the mechanism gave its usual annoyed buzz, acknowledging his right to enter. Security could be such a pain.

He could have entered Benjamin Harrison Town Project Rezcom Cluster 3 through the commercial entrance and avoided beeping his own way in, but that would have meant a walk around half the building, a waste of the shortcut up the hill through the park zone. He opened the inner door, waited his habitual half-second, and walked in and across the hall to the elevators. A glance at the mail dispenser showed the light on the Reddy box dark. Either nothing had come today or his mom had already cleaned it out. He hoped that it was the latter. He punched the call button, wishing for the car's instant arrival.

A soft chuffing noise announced the arrival of the lobby's cleaning 'bot. The toaster-sized cart wheeled out of its dark alcove and headed straight for John's muddy footprints. It gurgled happily to itself as it spit out soapy water and buffed the tile back to its original luster. Print by print, it advanced on him. When it was two away, he deliberately made a wall of fresh prints around himself. He hated the way the thing whined and hung around when it ran out of dirt on the floor and could still sense the mud on your shoes. He hoped the elevator would arrive before the 'bot finished with his impromptu defense.

It did.

John escaped the deranged and almost certainly dangerous 'bot with an astonishingly agile leap into the waiting car. He landed in a crouch, then rose on one toe, turning as he did. His jacket spread out around him like a swirling cloak. Without pause, he snapped a single finger out to spear the desired button as it flashed past. He stopped, facing out the transparent outer wall of the car, and dipped his head in acknowledgment of his audience's wild applause for his outstanding athletic prowess.

That was when he realized that he actually did have an audience.

Mister Johnson harrumphed at his performance.

"Hello, Mr. J." Geez, why did it have to be one of their neighbors to catch him cavorting about? Why couldn't it have been one of the billion strangers who shared the rezcom? And why Mr. Johnson, of all people? The old guy was so old that he probably couldn't remember how to *spell* young, let alone *be* it. John hoped his face wasn't too red. A tinkling sound in his ear, which might have been laughter or might have been distant machinery, turned up the heat and ensured that he was glowing enough to give off light.

Mister Johnson's mouth twitched, his usual grumpy hello.

"Nice night," John said, eliciting another twitch. "Or it will be, anyway."

Outside the lights of the city were beginning to wink on, to join the always-lit advertising banners and signs. Off to the east the first stars were showing in the sky, where the glow of the sprawl wasn't drowning them out. At least you could still see stars here in Worcester. Phil said you could really see stars where he came from, but John doubted he'd ever get out to Montana.

Then again, why would he want to? Other than to see the stars, that was? Phil's back-home tales made it really sound boring, aside from the Wild West history and all that Native American stuff, but there wasn't any *real* history. No kingdoms and empires, no armies marching proudly in their steel armor, no pyramids, no parthenons, no musketeers and no legionaries, no crusades—just miserable, coldhearted genocidal campaigns and resource exploitation, embarrassing rather than uplifting. And cows. Phil wouldn't like it if he forgot the cows. Like cows were important to anybody but Phil. Geez, you'd think he was from Vermont.

But even Vermont could seem exotic and far away to a guy who'd spent his whole life in one town. An "old-time safe haven," according to the Mitsutomo Keiretsu prop. John could see it all spread out beneath him as the elevator car rose: the old city, the Worcester Polytech campus, the Benjamin Harrison Project, the southwest hills where the old money still held out against the changes, the rebuilt commerce zone, and the Turnpike slicing through it all on its snaky way between Boston and upstate New York. It might not be an exciting place to live, but it didn't have the problems of, say, the Boston-Warwick corridor or the New York 'burb sprawl. Maybe those places should have had a Mitsutomo Keiretsu to look after them the way Worcester had.

John had scanned some of the old newscasts and seen how a lot of people had been upset to learn that Mitsutomo and its trading partners had bought up most of the land and businesses in the area. The biggest gripe seemed to be that Mitsutomo had done it secretly. But the old Disney Corp had done the same thing down in Florida when they were setting up their empire, and they had *made* the Orlando economy. And it wasn't like Mitsutomo was turning the town into some kind of *daimyo* fief. The prop said they wanted to make Worcester a real American town, and for once the prop hadn't been a lie.

Mitsutomo had a right to be proud of the work they had done in rehabilitating this old steel town. Their idea of "quintessentially American" was a little odd at times, but what could you expect from foreigners? Important thing was that they did something while the native governments sat and twiddled their thumbs. They had kept Worcester and much of western Massachusetts from tumbling into slum sprawl and urban blight zones like most of the East Coast cities. The old town might be a little kitschy for the mainstream these days, but old-fashioned didn't necessarily mean unfashionable. And what was wrong with old-fashioned, anyway?

Nothing, a little voice said.

John could only nod in agreement; some of the best things in life were old-fashioned.

He bolted the elevator before the doors were fully open and was around the corner before old Mr. Johnson was out of the car. He took the turn, and it was a race down the corridor. He lost, but he did reach the door to the apartment he shared with his mother before Mr. J made the corner. He popped his card and slapped the plate, tapping toe beating a nervous rhythm while he chanted, "Come on, come on, come on." The door finally recognized him and he bounced through just as Mr. J turned into the corridor.

Safe.

Of course, John. No threat.

So what? Speed and quickness. Dash and style. Ever ready, never lost.

Pointless platitudes.

He shrugged.

When he stepped out of the foyer, the first thing he noticed, as always, was the vid wall. *Happy Lifestyles* was running in timeshift. Perish any thought of Mom missing that mainline straightline. How would she know how to decorate the apt? Marianne Reddy wouldn't be happy unless her place was the way it should be. Nothing else would satisfy.

His mom was planted on the couch, taking in the latest and most proper corporate style. She had a half-dozen subscreens running through catalogs, looking for matches to the furnishings shown on the main screen. A seventh subscreen was running an interior design program on which their apartment plan hung, halfway through a metamorphosis into something like the one in the main screen, and she was absorbed inputting commands into the remote on her lap.

He popped into the kitchen and dug out some Cheez Snax™. On his way to the perscomp, he asked, "Any mail?"

"Yes, dear." She waved hello, but continued to give her attention to her program. "The confirm on your scholarship came today. Isn't that nice?"

"Wonderful."

"I was getting worried."

"No need to frown down. You know the corp's good for it." Mitsutomo's paternalistic compensation programs covered the education of corporate dependents. No problem. "I meant was there any mail for me?"

"In the file, Johnny."

It might be. It might be. There'd been barely enough time for his application to get through all the hoops it would have to go through. Barely. Slipping into the seat in front of the console, John tapped in his code. He shunted to the mail box and popped up the "in" box. There was only one entry. The com code burned a deadly disappointing green, and the ID code told him it was a notice from Dr. Block, his least favorite person in the world.

Shit.

His mother looked up, and he knew he'd said *that* aloud.

"Now, Johnny, it's just a checkup."

Block was a psychiatrist, not a physician. John was tired of the blockhead's probes. The bastard was always trying to trip John up, trying to get him to admit that he was still talking to Faye. Years of counseling had cured him, though, cured him of letting on to Block that Faye was real. Everything went so much smoother when he had Block believing that *he* believed that Faye was just another invisible childhood friend, the same as other kids had. Block liked to believe Faye was a psychological crutch, a manifestation of a troubled reaction to the death of John's father; such an answer made the blockhead happy, and John liked it better when Block was happy. The bastard left him alone then. "I don't need to see Dr. Block."

"Dr. Bloch is only interested in seeing that you're doing well."

Seeing that the blockhead's record stayed clean, more like. Unresolved cases didn't look good when you were up for promotion. But bringing that up would only unsettle Mom. She took Block's pronouncements for truth, 'scuse me, Truth. He was a psychiatrist, after all. "Block's only interested in drawing his checks."

"Now, Johnny."

"It's okay, Mom. I'll go."

Immediately, she looked relieved. She'd never believed in Faye, and was always nice to him after the blockhead's reports that said John's progression was satisfactory. If only she knew the truth. She was all corporate conformity, and the whole mainline straightline was just extruded plastic trash to him, so they butted heads often enough, but he knew she meant well, that she really loved him. She had to. Otherwise she'd never put up with him. But love, they said, was blind, though they usually didn't mean this context. And blind she was where Faye was concerned. Right?

Right.

But while love might be blind, it wasn't necessarily stupid. "Shall I make you an appointment?"

"I can take care of it."

"Now, Johnny. You know how you forget sometimes to do things you're supposed to."

Believe it.

"You'll be running off to the museum or working on your homework and the next thing, Dr. Bloch will be calling back, wondering what happened to you. Missing psych evaluations won't look good on your record."

And having them would? Logic jar, there. "I'll do it now if you want to watch."

"Now, Johnny. You know I trust you."

Uh-huh. Which is why you nag. John sighed. When the corporation paid for you, they expected you to fit *their* image of what you should be. It was easier to pretend to go along. You had to fit into the corporate image and lifestyle if you wanted to have any privacy at all, and John had long ago found that he liked his privacy. He'd deal with Block. Maybe this would be the last time.

Go along.

Yeah, that was the best thing. He keyed the respond menu and selected *make appointment*. He took an opening between his Heroic Literature seminar and fencing practice. He'd have just enough time to shuttle into the med center and back, if the trolley line was running on time. And if it wasn't, Coach would just have to understand. Medical, you know. Healthy mind in a healthy body, you know.

"I'll go Tuesday."

His mom smiled her well-satisfied smile and returned to her redecorating, leaving him to get on with his life.

"I might have known."

John looked up from his reader. Yael Haasmann's voice had sounded annoyed, but he had a stupid smirk on his face.

"Hey, Mom, call security. We've got a burglar."

Not really. Just an obnoxious fiend.

Friend, John corrected. Obnoxious friend.

Whatever.

In any case, there was no response from the other room. Yael stuck his hand under his jacket and pulled it out again, thumb pointing up and index finger extended. A maniacal look on his face, he pointed at John. "Too late, drone. She let me in. There's no one to save you now. One more twitch and you're vapor."

John put down the reader but declined to raise his hands. "It's 'there's no hope for you now.' "

The pretend blaster dissolved as Yael shrugged. "With all the times I'd seen the vid, you'd think I could get the lines right. I mean, *Stellar Wars, the Final Generation* is, like, the formative vid of our generation."

"Keep working on it." He waved a hand. "Grab some space."

Yael snatched a stack of reports, disks, and magazines from the desk chair and deposited it on the foot of John's bed. The pile dissolved into an avalanche that buried John's stocking feet. Promising himself he would put all that stuff away where it belonged, he pulled his feet free and sat up straighter.

"What brings you to this part of the galaxy, stranger?"

"I missed Zalinger's class today."

"So I noticed. Oversleep?"

"In a manner of speaking." Yael grinned wickedly. "But ask no more, for I will sully no lady's reputation."

"That's a new attitude."

"Simple practicality. I'm always discreet when it's useful."

"You've got a new line, anyway."

"Like it? I thought you would. Sounds like something you'd come up with. If you ever had to, of course."

"We were talking about your love life, not mine. She anyone I know?"

"Only in your dreams."

"Let's leave my dreams out of it."

"Okay. But I do need the reading assignment."

"Next three chapters. So, who is she?"

"I'm not telling. Three chapters! Doesn't Zalinger know we have lives outside his class?"

"I don't think he believes there is life outside his class. Not intelligent life, anyway. Her name, freund?"

"When you meet her. If you meet her. But I will tell you that *she* knows there's life outside the classroom."

"I'll bet."

"You'll win." Yael waggled his eyebrows and grinned foolishly. "Hey, just got the word. Zephyr Scream is gonna be playing down at the student center. We can drop over there after practice Tuesday night and catch the second set. And maybe, just maybe, you'll meet the elusive mystery woman."

"Who's Zephyr Scream?"

"Who's Zephyr Scream!" Yael smote his brow with broad theatricality. "They were right, you *must* be from another planet. No, wait. I know! Your brain has rotted from too many books. But don't worry, I'll save you from intellectual despair and share with you my secret knowledge of Earth's darkest secrets. Zephyr Scream is nothing less than the hottest buzz-rock band this side of Boston. When they play, it's like communing with the infinite. They pump, man."

"Sonic shock." John tapped the side of his head with a long, slender finger. "Cuts out all the higher functions of the mind."

"At least it's music." Yael pointedly looked at John's autographed Bard Taliesin poster and held his nose. "They don't do that retro downer stuff you listen to. This crew is alive. Crest of the wave."

"Last month you said those neomonowave shriekers were the crest."

"Yeah. Too true. But that was last month. World's a happening place, happening all the time. Not frozen like these books of yours." Yael kicked a dog-eared copy of *The Two Towers,* sending it sliding under the desk. The book connected with a pile of papers and disks, which promptly collapsed upon it and buried it. The shifting debris plowed into the table leg, the shock setting a Lego castle tower to teetering. The toy castle rocked, almost overbalancing before settling back to sit firmly again on the desktop. John shook his head. A little bit harder and it would have gone over, and no one would have been able to do anything about it. The old plastic was too brittle to survive the fall.

Barbarian.

Not really. Just ignorant of the finer things of life. Books, even secondhand ones, weren't cheap anymore. And the castle—they just didn't make *those* anymore. At least it hadn't been part of the Robin Hood set; *that* was truly irreplaceable. Still, friend or not, the incident couldn't pass unremarked.

"Watch the merchandise," John said with a growl. "Men have died for less than that."

Yael started as though John had made a real threat. "Hey, easy, freund. Nothing happened."

No thanks to him.

John chuckled. No, not to *him.*

"That tower is built from a prerecall, first pressing of the 1995 Earl's Keep set. My mom got it for me two years ago. It took her months of scouring the antique shops."

"Hey, like I'm sorry. Okay?" Yael's apology sounded only half sincere. "Look, I, uh, gotta go. Thanks for the assignment. See ya in class."

"Yeah. See ya."

John heard his mother saying good-bye as Yael let himself out. He should have been polite and seen Yael to the door, but he didn't feel very polite. Yael was difficult to get along with, and this latest interruption had almost cost John one of his favorite pieces. The guy could have phoned. John fished *The Two Towers* out from under the desk. Yael had no respect for anything important. Abandoning the homework assignment in his reader, John settled back on his bed and opened the book.

The Orcs were closing in on Frodo.

CHAPTER 2

Charley Gordon sat on the railing and watched the crime scene crew do their work. The body hadn't been in very good shape when Charley found it. No surprise there; the death had been violent, and the victim had lost a lot of blood. Up here in the mountains there still were wild animals to be drawn to the smell of blood. Scavengers, he told himself. He shivered a little and blamed it on the morning chill. What the wild animals had done was no worse than what rats did, he supposed. But you expected things like that in the city. Out here things were supposed to be cleaner, nicer.

Manuel Salazar was a good partner; he brought an extra cup of coffee when he came to sit next to Charley. Manny's badge wallet was tucked into his parka's chest pocket. The parka was civilian but the badge vouched for Manny's right to be here, even if you didn't notice the uniform under the coat. Charley didn't have either badge or uniform, since he wasn't here officially, at least not in the usual way. He was here as a witness, the finder of the corpse. He was supposed to be on vacation; he was supposed to have left all of this kind of shit in the Sprawl.

He took a pull from the steaming cup. The coffee wasn't as hot as it looked; most of the steam was air-temp differential. It'd be too cold to drink soon. Which might not be so bad; this swill was near as bad as Sergeant Kowalski's squad-room acid.

"Ranger says no bears this time of year," Manny said.

"Wasn't a bear."

"Forensics say so?"

"No."

"Then how do you know?"

Poor Manny. Nothing was real till some authority confirmed it for him. "Ranger's right about the time of year. Besides, that's not a bear kill."

"Come on, Charley. The poor bastard's been knocked to shit, slit up, and bloody half eaten."

True as far as it went. "Bears don't ride motorcycles away from crime scenes."

Manny was unimpressed. "Any tramp could have done that. He comes along, sees the thing. A free bike. Nobody around here to complain. Or see him. Especially the corpse. Tramp just takes it and rides."

"Body was still oozing when the bike left."

"How you know that? You been talking to Forensics without telling me?"

Charley took a sip of the cooling, coffee-colored swill. "I looked."

Manny grumbled into his cup. As usual when he wanted to vent, in Spanish. As usual, Charley pretended he didn't understand the language. Charley waited until Manny ran down.

"Glad you came up."

"Hey, we're partners. Couldn't leave you to the mercy of the locals. These country boys ain't got no respect for real cops."

"They're doing okay." Once Lieutenant Cullen, the local in charge of the investigation, had gone through the "you're off duty and we're not and it's not your jurisdiction anyway" speech, they'd been pretty decent. He even believed Cullen when the guy had said that making Charley wait around wasn't his idea, even though the lieutenant wouldn't spill on who Charley was supposed to be waiting around for. Charley understood that kind of jam; he'd had to do the same thing to a witness in the Gossamer case last year. "Lucky this wasn't on corp turf."

Manny nodded knowingly. Dealing with private cops and all their bullshit about company confidentiality made any investigation a pain. Murders like Gossamer's were the worst. The local boys were lucky they weren't going to have to deal with that kind of shit.

Sipping his coffee, Manny helped Charley watch the forensics team. Slowly his face screwed up into the grimace that meant he was thinking hard about something. Charley waited. Manny would talk when he was ready.

"So what's so important about this Churdy guy?"

"Don't know."

"You ain't figured an angle on it yet?"

"No."

"Maybe it *was* a bear, then."

Manny was persistent; you had to give him that. Captain Milton called it boneheaded, but then Captain Milton didn't think much of Manny. Charley didn't think much of Captain Milton. "Like I said, no bear."

"Maybe it's a hit by the Barrington creepo? That bastard tears 'em up pretty good."

"That slasher's got a pattern. Timing's not right."

Manny grunted. He didn't like that answer either. "Copycat?"

"Out here? Get real."

"Yeah." He looked disappointed. "Still. It's gotta be *something,* if they want you to hang out here and talk to whoever it is they want you to talk to."

"So they won't tell you either?"

"Lieutenant Cullen says I gotta wait if I wanna see. 'Jurisdiction,' he says. Jurisdiction, my ass. Bugger likes being one up."

Charley nodded. He had assumed the lack of info was just due to his being a witness. "Never tell the civs anything" was usually the safest rule, and in this case Charley counted as a civ. But if the locals weren't telling Manny either, they might be under some kind of gag order. Or maybe that lieutenant just didn't like outsiders breathing down his neck.

Aircraft noise made the lieutenant look up. Charley gave a glance, but only a glance; Manny gawked. Even the lab boys looked up from their work. One of them cursed and scrambled to unfold a tarp to cover the body.

"This them?" Manny asked.

"Good guess."

A Boeing Swingjet™ appeared from behind the mountain and banked toward them. The engines perched on the ends of the stubby wings looked ominous, almost like rocket pods on a ground-attack helo. Charley knew better, but he couldn't help flashing on the image. He felt better when the Swingjet's nose turned away from him, lining up with the highway for a landing. The plane had no markings, but its sleekness said money or connections, or both. Maybe this killing did have corporate connections, after all. Charley's stomach felt tight. The engines kicked up clouds of debris and gusted hot, oily air over him as the Swingjet settled.

Before the engines cut out, the door swung down into a ramp. As the stairs popped up, a quartet of tough-looking guys in suits pounded down them. Fancy boys in tailored suits. They didn't show any weapons, but Charley had no doubt they were carrying. The first one made a beeline for Cullen, while the rest spread out around the Swingjet.

A couple of tech types—in goddamn white coats, for Christ sakes—struggled down the ramp. Their satchels made the narrow passageway difficult for them to negotiate. The last guy out of the Swingjet had a little trouble squeezing through the narrow hatchway even though he didn't have to bend over to keep his head from bumping the coaming as the others had. The guy wasn't very tall, but he sure was wide, nearly as wide as he was tall, making Charley think of a drill sergeant he'd once had; this guy looked a lot like old Jonesy if you took a couple feet out of Jonesy's middle and lightened his skin tone a dozen shades.

The shrimp was clearly in charge. Charley heard one of the techs call him Mr. Sörli. Very deferentially. Sörli pointed at the tarp-covered body and the techs scurried off. The locals pulled off the tarp, then stayed out of the whitecoats' way. The new boys opened up their bags and started to do the same things the crime scene crew had been doing.

Redundancy, sweet redundancy. These guys had to be feds.

"Lotta muscle for hunting bear," Manny commented.

Manny just wasn't going to give up on the bear theory.

"They're feds. Haven't met the fed yet who's going to worry about a bear."

"Feds?" Manny's face darkened, then lightened a bit. "So much for no pattern. This *must* be some kind of psycho killing. Interstate stuff. Bet the perp's been cutting people up in half a dozen states. More of that luck of yours, Charley. Bet this is the closest they've come yet. You're gonna get yourself famous like Billy Kent down in Philly, Charley-boy."

Charley felt a sudden nostalgia for the bear theory.

The whitecoats went diligently about their task while the first suit talked to Lieutenant Cullen. Sörli stood by the Swingjet, arms folded, surveying his team at work. Two of his pet suits towered behind him like a pro linebacker's Masai bodyguards.

Finally Cullen pointed toward Manny and Charley, and the suit headed in their direction. When he arrived, he addressed Manny.

"Officer Gordon?"

"That's me," Charley said. The twitch of annoyance in the suit's face as he turned gladdened Charley's heart.

"Come with me, please," the suit said stiffly.

Why the hell not? A few questions and he could be headed someplace warm. Charley went along. The suit led him toward the shrimp. When they arrived in the shadow of the

Swingjet's wing, the suit stepped aside, leaving Charley face to face with—well, facing anyway—the shrimp.

Sörli's hands were in his pockets, and he didn't pull one out to offer a handshake. "Gordon?"

"That's me."

"You are the one who found the body?" asked the suit on the left.

"Yup."

The guy held out a reader. "Would you please read your statement?" Charley did so. "Is there anything you would like to add?" Charley shook his head as he handed the reader back. "Anything you would like to alter?"

"Nope."

"This is a serious investigation, Officer Gordon. Your superiors have promised complete cooperation. I do not believe that you understand the gravity of the situation."

"Damn straight."

"Your levity is not appreciated, Officer Gordon."

Too bad. You don't own the country. You don't own me. "I don't much appreciate being told to hang around here in the cold."

"We would appreciate your cooperation."

"I've been cooperating by hanging around out here, and you're acting like I'm the one putting *you* out."

"This is a serious investigation, Officer. We have no interest in wasting our time, or any citizen's time for that matter. I am sure that we all will be quite happy to get on to other things."

The sooner the better. "Look. If you got specific questions, ask them."

The suit looked as though he'd bitten into a lemon. A real one, good and sour. When he asked it, his question sounded more like a statement. "You saw no one near the body, nothing out of the ordinary."

"A bloody corpse on a mountain road is not ordinary. Leastwise when it's not a deer."

"Quite. I meant to ask if you saw anything unusual that might be related to the killing."

"Nope."

"The report you gave was very clear, but totally lacking in supposition. You are a police officer and surely you have some observations concerning the crime. Some thoughts."

More all the time. "I found the body, but I'm off duty."

"You are a police officer, are you not?"

"I'm on leave, and even if I wasn't, this isn't my jurisdiction. I reported the find like a good citizen, and like a good citizen, I'm content to leave the investigation to the local law officers. I have plenty to do back home."

"Ah, yes. You are involved in the Barrington slasher-killer investigation, are you not?"

"Peripherally."

"You found one of the bodies in that case as well."

"Yup."

"Do you see any connection between the two?"

Other than dead bodies? "Different killer."

"You are sure of this?"

He'd thought so. Now? Maybe not. "Got no evidence. You're the boys been collecting that."

"Quite. Do you have any supposition concerning—"

Sörli interrupted him. "Are you related to the victim?"

Just before Charley turned his eyes to the shrimp, he caught a flash of annoyance on the suit's face. Discord in the ranks? Sörli either didn't notice or didn't care; he stared at Charley with a hard expression. His dark eyes glinted coldly above his bearded cheeks.

The question didn't make any sense to Charley, but he answered anyway.

"Never saw him before."

"You are sure?" the suit prompted.

"Yup."

Sörli's flinty eyes stayed on Charley for a moment. Then he seemed to sink into himself, thinking. After a while he mumbled something. It sounded like, "These things are often tied together."

Tied together, huh? "What things?"

Sörli stared up at him, clearly irritated. The shrimp probably thought he hadn't spoken aloud. Interesting. The annoyance in Sörli's voice made his words sound like concrete blocks grinding together.

"You are a conscientious man, Officer Gordon. It is a quality that I appreciate. I am also told that you are lucky and inquisitive. Stay lucky. Don't be inquisitive."

"Why not?"

"If you are lucky, you won't find out."

The shrimp turned his back on Charley and headed for the Swingjet. Several of the suits filed after him. The one doing the interrogation said, "That will be all, Officer Gordon," before following the others.

For once, John was glad that Coach wasn't present for the Tuesday night practice. Lack of corporate interest in fencing meant a lack of funding as well, and the team had to practice when none of the other teams wanted school facilities, which wasn't very often. They had to make do where they could, which meant shifting sites and times. The odd scheduling meant that Coach Montoya, obliged by other, more mainline commitments, couldn't always make practices. Especially when the team was slipped into a gap in off-campus facilities like Rezcom 7's gym, as they were today.

The coach's no-show was still a mystery, but John knew all too well why he was late. His appointment with Dr. Block—praise the powers that be, it had been short—and the problems getting to the rezcom; the trolley had been half an hour late. Across the room, Yael, Will Brenner, and Philip Skyler were already going through their warm-up exercises.

John dug into the bottom of his duffel, groping for the box with the sensor tips. He finally found it, tucked inside his mask. He pulled both out and set the mask down. Opening the hard plastic case, he took one of the tips from the foam-lined compartment and fitted it to his foil.

The sensor tips were the latest in high-tech fencing equipment, and had consumed most of the team's budget for the year. The tips combined the protective cover for the metal point of the blade with a chip-driven monitor. A sensor registered the pressure of a thrust, while another monitored blade angle and motion. The feedback allowed the chip to score hits for quality. A trigger on the grip allowed a fencer to register intent to attack, and a continuous communication loop between two opposing tips allowed the right of way only to the first fencer to register his intent. The freedom from monitor cords had changed the face of the sport, taking it away from the single line of the mats and returning it to the freer styles of ancient sword fights. John pulled on his glove and ran the chip's self-check, receiving the reassuring "right of way" buzz in his palm.

Yael and Phil were sparring by the time he got his mask on. Will, the usual laggard, was having trouble getting the straps on his mask adjusted. John stepped over to give him a hand. Will was a senior and had been a member of the team longer than any of the rest of them, but he was still something of a klutz. Only conference rules and a lack of interested athletes kept him on the team.

Once Will was ready, they set frequencies, squared off, and set to. The physical action felt good after the frustrations of psychological sparring with Dr. Block. John trounced Will in three passes running before easing off. Calmed, he stretched himself by letting his point drop and offering Will openings. Will took the offerings, but John was still too quick for him. On the next pass, John opened his guard further.

He felt good, elated not so much for his easy defense against the clumsy Will, but by his control, form, and mastery of the weapon. Fencing was much better than basketball. Not that he didn't like B-ball. He had enjoyed playing in high school, but his first semester on the 'Tech frosh team had taught him how different things were between high school and college. Even on the freshman team, the pressure of collegiate play had been omnipresent. And if the pressure to make the cut wasn't enough of a distraction, there was always the intrusive attention of the corporate sportsmongers. College B-ball had a media following, and that meant that every team, even 'Tech's bargain-basement squad, had a following. Of media hacks, at least. John had found the artificiality of the whole thing nauseating.

The heavy corporate promotion of the sport had soured him on playing. The sponsorship required everything to be so rigid, made it seem so controlled. That wasn't what sports were supposed to be about. So he had quit the team halfway through the season and tried looking for something else, but none of the other sponsored teams had wanted him after that. He had spent his second semester without any organized physical activity at all and discovered that he liked that even less. During the summer he tried the rezcom athletic programs, but they were full of screaming kids and geezers, and so instead of doing something, he spent a lot of his time trying to figure out what sort of sport he could live with when the fall semester rolled around. He made it through the summer mostly because his docent work at the Armory Museum had kept him busy. It wasn't active, but it did fill the time. While he was at the museum, anyway. Then Will, a member of a medieval reconstruction group, had visited the museum. They got talking about swords and Will happened to mention the fencing program at 'Tech and John was immediately fascinated. The idea of swinging a sword brought images that fit snugly with John's dreams of knights, fairies, castles, and damsels. Better still, the corporate media mostly ignored fencing. Best of all, some of his teammates had the same fascinations with the romance of swordplay that he did.

Over the years, John had found few friends who shared his interests, but he still shied away from organized groups, even those that seemed to focus on those very interests. He'd heard of re-creation groups like the Society for Creative Anachronism but had always been too embarrassed to participate. They seemed a little too out of sync with the real world. John had been accused of asynchronous behavior too often as it was.

John laid his point against the heart target on Will's jacket for—what?—the tenth time? The grip of John's sword signaled cutoff; Will was conceding the match.

"You're too good for me tonight, John. I need a break." Will pulled his mask from his sweaty head. "Gotta save some energy for later. Hey, wanna come to the Society meeting tonight?"

"Not that Sca crap again, Will." Phil stood nearby, mask tucked under one arm, sword under the other. He had his usual disapproving frown on his face.

"Who asked you, Phil-uptight?"

"Certainly not you, my history-besotted freund." Phil stepped between Will and John and swept his blade up into a salute at John. "This is a fencing practice, not a costume-party club. You ready, Reddy?"

John took two steps back to open space and returned the salute. Will walked away, shaking his head, as Phil slipped on his mask. Yael joined Will and the two started to talk, but John had no time to pay attention because Phil started to attack.

John's height gave him almost as much of an advantage in fencing as it had in B-ball, for his reach allowed him to strike at much greater distances than most of his opponents. This was an especial advantage against the short and compact Phil, but the pugnacious Phil always insisted that he didn't mind, that he liked the challenge. Dogged determination and skill were what Phil relied upon, and he was constantly working on ways to make the initial slip past John's point. Tonight, Phil immediately started pushing, pressing John to fall back or allow him within reach. John retreated and maintained distance, content to allow Phil's attacks to play out. On the switchovers, John regained all the ground he had surrendered. Will shouted encouragement and John responded, "It's always easy when you fight people who can't reach you."

Within his mask, Phil snorted in reply to the taunt and took up his attack with renewed vigor. Will's catcalls and John's quips seemed to fire him. His attacks stepped up and began to get a little wilder, but John covered, parrying and retreating. John's counters reached through Phil's defense to score, and each score brought a whoop from Will, but seemed only to add to Phil's determination. John's blade rang as Phil's strikes came harder and faster.

In the next pass, John found Phil slipping inside his line with a move he hadn't expected. Their swords shrilled, as blade ran along blade until the hilts smashed up against each other. Phil whipped his foil down with a shriek of metal against metal. As the pressure of his opponent's weight left his blade, John skipped back to prepare for a counterattack. John cocked his wrist to activate the pass-over signal, but Phil still attacked, ignoring the right of way. He bore in, blade flashing. Caught off guard, John started to circle but misjudged the impetus of Phil's lunge.

Phil's point rushed toward John, and he knew he would not be able to parry in time. He tried to twist out of the way, hoping to let the point pass by. As he shifted, his knee buckled, the tendons robbed of their tension as though someone had shoved his foot against them. Instead of twisting away from the attack, John collapsed. As he fell, the tip of Phil's blade ripped through his jacket, plowing a burning furrow through the skin of his shoulder.

John gasped in shock. He was wounded, really wounded. Somehow the sensor tip had fallen from Phil's blade. Had John not fallen, the sword would have pierced his body. He could have been killed.

Phil had his mask off in an instant. "You all right, John?"

"Hell, Phil, you coulda killed him!" Will shouted.

"I didn't know the tip was off," Phil protested.

"Didn't you get the cut-out signal?" Yael asked. He sounded calmer than either of the other two.

Phil shook his head. He was shaking. "I didn't feel anything."

"I think we'd better quit for today," John said shakily.

"John." Phil looked worried. "You gonna tell Coach?"

"Going to have to." He plucked at the ripped jacket. The bloodstains were hard to miss on the white fabric. "I think he'll notice."

"You gonna tell him I did it? It was an accident."

"I know that, Phil. Look, it's okay. Really." Phil didn't look convinced. "Look, help me out of the jacket so I don't bleed on it any more."

With Yael and Will's help, they got the jacket off without getting much more blood on it. They didn't jar John's arm much, either. Yael frowned at the wound. "Better get you patched, John."

The jacket got tossed into the showers while Yael swabbed John's wound with disinfectant. By the time John was bandaged, everyone seemed calmer. Phil handed the soggy jacket to John. The rip was more noticeable than the bloodstains now, and John rolled it up without a word. They took a vow not to mention the incident to anyone until John determined what they'd tell Coach Montoya, at which point they would back whatever John said. The evidence of the accident put away, the talk turned deliberately to other things. Save for a lingering nervousness in voices and hesitancy in speech, the accident might never have happened.

"I saw Kelley yesterday," Yael said.

"Kelley Donaghue?" John knew the question was stupid even as he asked it.

"Yeah, Donaghue. You chasing some other Kelley?"

"I'm not chasing her."

"The way you pant every time she walks by, I'd assumed you were running hard," Phil observed.

"Hormones," Yael commented sagely. "Worse for the brain than books."

"Have you asked her for a date yet?" Will asked.

"Bet she'll be at the Zephyr concert," Yael said.

"Maybe I'll check it out." John hated buzz rock. But if Kelley was going to be there, he might go have a listen.

"Must be true love for you to be considering that," Phil said.

"Ease up, guys," Will said.

Phil gave him a sour look. "Aren't you supposed to be somewhere else?"

Will glanced at his watch. "Shit! I gotta run if I'm gonna make the meeting. Sure you don't wanta come, John?"

"Kelley Donaghue won't be there," Yael pointed out.

"Maybe next time, Will."

Politely, Will made no mention that John's response was the same as always. John wondered if Will believed him.

Phil also had something else to do, so it was only Yael and John who headed over to the student center.

The concert was a toxic spill of sound, but Kelley Donaghue was there. She seemed surprised to see him, but not unpleasantly. John's attempts at conversation at any volume less than a shout didn't get anywhere. Even shouting he couldn't hear half of what he was saying himself. Kelley's words were lost even more completely. Fortunately, Kelley seemed as frustrated as John over their inability to say anything to each other.

The gang with whom Kelley had come was headed off to the Frilly Cow for a late-night snack, but John was broke. Since he hadn't really been expecting to go anywhere but home after practice, he hadn't brought any money with him. Bad form to mooch, or sit around with nothing in front of you. Afraid she'd think less of him, he mumbled an excuse that involved some kind of heavy assignment. She seemed disappointed, and that was encouraging. John did come away with one treasure, a promise from Kelley to go to another concert with him. A quieter one. He whistled "Jolly Drover Boy" all the way back to the rezcom.

Kim Murphey was doing sets down at the Northsider Club.

Was that a good choice?

Maybe. Kelley *had* said a quieter place, and she really liked music. She was a music major; she had to like lots of different kinds of music, didn't she?

Maybe.

Maybe not. She might be like the others. As soon as any of his potential girlfriends saw his room or went on a date to a folk concert, they took off like a rocket, blasting back to corporate mainline straightline.

It was their fault. They had no appreciation. And not just for the music.

Meaning no appreciation for me. Well, a nice thought. But how could you tell for sure?

He waited, but he got no answer.

Ah, well. Faye wasn't always there.

CHAPTER
3

Maybe the distant rumble of thunder and the threat of a storm had put Helen on edge, but the woman pulling up on the motorcycle gave her a shiver. She didn't really look like trouble. Not like those biker babes. No leather jacket, no freaky haircut, no gloss makeup. This one looked almost old-fashioned with her long hair, ratty knapsack, denim jacket and jeans. And a helmet. The wild ones never wore helmets.

Shifting for a better look, Helen kicked the sign lying under the counter for the twentieth time tonight. Why hadn't Sam gotten around to putting the damn thing up? All well and good that he was bright enough to think of a placard advertising their store as the first convenience in Maine. Sam was the manager; he was supposed to think up things like that. He'd even done the work of making the damned thing himself, instead of sticking her or one of the other employees with the job, but he hadn't finished it. Sign didn't do any good if no one saw it. The counter help had been tripping over the damn thing for nearly a week now.

Helen watched the woman leave the helmet balanced on the bike's fuel tank. Stupid move. She might get away with it, though. It was only Tuesday. If this were a weekend the lot would have been full, and the helmet would have been gone before the woman got into the store.

The woman's features were sharp, and might have been really pretty when she was younger. She looked tired and a little worn out. When she came through the door, she looked around as if trying to put everything into its place.

As if this shop were different from millions of other convenience stores.

The woman headed toward the back, down the aisle leading to the microwave and coffee bar. As she passed, Helen pretended to be busy with work at the counter. Her act wouldn't fool anybody who'd worked a store, but most people didn't know how little there was to do. The woman didn't even look at her. Helen continued to watch the woman surreptitiously. She didn't look dangerous, but there was something about her. Better to keep an eye on her. You could never be sure about someone who rode a motorcycle.

By the time José finally emerged from the back, the woman had gotten her coffee and had put a burrito into the 'wave. José caught sight of her and gave her a look, a lingering look. That kind of business was normal for him; the boy would jump anything with the right genitals. Almost anything, she amended. Like Helen, this woman was too old for him.

On second thought, maybe the woman wasn't that old. Real exhaustion made a person look older than she was. The way the woman had fumbled with the 'wave showed that she was really out of it.

José sauntered past her in the aisle, pretending that he had business at the self-service counter instead of joining Helen at the counter as he was supposed to. He might as well have just come up front. She didn't even look at him when he bumped her elbow; she just sidestepped away from him. José finally looked in Helen's direction, and she gave him a scowl. He grinned sheepishly and abandoned his stalk, bringing the rolls of change she'd sent him to the back for.

Just as José lifted the panel to enter the counter section, there was a flicker from the parking lot. Power surge? No, the store lights had stayed steady. She hadn't heard a truck. Probably just her imagination. Sam always said she had an active imagination. If he only knew what she imagined about *him*.

She had to slap José lightly on the shoulder to get his attention long enough for him to turn over the change. The boy was still checking out the woman.

"Forget it, José."

"But she's so pretty."

Helen looked again. The plastic food seemed to agree with the woman; she didn't look near as bad as when she had walked in. Yeah, you could say she was pretty, if you liked the angular, foxy-featured type. José would like the type; he liked all types. The boy mumbled something to himself in Spanish, and Helen just shook her head. Young and headstrong. She had work to do. She rang the "No Sale" to open the register for the coins, and the store went dark.

Damn!

Storm must have caught a power line somewhere. Even the streetlights were out. A car went by, headlamps throwing a wash of light across the lot. Nothing out there but the woman's bike. No more helmet.

Even on a weeknight.

With the power out, Helen had to secure the till. Telling José to close the register's drawer, she stepped out from behind the counter. Best to lock the doors until the power came back.

Impulsively, she stepped outside to see how extensive the outage was. Funny, there wasn't any wind. Must have been a lightning strike, then. Just took out the local stuff, though; she could see lights down at Duffy's Tavern and most of the houses beyond it. The streetlights along Route 4 were on, too. But for at least a quarter mile either side of the store everything was dark.

Amazing how quiet things got when it was dark.

She heard a scuffling by the dumpster and turned quickly enough to catch a glimpse of a pair of kids ducking behind it.

The helmet thieves, no doubt. She took a step back toward the door, knowing she'd best lock it up.

With a shock, she realized that the kids were running toward her, not away. One of them held something in his hand, something that glinted.

The helmet?

Shit, the kid had a knife!

She stepped back again, hand groping for the door she'd let close behind her. Instead of metal, her hand touched leather. Warm, slick leather. She spun to find a tall man standing between her and the door.

"Help me, mister."

"You're not her," he said. He sounded disappointed.

Pain shocked a scream from her as fire lanced into her back. Her grasping hands reached out for the man, but he stepped away from her. Her knees hit the cement. Her spine seemed on fire. She'd been knifed in the back.

Why was the guy just standing there?

Fuck him!

Helen heaved herself up. One of the kids was tugging on her. Little bastard was wearing a mask. His buddy was pawing at her too, his nails gouging like claws. God, were they going to rape her while she bled her life away?

She kicked one of the little bastards and he staggered back. She backhanded the other, sending him staggering away too. She was surprised at her strength. Where was it coming from? Her back felt cold now.

Her knees buckled again, dropping her. She reached up for the door handle, but one of the punks grabbed her arm. She felt his stinking breath on her cheek and his nails digging into her flesh. He twisted her arm back, painfully. Her knees left the cement. She flailed helplessly as he heaved her up. The kid was laughing as he held her over his head.

What the hell was he on?

His partner chattered something in a gutter dialect, and both of them laughed. The jazzed punk grunted and heaved her straight at the store window.

She hit it, hard, and smashed through. The impact was worse than that night her ex-boyfriend Billy had thrown her against the wall. She clipped the video rack and sent it spinning in a clatter of cassettes. She heard a distant sound like steak hitting a counter, and she was gasping for breath on the floor.

Much worse than what Billy had done.

There was glass everywhere. She felt it slicing her skin, shredding her clothes. More of it tinkled down on her in a sharp-edged rain.

"Madre de Díos!"

José's voice was halfway between surprise and fear.

Something flew in through the smashed window, something about the size of one of the punks. They had to be jazzed, really jazzed, to jump like that. José, standing frozen in shock, was nearly bowled over. The other one piled in too. The three of them went down in a heap of flailing limbs.

Helen's legs wouldn't move and her right arm lay twisted beneath her. She was broken, dying. Her chest was afire, leaving her no breath to scream. A warm stickiness was oozing along her thigh. She began to cry. It was all she could do.

The sounds of struggle by the counter stopped, but she didn't care. No point. No point at all.

Nym started moving as soon as she saw the shadows flickering outside. She went through the door the male shopkeeper had used to enter the public portion of the store. She found herself in a stockroom. Off to the right was another room, a window separating it from this one. Through the window she saw a man sitting at a desk. Through the partly open door leaked loud, rhythmic sound, almost music; all bass, no melody. Noise. The noise drowned out the struggle behind her. The man looked up from the papers in front of him, and his brows furrowed when he saw her.

She ignored him.

The back door was bolted. She threw the bolt and flung the door open, stepping to one side as she did so. Nothing rushed in, so she ran out. Keeping next to the building, she circled around to the front.

At the front corner she stopped, glancing cautiously around. She could see no one. The sounds of struggle still emanated from the store.

She ran to the bike.

The helmet was gone, but that wasn't important. She hopped on and kicked the engine to life, revving it hard. She bumped jarringly over the parking stop as she made her turn. Fighting the bike's attempt to twist out of her control, she barely avoided the dumpster. But then she was clear of obstructions and pointed toward the road.

Something whooshed past and fire blossomed behind her. A glance showed her the convenience store engulfed in a growing fireball. The tall silhouette of a man moved between her and the fire. She throttled up, ducking low against the bike. Her hair streamed behind her and she pushed the bike as hard as she could.

The air crackled.

She was still too close. And no protection.

Slowing as much as she dared, she cut around a parked car to put it between her and the store. Almost instantly, the vehicle burst into flame. Heat washed over her.

She opened the throttle. Distance was the only answer now.

Something else ignited behind her, but not so close.

She left it all behind.

Enviro lab had gone on forever. Sharon, John's partner, was a real scijock, always concerned for two or three decimal places past what John thought necessary. They'd been the last ones done. By the time John got cleaned up and out, the campus was emptying. Students in ones and twos were hustling back to the dorms and out to the rezcoms. John ambled along, content to take his time. A band of raucous frat boys from one of the jock houses, already well into celebrating the weekend, tumbled past. He indulgently endured their jostling. Who was he to complain? He had his own celebrating to do tonight.

Right?

. . .

Ah, well. He supposed this was one situation Faye would not be keen to comment on. Faye had seemed worried about him all week, even before the fencing incident with Phil, but she hadn't responded to his questions about her fretfulness, which was a little unusual; she was usually frank about her feelings. She was probably just in a funk because John had a date tonight.

He didn't like it when she acted this way, and had hoped he and she could talk it out. But she had made herself scarce, and they hadn't talked much. Even when she was around, she was far less communicative than usual, so he really didn't know if he was right or wrong in his suppositions.

She'd get over it.

He had just begun to think he detected her lurking around, when he noticed that the frat boys had pulled up and were blocking the entire walkway in front of him. They were hooting and hollering and egging on one of their number, a hulking jock by the name of Winston whom John remembered from his days on the frosh B-ball squad. Winston had been long on brawn and short on brain, and something of a bully. He and John hadn't gotten along at all. Winston was shoving a smaller kid around and shouting slurred insults. Some things never changed.

Winston's victim was much smaller than he was, a slender kid wearing glasses. Glasses! Nobody but geeks wore glasses anymore. The kid looked vaguely familiar, but John couldn't recall his name. It came to him when he heard the kid's reedy voice yelping in protest when Winston snatched his glasses. This geek was one of the freshmen who had made advanced placement into John's second-year Global Studies program. Trahn was his name.

Jocks and geeks, a natural antipathy, and not something to get involved in. John edged his way through the outer fringes of Winston's frat brothers. Intent on their brother's harassment of a lower life-form, they let him pass. John felt sympathy for the kid and hoped things wouldn't get too physical; in the past, he'd received more than enough similar attention. John cleared the knot of jocks and jock sympathizers and headed north. It wasn't his problem.

Hardly a noble reaction. Would D'Artagnon look the other way?

John felt his cheeks grow hot. I'm not D'Artagnon.

No. Just John Reddy.

Right. John Reddy, not D'Artagnon. John Reddy, who's got a date tonight. John upped his speed a notch. The sooner he was out of earshot of the hazing, the sooner he could forget it.

So much for nobility, John Unready.

A couple hundred yards ahead, a group of women turned the corner onto the lane. A dozen or so of them, more than twice the number in the hazing party. The girls would see what was going on and hurry prudently on their way. They'd be all right.

John spotted Kelley among the approaching group. If the girls saw what was happening, they'd know he had seen it as well. What would Kelley think if John just walked away from someone who needed help? He was back on the fringes of the hazing group in a few quick strides.

"Hey, Winston. You're not being very sporting."

Hand still gripping Trahn's bunched shirt, Winston looked over at John. His eyes narrowed in recognition. "If it ain't the ghostly broomstick. Fade, or you're next."

Winston turned back to Trahn, giving him a slap across the cheek. John elbowed his way past one of the jocks and grabbed Winston's upraised wrist. "Guy like this isn't much of a challenge for one of your obvious attributes."

"You want the same?"

"No."

"Then walk away."

They stared into each other's eyes. Winston was partly drunk; John could smell the alcohol on his breath. Not a lot of judgment left behind those piggy eyes. At the periphery of his senses, John could tell more of a crowd was gathering. Was Kelley among them? He didn't want to look around and see. There were too many people watching. Unlikely a bully like Winston would back down now.

Still, John wanted to give him a chance. He released the jock's wrist and offered a placating smile. "You've had your fun. Leave him alone now and nobody'll complain. Isn't that right, Trahn?"

"Ain't your business," Winston growled. "Ain't that right, Trahn?"

"I've made it my business," John said, dropping the smile. "You've made it your trouble."

Winston released Trahn and swung on John. John stepped back into one of the jocks, who shoved him right back at Winston. Winston's second punch caught John in the stomach, doubling him over.

Winston laughed. "Don't need your help, Vinny. The ghostly broomstick's all shadow, no substance."

John's punch caught Winston in the stomach, but the jock didn't double over; he just whuffed, more from surprise than from pain. The guy was built like a wall. But the attack bought John time to get out of Winston's reach.

He danced away from Winston's next swing and punched back. John's long reach let him strike while staying out of Winston's range. He took advantage of it, lashing out to belabor the jock as he tried to close. But Winston wasn't stymied for long. Ducking his head down, he charged, apparently willing to take punishment in order to get to grips with John. The guy was a pig-head like Phil. Like Phil, he was successful. He slipped past John's fists and slammed into him. They both went down, John landing on the shoulder that Phil had slashed.

It hurt.

Heat flared through him. Thrashing his way free of Winston's clutching paws, he rolled to his feet. The jock was up too, and charging again. Ready for that tactic now, John stepped aside and clipped him on the side of the head. The pig-head tried again just the same. John gave him fists.

He felt giddy. This was not like fighting Phil. No swords here, just flesh and bone. And blood. John caught the jock on the right temple and opened the skin. Winston was spending more time blocking now. John's knuckles were raw, but he kept punching, because Winston kept coming. John was glad to oblige him. The jock's defenses were getting sloppier, and John scored again and again. Winston's own attacks were becoming less coordinated. John caught him on the nose and felt it crunch. Winston staggered back.

"So, mister tough guy. Like the other side of it?"

Somebody in the crowd laughed.

Winston flung himself forward, catching John off guard. The jock's head came up under John's chin, shocking John's teeth together. He tasted blood. His own.

Grappling, Winston tried to squeeze the breath out of John. John hammered Winston's shoulders, to little avail. John's vision grayed as the jock squeezed harder. Dizzy, John brought his fists together against Winston's ears. The jock howled and let go. John pummeled his unprotected midsection.

"Hurt me, will you?"

John hit him again. And again. Winston started to stagger, but John was not going to let him off easily. He kept punching, harder and faster. Winston went down.

Not easy at all. Gonna pay, Winston.

John pounced on Winston and pinned the jock's flailing arms under his knees. Winston's head rocked back and forth under John's fists. Someone was yelling somewhere. It sounded like Trahn. Let him yell; Winston was getting what he deserved.

John raised his fist for another punch, but it didn't fall. Someone was restraining his arm. He tried his other hand, but that was held as well.

At first, all John saw was the uniform.

Police.

He looked down at Winston's battered face. The guy's eyes were shut, his jaw slack. John's brain slowed down into something like normal thought. Shit! He was in trouble now.

He looked up at the cop.

Who wasn't a cop. The man was wearing a campus sanitation uniform. John stared into the ugly face of Trashcan Harry. Not a cop. Just Trashcan. Nobody important.

Trashcan Harry was a custodian on campus, and his nickname was as much for his odor as his job. He was a hairy old prole who made Winston look thin and anemic. Harry's nose had met somebody's fist too many times and his ears had been on the receiving end of cosmetic surgery performed by a blind butcher. He had an odd accent as thick as Winston's head, and was the butt of more campus humor than John could recall. But Trashcan's grip wasn't funny; John thought he could feel his wrist bones grating together.

Finally John realized that Trashcan Harry was saying something to him. The same thing, over and over, like a chant.

"You stop now."

He stopped resisting the custodian's iron grip.

At least Trashcan Harry wasn't a cop. But relief faded as fast as it had come. Trashcan's work-relief job probably required him to report anything that disturbed the peace of the campus.

John looked around. Trahn was the only one left, and he was looking at John with wide eyes. Even Winston's buddies had deserted him. Kelley wasn't present either. Had she ever been?

Winston lay on the pavement, bloody and breathing raggedly. Had John done all that damage? He didn't remember.

"Where'd everyone go?"

"Nobody likes trouble," Trashcan said.

Trouble. Yeah, there'd be trouble, all right. Winston was not in good shape.

Trashcan tugged on John's arm. "You go get cleaned up."

"What about him?"

Trashcan Harry looked down at the fallen bully. "I take care. You not worry."

Worry? An incident like this would trash his new job at the museum. Worse, it'd mean more sessions with Dr. Block. Regular sessions. Probably cost him his place on the fencing team, as well. Sure, why worry?

And Kelley. Had Kelley seen it all?

There was no one in sight along the lane. The campus was quiet at the end of its day. No one here to stand over Winston but John, Trashcan, and Trahn. And Trashcan was chasing Trahn off, exhorting him to go home and be quiet. John just stood there, pinned by Trahn's accusing stare.

What had he done?

Trashcan tugged on his arm again. "Go get cleaned up."

"I've got to do something about him."

"Done enough. Go."

Embarrassed and scared, John went. He didn't run home, but he wanted to.

Faye, what am I going to do?

. . .

Faye?

CHAPTER 4

Technically, Mr. Sörli was a dwarf, his legs being far shorter than normal for a man with his breadth of shoulder. Yet he showed neither the unsteadiness of gait so characteristic of those afflicted with dwarfism, nor any of the other deformities common among ordinary dwarves. But then, Sörli was not ordinary. If he had been, he would have had no business taking up any of Pamela Martinez's time.

He walked into the room and headed for the chair—just one special chair today—facing her desk. He walked confidently, paying no attention to the rich furnishings. Most people could not stop themselves from gawking at the art on the walls, the fine furniture, or, at the very least, the soft thick carpet under their feet. This office was of a quality beyond the means of most, a chamber suitable to the president of the North American Group of the Mitsutomo Keiretsu. Sörli paid it no more attention than a commuter might pay to a subway platform. The dwarf's indifference to her office irked her more than his brusque manner.

She let him sit long enough for the chair to take a baseline and match it against the file readings. While he waited for her, she watched the tracings fall into line on her desktop monitor. For all he would know, she was reading the *Wall Street Journal*.

Sörli didn't wait for her to speak.

"I'm busy."

Was that irritation in his voice? Yes, the monitor confirmed it; she was getting better at reading him. She was pleased; it made him a little less mysterious. But she was also displeased that he would have the temerity to imply that his time was more valuable than hers. *He* was on *her* payroll, after all. Besides, she knew he was busy; she'd read her watchdog's report. As she pretended to cut off the monitor, she said, "You did not report to me when you returned from Maine."

He shrugged. "There was nothing conclusive."

"We expended resources at your request. I expect a report. From you."

"Very well." Sörli drew a breath. "Al Churdy was killed by a creature of the otherworld, probably one of the Red Cap cult."

The otherworld. She'd been hearing about it for years now, and still the very mention of it sent shivers down her spine.

Though the monitor said he was telling the truth, she asked, "You can verify this intrusion?"

"Probably not to your satisfaction, Ms. Martinez. But then, the proof you want will only be obtainable after it is too late."

It was his standard response. When Sörli had first mentioned the otherworld to her, she had thought he was joking. The very idea of a dimension coexisting with the normal world was weird enough, though it had some justification, according to some of the more abstruse philosophers of physics. But to claim that this other dimension was one in which magic worked and chaos ruled! That was an insane concept, the stuff of tabloid journalism and instant video documentaries. Sörli's hypothesis of an otherworld went far in explaining many of the strange things that happened in the world. If one accepted his basic assumptions. But asking acceptance was asking a lot.

"Churdy was a motorcycle racer. What kind of connection could he have had with the otherworld?"

"We have not been able to ascertain any connection at all. This leaves the inescapable conclusion that the connection lay with his passenger. It is likely that the passenger was the real target of the attack."

"Passenger?"

"A woman. As yet unidentified."

"There was no mention of a woman in the police report."

If Sörli was surprised by her mention of the police report he didn't show it, either visually or on the monitor. All he said was, "Good."

Confidence, or overconfidence? Or simple insanity?

"I did not get to where I am today by being a fool." No, indeed. She had taken advantage of every opportunity, equal or otherwise, and gained a high position. She had clawed her way up through the corporate world to her current post with Mitsutomo, and men and women who had thought her a fool had learned otherwise, to their regret. "You have used Mitsutomo resources, and you bring me no results. I have to answer for these expenditures. What am I to tell my superiors?"

"The truth."

"That we are being invaded by goblins and fairies?"

"Your words."

"Give me other words, then. Something to make this alleged threat more credible."

"Names aren't important." The monitor jumped a little there. "Call them what you want, it won't change their nature. But do not deny their existence."

"Bring me proof."

"In time."

It was the same promise he had made when he had first asked for her help in combating the intrusions of the otherworld. She hadn't believed him, of course, expecting to find real-world monsters behind his fairy-tale dangers. She had gone along assuming that the information he gathered would eventually turn out to be useful; she had never found information-gathering to be a waste of resources. An organization as diverse as Mitsutomo Keiretsu had many places to apply information.

Sörli's investigations had given her some of what she sought, but they had also turned up situations that were less understandable. That was unless one accepted his otherworld hypothesis. But there was never anything concrete, incontrovertible. Proof, hard proof, continued to be elusive, and each day she found herself locked tighter and tighter into his intricate schemes. He was leading her farther and farther down the path he walked. No longer could she deny that *something* was happening. Whatever that something was, Sörli had some sort of inside line on it. Each day, she found herself closer to accepting his explanation.

Perhaps it was she who was mad?

No. That was an unacceptable explanation. There *was* something real going on, and Sörli knew more about it than he was telling.

"Tell me about this woman."

He shrugged. "The powers of the otherworld have agents here. Those agents are working to bring about a full convergence of the worlds."

The monitor suggested that he was withholding information, but the confidence quotient was not high enough for her to call him on it. "Are you saying that she is some kind of fairy?"

"My information concerning her origins is insufficient at this time. However, I suggest that we must be prepared to act. It is likely that she is an agent of the otherworld. In that case, she must be stopped."

"Are you proposing what I think?"

He smiled at her. He might have been a cat contemplating a trapped mouse. She considered his sanity again. If he was suggesting a murder, perhaps his delusions had taken too dangerous a turn. In fact, she detected a flaw in his logic.

"You said you thought that this woman was the target of the attack. If she is an agent working for the otherworld's interests, attacking her makes no sense. Why would the powers of the otherworld, wishing to see a convergence, try to kill their own agent?"

As always, he had an answer. "There are factions on the other side, and they do not always work in concert. This is fortunate, a factor in our favor."

"Why not leave her to this opposing faction, then?"

"As well trust a work-relief prole to do your own job. Stopping the convergence must be our highest priority." He slipped out of the chair and leaned on her desk. "The intrusion of magic into this world would be disastrous. You cannot begin to imagine the chaos that would result. Not only governments would collapse."

For once, Sörli was wrong; she had *often* imagined the chaos of a world gone magical. In fact, she had done such a good job of constructing that nightmare scenario of unbearable instability that it was costing her sleep. Magic did not belong in the world. Not in *her* world. *Her* world was a rational one; dangerous, perhaps, but predictable. She knew how to survive in it. She had built herself an island of stability in the turmoil of the world, and she had no intention of seeing her hard-won stability torn away from her.

Magic was the wildest of wild cards, capable of destroying all stability, everything she had made for herself. In a world confused by magic, the corporations would lose control; and by extension, so would she. Unacceptable! She could not—would not—let that happen. She had to take action. But what should she do? She hated herself for dithering. She'd thought she'd been long done with such indecision. Her uncertainty reminded her too much of who she'd been.

The threat of chaos reminded her of things, too. Past things, things she had walked away from or buried, things she had sworn never to let affect her life again. She'd banished chaos from her life once, she was never going back there. Never!

Sörli was still asking her to take a lot on faith, but could she afford not to believe him? What he'd shown and told her was so nebulous. Why hadn't he been able to provide her with more than hints and suggested interpretations? She wanted real, solid evidence, which Sörli had so far been unwilling or unable to supply. Without evidence, acting involved risk. She didn't like to take chances, but she had survived times when a gamble was the only answer, the only way to remain in control, and this was looking more and more like one of those times. But if she played this wrong, there'd be a scandal; a scandal could prove very hard to survive.

The fear of chaos haunted her. If there *was* an otherworld, and if Sörli's mystery woman *was* working to bring it into convergence with the world as Pamela knew it, that woman had to be stopped. Pamela had never lacked resolution in the past; she had always had enough guts to do whatever had to be done. So why was she hesitating? Was it just prudent caution, or was it more than that? Was she afraid of being embarrassed if Sörli pushed her into unjustifiable actions? Or was she afraid that Sörli's fears might be all too correct, and that there might be nothing she could do to stop the advent of the chaos? She needed to know more about what was *really* going on.

"I want you to find out more about the woman before you take any action."

"We may not have the luxury of discussing this at leisure."

"*I* don't have the luxury of making a mistake." She fixed him with a stare. "Neither do you."

"The biggest mistake would be to let this woman continue to operate."

"Convince me."

Scowling, Sörli said, "If I have not yet convinced you of the danger, we are lost." He tapped the privacy screen around her monitor. "Your tools tell you that I do not lie. Believe them, if you will not believe me. We come to the cusp. We must act."

"Convince me."

Sörli drew himself up. Without further argument, he turned and departed. As the door slid shut behind him, Pamela touched the intercom.

"Get Mr. McAlister on the line."

She needed a word with her watchdog.

Making himself presentable after his fight with Winston took time. John considered getting Kelley on the phone and calling off the date, but Faye convinced him otherwise. By the time he had cleaned himself up, he was running half an hour late. He snatched bits and pieces of an outfit from his closet, mostly with an eye to hiding the bruises. The only way to hide his bruised and scraped hands was to wear gloves; he hoped Kelley would take it as a fashion statement.

He was pushing an hour late when he arrived at her dorm. To his relief, she buzzed him in rather than just telling him to get lost. She came down to the lobby promptly, but stayed aloof all the way to the Northsider Club. They had missed the first set and Kim Murphey was well into her second set when they arrived, but the music soon mellowed Kelley and by the end of the third and final set, she was talking easily. Neither of them mentioned the afternoon's fight, encouraging John to hope that she had either missed it or not realized it had been he.

He wanted the evening to last forever, forever delaying the time when he'd have to deal with the repercussions of the afternoon's fight. He suggested they go to the Frilly Cow for a snack, and she agreed. When they were settled in a booth and had put in their order, he started on a topic that seemed safe.

"You seemed to like the concert."

"Yeah. It was good. It's nice to hear real instruments once in a while."

"Real instruments?"

"Yeah. You know, instead of synthesized sound. The boards are light-years ahead of what they used to be, but there's something different about a real instrument that even an individuator can't dupe."

"Maybe it's the player."

"Or the company."

The company? Had she really said that?

Their order arrived, saving John from immediately saying something stupid. Once the Cokes and burgers were on the table, their talk took a sudden turn to other, safer things like classes and assignments and professors. Eventually, the conversation rolled around to the music again.

"Yeah. The music's fine. But the lyrics." She rolled her eyes. "The lyrics are always so, like, imaginative."

"You think so? I've always been fascinated by the stories they tell. Do you ever think that there might be something more than simple imagination behind the stories in the songs?"

"Like what?"

"I don't know. Like, maybe some of the stories aren't just stories. Like, maybe they're some kind of distorted history."

"History? With all those witches and ghosts and magic talismans and stuff?"

"Why not?" Kelley quirked an eyebrow at him, so he tried another tack. "I mean, couldn't stuff like that be symbolism for other things?"

"I suppose." Her agreement was hesitant.

"Suppose it was. For the sake of argument. Don't you have to wonder what might be behind those stories?"

She looked dubious. She was clearly beginning to think he was an idiot. If he shut up now, she'd know for sure. His only hope was to keep talking and bring the conversation back to a place she found more acceptable. But how? Since dropping the subject cold would just freeze ideas about his weirdness in her head, he'd have to work himself out into safer areas.

"Give me a minute, here. If you suppose that there *is* a real story behind the song, you have to suppose that there are real events and real people in it, right?" She nodded dubiously. "Given that. And given that there isn't anything like magic in the real world . . ." That seemed to score points. Keep talking, boy. "A lot of seemingly magical effects can be explained by chemistry and psychological manipulation, participatory hallucination, and stuff like that. You get a bunch of people believing in a thing and telling each other about it, and then they start believing that it really does exist and when they see anything that could by the furthest stretch of the imagination be that thing, it is. That's the way a crocodile becomes a dragon. It's imagination at work, but it's not making it up out of whole cloth, you see?"

"I suppose."

"Right. It's the same sort of thing with the people in the stories. You take someone like Tam Lin. Here's a guy, a landed lord, that nobody has seen for a while. He's, like, disappeared. The song says he went to Faery, but who knows where he really went? Maybe the Faery riff is a cover story, to hide the fact that he was off doing something he wasn't supposed to be doing. Remember, the old-time folk *believe* in this Faery stuff. Who'd ask what he was *really* doing? Point is, he comes back and finds somebody, Fair Janet, has taken over his turf. Maybe he's been gone so long that he's been declared legally dead. His problem: he wants his turf back, but can't do it legally. Her problem: she's pregnant, and won't or can't tell who the father is. Maybe she doesn't know. Anyway, she needs protection. Maybe from the father himself, maybe from *her* father. This Tam Lin cooks up a scheme. By getting married, he gets back his claim on the turf, she gets to keep it too, and the kid gets a father. The Faery stuff gives it all a fancy gloss."

"You make it sound almost possible."

"No *almost* about it."

"So who's the Queen of Faery?"

He wished he knew. He also wished he had an answer for her.

A shadow fell across the table between them, chilling the conversation. John looked up to see a tall man partially silhouetted against the Cow's lights. The light leaked around from behind the stranger lit enough of his long face to show his somber expression. It was an official business kind of expression. John didn't recognize the man, but he got the impression that he should know him, or at least what organization he represented.

There was no corporate affiliation pin on the lapel of the stranger's long leather coat. The coat was dark on the shoulders, as if it was wet, but it hadn't been raining. If it had been, his hair, white-blond and finely styled, would have been plastered to his head.

The stranger waited several heartbeats before he spoke.

"Excuse me. I'm looking for John Reddy."

Police was John's first thought. *Winston,* his second. Was this about the fight? Had Winston . . . died? The man's intense stare didn't leave any doubt that he knew he'd found John Reddy, so there didn't seem to be any point in denying it.

"I'm John."

"I'd like to ask you a few questions."

"You a cop?" Kelley asked nervously. Her sidelong glance at John suggested that she had seen at least part of the afternoon's fight.

"Not exactly, miss. But I am part of an ongoing investigation."

"You with the feds?"

"I'm not really at liberty to say."

"Oh, man." Kelley looked frightened. "Look, John. I gotta go. Okay?" She started to shuck into her jacket, then looked nervously up at the cop.

"This doesn't concern you, miss," he said, and Kelley looked visibly relieved.

She gave John a look that was a cross between pity and sympathy. "I'll, like, I'll see you around."

She slid out of the booth, skinned past the cop, and practically ran out of the Cow. And that was the end of it. Thank you, Mr. Federal Policeman. Then again, maybe you just finished off what I had already started. In any case, here's another date shot to hell, another big score for John.

"May I sit down?" asked the man pointlessly as he sat in Kelley's vacated seat. Flashing something that looked like a badge and a federal ID card, he said, "My name is Bennett."

Mr. Bennett was not your usual federal investigator, or so John supposed. Weren't those guys supposed to be inconspicuous? Beyond his slick good looks, noticeable enough in any crowd, this guy was tall and thin like John, and John knew from personal experience that such a physique did not blend easily into a crowd. Bennett's eyes were as clear and gray as John's, but they had a hard quality that would have frightened John if he had seen them staring back at him in a mirror.

"They pick you special to còme talk to me?"

"Excuse me?"

John waved a hand up and down. "Your look. The pale-scarecrow effect. Not too many people with our phenotype. This a coincidence, or what?"

"I don't believe in coincidence," Bennett said quietly. "Matters of appearance are trivial. John, there is a very serious matter to hand."

It had to be Winston. Had Mitsutomo disowned him? Was he being turned over to some kind of federal rehabilitation program? "Look, Mr. Bennett, I'm really sorry. It was, like, an accident. I didn't mean to hurt him."

"Hurt him?"

"Winston."

"Ah, the other student. That's not important." Bennett pulled a photograph out of his pocket and tossed it on the table. The false three-dimensional image showed a woman with long hair. "Ever seen her?"

John stared stupidly at the photograph. What was this? Bennett wasn't here about Winston? It was something else entirely. What was going on? Bennett had to ask again if John had ever seen the woman before he paid attention to the image in the pic.

"No."

"Are you sure?"

The intensity in Bennett's voice made John look up. The federal agent was staring at him. The ice in those gray eyes made John uneasy. "What did she do?"

"It's not so much what she has done as what she might do." Bennett gathered up his photograph and tossed a business card down to replace it. When John picked it up, he saw that there was nothing on the card but a number. "I would appreciate it if you would call me if you should happen to see this woman. Please feel free to call at any time."

Knowing that Bennett was not after him was strangely liberating. John felt light-headed, cocky. "What's this all about?"

"I'm afraid I'm not at liberty to discuss that."

" 'Not at liberty' seems to be your chorus. What *can* you discuss?"

Bennett ignored the question. "John, this is a very serious matter. I'd appreciate it if you would take it seriously. This woman is potentially dangerous. Call me if you see her." He slid out of the booth. "And don't try to do anything yourself."

Bennett walked out of the Frilly Cow, leaving John alone. The waitress, who had never bothered to come for the cop's order, stayed away as if John had been contaminated by Bennett's presence. John's head was full of questions.

Who was Bennett, and why had he come to John?

Bennett's looks had to be more than coincidence. John knew he had relatives on his father's side somewhere, even if his mother never talked about them much. He'd never met any of them. Whenever he'd asked his mother, she had always said it was too painful for her to spend time with them. John had accepted that answer. Sometimes it had been better to have a mysterious, dead father. One could always make up suitably heroic pasts for an unremembered father.

So Bennett might be a relative.

His mother had once said something about one of his relatives being some kind of cop. Just now, he couldn't recall which side of the family this cop was supposed to be on, but he remembered the reference. Sometimes people called special investigators "cops," as if they were ordinary policemen. Also he'd heard about federal agents claiming they were undercover detectives when they couldn't get away with the old

"I work for the government" dodge. The special ones had to keep their real jobs quiet. Maybe Bennett was John's cousin, a special investigator on a secret federal mission, who had come to seek out a relative because there was no one else he could trust. Only John would be able to help him find this woman and save the country from some dire peril. Maybe she was a mole for the Sino-Asian Alliance, or maybe she was a connection for a Latin cartel.

This was exciting.

He wondered who the woman was and what she had done. Wait a minute: Bennett had said that what she *might* do was more important. John wondered who she was and what she was going to do.

This was better than a date.

Wasn't it?

He looked at the empty seat across from him.

It was better, wasn't it?

CHAPTER
5

The sign said that the Schmidt Institute was a Psychological Trauma Center, but Holger Kun knew better. He knew a nut house when he was in one. Better than most people. This place made the back of his neck itch. And the insides of his elbows. He suppressed the urge to scratch. Not good form, that. Made the orderlies notice. They knew. They knew.

The woman at the reception desk gave him directions to the research department. Having no desire to get lost, he followed them precisely, even though it meant waiting five minutes for the elevator. He could have burned off some of his nervous energy climbing the stairs, but she had said, "Take the elevator to seven." Explicit directions. He followed them.

The entry to the research department was secure. Holger buzzed and waited for the orderly inside the first door to open the lock. Once inside, he showed the man his pass. The man's mouth twitched and he spent an inordinate amount of time reading the pass. Finally he nodded and, using the controls at his desk, closed the outer doors. The inner doors wouldn't open until the outer panels were locked again. A decent enough system, though far better for keeping people in than out. But then, that's what this system was supposed to do.

A blast of chemical stink hit him when the inner doors opened. Underneath it, he could smell the vomit and the piss and all the other foul odors that went with these places.

"First left, then last door on the left," the orderly said just before the inner doors closed behind Holger.

Those doors wouldn't open again until the orderly gave them the command. Or until Holger did something about them. But there wouldn't be any need for that, would there?

The doors along the corridor were all fitted for security and observation. They had heavy locks with keypads, pass-through drawers, and peepholes to supplement the monitors set into the walls beside each frame. Holger avoided looking at the monitors.

The rooms were well insulated; he heard nothing save the sound of the air-conditioning equipment.

He took the turn. The door he was looking for would have been obvious even without the orderly's directions. It was the only one that was open.

The room was bigger than he expected, part of it out of his sight around a corner. There were several workstations scattered around, but only one was occupied. The woman seated there was middle-aged; her hair, cropped tight to her head, was more gray than brown. She wore no makeup to soften the lines of her face. From what he could see beneath the obligatory lab coat, she was well formed, if skinny. She matched the ident file perfectly.

His new boss.

Yeah, but he didn't have to like it. His request for transfer to another department had only gotten him an internal shift to Spae's team. A demotion, too, since he *was* Spae's team. The doctor was in no better odor with the big butts than he was. He knew why he was on their shitlist, but her file didn't show what she'd done to piss the bastards off. Spae had been one of the Department's first recruits. What had she done to fall from favor?

He stepped to the side of her chair.

"Dr. Spae?"

She made a noise without bothering to look up from the console she studied. After a moment, he decided that she probably had meant her noise as a confirmation that she had heard him. Self-important whitecoat.

"I'm Kun."

This time she looked up. She showed no sign of recognition.

"From the Department."

"Kun?" The light of understanding lit in her mismatched green and blue eyes. "Ah. The new bullyboy. Sit down. I'm working now, we'll push the papers later."

Holger found himself a place where he could keep an eye on both the door and the unseen portion of the room, pulled a chair over to his chosen spot, and sat. There wasn't much you could do with whitecoats. At least not when you were under orders to protect and assist them.

A whitecoat rounded the corner from the other part of the room. The stethoscope around his neck said M.D., and old-fashioned to boot. The frown of annoyance on his bearded face was old-fashioned, too.

"What are you doing here? Let's see your authorization."

Holger just stared at him. They didn't like that.

The doc blustered up, armored in his importance. Holger let him blow. Well before he got on Holger's nerves, Spae noticed.

"It's all right, Kevin. He's Department."

"Oh," Kevin said.

Bright boy, the doc.

Naturally, it turned out that the doc had come to talk to Spae. About a patient named Lambe. Holger listened closely; Lambe was the sleeper they were supposed to be investigating. From the way Spae was talking to this Kevin, he knew almost as much about the Department as Holger did. Certainly more than Holger had known when he had requested transfer to the then newly formed Department M. Back then, all he'd known was that the Department was where all the hotshots in the European Community Special Services were headed. Supposed to be the fast track.

Fast track to hell.

He cut off the memories. This was no time to dredge them up. This place was too much like where he'd spent the last two years. Focus, he ordered himself. Focus on the current mission. There is nothing else.

Like hell.

Hell was where you lived when you died.

You and all your friends.

Friends die.

And go to hell.

Like hell!

Do you like hell, Mr. Kun? Is that why you stay there? No, Doctor. I hate hell. Very good, Mr. Kun. We're making progress.

On hell?

Like hell!

Focus! The mission! Nothing else!

He pictured his orders, grabbing for the memory as if it were a rope and he was in water over his head. He hated water. He didn't think much of his orders either.

Assignment: Dr. Elizabeth Spae, thaumaturgic theorist.

Holger Kun to assist as resource specialist and expediter.

And bullyboy.

That part was never in the orders.

But then, there was a lot that wasn't in the written orders. The Department was a covert group, which meant they put nothing in writing unless forced to. Paper trails made covering your ass more than usually difficult.

The Department's putative mission was to investigate unusual phenomena. They were supposed to be a scientific inquiry operation. And they were that. That and more. The Department's whitecoats worked to gain an understanding of so-called magical effects. It was the expediter's job to acquire anything that the whitecoats confirmed for the use—preferably exclusive use—of the ECSS in specific and the European Community in general.

All without letting anyone know what they were doing.

Beyond all the usual reasons for secrecy, there was the issue of credibility. Who would vote for a politician who believed in fairies? Beyond that, or maybe it was just an extension of the credibility thing, was the issue of power. It always really came down to that, didn't it? The bosses of the ECSS wanted power in the EC, and the bosses of the EC wanted power in the world. And who would have more power than the saviors of the world?

Holger listened to Spae and Kevin wrangle loudly over the validity of some of the tests the doc had conducted. The technical details were beyond him, but he knew an argument doomed by underlying disagreement when he heard one. Some saviors.

When the shouting match was over and Kevin had left, Spae turned to Holger.

"You want to monitor the call?"

"Of course." She would have to report her conclusions to the Department. It wasn't in his orders that he monitor her communications, but he wasn't about to refuse an offer. The more he knew about what she thought she was doing, the safer he'd be.

Holger set up a tap feed from her console to piggyback the incoming signal and set up an inset window to show her outgoing signal. When she placed the call, he was not surprised to see that her security clearance was several grades above his. The machines did their handshake protocol, but the security systems didn't register Holger's tap as a violation; his own clearance was high enough for that. Once the line was secured, a broad-faced man with a Gallic cast to his features appeared on the screen. Holger was impressed. He hadn't expected Spae to have such ready access to Magnus.

"This trip is a waste," she said without preamble.

"Ah, Dr. Spae. How are you?"

Holger thought he detected a weary amusement in Magnus's tone. Spae answered him acidly.

"Tired. Annoyed. Lambe's not a sleeper."

That was fine with Holger, but Magnus didn't look pleased.

"Are you sure? Dagastino's been right before."

"So have I. More often than he has, as you well know. I'm telling you, we don't have a sleeper here."

Magnus frowned. "We had the lead on this one. I would rather not lose Lambe to the CIA."

"They can have him. He's just a garden-variety lunatic."

"But Dr. Dagastino's preliminary tests—"

"Looked good from the other side of the puddle, but over here it's plain to see the truth. It didn't take me long to ascertain that Lambe's got no aura to speak of. Dagastino's got nothing more than Lambe's ramblings to base a case on. He's a nut case, a waste of time."

"Still, we must be absolutely sure, Doctor. I cannot emphasize enough the importance of this mission. Each and every sleeper is vital. They are the key to the future, perhaps the only hope for mankind."

"Can the pep talk. It won't change anything."

"Dr. Spae, as a specialist, you understand—"

Spae slammed her fist against her keyboard, forcing a protesting beep from the system. "I understand that I'm chasing phantoms while the real work is being done on the Cornwall project."

"This channel does not have a high enough security rating for discussion—"

"Anybody with access to this channel knows about the project. I want to work on Arthur."

Magnus shifted his tone, speaking softly but firmly. "This Department, of which you are a part, has a mandate that includes investigation of all unusual phenomena which may have a magical origin. Since you left, we have received several reports of incidents on the East Coast of North America. You are our closest expert, Dr. Spae, and you will investigate. The Department is relying on you to do necessary, and I must add, vital, work."

"Boondoggles," Spae muttered.

"What was that, Doctor?"

She cut the line. Holger began to understand why she was in bad odor with the higher-ups.

CHAPTER
6

She walked, the soles of her shoes scuffing a rapid beat on the concrete sidewalk. The bike was gone, stolen her first night in the sprawl. Normally, she wouldn't have minded. Normally, she had no need of hurry, but now the stars, wheeling in their marshaled array, offered little time, and she knew she was not as well hidden as usual. What the stars allowed, others sought to deny.

She didn't recognize her surroundings, but that was no surprise. It had been a long time since she had been in Massachusetts, and then it had been in another part. The signs proclaiming "Tewksbury this" or "Tewksbury that" suggested that the area was called Tewksbury. The name was vaguely familiar, but she didn't remember the crowds. Or the presence of skyscrapers, rezcoms, apartment blocks, and industrial centers. Or the decay.

The temperature was dropping along with the sun, and the wind was rising. She pulled her jacket tighter. Walking was easier at night, but tonight the wind would be a danger; she'd need a place for the night, somewhere out of the wind. But it was still only evening, and there was still time to cover ground, so she walked on.

Tewksbury was one of the northern fringe districts of the Northeast sprawl. Only the fringe, but still an unfriendly place. The sprawl was a principal battleground in the war between the ordered forces of urban professionals and the chaotic hordes of urban victims and predators. Victory lay unclaimed, but whichever side was the ultimate winner, the land would lose.

It was cold on the streets and getting colder.

Evening rush hour choked the street and the sidewalks. Cars and people, all moving in a complex dance. She moved along with the flow, fitting herself into its rhythms. She didn't look out of place, and that was good; being noticed held danger.

A large black limousine cruised slowly down the other side of the street. It was clean and had all of its trim, making it look out of place among the smoking heaps and battered E-cars through which it cruised. It might have been a giant grouper, cruising the reef of the sprawl among shoals of lesser automotive fish. It passed from her sight, and from her mind.

The people around her were a mix of types: workers of many kinds, homeless old men and women, drug addicts and pushers, whores, pimps, and their users, street vendors, and gangers. Some sorts were familiar to her from other cities and other times. Others, like the man and woman in matching, multicolored spandex bodysuits with shaved heads and flashing visors, were sights so strange as to defy categorization.

She sensed a presence at her back coming closer and found it convenient to stop and adjust her knapsack strap. People. Cars. The bald couple, arms locked around each other's waist, strolled past her; she heard music coming from their visors. The black limousine was now on this side of the road, cruising barely faster than a person might walk. Accompanied by honking, and rude gestures and suggestions, traffic flowed out around it.

She reslung her pack and walked on.

The limousine passed her, then slowed, nosing in toward the curb. As she drew abreast of the fender, the rear door opened. She halted, ready to bolt, and a man stumbled into her from behind. Cursing, he gave her a shove that sent her toward the limousine. She landed quivering against its fender, but nothing leapt out of the car.

Instead, a broad hand with pudgy fingers appeared and grasped the armrest on the door. Gold rings glinted on most of the fingers and a heavy silver bracelet dangled from the wrist. A face appeared, eyes hidden behind dark glasses. Full lips beneath a thin mustache curled up in a smile.

"Sorry. Didn't mean to scare you. In fact, quite the opposite. I'd hoped we'd be friends."

She straightened up and shifted to where she could see more of the interior of the car. It was clean, sparklingly clean. An array of gadgets studded the partition between the large rear compartment and the front seat. She recognized the faucet next to the rack of decanters and the video screen was obvious, but there were other fixtures of gleaming chrome and dark, lustrous plastic that were complete mysteries to her.

The eyes behind those dark glasses were mysteries, too.

"I don't know you," she said.

"But you could. My name's John."

"Nym."

"We could have lots of fun together, Nym."

Something moved within the limousine, and Nym caught sight of a white ankle. She shifted for a better look. John was not alone in the back seat of his limousine; he had a woman beside him, nestling close to him and clinging like soft wax. From what Nym could see of her face, she was pretty, beneath a light scuffing of street dirt. She was definitely young and well endowed. Her clothes were shabby and she wore no shoes, but a change in shade beneath her ankle showed she had until recently. A gold bracelet encircled one wrist. Gold and torn, dirty jeans added to an obvious conclusion.

John noticed where Nym was looking and drew his own conclusions. "I give presents to my friends. Nice presents."

"I have to be somewhere."

His smile dampened a little, but he didn't relent. "Riding is faster than walking, my dear. More comfortable, too."

It would be night soon. "You'll take me there?"

His smile returned, broadening to reveal his teeth. One of them was gold. "I'll take you places you haven't even thought of yet."

"Okay." She unslung her knapsack and dropped it on the floor of the car. She climbed in beside him and swung the door closed. "Let's go."

Even before Nym was settled, the other woman started squirming against John, nibbling at his ear and murmuring soft, meaningless words. John's reaction to the attentions of the strumpet made clear what sort of fun he enjoyed. In the midst of an embrace, one of his hands left the woman and found its way to Nym's knee. She removed it.

John came up for air. "What's the matter, pretty lady? Don't you want to play too?"

"You said you'd take me there."

"And I will." The woman was continuing to nuzzle him. "But we can have fun along the way. It's nice and private in here." As if on cue, the woman's hands slid to his belt and unhooked it. Her fingers started in on the fastenings beneath. "Don't let Cherie here inhibit you. There's plenty for everyone."

It was not an unfamiliar coin she was being asked to pay.

John gasped as Cherie found what she sought. Her head dropped to his lap. She quickly established a rhythm and one hand rose up to tug open his shirt. Dark-tinted nails traced intricate patterns on his body.

"Join the party," John panted.

Nym stared at Cherie's hand. The woman's sharp nails left pale marks on John's skin. Occasionally tiny drops of blood welled up. John begged for more. Cherie's nails dug deeper.

"Maybe you need a woman's touch to get warmed up."
John stroked Cherie's hair, then slid a hand under her chin.
He sighed reluctantly when she released him.

Cherie lifted her head, languid lids hooding her dark eyes.
She turned in Nym's direction and, apparently for the first
time, looked at her. Her eyes snapped wide, dark orbs
flashing in recognition. Cherie's face contorted and her lip
rose in a snarl, revealing white, white teeth. Her canines
were long and pointed. She hissed.

John went pale and tried to squirm away from his suddenly transformed inamorata. Cherie lunged at Nym, but
their mutual host got in the way. Cherie clawed at him,
tearing cloth and flesh. Nym battered at the controls for the
door. John was screaming, struggling to fend off the harridan
assaulting him. Some of the violence of their grappling escaped and buffeted Nym, but John's frantic struggles, as un-
coordinated as they were, proved a mostly effective barrier;
only once did Cherie's claws snake through to rake Nym before the door mechanism finally released and the panel
swung open. Fortunately the car wasn't moving very fast.
Nym tumbled out, snagging her knapsack as she went. She
hit pavement and rolled.

The limousine continued forward, rocking back and forth
on its springs as the struggle inside intensified. People noticed and pointed; some laughed. Nym heard the sound of
smashing glass. The car turned slightly toward the oncoming
lane of traffic, then swerved hard in the other direction, ac-
celerating. It jumped the curb, scattering screaming pedes-
trians. One fell beneath its wheels before it slammed into a
building with crumpling force. The horn began to blare and
the car began to shout, "Help! I'm being stolen!" in a me-
chanical voice. A calmer voice requested that all passengers
fasten their seat belts. Nym couldn't hear John's voice
among the cacophony.

Nothing but smoke emerged from the wreck, but Nym
didn't wait to see if the situation would change. She ran
down the street away from the scene. Behind her a fierce
bestial howling filled the air.

It wasn't the car.
She ran faster.

Monday's classes dragged. John kept expecting someone from the administration to show up and haul him away, but no one ever came. To all appearances, nothing had changed. It wasn't what John had been expecting.

By the time he got to Global Studies, he had almost convinced himself that Friday's incident was a dream, but Trahn didn't show up for class and John didn't know what to make of that. If Friday's incident was a dream, Trahn should have been present. GS class was longer than the rest of the day combined.

Yael found him while he was scouting the athletic facility for any sign of Winston.

"Missed you at the meet on Saturday. Coach is going to hand you your head at practice tomorrow."

Yael grinned cheerfully as he made throat-cutting sounds and swept his finger across his neck in an exaggerated arc. John wasn't in the mood.

"Something came up."

Yael's eyebrows shot up. "I can hardly wait to hear."

"I don't want to talk about it."

Yael followed him out of the facility. "Coach won't take that for an answer. You don't miss a home meet unless you're dead. You don't look dead to me, mein freund. Just almost dead."

"Didn't get a lot of sleep."

Stopping in his tracks, Yael grabbed John's arm and forced him to stop as well. "Kelley! You got lucky!"

"I did not," John snapped, and immediately regretted it. That would have been an excuse Yael could have understood.

"But is the protest real, or simply a clever subterfuge?"

"Your choice," John said. Let him think what he wanted. It was better than the truth. "Look, I gotta get going. Got stuff to do."

Extricating himself from Yael took only a few more ambiguous comments, the capper being one that implied John might be going to see Kelley. John wished that it were so; she hadn't returned his calls all weekend and he hadn't seen her all day save at a distance or in a large group.

There was mail waiting for him when he got home. Physical mail. His mom was out, so no one heard the yelp he gave when he saw the return address. It was from the Woodman Armory Museum. Physical mail took a lot longer than the usual electronic kind; no wonder it had taken so long to come.

But come it had.

He tore it open. It was the job offer he was hoping for. Only now that he held it in his hands, it didn't seem like such a magic thing, and his excitement faded as quickly as it had come. The incident with Winston would probably destroy this opportunity. Once the museum heard about the beating, they'd withdraw the offer. How could they trust someone with such violent tendencies? Wouldn't matter that the position was only a night watchman's post; criminal behavior was criminal behavior. They'd probably also tell him that his services as a docent were no longer desired. Bad for public relations, to have a brutal brawler talking with impressionable young kids.

He almost threw the letter in the disposal.

But he didn't. He and his mother could use the extra income. The company stipend kept them fed and clothed, but it wasn't really enough for those extras that made life comfortable. His mother was always passing up something for herself in order to spend the money on him. As much as he wanted her to stop denying her own happiness, he didn't want to go without those things she bought for him either.

The museum job offered more than just money. Sure, there would be extra income and, since Mitsutomo was a major sponsor of the museum, he would be able to convert his pay easily into company credit. But more important, he'd be working close to something he liked. Sure, it was just a prole's job, but it was *in* the museum. On the museum payroll. Once on the inside he could get to know the curators, show them how much he cared about the armor and knights and all that stuff. He could impress them. Once they got to know him, they'd see he had potential. He could work with the curatorial staff in his off hours, and once they saw how much he cared, things would change. Maybe he'd get to spend a few hours cleaning stuff, then to do some work on a display. He'd work his way up. It would be far, far better than working in an office in front of a console.

He reread the letter. They wanted to have an orientation session. The letter said at John's convenience, but there was an unstated sense of urgency. John thought he understood that; Jenny in the gift shop had told him that the museum was having quite a bit of turnover among the guards.

Maybe they'd want a watchman enough to take him despite the thing with Winston.

Don't get your hopes up.

Who asked you?

There are safer places to be.

What do you mean?

Think about other things. You'll be less disappointed.

I'm not afraid. What can they do, say they don't want me?

Mitsutomo may have a more severe reaction.

About Winston, you mean.

Winston.

It was an accident! I lost control, okay? Everybody loses control once in a while. I'll apologize to him as soon as I see him. What do you want from me, anyway?

. . .

John spent a half hour fretting and fuming alone in his room, before he could convince himself that he'd have to go on with things. If they were going to do something to him for beating up Winston, they would. Why should he help them by pummeling himself? He placed a call to the museum compsec and scheduled the orientation session for Tuesday night, opposite fencing practice. A job demand was an excuse Coach would have to accept. Missing practice would allow John to postpone the confrontation for a while longer. Maybe by the time it happened, he'd have figured out a story that wouldn't make him out to be a homicidal lunatic.

CHAPTER
7

Sörli droned through his report on Friday night's fire bombing in the village of Blaisdell Corners, and Pamela Martinez listened dutifully. She was only receiving what she had asked for, after all.

The eyewitness accounts were vague, but there was nothing vague about the three deaths and the nearly one million dollars in property damage. Sörli seemed more interested in a report by the keeper of a local tavern that one of his regulars, a known drunkard, had claimed to have seen a lone female motorcyclist fleeing from a pack of fiery hounds. He found it especially significant that the drunkard in question was found dead in the bushes the morning after the attack. The preliminary police report said that the man had died of exposure.

"Of course, that was only the *apparent* cause of death," Sörli said.

"Of course." She checked the monitor to ensure that the record function was activated; last time, their conversation had not been stored in her console's memory. "And the real cause?"

"He saw those who hunted the woman. They are not yet ready to reveal themselves, and so they silence those who are unfortunate enough to discover their existence."

"Of course." Sörli's was a relentless obsession. "Yet *we* know of them. Why do they not seek to silence us?"

"They do not know that we are aware of them."

"How can you be sure?"

"By the very fact that they *haven't* made any attempts to silence us."

Neatly circular. "They have taken no notice of your investigative efforts?"

"*They* have always been gone by the time we learn of their activities. This is both fortunate and unfortunate. Fortunate in that they are as yet ignorant of our opposition to them, and unfortunate in that we have been unable to act effectively against them. This will change.

"And soon, I think. This morning I learned of an incident which occurred last night in the Tewksbury District." He spoke of a car crash resulting in the death of the driver and his passenger and the crippling of a pedestrian. She had heard of it already; the pedestrian was a Mitsutomo dependent. The only new piece of data he provided was an account of a woman seen running from the scene. "We have people looking into it, but I do not expect more than confirmation of the details we already know."

"And why is that?"

Sörli frowned. "My team cannot investigate this incident directly."

This was new. "Why not?"

"One of the officers involved in the investigation is Charles Gordon, the man who found Churdy's body. Were any of my team to appear on the scene, he would undoubtedly recognize us and make connections between the incidents which would be best left unmade at this time. We need freedom of action if we are to successfully combat the danger."

"Meaning the convergence?"

"Exactly." Smiling, he added, "I knew I was correct in coming to you."

The lame attempt at flattery surprised her. "Your point?"

"These most recent incidents are clear evidence of the destructive nature of the otherworld, and the lack of regard in which they hold our world."

"But the existence of the otherworld remains unproven." She waved down his protest. "The media is labeling the fires a terrorist attack, despite the lack of motive or claimants to the responsibility, and they have described the car crash as a 'drug-related incident.'"

"They are correct in the first case, although not in the way they think. There will be no one taking responsibility for the attack. As to the drugs, the only ones involved are those taken by the media hacks. *They* may be blind to the approaching danger, but *we* must not allow ourselves to be blinded. There is a pattern to these disturbances."

"What sort of pattern?"

"The presence of the woman."

"Half the population is female, and we don't know if all these incidents involve the same woman."

"Perhaps *pattern* is too strong a word," he conceded. "Rather let us say that we have a progression. First the Churdy killing in the mountains, then the incident on the Main–New Hampshire border, now this one in the Tewksbury, an outer district of the Northeast sprawl. The disturbance is moving south and west."

"If this is a progression, what is the goal?"

"That is unknown. Certainly it is related to an attempt at convergence."

"How is it certain?"

"Other sources confirm that the woman is an agent seeking the convergence. It is foolish to ignore the likelihood that these incidents center around her. We cannot afford to be foolish, Ms. Martinez."

I certainly can't, little man. "What are these 'other sources'?"

He tilted his chin down in a defiant manner and stared her straight in the eyes. "I will not say."

"*Will* not? I could insist otherwise."

"You would not be wise to do so. We cannot afford a rift in our ranks. This woman must be stopped before she achieves her goal."

"Your otherworld faction seems intent on that."

"They are not *mine,*" he snapped. His vehemence vanished as quickly as it had risen. He continued, "But, yes, it would seem that a faction is intent on stopping her. However, they have had notably little success. It is possible that these attempts are merely a device to lull us, to keep us from acting."

"I thought you said they didn't know about us."

"I could be wrong. But such actions could have nothing to do with confusing a known or specific party. The rulers of the otherworld are devious and have strange ways. They have a passion for confusion, even when it has no discernible purpose."

A passion for confusion, eh? Like Sörli's? If they had half the mesmeric force of this man, those rulers would be dangerous. Through implication, inference, suggestion, and only the most circumstantial of evidence he had drawn her into his delusion, if delusion it was. How could belief as intense as Sörli's be based on anything short of reality?

Sörli had to be worried if he would admit to a possible error, even if he backpedaled immediately, and seeing him worried made her anxious. "What do you propose?"

"We must spread a net for this woman. We must start surveillance on all possible otherworld agents along the path of the disturbance, and I need your authority to requisition the necessary resources. Further, we must prepare to stop her."

"Capture her, you mean."

He stared at her, saying nothing.

"For interrogation."

He remained silent.

"You want to kill her," she accused.

"She is too dangerous to deal with any other way," he said matter-of-factly.

"I will not be a party to a private murder."

He tilted his head and gave her an indulgent smile, then his expression sobered. "This is a matter well beyond private concerns. With the fate of the planet lying in the balance, will you let one woman outweigh all? Will you let her tip that balance and send us all into chaos?"

"I want to know more."

"There is little time. We must act."

"So you say."

"Yes, so I say."

"Where's the proof you've always promised?"

"By the time—"

"Yes, yes. I know. It'll be too late."

"We face dangerous opponents."

"I believe you." We have dangerous friends, too. "I'm not asking you to risk your life. Mitsutomo has no policy against employees' carrying defensive weapons."

"A sound policy."

"*Defensive* weapons. If you involve Mitsutomo in murder, I will disown you. And don't look so smug; I can make sure you don't work for any corporation in the Northern Hemisphere. You know I can."

"I am aware of your influence, Ms. Martinez," he said, still looking smug.

"Keep it in mind. Now go, set your snares. Capture this woman and bring her to me."

He stood, but did not immediately turn to leave. When she looked at him, he said quietly, "She may resist."

"If she does, use force, but not lethal force. I want to interview this agent of the otherworld."

"She may have allies who will oppose us."

"There hasn't been any sign of 'allies' so far. But if any show up, oppose *them*. I'm tired of stumbling around in the dark. I want hard information and I want it soon. You understand?"

"Quite."

"Understand this, too. I want this operation quiet, and we both know that you know how to be quiet. If things don't stay that way, you'd better have a very good reason."

"I do nothing without good reason."

"Your good reasons do not always accord with mine. This time, they had better." He nodded and started for the door. She let him get halfway there. "If you start shooting, you'd better bring me back a goblin's head to mount on the wall—because if you don't, I'll mount *your* head up there."

On Thursday the media announced the whereabouts of the missing Winston. His severely beaten body was found over on the south side, near the old train station. It wasn't a nice part of town, so Winston's being dead wasn't as shocking as it would have been if his corpse had turned up in the middle of the Polytech campus. There were lots of burned-out injectors and empty capsules around, so the media naturally picked a drug angle: STUDENT BEATEN TO DEATH AS DRUG DEAL TURNS SOUR.

It was big news all over campus that morning. John cut his classes and spent most of the morning in the student center, where live reports and taped segments fed in from a news service ran almost uninterrupted on the vid wall. In one, Winston's roommate, clearly badly shaken up, told a reporter that Winston had been talking and acting oddly on Saturday night. In another, a solemn-faced reporter babbled about an unnamed university custodian having said that he'd seen Winston get into an argument with another student. Supposedly the argument had devolved into a shoving match and after the two were separated, Winston made some threats. The custodian allegedly saw Winston meet with a man in a dark raincoat, the two of them departing in a late-model sedan with out-of-state plates. All very mysterious and "suggestive of the tragedy to come," according to the reporter.

John wondered if the "unnamed custodian" was Trashcan Harry.

Of all the students talking about it, on or off the screen, only Winston's roommate spoke of seeing the dead jock after Friday afternoon. One of Winston's frat brothers collected an audience for himself by repeating in person his interviewed statement denying that Winston had ever done drugs. In the background, on screen, official spokespersons for the university denied prevalent drug abuse on campus and agreed with the frat rat, but many of the live audience weren't buying. One loudmouth in the crowd made a point of recalling Winston's reputation as a hard partyer.

Sitting sunk in one of the lounge chairs, John stayed out of the discussion. He stared at the screen and listened to the reports, ignoring the few students who spoke to him. Mostly he saw Winston's still body lying on the ground outside of the Dunstan Building.

He felt a little sick.

There was a hole in the reporting, and it wasn't just the failure to mention John's brawl with Winston on Friday. None of the reports mentioned anything unusual about the body's condition, which puzzled John. If Winston had died of the beating John had given him—too likely a possibility—the body should have been decomposing. But it wasn't. So John was not the killer.

Right?

. . .

If John hadn't killed Winston, the jock had gone on with his life after their encounter on Friday. But if Winston *had* gone on with his life, some of the bruises would have begun healing. There wasn't any mention of evidence of "systematic abuse," as the media liked to call repeated beatings. To all appearances, Winston had been beaten and killed on Wednesday night.

The coroner was reported to place the time of death at one in the morning, a not uncommon time for drug deals. Who else would be out there at that time of night?

The killer, for one. But not John. John had been home in bed. Asleep. Which was where Winston should have been.

For all John thought Winston had been an ass, he had never known the jock to use more than alcohol or mild stimulants. Just over-the-counter stuff. Being on the basketball team meant too much to Winston; he wouldn't have risked losing that. Winston's being down on the south side didn't make sense.

There had to be more to the story. Where had Winston been for five days? And had he spent those days dead or alive? Normally John liked mysteries. But normally he wasn't a part of them, one of the suspects. Suspects? Not really. He seemed to be the only one who suspected him.

His stomach flopped and he thought about heading for the men's room. He waited it out, scowling at the vid wall. When he felt as though he could walk safely, he headed home. He took the shortcuts, not for speed but because there were fewer people to see him along those byways. Once home, he shut himself in his room. He even told Faye to shut up and go away.

Mysteries, but not mysteries for him to solve. He was just a student. Maybe a killer. He didn't sleep much that night, worrying at the problem.

He stumbled through his Friday morning classes in a daze, struggling to piece the facts he knew into a picture that made sense. He spent the dead time between classes wandering around the campus with no real destination in mind. The walking seemed to keep him calmer, let him think more clearly. Slowly he came to the conclusion that it was physically impossible for him to have beaten Winston to death. Dead men don't lie around for five days without decomposing. The bruises of the fatal beating must have overlain those that John had given the jock. The south side thing had to be what it appeared to be. Winston must have had a hidden side that his friends didn't know. That kind of thing happened all the time with serial killers. Why not with victims?

Feeling better, he headed for the student-center cafeteria. He put a Coke and a plate of the daily special on his card. The anonymous collection of brown, green, and yellow things on the plate didn't look much like food, but state law required the mess to be nutritious. A day without solid food had left him hungry enough to enjoy it. By the time he was washing down the last of it with his Coke, his attitude was improved considerably.

Awake, awake, sleeping beauty. You are being followed.
What?
Two men over by the concession stand.

John thought they looked more interested in the magazines than they did in him.

But they haven't been more than a block away all morning.
Really?
Really.

Dredging his memory, he realized that he had seen those two before. One or the other of them had been somewhere nearby all morning. Coincidence, surely. They had business on campus and just happened to be in the same places. Yet there was something ominous about their presence.

His watch beeped. He had lab in ten minutes, and he'd be late if he didn't hurry. Enviro lab in the Dunstan Building. Just like last week. But not like last week—Winston wouldn't be carousing along the walk when John got out.

Telling himself that the past was behind him, he gathered his stuff. He noticed that the two men finished looking at the magazines about the time he went past the concession stand. They didn't buy anything.

They walked on past when he entered the Dunstan Building. Though they had apparently gone on about their business, they stayed on John's mind throughout the lab. After he'd turned in his assignment, he decided he wouldn't go out the usual way. He took the side door he used on rainy days; the cut across to the trolley station was shorter that way. Before leaving the building, he took a look around. He didn't see anyone.

While he was waiting for the trolley, the two men showed up again, one at a time. Neither approached him and neither paid attention to the other, but they both boarded the trolley when John did. To see what would happen, John got off before his regular stop. The two men got off as well.

The men of grim intent stay on your trail.

That was obvious.

He headed up the street toward Stetson Mall. There were always a lot of people at the mall. Bad guys didn't start trouble around lots of people.

What was he expecting from these men? He didn't even know who they were. Why was he assuming they were the bad guys?

Pretending to make a phone call just outside the mall gave him a chance to look them over. They were nondescript fellows: average height, average build, ordinary haircuts, regular features, and simple, slightly conservative suits. One was a blond Caucasian, the other an Asian. The suits were the only thing that made them stand out on campus. John couldn't remember seeing either of them before.

Were they cops? Mitsutomo men checking on him? Associates of the mysterious Mr. Bennett? Did it matter who they were? Of course it did, especially if it involved Winston's death. The only safe assumption seemed to be that they were not thugs out to rob him; thugs didn't wear tailored suits.

So why were they following him? The answer would be intimately tied to who they were, the one answering the other. Whoever they were and whyever they were tailing him, he didn't like the idea of strangers following him around, watching everything he did. There wasn't much he could do about it without knowing who they were. There might not be anything even he could do if he did know, but knowing was better than not knowing.

There was no one available to ask about these guys except the guys themselves. Confronting them in the middle of the street seemed inappropriate; this was some sort of cloak-and-dagger game. John started looking for a suitable place. As he approached the mall entrance he remembered a serviceway that ran behind the Lechmere's. It was a narrow place, usually full of trash, private but still near enough to the crowded bus stop at the mall entrance that any shouts for help would be heard.

He passed the mall entrance, checking in the glass to see if they were still following him. They were. The walk along the wall under the Lechmere sign seemed longer than usual. He spelled out the store's name, whispering each letter as he passed under it. Two steps past the last "e" and a couple yards from the entrance to the serviceway, he started to sprint. Three strides put him in the alley, moving at speed, but instead of racing down the lane, he kept turning, fetching up against the wall of the building.

Stay still.

Okay.

He leaned against the wall, folding his arms and adopting a casual posture. The shadows should hide him from immediate discovery. The guys came around the corner, moving faster than he had seen them do so far. They slowed and stopped just inside the alley mouth. They scanned their surroundings, looking for their quarry. For him.

He kicked his heel against the wall to attract their attention. "Nice day, guys. What brings gentlemen like you to this part of town?"

They started. The Asian started to reach under his jacket, but aborted the action. The looks on their faces were priceless. Surprise, anger, frustration, embarrassment, and just the faintest, most fleeting hint of fear. Annoyance surfaced and took over.

Probably directed at themselves.

Deservedly.

They'll have to be better to catch us, won't they?

Assuredly.

The blond one interrupted John's conversation. "John Reddy?"

John felt annoyed himself. Here were more strangers who knew who he was. He didn't like it. "Yes."

"I'm Agent McAlister. This is Agent Surimato. FBI. We'd like to ask you a few questions."

Damn, the guy recovered quickly. Agent McAlister was talking as if he was standing in an office, not an alley. "About what?"

"There's no reason to be upset, Mr. Reddy. We're not after you."

"Then why were you following me?"

The two agents exchanged glances. McAlister said, "We are investigating a series of terrorist attacks. We have been given reason to believe that you might have had contact with one of our suspects."

"I'm not a terrorist."

"Of course not, Mr. Reddy. We are aware of that. But you may have had contact with one or more of these people without knowing their true aspect. We need your help in this matter. Would you be willing to look at some pictures and tell us if you've seen any of the people in them?"

"Do we need to go to your office?"

McAlister smiled. "If you like. Or we can do it here. It shouldn't take long."

"Let's see them."

Agent Surimato reached into his jacket, the other side this time, and pulled out a handful of four-by-sixes. He held them out, and John took them.

The pictures were of varying quality, but all were cropped to show no more than a head and shoulders. Some of the pictures were very grainy, clearly computer-enhanced versions of other photographs. Halfway through the stack, he came across a picture of the woman in Bennett's photograph. It was a different angle and she looked younger, but John was sure it was the same woman.

"You know, you guys ought to keep better track of your investigations. I've already talked to an agent."

The agents exchanged glances again, concerned looks flashing across their faces. McAlister gave a slight nod. Surimato said, "Could you describe this agent?"

"A bit taller than me, pale, blond. Why?"

"Very thin?" Surimato asked.

"Male?" McAlister asked.

John nodded yes to both questions.

"You don't see him in the pictures, do you?"

John shook his head. "Naw."

"Did he give you a name? Show you a badge?"

"Said his name was Bennett. I didn't get a good look at the badge. Come to think of it, I haven't seen your badges either."

"Sorry," McAlister said.

Both of them pulled out wallets, flipped them open, and handed them to John. John looked carefully this time. The badges said Federal Bureau of Investigation, and the ID cards looked very official. The photos on the cards matched the two agents exactly. He handed them back.

"This Mr. Bennett is not a federal agent," Surimato said solemnly.

"If he is who we believe him to be, he is a very dangerous man," McAlister added.

"And just who do you believe him to be?"

"We're not at liberty to say," McAlister said.

"How did I know you were going to say that?" John thrust the stack of photos back at Surimato. "I haven't seen any of these people."

"You're sure?" McAlister asked.

"Yeah. I'm sure."

McAlister held out a card. John could see a phone number printed on it. "It's very important that you call us if you see any of these people. It would also be wise to call us if this Mr. Bennett contacts you again. Be very careful around him, and don't take any chances. Most especially, don't let him know you have spoken with us."

"You guys afraid of Bennett?"

The agents exchanged looks again. McAlister smiled reassuringly at John. "As I said, this man may be very dangerous. He could get you into a lot of trouble."

"I'll be careful."

"Good boy." Surimato started to leave, but McAlister lingered. "Remember to call that number if you see any of these people."

"I won't lose the number."

"Good boy."

Of course I didn't say I'd use it, either, John said silently to the backs of the departing agents.

The advice to be cautious was good advice. Something strange was going on, and more than one party thought that John had some connection to it. Intriguing. And a little scary. He was getting worried all over again.

What the hell is going on?

. . .

Some people are never around when you need them.

John cut back around to the mall entrance. The federal agents were nowhere in sight. He went inside. The noise and people made a comforting blanket. So very, very normal. He dropped by the arcade. Slipping his card into The Dragonknight, he bought himself some safe adventure for a while.

Worcester looked like a nicer district than Tewksbury. It was less built up, less paved over. There were more parks, more grass. The streets were cleaner, the people less unkempt. In many ways, it was more like the Massachusetts she remembered.

The driver dropped her off where 190 split from 290. He was going north, away from where she needed to be. The only payment he took was a smile.

Yes, Worcester was a more pleasant place.

She hiked down off the highway and skirted the fence separating it from the local streets. Up beyond the interchange she could see the Mitsutomo Light Metals fabrication facility spreading out along the base and lower slopes of the hill. At the upper boundary of the facility, the antique steel and glass structure of the Woodman Armory Museum stood silhouetted against the sleek sides of the rezcom units that topped the hill.

The streets here were a snarl of passageways passing over and under each other and snaking every which way. She walked along one that seemed headed in the direction of the hill.

There was still time.

Dr. Spae insisted that she had detected a ripple in the ambient psychic aura. Holger was just her bullyboy and no expert on such things, so his opinion of the reasoning behind the rush trip didn't matter. No one cared to listen to his opinion that she was just playing a hunch, Spae herself least of all. It only confirmed his opinion that she really didn't have a good reason to drag them to this corporate exurb.

"You're an expediter," she had said after deciding that they go directly to one of the sites of alleged activity. "Expedite our trip."

He had. Now here they were in downtown Mitsutomoland. All the maps said Worcester, Massachusetts, but maps always lagged behind reality.

The security at the airport had been lax; they hadn't seen what they should have seen, which suited Holger fine. He hadn't been obliged to produce his UN permits, always good for at least a half hour of hassle while the locals proved to themselves that they still had some authority over their jurisdictions. The easy pass-through meant that he and the good doctor had a lower profile. The Department appreciated low profiles.

The Department also appreciated results, which they didn't seem to be achieving. Of course, he couldn't be sure, because he was only a bullyboy and Spae was the special expert, but cruising the town seemed an unlikely way to turn up much of anything. Still, he followed the doctor's vague directions as best he could. Moving in a straight line was not easy while driving through the warren of one-way streets and narrow cowpaths-turned-roads that was the heart of the exurb's transportation net. The layout of the city reminded him a little of home, which was odd; he'd thought all American cities were served by broad highways and grid-planned streets.

One always has to adjust expectations in new places.

The morning had vanished and the afternoon was well on its way to following. Holger had stopped excusing himself when his stomach grumbled, but the doctor didn't seem to notice the difference. The sun was almost touching the western hills when she finally agreed to one of his suggestions that they stop for some food.

"May as well, I've lost focus anyway," she said, massaging her forehead as though she had a headache. She vetoed the restaurant when he pulled into the parking lot, saying, "I'm not sure we'll have enough time to sit down."

"Why not?"

"I don't know."

He nosed the rental car back out onto Park Avenue. He hated working with specialists. All vague feelings and no hard data. "McDonald's?"

"Hate the place."

Good. So did he. They passed it by.

"I think we should have people around," she said.

He'd prefer not. "Professional opinion?"

She mumbled something that sounded like "Yes."

There was a mall ahead on the right. Malls had food courts. Almost as fast as McDonald's, but more variety. Food could be better, could be worse. No way of knowing till you tried it, but the food was rarely as bad as that served in certain institutions.

"Try the mall?"

She opened her mouth, then closed it again. After a moment, she said, "Yes." She sounded unsure.

Parking took a while. It was late Friday afternoon and the mall traffic was picking up. Spae would certainly have people around. Holger located the food court on the map just inside the entrance and directed Spae toward it. Partway down the stairs, Spae stopped dead. Blocking traffic attracted attention. Holger urged her back into motion, pulling her to one side once they'd reached the lower level. She stared across the crowded walkway.

"Look over there," she said, starting to point.

He caught her hand and pulled it down. Bad tradecraft. People who were pointed at often noticed the people who were pointing at them. "Tell me, Doctor. There's no need to point."

"Over there by the sculpture."

Holger saw nothing out of the ordinary. No fireworks, no gun-waving thugs, no monsters. Just a crowd of mall crawlers, kids, old folks, shoppers, idlers, and working folk. Ordinary, everyday people. "Could you be more specific?"

"The dwarf."

Holger spotted her obvious referent: a dark, bearded man little taller than the lunchstand table by which he stood. He was short enough to be termed a dwarf, but he stood with an aggressive stance that suggested no one would call him one unless he gave them permission. Two other men, a Caucasian and an Asian, shared the table. They were holding a conversation, which suggested that they knew each other.

"I see him, Doctor. Why have you pointed him out?"

"Seeing him here tells me we've come to the right place."

This mall? She must mean Worcester. "How so?"

"He's turned up before."

"CIA?"

"Don't be ridiculous."

He hadn't thought he was being ridiculous. They were supposed to be stealing a march on the rival agency, and her reaction hadn't been strong enough to suggest that the dwarf was an enemy.

"So who is he?"

"I don't really know. He's used the name Sörli more than once. Fits if you like cross-language puns; he's a surly little bastard."

"Will we be coordinating efforts, then?"

"Over my dead body. The bastard's trouble."

"Is he a—" The therapy hadn't been totally effective. Holger couldn't bring himself to say the word, so he opted for the euphemism so popular in the Department. "Is he a specialist?"

Spae snorted a laugh. "No more sensitive than a rock. On all counts."

Holger was glad of that. It was always bad enough dealing with a situation when you didn't understand what was going on or who the players were, but to have some of them be—be *magicians* . . . Well, that would be too much.

Too much like before.

"Let's get out of here before he sees us," Spae said.

Holger was happy to comply. Fresh air and sunlight would be good right now. Spae and her search would wait. Questions about the dwarf would wait.

He needed to see the sky.

CHAPTER
8

John slept better Friday night. Not well, just better. He kept waking, thinking he heard someone calling. It wasn't Faye. She wasn't around. He stayed in bed late, chasing the elusive rest, and only rose when his mother called him to the phone. He wouldn't have bothered if she hadn't said it was the Armory Museum calling.

It was Mrs. Bartholomew, the personnel director. John had a moment of anxiety when she asked how his orientation session had gone; he was afraid she was going to rescind the job offer. But it turned out that one of the guards had just quit and the museum was caught in a scheduling bind. Mrs. Bartholomew told him that the museum was in a budget crunch, and hiring a substitute from a private guard agency would cost money better spent on the museum's mission. She wanted to know if he could start tonight. He said he could. Who really needed sleep anyway? She went on about some details, but John didn't listen very closely; he was too excited. He had to ask her to repeat what she said about uniforms.

The uniform shop didn't have any shirts with sleeves long enough for him and the pants had to be taken in at the waist.

While he waited, he tried to avoid thinking about the Winston situation. He wasn't entirely successful. Obviously the museum had not gotten word of his involvement in the beating incident. He supposed that he shouldn't be surprised, since apparently no one else had either. He hoped they wouldn't, but he couldn't count on it. In the past, the flare-ups of his temper had always brought official notice. It was probably only a matter of time. He resolved to enjoy his time with the Museum while he could.

Following Mrs. Bartholomew's instructions, he arrived about an hour before the Museum closed for the day. He waded through a crowd of school kids and around to the side door of the small room that served as the ticket office. It also doubled as the nighttime guard station. John tapped on the door and Mrs. Hanson opened it. He chatted with her while he signed in. When a late-arriving visitor took her attention, he went off to the staff room to change into his new uniform. The gift-shop staff came in while he was admiring himself in the mirror, so he had to put up with Jenny's smart remarks about how handsome men looked in uniform. With the museum about to close, he had the excuse of business to extricate himself.

Mrs. Bartholomew herself showed him the watch station and how all the controls worked. When the last of the office and shop staff had departed, she turned on the security system and sat with him through the fifteen-minute diagnostic and setup program. They watched the motion sensors report the movements of the janitor as he finished the last of his chores and followed the janitorial dot as it wandered about on the console screen's map of the museum. Mrs. Bartholomew showed him how to call up identification data; the computer said the dot was Mr. Revirez, janitor, and cited a ninety-seven-percent probability. Standard margin of error, Mrs. Bartholomew told him. The dot approached the watch station and John couldn't resist greeting Mr. Revirez just before he came into sight. Revirez gave John a perfunctory "good night" and a considerably friendlier one to Mrs. Bartholomew. He left, and for the next five minutes the motion sensors reported nothing. The computer reported the galleries and all of the staff areas except the guard station cleared of people.

With only the two of them left in the building, Mrs. Bartholomew demonstrated how to key the system up to the next level of security. Once it was activated, she had three minutes to exit the building without setting off an alarm. The combox on John's belt exempted him from the same requirement. The box was a call unit as well as a part of the security system loop, and broadcast continually to the system's scattered sensors; the system would ignore any readings generated within two feet of him. Mrs. Bartholomew said good night and wished him a pleasant first night on the job. He waved to her through the window as she passed through the lobby and listened until he heard the heavy steel doors thud closed behind her. The console flashed its green lights. The Woodman Armory Museum was secured for the night.

The position of night watchman didn't really require a lot of effort. The electronics did most of the work. All of it, really. The watchman was more a concession to tradition, a sort of honor accorded the men who had worn the armor and used the weapons that the museum so proudly displayed. It was better to think of the position that way than as a pointless redundancy in the security system.

Pointless or not, John was glad to be there. The museum felt different at night. Different even from just being closed. He'd been around when it was closed before, and then the arguments and jokes of the staff had still given the place a sort of ordinary life. Now with everyone gone but him, it was quiet in an absolute way. There was only John.

John and the armor.

He couldn't stand sitting in the watch room any longer. He had to get out and experience the great quiet in person. He wanted to see those hollow knights in all their solitude.

He took the back elevator up to the great hall. His passkey opened the lock on the ancient wooden door and he entered. The gallery lights were on their lowest setting, adequate for a slow amble and soaking up the somber, glinting magnificence of burnished steel, but not enough to see very far with any clarity. He liked the ambiance.

A suit of seventeenth-century three-quarter armor faced him. It was a new acquisition, said to have belonged to one of Oliver Cromwell's generals. It was a fine piece, but not the sort that John favored. He turned right, toward the medieval wing. The Middle Ages, when knights were knights.

The center of the hall was dominated by the jousting display, two mounted knights in full tourney armor aiming their lances at each other over a section of tilting barrier. Beyond them two English men-at-arms attacked a mounted French knight of the Hundred Years' War. Beyond them a pair of sixteenth-century knights fought with poll axes within the confines of a tiny list. The freestanding displays were only the highlights. More suits and isolated pieces of armor filled the alcoves on either side. The museum was blessed with a number of fine suits and had commissioned an equal number of fine replicas. All were carefully labeled as to which was which. He liked the replica displays better; they were generally mounted in more interesting ways.

Tonight, they all belonged to John.

He leaned on the railing around the Hundred Years' Warriors, admiring the narrow, tapering shape of the French knight's blade. John recalled the curator saying that the sword was the only real piece in the display, the only omission in the museum's labeling. It certainly looked real enough to slash unarmored men and thrust its diamond-shaped point through any gaps in a foe's armored protection. John imagined himself in the armor. He had survived the English arrow storm, and his horse, half mad with wounds and excitement, now reared and plunged among the scrambling English. They feared his good Bordeaux steel, these English dogs. As they should. John raised his blade high, ready for another slash.

A noise, half heard, made him spin around, reaching for his flashlight. He turned on the beam and sent it searching through the alcoves. The light played across glass cases, past wall-mounted weapons, and over suits of armor standing tall, proud, and motionless. The shadows of the armorer's shop display parted, but nothing moved among the anvils, tools, and half-finished pieces.

He heard the sound again, a soft, furtive shuffling. This time it came from his left, toward the new addition that housed traveling exhibitions. His light fell across the gallery sign: "Romano-Brithonic Warriors of the Dark Ages." There were a lot of rare pieces in there, many of which had never left England before. If John had been a thief, he would have considered it a target. From where he stood, his flashlight showed nothing of the gallery itself.

He thought about heading back to the watch station and calling the police, but he'd look awfully foolish if it was a false alarm. Checking out strange noises was part of his job. Cautiously he moved toward the gallery.

What if there really was someone there? What would he do about it? He couldn't hold a thief at gunpoint; he wasn't armed. He tried to convince himself that no one would be there, that it was just a random noise. Maybe it was a rat. Old buildings had rats, didn't they? Old buildings made all sorts of strange noises, too, didn't they?

From the doorway, he swept the flashlight beam around the gallery. The room was less crowded than the rest of the museum.

The walls were white and the carpet cream, a strong contrast to the dark wood-framed cases and the darker relics within them. The cases around the walls held minor artifacts and interactive displays covering the history of the time, detailing the various archaeological digs that had resulted in the exhibit, and even one covering legends associated with the countryside from which the finds had come. But the important stuff had pride of place in a large central case.

That case was set up like a grave mound for a warrior—a prince or king, from the quality and quantity of the grave goods laid around him on the bier. An armored form lay upon a carefully reconstructed cloak of handwoven cloth, rich with embroidery. The cloth itself was a minor, if modern, treasure. But the real treasures were the armor and weapons. The scraps of ancient armor that had survived were pieced together, missing parts reconstructed in plastic, and adorned blank-faced mannequins. The gold decoration of the real pieces glinted tawnily in the light. Four of the armored mannequins stood around the bier, one in each corner of the case, martial mourners for their dead mannequin king.

The five figures represented the best parts of three burial finds and the most complete martial suites yet recovered from post-Roman Britain. Each was more complete than the famed Sutton Hoo find, of which a few minor pieces resided in a case on the far wall. Each item was priceless; together their worth was even more priceless, if such a thing made sense.

To John's relief, nothing looked amiss. There were no thieves cutting their way into cases, no burglars tucking helmets under their arms.

The noise must have been a rat; Jenny had told him that the museum had been plagued with them recently. They were supposedly smart rats, too. So far all the traps had come up empty—sometimes sprung, but always empty. The curator had only just given permission for exterminators to be called in. Certainly the rats were smart enough to avoid John's light.

Seeing nothing amiss, he cut off the beam and walked back to the door to the central stairwell. Deciding against the antique elevator, he took the stairs that wound around the shaft. The building's outer wall here was glass and offered a view of the city and the hills beyond. The valley sparkled in the clear night like a sky gone mad with stars. The real sky might once have had so many lights, before man's cities stole away the night's natural brilliance, but there was little of it to be seen now. Still, Worcester wasn't as bad as some places. He couldn't recall having seen a single star on his last trip to Boston.

Thinking that simpler times had to have been pleasanter, he reached the landing and opened the door to the balcony galleries. The older stuff was arrayed here. He turned right toward the oldest. Green, half-corroded Greek helmets whispered to him of the glory of god-ridden heroes and the broad-brimmed gladiator's helmet echoed the roar of the crowds cheering the skill of the Thracian who had proudly worn the highly decorated piece. He ran his hand along the case that held the Roman horse armor from Dura Europa. He pictured the iron legions marching dusty roads on their way to keeping the Pax Romanum.

A noise from the great hall below drew him out of his imaginings. He crossed between cases dedicated to the hunt. He leaned over the railing and played his flashlight beam across the floor. The light cast strange shadows, eerie, jagged shapes. Something skittered away in the dark, scampering ahead of his light and disappearing behind the tournament display.

A rat. It had to be.

But were rats so big? From the glimpse he had caught, the thing had looked as big as a cat. It was creepy to think about animals sneaking around just out of sight. Furry wild things with beady eyes could be watching him from the shadows. He felt creeped out. There weren't any rats in the rezcoms. The cleaning 'bots would take care of them. This old hulk of a building wasn't fitted for cleaning 'bots. Historic register and all that.

The exhibits didn't seem so friendly anymore. With so many nooks and crannies, rats could be anywhere, just waiting to spring out. He headed back to the watch room, where there were lights. Opening the door, he surprised something that fell, or jumped, from the desk with a thump. By the time he got around the desk to see what it was, it was gone. He was left with what the rat had left behind.

Crumbs of bread, shards of plastic wrap, bits of paper, scraps of turkey roll, and shreds of lettuce littered the desktop. His lunch bag had been mauled, the sack ripped to pieces and the contents spread around the desk. His can of soda, its Chilseal™ gnawed, lay on the floor. No place in the museum was safe from the marauding beasts.

Cursing the little monsters, he picked up the dented can and tossed it into the recycle bin, then started scraping the desktop mess into a trash can. All the while, he hoped the exterminators would be successful.

An all-nighter without fuel was difficult to contemplate. The cafeteria was closed, but there were vending machines in the staff room, although they didn't offer much that was humanly edible. He tossed the last of the shredded bag and the scattered remains of his mother's handiwork. These rats deserved to die. It was not as though the species was endangered or something. He thought about going out and hunting them down himself. He couldn't get at any of the crossbows, all safely locked in their cases, but there were some demonstration swords in the closet with the gear for the outreach program. He could chase the rats down and slice off their heads. But then he'd have to deal with their bodies. And the damned things would probably bleed on some of the armor and he'd get in trouble with the curator. He gave the plan up as a bad one.

At least they hadn't messed up his reader. He called up the novels and selected R. Norman Carter's *The Heirs of Prester John*. He'd have more than enough time to finish it before his relief showed up at two. He settled in.

By eleven, his stomach was complaining regularly enough that he visited the machines in the staff room, settling on the Cheese Winks™ as the most nourishing and least likely to have been spoiled by a couple of centuries inside the machine. Occasionally he heard some of the rats skittering about on their nocturnal wanderings. Hunting for food, whatever it was they ate when they weren't depriving him of his lunch. Most of them probably lived on scraps from the cafeteria; they surely couldn't survive on things like Cheese Winks.

Fortified by his fine repast, he felt a little foolish about his reaction to the rats. Why should he let them rob him of the pleasure of having the armor all to himself? They were just animals, doing their animal thing, and their day was coming, along with the exterminator.

His own days might be numbered, at least as far as the museum was concerned. He might never have another opportunity to wander the museum like this. Would he let a few rodents, who now that he thought about it were acting more scared of him than he of them, keep him from enjoying himself?

No. He wouldn't. He had more right to the galleries than they did. He would go on with his private tour.

He considered turning on the lights from the watch station, but that would mean the rats had won, creeping him out. It would also mean he'd have to explain to Mrs. Bartholomew why he had burned the power. Lights or no lights, he was going. He had the flashlight, and he'd always been able to get around in the dark. He didn't need the lights.

With some vague idea of sneaking up on the rats, he took the stairs. Before he reached the landing, he could hear them scampering about. No wonder, the door to the great hall was open. Hadn't he closed it? He felt sure he had; but he must not have, because rats couldn't open doors.

He stood by the door and listened. There seemed to be an almost continuous shuffling of padded feet. Sometimes they squeaked, but not often. There were either a lot of them, or a few of them who were very busy. But why were they hanging out in the galleries? Armor certainly wouldn't be to their taste, but the leather straps on the suits might offer some sustenance. That was probably why the curator finally decided to do something about them. That, or the fear that one would pop up during the day and scare some of the visiting schoolchildren—or, more likely, one of their teachers. Bad for public relations.

A sharp rap, like something hitting glass, echoed from the south end of the hall. One of the damned rats must have run into one of the cases. He knew birds did that sort of thing; maybe rats did too. He didn't think they could break into the cases, and he hadn't heard the tinkle of shattered glass, but he thought he ought to check it out.

None of the cases in the galleries off the main floor were damaged. John headed for the special-exhibit gallery.

Standing at the door, he pointed his flashlight. The beam reflected in an unexpected place. With a shock he realized he was looking at the open door of the central exhibit case. The reflections made it hard to see, but he thought he counted five standing human shapes in the case. There should have been only four.

One of them moved and John turned his beam on it, expecting to see a dark-clad thief. Instead, the light revealed a short, willowy woman dressed in jeans and a tattered T-shirt. Back to him and rocking back and forth on her heels, she seemed oblivious to his presence and to the harsh glare of the flashlight beam.

Behind him something skittered and he spun in reflex. His flashlight's beam fell on a spindly scarecrow figure barely two feet tall. The thing crouched, squinting against the light. He stared at it and it stared back with slitted eyes beneath a shielding paw, hissing and baring sharp, yellowed teeth.

"Pay it no mind," the woman said. "They always gather near a working."

John turned his head at her words, then heard the thing move. He snapped his head back around, but it was gone. Tiny feet scampered in the darkness to his left. And to his right.

There was more than one of them!

Were they dangerous? He hoped not. If these things were what he had been hearing all night, there were a lot of them.

"What the hell are those things?"

"Boggles. Harmless, really."

One of the things she called a boggle peered around the case at John. Another dropped to the floor from the top of the case. The two of them grinned at him. Evilly. Anything with that many teeth had to grin evilly.

John forced himself to take his eyes off the boggles and check his combox. According to the black box, the security system was still working, despite its failure to note the entry and presence of this woman. How had she managed that?

"Who are you? How'd you get in here?"

"Sideways."

"There is no side door."

"Whatever." She shushed at him. "Now be quiet. I have to get to work now."

Work? Doing what? Why was he asking himself instead of her?

John watched her dig into a knapsack and pull out a jar. She unscrewed the lid and poured something into her hand. Putting the jar down, she began to scatter the stuff like a Sumo wrestler tossing the ceremonial rice before a bout. The stuff sparkled like carnival glitter. As she turned within the beam of his flashlight, he finally got a good look at her face; it was a face he'd seen before—twice—in pictures.

This was the woman both Bennett and the FBI were looking for. John was confused. She wasn't acting like a thief caught in the act, or a fugitive. Just what was she? Whoever she was, she wasn't supposed to be here, and whatever she was doing, she probably wasn't supposed to be doing. But what was he going to do about it? And why wasn't the alarm going off? The alarm *should* be going off.

"Turn the light off, please," she said. "It's distracting."

He did as she asked, feeling satisfaction that he had pleased her.

What business did he have pleasing her?

Sure, she was pretty, beautiful even; but she wasn't supposed to be here. God only knew what she was doing to the exhibit. So why wasn't he doing anything about her?

One of the boggles scampered up to him and sat at his feet. It watched the woman. John stared down at it, dumbfounded.

The woman started speaking in a low monotone. John didn't understand her words; she wasn't speaking English or Japanese. It sounded a little like Spanish, but only a little.

Moving about within the display, she touched several of the artifacts, crooning to each. Each object she touched began to glow with a blue light.

John blinked. All he could think of was that she shouldn't have been touching the artifacts without wearing white cotton gloves. He began to feel a pressure in his head as though he were in a rapidly rising elevator car. Cool air drifted across his skin. Was that frost forming on the glass of the case?

The boggle at his feet was joined by two more. They chittered together for a moment, then quieted.

The pale blue nimbus limning the artifacts strengthened, filling the display with azure light. Each of the objects the woman had touched shone now. The dead king's belt, the greave on one of his mourners, and the body armor and helmet of another were all glimmering brightly, but the crown enfolded in the king's hands gleamed more brightly still.

It was a hell of a show. Kind of like being in a virtual reality simulation, but the effects were better. Realer. But then, this wasn't a simulator, this was real. Wasn't it? If it was, and all of his senses told him that it was, this woman was working magic. Real magic.

John's throat was dry.

Real magic.

The light swelled, filled the entire gallery. A stronger light of almost painful intensity appeared as a pinpoint in the air above the bier. It grew, rainbow colors rippling along its edges, into a sphere the size of a basketball. With a flash that forced John's eyes shut, it expanded. When he could see again, the globe of light was less bright but it had a diameter large enough for John to walk through.

The woman giggled. "Great and small, need them all."

A figure appeared within the flickering light, slowly resolving to clarity like a video fade-in. The image was man-shaped. His feet almost touched the surface of the bier and the top of the case intersected his chest.

As the resolution of the image improved, John could see that the man was naked. He had broad shoulders and was thick-bodied, his skin tracked with white scars. His hair fell to his shoulders and he wore a full beard. Both hair and beard were dirty blond and shot with gray. His eyes were closed, but his expression was troubled.

The man hung suspended within the cloud of light, floating in the air. He might have been lying on a bed, save that he was vertical. The pose was odd, in a way more unnerving than the fact that the man was suspended without any visible support.

The woman faced the man and spoke. Her words were still incomprehensible to John, but he recognized her tone as one of entreaty. Her gestures were those one would use to call a small child.

The man floated within the glowing ball, drifting a little closer, then a little farther away. The woman spoke faster. Silent sparks jetted out from the floating man, leaping out to ground against the metal fittings of the case and the reproduction weapons within it. One jumped to the forgotten flashlight in John's hand, and he dropped it.

The woman stood serenely within this electrical microstorm. Her words became a chant and the floating man drifted free of the case. Slowly, he settled toward the floor. He was looking more solid now. More real, somehow.

The woman held out a hand toward him.

"Come, lord," she said. "Waken. 'Tis time."

CHAPTER
9

The man started to collapse as soon as his bare foot touched the stone floor, crumpling bonelessly toward the paving flags. His obvious helplessness and need broke through the awe and fear that had paralyzed John. Rushing forward, he caught the man before his head struck the stone. The limp body was a deadweight, too much for John's strength, and pulled him off balance. They both landed sprawling on the floor.

The man lay there twitching, his eyes screwed closed. Arms enfolding his head, he curled into a ball and started mumbling. John couldn't quite catch what he was saying; it sounded like a foreign language, something Germanic. Whatever the language was, the short phrases and stuttering delivery made his words sound disjointed. Although he couldn't tell for sure, John suspected the man's speech was slurred. He seemed to be in shock.

John knelt beside the man and gently tugged his hands away from his head. Brushing aside feebly flailing arms, he shifted the man around so that his head could rest against John's thighs. That seemed to relax him; he stopped fighting, at any rate. The babbling stopped too.

John was thinking about where he'd find something to keep the guy warm when the woman laid her hand on his shoulder, startling him, and spoke.

"Take good care of this man."

John recovered enough to say, "But—"

"Artos needs your help."

John was befuddled. Who was Artos? "What are you talking about?"

"Artos has slept a long while, but the time is come. He is needed." She giggled. "All of them. Great and small, need them all."

This woman—this sorceress—was crazy. Then again, maybe *she* wasn't the crazy one. "I really don't understand what's going on here."

She smiled a sad smile and touched his cheek with her hand. "Such enviable innocence."

"Who are you?"

"Nym." She smiled beatifically at him, as if that explained it all.

Right. Try again. "Who's he?"

"Artos."

Nym looked at him expectantly. Was he supposed to know this guy? John didn't exactly make a habit of hanging out with naked men in closed museums. "Be careful of strange men," his mother used to tell him when he was little. How much stranger did you get than appearing out of nowhere when a ditsy sorceress called you up with a spell?

Or had she? What if this guy wasn't a *man*? The head lying against his thigh suddenly seemed far warmer than it should be. What if she had called up something else, and it just had the *shape* of a man? What if—

What the hell was he thinking about? This couldn't be real. It had to be a trick of some kind, but he couldn't imagine anyone with the resources or the reason to pull such a thing off.

Nym frowned, apparently displeased by his reaction, then she brightened. "Oh, sorry," she said. "It gets a little confusing sometimes. So many, you know. And things get a little fuzzy over time. You'd probably call him Arthur."

"Arthur?" No. It couldn't be. *"Arthur?"*

She nodded.

His eyes flashed to the case behind her. It held a few artifacts of gold and silver, a Caxton printing of Malory's *Morte D'Artur,* photoprints of several manuscript illustrations, an original cel from Disney's *The Sword in the Stone,* and a block of text headed "The Matter of Britain: Arthur, Myth or Reality?" The screen that showed a clip from Sandler's *Legacy of the Round Table* was dark. Centuries of legends about the king who waits.

"As in King Arthur?"

She nodded again.

"The King Arthur?"

She smiled radiantly. "Sleeping no longer." Bending down, she kissed the man on the forehead. "Rise, O king. The fight is to be fought."

The man groaned. She nodded in satisfaction and started gathering her things into her knapsack.

"It can't be," John said.

"Were you there?" she asked.

"Where?"

"I thought not. You're a bit young. That being the case, who are you to talk? One must have knowledge beyond learning or wisdom beyond understanding to say what can and cannot be." She leaned over and murmured in his ear, "The stars have whispered to me. They have told me that the time for sleeping is over. The time of need is upon us."

"I—" He decided it was better not to voice his doubts about her story. This woman, whoever she was—whatever she was—was not entirely fastened down. It would be best to humor her until he could find somebody who might have some idea of what was going on. He decided to try to talk her into helping him get this guy down to the watch station. From there he could call the police; they'd have somebody who could make some sense of this. Hoping he'd be inspired to say the right things, he started, "I—"

"Yes, you. You surely have a place in this. I had not foreseen you, but *something* is sure to come of this. You are here, and he is here, and—" She cocked her head as though listening. Eyes narrowing, her expression hardened. John hoped that it did not presage violence. She shouldered her pack, then leaned down again, whispering, "And *he* is here as well."

Her hand brushed John's waist, shifting the combox. The lights came on in the great hall. How did that happen? A shaft of illumination fell through the doorway into the still-shadowy exhibit gallery. Arthur—if he was Arthur—groaned again and raised a hand to shield his still-closed eyes.

The light dimmed as a man stepped into the doorway. The backlighting and the dark trench coat that he wore made a lean column of his figure, and silver hair glowed in a halo around his head. He took a step forward and his face came into the light. It was Bennett.

For a moment, John was overjoyed. Here was someone who knew about Nym. Bennett would know what was going on. Then he remembered that the FBI agents had said that Bennett was an impostor. The agents hadn't said what Bennett really was except dangerous.

A handful of boggles scampered past Bennett. He didn't seem surprised by them. The light behind him diminished for an instant as something moved out there. Whatever it was, it didn't stray into John's line of sight, but he sensed it lurking out there. Bennett remained undisturbed by its presence, but Nym stared worriedly over his shoulder.

As with Nym, there had been no alarm to mark Bennett's entry into the building. John checked his combox. The status light still burned green, falsely claiming that the building's security remained unbreached. That wasn't right. Couldn't be, could it? He had to be dreaming all this, didn't he? The weight of the man's head in his lap was real, and when Bennett spoke his voice sounded as real as it had in the Frilly Cow.

"I see I'm too late for the show."

Apparently galvanized by Bennett's voice, Arthur rolled out of John's lap and struggled to rise. His muscles trembled and his arms gave out on the first attempt. John helped him with the second and the man got to his knees. His eyes, open now, were fixed on Bennett. John would not have liked to have been the recipient of that venomous glare.

Arthur said something in his guttural language. His stutter was gone, his voice stronger, almost compelling in its power.

"I've seen stronger puppies, man," Bennett replied to him in English.

"What can you expect from a day that begins with getting out of bed?" Nym said.

Bennett ignored her. "Really, John, you should have told me when you began to keep such bad company."

"You're not a federal agent," John accused.

"According to whom?" Bennett asked.

"Some real federal agents."

"Are you sure *they* were federal agents?"

"I saw their badges. Who are you, really?"

"A person very concerned about what this woman is trying to do." He took a step into the gallery, and though his hands remained in his pockets, Nym flinched back.

"Don't trust him," she said to John.

"She is a liar, John," Bennett said. "Pathological."

"I am not," Nym protested.

"Do you know what she's done, John?" He paused, more for effect than to allow John to answer. "She's summoned a murderer. A hunter. A maker of war. You were here; you saw the anchors she used for her summoning. Weapons. The tools of a killer. The man you so tenderly held in your lap is very dangerous. A veritable demon in man form. He will deceive you into betraying all you hold dear. He has done so before, with others."

"You are the deceiver," Nym stated.

"Will you deny what I have told John about this man?"

Nym bit her lip.

"Her silence is the answer, John. This man is all that I have told you and more. He should be destroyed like the mad dog he is."

"He is needed," Nym protested.

"Not by me," Bennett said. A boggle tugged on his pants leg. He kicked the thing away and it ran away into the darkness, whimpering. A melody, faint and hauntingly sweet, floated in the air. Bennett tilted his head and listened, smiling. "Ah. However, his wakening does have benefits, and so for that I thank you."

Nym glared at him. "I did not do this for you."

"Of course not, woman. But whatever your motives, your results seem less than complete. Your champion doesn't look as though he will be much good to anyone."

Nym drew herself up, raising her chin loftily, and said, "He's still half asleep."

"Still? Not handling the transition well, is he? Or a fault in your spell, perhaps? Too bad. I'd rather have had him aware for this."

Bennett withdrew his right hand from the pocket of his trench coat. He flicked his wrist, and instantly a ball of crackling energy sprang to flickering green life around his hand. Boggles scattered.

"No," Nym protested, stepping between Bennett and Arthur.

Arthur mumbled something. Reaching out a hand, he tried to draw her back, but she shrugged off his hand.

"Leave," she whispered to him over her shoulder. "Get far away."

"You can't protect him from me," Bennett said.

"Can't I?"

"Don't overestimate your skills. I know you must be feeling quite strong now, frisky even, but it is a false confidence.

"Step away, John."

Mouth dry, John asked Bennett, "What are you going to do?"

"Something that should have been done long ago. Now step away."

John hesitated.

"Very well," Bennett said. He flicked his hand forward, and the energy rolled off his fingers. The ball of lambent green fire floated toward Nym, Arthur, and John.

Nym held up both her hands, palms out, and crossed her arms. The fire vanished inches from her hands. John could only stare, wide-eyed.

"Not bad," Bennett said.

"I've been practicing," she said coyly.

"But not enough. If you insist on interfering, I will simply have to settle with you before I settle with him."

"I insist."

Nym slashed her hands down and a wall of shimmer appeared between her and Bennett. Bennett gestured again and sent another, larger ball of fire at them. The sphere burst on Nym's shield. John felt the heat. That was enough for him. He grabbed Arthur's arm.

"We've got to get out of here."

Bennett's hands started weaving in complex patterns; Nym's too. Lights flashed as energies leapt between them. John's hair stood on end and he felt flares of heat wash over him.

There was a service elevator in the back of the exhibit gallery. It was installed for the convenience of the preparators, but it offered another way out than the doorway that Bennett blocked. John's combox would unlock it. He tugged on Arthur's arm.

"Come on."

The man resisted. In the glare of the flaring energies, John could see the man's expression shift rapidly. There was naked fear there, and other emotions as well: determination, anger, and frustration. Beneath John's hand, he trembled with passions. Clearly Arthur wanted to do something more than stand and watch this wizardly duel. The fear seemed strongest.

That was something John understood. This magic stuff was scary, real scary, when it wasn't in a book or a vid. His guts felt like something was stirring them around. He hoped that all he was feeling was fear, and not the insidious effects of some spell designed to turn him inside out. All John wanted right now was to get out of there.

"Unless you can throw spells, there's nothing to be done. Come on."

Arthur let John tug him behind the case, putting something between them and the sorcerers, before stopping again. He stared at the contending magicians.

"Sure, it's a great show," John babbled. "But, like, we're outclassed. Come on."

John tugged on Arthur's arm, but again he resisted. Some weak puppy. It was like trying to move a statue.

Maybe he had a reason to stay. Maybe there *was* something he could do. John had to ask. "Can you do magic?"

"No."

With that word, Arthur gave in to John's insistent tugging, allowing himself to be led away. John got him around the corner before releasing his arm and racing ahead to punch the call button for the elevator. For a miracle, the car was on their floor, and the doors hissed open immediately. The doors were closing, sealing them in the elevator car, when John realized that Arthur had spoken comprehensibly.

"You speak English?"

"Speak."

Was that an answer or a command? "Then maybe you can tell me what's going on?"

"Slow."

What was slow? Geez, don't tell me King Arthur is an idiot. Maybe his brain was fried from sleeping too long. The doors opened; it was time to move again. Once John got somebody to take charge, everything would get sorted out. He bolted from the elevator.

"Come on. Come on. We'll call the police."

After a moment's hesitation, Arthur followed him. John didn't wait for him, but hurried through the staff areas behind the gift shop. The lobby was lit with strange lights flickering down through the stairwell, and a gaggle of screeching boggles scattered from the landing as John raced across the open space. He nearly fell over one of the things, but caught himself on the framework of the archway into the orientation wing.

Almost there. He looked back to see Arthur trotting after him. The guy was looking around like a lost tourist.

"Come on!"

Arthur picked up his pace. Satisfied, John took the last few yards to the entrance of the watch room. John slammed the door open and flung himself down in front of the security console. Before he called the cops, he wanted to see what was happening upstairs. There was still a small chance that this was all a dream.

Damn small.

John punched in the commands to put the gallery camera on screen while Arthur started prowling the watch room. John heard him open the closet door just as the gallery vid camera came on line.

When it came up, the image was almost white, all glare and flash. John had to turn the contrast all the way down before he could see anything. Even then, it was hard to be sure what was going on through all the fireworks. He checked the motion sensors. As far as they were concerned, nothing was moving up there. Bizarre.

Arthur returned to his side. In his right hand, the guy held one of the demo swords from the outreach collection. Naked as a jaybird and the first thing he grabs is a weapon! Hope he knows how to handle that thing. The blade's edge glittered coldly. Geez, he'd picked the only sharp one in the bunch. Maybe it would be better if this guy *didn't* know how to handle a sword.

Time to call the cops.

As he reached for the phone, a prompt appeared on the monitor and started flashing: "Malfunction station three."

Now what? Station three was the rear service entrance. Before John could acknowledge the prompt, it disappeared. It wasn't supposed to do that.

The motion sensors were registering movement near the service entrance, so John called up the vid camera that covered the rear entrance. The magical battle in the gallery disappeared from the screen, replaced by a much darker scene. Cloaked in the night, several figures hunched against the wall of the museum building. One of them, considerably shorter than the others, stood by the control box with a dark object in his hand. Several wires led from that object to the control box. That was all John saw before the image went black.

John heard the distant rumble of the loading-dock door opening. Pointlessly, he looked in that general direction. From the corner of his eye, he saw Arthur look up, as though he was searching the sky for thunder. John turned back to the console, cutting in the camera inside the loading bay. Men carrying guns rushed in. John recognized two of them: McAlister and Surimato. What the hell was the FBI doing raiding the museum?

The camera went dead, then the whole security console blinked: telltale lights, monitor, submonitor, everything. When they flickered back to life, everything looked normal, but somehow John didn't think everything was normal. He tried to call up a diagnostic, but the console didn't acknowledge his attempt.

Things were getting very strange.

A gunshot thundered somewhere in the building.

Weren't federal agents supposed to issue warnings first? He hadn't heard anything like a warning. He picked up the phone and found the line dead.

More gunshots erupted from upstairs, then a whumping noise like nothing John had ever heard. Someone started to scream in agony.

John didn't understand what was going on, but it was obvious that the museum was not a healthy place to be at the moment. Nym's advice to leave sounded very good. Very wise.

He shoved his chair back, Arthur's nakedness flashing in his peripheral vision. It was cold outside; the guy would freeze. John panicked for a second, then remembered that there were clothes where Arthur had found the sword. Stupid costume stuff, but warmer than naked skin. John dove for the closet and hauled out the first things he saw. He tossed the handful to Arthur, who caught the floppy mass without fouling his blade.

Maybe he did know how to handle that thing.

"Let's go," John said as he ran out of the room.

At least this Arthur guy wasn't completely in the ozone. He followed John to the door and shrugged into one of the long robes while John fiddled with the lock. The noise from upstairs made John nervous, and he kept fumbling with the key.

"Haste," said Arthur.

John looked up to see him, sword held ready, staring across the lobby to the stairwell. Something heavy was clumping down the stairs. Motivated, John slotted the key and turned the heavy mechanism. He tugged on the door, but the massive steel valve resisted. Arthur gripped it with his free hand, and together they swung it open.

Chill air blasted in. It *was* cold outside, but they ran out into the night anyway. Intent on putting distance between himself and the museum, John didn't look back. He headed up Randolph Road, toward the rezcoms. The only thing he heard behind him was the slap of Arthur's bare feet on the road surface.

CHAPTER
10

The Woodman Armory Museum looked dark and quiet as Holger cut the engine and let the rental car roll down the hill from the rezcoms. The streets were deserted: not surprising; it was half past one in the morning and this was a quiet town. But the parking lot was empty too, not even the watchman's car.

Something wasn't right.

He pulled over where Randolph Road met Barber Avenue, instead of proceeding ahead into the lot as he had planned. The museum sat across the intersection. He scanned the area. No obvious damage, no suspicious activity. The banner announcing the imminent opening of an exhibit on Romano-Brithonic things rippled in the cold breeze. Beneath it one of the main entrance's heavy steel doors was open, offering an incongruous invitation.

Dr. Spae reached for her door handle and Holger hit the lock override before she could get it open. She turned to him, ready to question his judgment, but her mouth snapped shut when she saw him draw his Glock. The appearance of the pistol put a disapproving glare on her face.

He nodded toward the museum. "Door's open, Doctor. Alarm must be going off."

"I don't hear anything."

"Some alarms are silent. The local police are likely on their way."

"I don't hear any sirens."

"That doesn't mean the police are not responding."

"Unlock the door," she demanded.

"We should wait a little bit, Doctor."

"You wait. I need to see inside."

"I don't think that it is advisable at this time."

"The activity has stopped now. The traces will soon fade and there won't be any point in getting inside."

"The lack of activity doesn't mean that whoever attracted your attention has left."

"You are obstructing this investigation."

"I'm trying to avoid problems. There may not be a threat just now, but the situation remains difficult. If we are found in there by the local police, we will have to do more explaining than the Department would care for."

"We'll just have to be gone before they arrive."

"Too late. The locals are already arriving," he told her.

A police car had just taken the turnoff from Route 12 onto the lower end of Barber Avenue. It pulled over and cut its lights. Though Holger had a clear view, the position selected by the cruiser's driver would be concealed from the museum by the slope of the hill. Two officers got out of the vehicle; their watchful looks up the hill toward the museum confirmed that they had come to investigate, but they made no move to start up the hill. As yet, they showed no interest in Holger and Spae's car.

Spae cursed the cops' arrival and cursed Holger for wasting her opportunity. He let her words roll past him; her safety was his responsibility. Charging into an unknown situation without backup was just plain stupid.

What were the cops waiting for? Reinforcements? That suggested they knew there was trouble inside. Maybe they were exercising simple, reasonable caution, although he wouldn't have expected that from Americans.

Two more cars arrived. A quartet of new arrivals joined the officers on the street corner for a conference. No immediate action was taken.

So the first pair hadn't just been waiting for reinforcements to conduct a simple search. One backup car would have been enough to respond to a silent alarm. Two indicated a more complicated situation, but the lack of anything other than patrolmen made a truly serious situation unlikely.

"Doctor," Holger said, formulating a plan as he spoke. "Will you agree that we cannot enter the building now without attracting the attention of the local police?"

"You've made sure of that."

"I think we might persuade them to take us in with them." He reholstered the Glock. "*If* you will follow my lead."

"Just get me in there."

They left the rental car and started down the hill. The air was colder than it had been earlier in the night. Holger refastened his coat; he shouldn't need to get to the Glock for a while. A cop noticed them approaching and nudged one of his fellows. The conversation among the officers faltered and they all turned to look.

"Let me do the talking," Holger whispered to Spae. "Try not to let them see your face clearly. Huddle in your coat like it's cold."

"It *is* cold."

"Exactly why they won't question it."

He hoped she'd go along. Specialists like her rarely showed common sense.

They were close enough to the policemen now.

He tugged at his hat in greeting, using the opportunity to pull it a little lower and put more of his face in shadow, and said, "Good evening, Officers."

Eyebrows were raised and glances exchanged among the officers. One, sergeant stripes showing on his heavy coat, stepped forward.

"Pretty cold for a late-night stroll, isn't it, folks?"

"Colder than I'd like. Later, too, Sergeant Willis." Holger got the name from the man's name badge. He held out his hand. "I'm Holger Kun, with the EC Commission on Antiquities. This is Dr. Spae, one of our specialists."

Puzzled but reacting to normal courtesy, the officer shook Holger's hand. One of the others whispered to his partner, "Yamana didn't waste any time, did he?"

"I'm sure you understand our concern," Holger said to the sergeant.

"Just what did Mr. Yamana tell you?"

Holger didn't know who Yamana was. "Actually Ms. Satsumi notified us. She wasn't very specific, though. Just what is the problem at the museum?"

Mentioning the museum seemed to be the last thing needed for the sergeant to place Holger's noncommittal statements into a framework that made sense to the officer. To the sergeant's mind, Holger had proven he was part of what was happening and, therefore, safe to speak to.

"We're not entirely sure, Mr. Kun. We had a blip in the security feed from the museum. Happens all the time, but when the duty monitor put in a call to the watchman to confirm the malfunction, all she got was a dead line. Monitor feed was still on line, though, so it's probably just a dead phone line. Standard procedure requires us to check it out."

"Oh, dear," Holger said, trying to sound as though he had just put something together. The sergeant's eyes narrowed satisfactorily. "I'm afraid things might be more serious. The front door was open."

"You didn't go in?" Willis asked.

"No. Of course not. We saw your cars down here at about the same time and thought you would know what was going on."

"Smart move. There could still be perps inside." Willis sounded relieved.

"Perps?" Spae asked.

"Perpetrators, ma'am. Criminals."

Spae harrumphed.

The sergeant gave her a flash smile of rigid politeness and turned back to Holger. "Did you see anyone near the museum?"

"Not a soul."

Spae snorted slightly.

"This weather can't be doing that cold of yours any good," Holger said to cover her slip, but she continued to press.

"Perhaps we could go inside now. I'm sure it will be warmer."

Sergeant Willis shook his head. "I don't think it would be a good idea just yet. We'll have to check it out first."

Holger nodded in agreement. "I understand your concern, Sergeant. Perhaps Dr. Spae could get out of the wind and wait in one of your vehicles. I'm afraid ours is parked just outside the building. Returning to it might not be the best of ideas just yet."

"I want to go inside," Spae protested.

"One of our vehicles would be better, ma'am."

"We all share your concerns, Doctor. The officer is only concerned for your safety, Doctor. As am I. We will get you in to check on your precious antiquities as soon as we may do so safely."

"I think it would be better if you waited out here too, Mr. Kun," Willis said.

"Whyever for, Sergeant? I *am* a licensed security technician. Interpol certified."

"Interpol, huh?"

Sergeant Willis seemed about to say more, but headlights flashed across them from Route 12, and he turned to check out their source. The lights swung away as the vehicle took the next curve, moving more slowly than necessary for a vehicle traveling about its business. The car was a late-model luxury sedan, a Nissan Silhouette.™ The Silhouette passed their position, slowing further as it took the corner onto Barber Avenue. The car pulled up behind one of the police vehicles. The car's windscreen bore a parking sticker with the Mitsutomo crest. Holger recalled from the travel guide he'd read that Mitsutomo was one of the museum's sponsors.

Having an interest in the place, they'd naturally be concerned over any problems. Sending a company rep demonstrated that concern; the Silhouette, a car expensive enough to be out of the reach of anyone below upper management, suggested that Mitsutomo's concern was quite serious.

The driver got out of the car and scampered around to open the door for his passenger. The man who emerged was a Japanese. No surprise there. He wore a heavy overcoat that added to an already substantial girth. The driver fell in behind him as he clumped over to the group. He greeted Willis by name and immediately asked who Holger and Spae were. The sergeant told him Holger's fabrication and introduced them to him, saying, "Mr. Yamana is the head of security for Mitsutomo Metal Fabrications."

Head of security? To check on a communications malfunction?

Holger stuck his hand out again. "I must say that I'm surprised to see such an elevated person as yourself here tonight."

"I do my job, Mr. Kun," Yamana said as he shook hands. "There are very valuable artifacts on loan to the museum. It would be unforgivable if something happened to them while they were in our care."

"You mean the museum's care."

Yamana inclined his head. "As you say."

"Why aren't some of the staff here?" Spae asked.

"They will be informed at the proper time, Dr. Spae. The important thing at the moment is to determine what has happened."

Spae nodded briskly. "I agree. Shall we go?"

"I think this is a matter for the police, Doctor."

"We've just been having that discussion with Sergeant Willis here," Holger said. "I'm sure you will be able to set the sergeant straight."

"The sergeant knows his responsibilities."

"Mr. Yamana," Holger said sternly. "I have responsibilities as well. The Commission of Antiquities will not be happy if I am excluded."

"Time is wasting," Spae put in.

"You are correct, Doctor." Yamana's stiffness suggested that he was annoyed, but his voice remained calm and level. "We've no wish to make this a political issue, Mr. Kun. If the sergeant is satisfied that you are safe to yourself as well as to his men, I will be satisfied. But I must insist that Doctor Spae remain outside for the moment."

The sergeant looked distinctly uncomfortable as he fumbled through a few more questions, which Holger answered. Holger had to produce his Interpol-certified gun permit before the man would agree to include Holger in the search party. Even then, he insisted that Holger stay in the back of the party with Mr. Yamana and his driver. They left one of the officers at the cars to stay with a still-protesting Spae when they marched up the hill to the museum.

The cops organized their entry with reasonable precision. Two officers split off to watch the back entrance and loading-dock area, while the rest prepared to go in the front door. Holger readied his Glock and was unsurprised to see that Yamana's driver was armed as well; the man moved too smoothly to be a simple chauffeur.

They advanced on the door, but didn't get past the threshold. There was a pile of empty clothes just inside the door.

Holger swallowed hard, but kept himself from taking a step back. Yamana eyed him suspiciously while one of the policemen poked the pile with his foot. Nothing but cloth. The sergeant gave the sign to proceed. The cops moved into the quiet lobby.

Holger couldn't pass the pile without knowing. He picked at the pile gingerly. It was an odd lot, costumes and not real clothes. More important, there were enough garments in the pile for two or three people of different sizes. There was no way for this lot to be the clothing of a single person.

Holger felt relief.

He straightened up, ready to get on with the search, and was nearly run over by Spae. She was out of breath but didn't seem frightened. Significantly, the doctor was alone.

"You should not be here."

"Shove it."

"Where is the officer who was with you?"

"He'll be along as soon as he realizes I left. What have you found?"

"Nothing much."

She frowned. Folding her hands before her, she took a deep breath and let it out slowly. Her eyes lost their focus. "We need to go upstairs."

"Why do you say that, Doctor?" Yamana emerged from the shadows of an archway. Holger hadn't known he was there.

Spae, only half aware of the real world around her, answered, "It's up there."

"What is, Doctor?"

"The exhibit, of course," Holger said, hoping he was right.

Clearly not satisfied by Holger's response, Yamana nevertheless was forced to postpone further questions as Sergeant Willis called him. Dragging Spae along, Holger followed the security chief into a small room just off the corridor. A glance told him that the room served as both a ticket office and a security station. Willis was showing Yamana the security arrangement.

The monitor console showed that all was secure—a patent incorrectness, given the open front door visible through the window into the lobby. According to Willis, access to the security system was locked out, but the regular computer functions were available. Obviously someone had tampered with the system.

Ordering Spae and Holger to remain in the watch room, Yamana went with the locals as they searched the entry floor. Holger didn't object; when they were out of sight, he called up the personnel files and scanned through them. It was all he had time to do before the party reassembled in the lobby. Willis reported that the entry floor was empty and nothing looked disturbed. All of the building's elevators were on this floor; the police used their emergency keys to lock them there, limiting access between the floors.

They moved up, finding the second floor with its offices and "touch" gallery as empty and undisturbed as the lower floor. On their way to the third floor and the main exhibits, Holger began to smell cooked meat. One of the cops made a crack about something smelling good. Holger said nothing. The cop would learn.

A body lay sprawled in the junction of the vee formed by the two arms of the great hall. The blackened corpse lay in a pool of dark, half-congealed fluid. The cadaver's contorted pose suggested the agony in which the victim had died. All was consistent with death by fire. Unfortunately, other than the corpse there were no signs of a conflagration.

Spontaneous combustion? Unlikely.

"Energies have been used here," Spae whispered.

No shit. Holger didn't need a specialist to tell him that.

Over in a corner, the hungry cop was barfing up his last meal. Holger considered joining him, but not because of the corpse; he'd seen messier deaths. It was how this death had been accomplished that made his stomach rebel.

A charred corpse and no other sign of flames could only mean one thing. Magic. Holger hated magic.

The south wing held what the police sought, definite signs of a break-in. The exhibit was a shambles. There and in that end of the great hall, armor and displays were disarrayed, smashed, and scattered. Bullet holes pockmarked the stone walls of the great hall, starred its false windows, and maimed the more modern paneling in the special-exhibit hall. A small war had been fought here, but beyond the charred corpse, the only casualties appeared to be mannequins, artifacts, and the building itself.

Spae didn't want to go any farther to continue with the search. Willis admonished Holger and Spae not to touch anything pending the arrival of the crime scene van, but allowed them to remain in the special-exhibit gallery. He actually seemed relieved to be able to do so. Once Yamana and the police had left to sweep the rest of the building, Spae spoke with awe in her whispering voice.

"Kun, there's more residual energy here than I've ever felt before. I feel invigorated just being here."

Holger did not consider the doctor's pronouncement good news. "Perhaps you can do something with this energy to preserve our cover."

"Who cares about the cover?"

"I care, Doctor. And the Department will care. It is our job to hide what happened here until we know more about what is going on. We will be able to do that better if we preserve our cover. Yamana will soon be asking us whether anything is missing from the damned exhibit. *I* certainly have no idea. If we are exposed, our access to this site will be limited."

She was quiet for a moment. "There is a spell I could try, but I've never had a lot of luck with it. Without my tools, I can't promise much."

"Anything might help."

"Very well."

She spent a minute or so in meditation, then began a quiet chant in Latin. Holger waited: frustrated, unhappy, and very uncomfortable. Seeking something to distract himself from the doctor's efforts, he stepped to the doorway. From there he could, if necessary, give warning of the approach of Yamana or the police. Spae stopped talking after three minutes but remained standing, swaying slightly. It was another three minutes before she spoke to him.

"It's wonderful. I've never seen auras so clearly."

Holger didn't want to hear about it. "What did you learn?"

She smiled indulgently. "I don't think anything is missing, but several of the items have an odd quality to their auras. Sort of a freshness. It's not like anything I've experienced before."

She babbled on about the auras and energies for several more minutes before he had to hush her. The police returned, bringing word that there was no one in the building other than the searchers.

"That corpse must be the night watchman," one of the cops said.

"It'll take the lab to be sure," Willis predicted.

Holger doubted that. Having scanned the personnel files, including the physical statistics on the fellow holding the first shift, he knew the corpse was too short by at least ten centimeters. Far more than incineration shrinkage would account for.

So where was Mister John Reddy? Run away at the first sign of magic, if he had any brains.

"Hi, Mom, I'm home."

Marianne Reddy walked out of the kitchen, momentarily startled that John was not alone. "Who's that with you, dear?"

"Oh. This is King Arthur. A mad sorceress just pulled him out of thin air, and since he's new in town, he needs a place to stay. I told him you wouldn't mind."

"Not at all," she said, smiling. "I'm always happy to meet your friends and it's so lovely to have foreign guests. Do men wear dresses in your country, Mr. Arthur?"

Arthur glowered at her.

"It's a robe, Mom. We stole it from the museum."

Neither Arthur's scowl nor John's admission of theft had any effect on her ebullient mood. "I see. Oh my, what's that in his hand?"

"It's a sword, Mom. We stole that from the museum too."

"How nice."

From somewhere behind John a gun opened fire. Small black holes stitched up his mother's body. A ball of fire roared over John's shoulder, engulfing her in a blazing inferno. Marianne Reddy smiled through it all, the grin as frozen and foolish as John's fantasy. The scene dissolved, forcing John back to the cold dark of the alley that served the commercial strip of Rezcom 3.

Not a good idea, John.

Now you show up. And not so loud, huh. People will hear.

Don't go home, John. It's not safe.

Where else is there to go?

Somewhere else. They know about you now. They will know to go there.

Maybe going home wasn't a real bright idea. An awful lot of people seemed to know who he was, while he had absolutely no idea who they were. Bennett, for one. Those two guys who said they were FBI, for another two. Wouldn't home be the first place anybody would come looking for him?

His mind shifted into replay. Screams and gunshots. Scampering boggles. Flashing magic like a war of fireworks. Just fine in a vid or a game, but not the sort of thing you wanted to bring home to your mother.

The "federal agents" were clearly capable of violence. Bennett, too. Who knew what that madwoman Nym was capable of? Magical spells, for sure.

She's still out there, John.

Yeah? How do you know?

Trust me.

She must have beaten Bennett, then. The feds, too.

Nothing is settled yet, John. Don't go home.

All that magic and all those gunshots. Surely something must have happened?

Something has.

What?

. . .

All right, don't tell me. I don't think you know.

I know you shouldn't go home.

John looked up at the building. This was Mitsutomo Keiretsu's Benjamin Harrison Town Project Rezcom Cluster 3, his home for as long as he could remember. It wasn't pretty. In fact, it was downright corporate ugly, but he'd always been safe here. Why should that change?

Flash rewind; play. Gunshots! Coruscating light! Shadowy strangeness creeping around the edges of his vision. A naked man with a sword.

He knew why he couldn't go home. If he wasn't there, they would have no reason to be there. If he avoided going home, they, whoever "they" were, might leave his mother alone.

Still, Mitsutomo Keiretsu was a powerful force in the world. No one in their right mind would want to antagonize Mitsutomo Keiretsu by bringing violence into one of their corporate buildings. Maybe he would be safe there. But at least one of the people John had met in the last few hours wasn't in her right mind. He looked over at where Arthur crouched staring out into the darkness, sword naked in his hand. Maybe two.

He thought about what he'd seen. Or thought he'd seen. If it was all in his head, there was only one crazy person involved. Him. Dr. Block would like that; it'd mean more business.

All of his senses said that it was real. His fingers and toes were just about solid ice, and the concrete of the rezcom was cold, rough, and scratchy where he rested his cheek against it. The sounds of traffic on Route 190 whined in his ears. All real.

The man beside him, shivering in the ratty old robe. The glint of light running along the sword blade as the man turned in his watchful survey of their surroundings. The sound of velvet rustling when the man moved. The smell of his sweat. All real.

"Are you really King Arthur?"

"Name is Artos," he said without looking at John.

"Like in Mary Stewart's books?"

This time the man looked at him. The sides of his mouth were drawn back. "Not Ar-tur, Ar-tos," he said in the tone usually reserved for small children and total idiots.

"Right. Artos."

That seemed to satisfy him, and he turned his attention back to the night.

Artos, not Arthur. So John wasn't running around the project with a half-dressed, sword-toting King Arthur. He was running around with a half-dressed, sword-toting guy named Artos, who was, according to his own vehement insistence, not Arthur. There was a lot less glamour in hiding out with a sword-wielding brute than with a reawakened King Arthur.

Without warning, Artos lunged forward, sword high, shouting, "Die, goblin!" John, his right foot on a fold of Artos's robe, was pulled off balance. He landed on his butt, grazing his head on the concrete wall as he fell. By the time he stopped seeing stars and got his feet under him, Artos was rolling around on the ground with someone. Light sparkled around them, snowflakes caught in a whirlwind.

John staggered toward them. The sword was nowhere in sight and Artos had his hands around the other guy's throat. He seemed intent on strangling the stranger.

Bennett had said this guy was a murderer.

The thrashing pair shifted, and light from the plaza illuminated the face of the person Artos was trying to strangle. It was Trashcan Harry!

"Let him go!" John shouted. "The guy's just a janitor!"

Artos ignored him.

John threw himself onto Artos's back, slipping his arms under the man's armpits and bringing his hands back up beside his head. He locked his fingers behind the madman's neck and wrenched back with all his strength. The man on the ground heaved and swatted until, between them, they broke Artos's grip. Trashcan Harry scrambled to his feet. When Artos stopped struggling, John released him and got shakily to his own feet. Artos stood and glared at both of them.

Satisfied that the man's mania had subsided for the moment, John looked over his shoulder. "You okay, Trash—ah, Harry?"

"Been worse." Trashcan Harry massaged his throat and glared venomously at Artos.

Artos stared back just as venomously.

"He tried to kill me," Trashcan said.

"Yes," Artos agreed. "Kill it. Very treacherous it. Kill now easier."

John stepped between them. "Nobody's killing anybody."

"Fool," Artos said disgustedly.

"Maybe so," John said. Definitely so, he thought. "But I can't stand here and let you kill this man in cold blood."

"Can."

"No! Now look, I owe this guy."

"He help you?" Artos sounded incredulous.

"Yeah. And you're not going to kill him."

Artos stared John in the eyes for nearly a minute. John felt the power of the man's will and knew he couldn't stand up to that gaze for long, but something made Artos falter. After an awkward moment, Artos turned away and started kicking through the debris in the alley.

Probably trying to find that damned sword.

Definitely. Won't, though.

Good girl.

"Thanks, John." Trashcan's ugly face held what had to be a grateful expression. "I can help you now."

"What makes you think I need help?"

Trashcan's face scrunched up; he was thinking hard. Finally he said, "There was a death at the museum."

John's throat went dry. "Who?"

"Don't know. Know it's bad for you, though."

Don't go home, John.

A police car, its lights flashing, moved past the alley mouth. Harry tugged John against the wall. The car appeared again as it rounded the plaza road, pulling up before the residential entrance. The stink of Trashcan Harry in his nose, John watched the officers get out and enter the building. Artos, having abandoned his search for the sword, stood frozen, staring at the flashing lights with wide eyes.

"They looking for you," Trashcan said to John.

"How do you know that? You can't know that." John felt panicky. He wanted to believe the police car's arrival was coincidence, but he couldn't. Not after what happened at the museum.

"We gotta go," Trashcan said. "Come on. I know a place."

Go, John.

John resisted the tug on his arm. "What about Artos?"

Trashcan spat. "Don't need him. Come on. Gotta go."

"We can't leave Artos."

"Can, too."

"Now you sound like him." John shrugged off Trashcan's grip and walked up to Artos. "They're looking for us."

Without taking his eyes from the car, Artos asked, "Fight them?"

"Are you crazy?"

Artos shook his head.

Yeah, right. "Come on."

Trashcan Harry led them away from the rezcom.

The buzz from her console woke Pamela Martinez. The office windows showed the sky to be lightening; she'd gotten a few hours of sleep, anyway. She checked to confirm the source of the call. Good. She'd have time to fix her makeup and otherwise make sure she looked ready for business before they cleared security. It wouldn't do for her to look as though she had been sleeping in her chair, even if that was the case.

McAlister's late-night message had simply been the code word indicating that Sörli had initiated an action. The time between the strange little man informing his staff of the imminent action and their departure had been short, too short for McAlister to do more than launch the prearranged code message. Not knowing how long the action would take, she had returned to the office at once to await results.

She wanted to be present when Sörli returned.

Now her console was signaling that Sörli had tried to communicate with her and been informed that she was in her office. The origin point of the call was the helipad on the roof of building three. Time enough to get ready.

She was groomed and seated behind her desk when the door to the outer office opened, revealing a handful of men in tight-fitting hoods and dark padded clothing festooned about with odd lumps of mysterious import. Some of their gear she recognized; Pamela knew very well what military-issue automatic rifles looked like. McAlister stood with the other men, explaining the lack of an update; Sörli must have kept her informer by his side the whole time.

Sörli was dressed like his commandos, but his hood was pulled down into a baggy crumple around his throat, the end of his beard still tucked away inside. Dark smudges surrounded his eyes like the mask of a raccoon, and he looked grimmer than usual.

He marched up to her desk and tugged a bag woven of metallic thread from the harness set into his vest. Without a word, he upended the bag, dumping an object slightly larger than a softball onto her desk. The thing rolled erratically about until it fetched up against her secondary monitor. Her gorge leapt to her throat when she saw that it was a severed head.

Cold, blind eyes stared at her from the thing's hideous parody of a human face. But it was not human. Though child-sized, the head was not that of a baby. Its skin was wizened and had an odd gray pallor. The mouth was locked half open in a tooth-baring grin. And those teeth! Yellowed tusks, stained and runneled from unimaginable feasts.

"What is it?" Her voice sounded weak in her own ears, adding embarrassment to her shock.

"You asked for proof."

Dropping the bag on her desk, Sörli turned on his heels and headed for the door. He was halfway through before she stammered out her next question.

"What happened?"

"We were too late. You'll get my report," he said without stopping.

The door shuffed shut, sealing her in with his grisly present.

She locked out her console, isolating herself from interruption, and sat contemplating the terrible goblin head in stunned awe. The light outside grew stronger, allowing her to see more clearly the awful face of magic made corporeal. Much as she wanted it to be a fake, it was too real to be something constructed to fool her. Its presence paralyzed her.

As the morning sunlight crept over her desk, a change began to occur before her eyes. When the light touched it, the head transformed, slowly turning from its natural—no! unnatural—colors to chalky white. Greasy hair, pocked skin, dark stained teeth—all of it—shifted into a pallid, lusterless uniformity. The head might as well have been a repulsive sculpture of ash, fresh from the hands of a lunatic sculptor who had spent too long among the post-Froudites.

Somehow, the new appearance of the head made it seem safer, less threatening. She reached out a finger to touch it. Her finger touched the cheek and for the barest instant she felt it, real and solid under her flesh, before it crumbled into a pile of ash and dust.

Her Tidibot™ emerged from her desk and started sucking away at the debris. Its tiny vacuum whined in protest at the load. The little machine needed a dozen trips to take it all away; intended for keeping an executive's desk clean and shiny, it wasn't built for such a volume of dust.

Pamela watched the Tidibot's struggle and knew her own was just beginning.

Part 2

————

NOT OF THE SAME ESTATE

CHAPTER
11

The police expected that it would take the museum staff at least two days to complete their inventory of the damage. Holger didn't waste the time. He got himself and Spae set up in a residential hotel on the south side of town, not allowing Spae to do anything until he had swept all the rooms of the suite. Finding it clean, he set up his countermeasures. When he was satisfied that their base of operations was reasonably secure from observation, he retreated to his room. The stuff she wanted to set up in the sitting room made him nervous. He left her to it.

By the time he logged in to the Worcester police computer, Holger had all the necessary documentation to certify him as a member of the EC Commission of Antiquities, including a very official-looking diplomatic request that the local police force cooperate with him by allowing him access to their investigation. He dropped that note on the system operator, and she gave him access to the investigation files after only the most minimal of delays.

The inventory was there, so he opened it. As Spae had suggested, although some artifacts from the Romano-Brithonic exhibit had sustained damage, all were accounted for. Holger wasn't sure how he felt about that. He didn't like having Spae's magical work made real; magic didn't belong in what, while it might have been chaotic, was at least a rational world. At the same time, he was supposed to be working with Spae, and partners were supposed to be familiar with each other's capabilities. She had shown that she was competent in one of the aspects of her specialty. But how could he have confidence in such an unnatural skill?

The only things shown missing were a robe and a replica sword belonging to the museum's outreach program. Too bad something important hadn't gone missing. The nature of such an object might have held a clue as to the perpetrators of the incident. And stolen objects were real, physical things, things that could be traced.

Holger switched over to Sergeant Willis's preliminary report. The missing objects weren't noted; Holger found them listed as missing, though, when he checked previous reports of petty theft at the museum. Curious. The night watchman—one John Reddy, a student at the university—was officially listed as missing. A patrol car sent to the rezcom where he lived with his mother reported that he had not returned home on the night of the incident. Mrs. Reddy had been asked to call the police if she heard from him, but no such call had been logged as yet. Willis speculated that the charred corpse was Reddy's, but noted that initial analysis of the corpse was inconclusive pending authorization of funds to do DNA matching. Willis offered no reason for the watchman's death or the shoot-out in the gallery. Clearly, the police were puzzled.

So was Holger. By now the police should have realized from a simple comparison of physical data that the corpse, whoever he was, was not John Reddy. Why hadn't they?

Disconnecting from the police system, Holger placed a call to the museum. Once he transmitted his Commission ID, he received courteous and efficient service. The head of personnel herself transmitted him the files on everyone present at the museum on the day of the incident. Holger was only interested in one. He opened Reddy's small file, called up the biographical data, and saw immediately that something had changed. Reddy's height and weight were not the same as they had been two nights ago.

Someone was working to make it appear that Reddy was the corpse.

The woods out in back of the school weren't much, but they were all Kari had. They were where she went to be alone, to get away from the things she didn't like, to pretend that the world was all a forest and she was the keeper. Today was one of those days when she really needed the peace of her safe forest. She headed for her favorite place, trying not to think about any of the awful things that were happening outside her forest.

Once she had settled into the hollow by the fallen tree, she knew today wasn't an ordinary day in her forest. Something was, well, not wrong exactly, but different. Maybe the birds were too quiet, or not quiet enough. Something, anyway.

She sat quietly, listening. She thought that, if she was very quiet, she would hear what was different. Her eyes roved the brush and trees, searching.

Slowly, she became certain that she was not alone in the woods today.

She got that itchy feeling she got when Kevin Luckner was looking at her when he thought she didn't know. She turned her head, but not all the way. She knew how to do that. She did that when she got the itchy feeling, turned her head just enough that she could see Kevin there, watching her, but not enough that he'd know she was noticing.

There was someone—or something—there. It wasn't Kevin Luckner, but she wasn't sure who or what it was. She turned her head a little farther and the watcher shifted warily. All she could see was a white shape among the trees.

She knew she ought to be scared, but she wasn't.

"Hello?"

The watcher didn't answer her. But didn't leave either. Very, very slowly she turned farther.

It was an animal. It looked like a pony, but it wasn't any breed she'd ever looked at in her vids. She didn't notice the long spiral horn on its forehead until the animal stepped around the fallen tree.

It couldn't be a unicorn; they were just in fairy stories.

With delicate, almost hesitant steps, the animal that couldn't be a unicorn came up to her and folded its front knees until it was kneeling at her side. She smelled the warm animal scent of it as it stretched out its neck toward her. The weight of its head was heavy as it rested its chin in her lap. Even through her jeans its breath felt hot and moist on her thigh. She stroked its mane and was amazed at how soft and silky it felt. Afraid that she would break the illusion, she reached out and touched the animal's horn. Hard, rough, and very, very solid.

It was real!

She buried her head against the unicorn's neck and cried for joy.

"Your report is somewhat lacking in detail, Mr. Sörli." Pamela Martinez shook the hardcopy report at him. She was not pleased, and she didn't mind letting her anger show. "Given the week you've taken to submit it, I expected something more substantive."

"Some things are best not recorded," he responded blandly.

"Such as your responsibility in the death of William Tobias?"

"It was unfortunate."

"It was unnecessary."

"Unfortunate," Sörli repeated emphatically. "There is no reason for the truth to be recorded where anyone can read it and learn of our investigations. Let the record show that his death was the result of an industrial accident, and that the body was sufficiently mutilated to preclude an open-coffin ceremony. No one will question such statements. Will you be attending the funeral service tomorrow?"

She ignored his question. "You perpetrated this lie without my permission."

"He died honorably and well. His family deserves the full benefits of his sacrifice. Without the lie, your generous Mitsutomo would dispense no benefits to his family."

True, employees killed or injured while engaged in illegal activities were divorced from the Keiretsu's family. But, she added, "That is not the issue."

Sörli had a ready answer for that. "I acted in accordance with your mandate that we conceal the true nature of our operations."

Damn the man! It *did* make sense, if only to cover their own butts. Still, she wanted to see him squirm over it; he deserved to squirm. "A good man has died and you have achieved nothing."

"Oh, not nothing." He folded his hands casually. "You have no head on your wall, but I think that you no longer doubt the existence of the otherworld. This is not only desirable but necessary. The stakes have increased and the task has grown more difficult."

"I'm not in the mood for your riddles." Or for his manipulation. But he was right, she did believe. God help her. He knew more of this matter than she did. She still needed him, but she'd be damned if she'd let him think he was in charge. "I am not satisfied with the results you have achieved."

"Nor am I," he interrupted.

"You have implicated a Mitsutomo dependent in these events, but there's nothing in the report of a substantive nature. More things best left unrecorded?"

"For the moment. I have ascertained that John Reddy was contacted by an agent of the otherworld operating under the name Bennett at least once prior to the museum breakthrough. Likely his presence that night was arranged. This incident and his subsequent disappearance confirm his collusion. We should have been more vigilant."

"Vigilant?"

"His name was on one of our lists of possible agents. Admittedly, a low-priority listing. Our enemy achieved a success against us with his placement."

"And who is this enemy?"

"That remains an open question."

"I want answers, not questions."

"There is more work to be done. More preparations to be made. You have my requests for funding. Grant them."

"You'll give me answers?"

"Whether you like them or not."

The requests were all listed on her monitor. All were reasonable in their phrasing, all looked legitimate. All were euphemisms or outright lies. She hit the execute key, authorizing the expenditures. "It's done. Now get out of here and do your job."

Damn! He'd thought he'd tightened that bolt.

The vibrations from working on the others must have loosened it. Carlos shook his head and set to it again. Once he got the battery bolted down, he could crawl out from under the car and go inside for supper. Oh, for the good old days when cars had real engines instead of these electric motors.

Down the street he could hear some kids giggling. Probably laughing at him. Why not? Everybody around his new neighborhood thought old Carlos was a little odd for doing his own mechanic work, but where Carlos had grown up there hadn't really been any choice. He had gotten used to it. He actually enjoyed it most of the time.

But he hadn't gotten used to the cramped quarters under these electric jobs. His hand slipped and skinned his knuckles on a strut. Wrenching his hand away, he banged it again. Damn, damn, damn! Heedless of the dirt and grease, he sucked on his bruised knuckles.

Above his head, the nut he'd been working on dropped from the bolt, pinging on the concrete beside his head. The car above him rocked. Damn kids! He started to shout at them to take off, but stopped, eyes wide, as he saw the battery shift, sliding free of its mount. It couldn't be! He had tightened the other bolts.

The kids were still laughing when the heavy battery slid free and crashed down against his head. The pain almost put him right out, but he held on.

Concussion for sure. Maybe worse. His vision was graying, tunneling down. Had to crawl out, get Morena. She'd call the ambulance. He tried to move, but all he could do was roll his head to the side.

A pair of tiny, naked legs ran between the front and back tires. Scrawny legs, ending in broad feet with splayed, horny-nailed toes.

Hallucinations. The pain was causing hallucinat—

Spae's screech brought Holger bounding across the sitting room, Glock in hand. He hit the wall by the door, ready for trouble, but found her railing at her computer screen. He stayed by the door, out of the angle of the pickup, where he could see her monitor reflected in the mirror. Holger would show up if the people on the other end analyzed the image, but they probably wouldn't bother, and even if they did, it probably wouldn't matter; he was Spae's security, after all. Still, he thought it advisable to keep his presence discreet; she was talking to Charles Magnus.

"It's been two bloody weeks! Why wasn't I informed?" Spae's voice was pure outrage.

Magnus's response was calm, exaggeratedly so. "There is still debate concerning the meaning of the data we have acquired. Certain individuals didn't want you told anything, but I thought it best that you be brought in."

"Certain individ— Dagastino, I'll bet."

There was a sputtering noise from off screen on Magnus's side, and Holger knew Spae had named her chief adversary correctly.

"Let us leave personalities out of this and stick to the business at hand. Your perspective on recent events could be valuable, but your opinions will not be looked upon favorably if you will not confine yourself to business."

"Business, eh? All right. Business. Have you finally real-ized that there's a connection with the incident here and having the Cornwall project blow up in your faces?"

"The timing is suggestive," Magnus agreed sourly. "Have you learned anything new?"

"I'm certain now that it was an important awakening. There were other forces involved."

"The team here agrees."

Spae went on to detail her procedures and their results. Magnus nodded and made encouraging murmurs, but Holger caught him glancing off to one side where, no doubt, one or more specialists were advising him as to the validity of Spae's procedures. No doubt the antagonistic Dr. Dagastino was among them.

"And the sleeper's identity?"

Spae snorted. "You know that as well as I."

"I *know* nothing of the sort, Doctor. I merely speculate, as do you. Until we can question this sleeper, we will not *know*."

"That's Dagastino talking. He wouldn't *know* his own name without questioning his mother under Pentatell™."

"We must be above petty rivalry, Doctor. If this sleeper is Arthur, we must acquire him."

"If you're so anxious to get him, send me some support. If I didn't have to do everything myself, I could be getting closer, faster."

"Frankly, Doctor, given the size of the energy fluctuation, several of us here feel that more than one sleeper may have been woken. There is no telling who your sleeper may be, but given your physical location, it seems unlikely that he is who you believe. Without solid data, we must continue to consider your operation in the USA as only one of several vital operations. Our resources are stretched trying to cover alternative possibilities."

Meaning that no more bodies were coming.

"Dagastino's got you tossing all of Wales and half of Eng-land, doesn't he?"

Magnus ignored her comment. "You and Mr. Kun will have to continue on your own for now. You will, of course, continue to have the Department's full computer and financial support."

"I'm sure."

"Bring your sleeper in, Doctor."

"Right." She cut the connection. Without turning she said, "We were close, Kun. So very close. And they're so far away, they have no idea at all. Won't even look at the evidence. It's up to us, Kun. We've got to find him by ourselves."

"Is he really Arthur?"

"Who else would he be?"

"Why here, then? This is America, not England."

"I don't know." She shook her head, her face empty of its usual arrogance. "I wish I did. It might tell me something that I could use."

"Maybe he can explain it."

"Maybe, but I doubt it. In any case, we have to find him before we can ask him."

He didn't want to, but he knew he had to ask. "Can you track him magically?"

"No. I have nothing of his to use."

"Nothing from the museum will help?"

She turned to face him, smiling slightly. "You know more about this stuff than you like to let on. Normally, one would expect that something in the exhibit was used as a key to call to the sleeper. Law of Contagion and all that. But I couldn't feel any resonance with any particular individual."

"Could the resonance have been blocked? You said you sensed more than one hand had shaped energies there."

"Perhaps." She thought for a while. "I don't think so, though. I didn't feel like I was facing a block. Maybe the connections were just too old, too tenuous for me to feel."

"So you can't find him with magic."

"No."

Good. They'd have to do it the old-fashioned way. His way.

* * *

Charley Gordon hated it when his beeper went off in the middle of the night. He ordered the lights on, wincing when the computer obeyed him efficiently and blasted with full wattage. "Lower lights," he pleaded, then ordered it to connect a line to whoever wanted him.

"Captain Milton," the machine informed him.

"Charley? You there?"

"Yeah, Captain."

"Sorry to wake you."

I'll bet. Milton didn't sound apologetic; he sounded as if he enjoyed it. "What is it?"

"The slasher's hit again."

Huh? "Two days early. You sure we ain't got a copycat?"

"Don't think so."

"Be right down."

"Comm Ave. The park," the captain said before he cut the connection.

Charley passed the word to Manny while he dressed. Manny said he'd meet Charley at the scene.

Two days early? Had to be a copycat. The Barrington slasher was a real stickler for timing.

When he got to the scene and saw the bodies, he didn't need the forensics boys to tell him that this was the real slasher. Nobody but the cops knew what body parts the slasher took away with him. Charley found a trash can and gave it his breakfast. He should have known better than to have eaten.

"We got a witness this time," Milton said to Charley after he'd stopped puking. "Said he saw the killer."

The captain didn't sound as though it was the break they'd all been hoping for, and once Charley talked to the witness, he understood why. No DA was gonna buy in to an eight-foot-tall, bat-winged lizard.

"I am tired of being interrupted," Sörli said as he sat in the chair. "Can't you think of some better way to ask your incessant questions other than demanding these pilgrimages to your office?"

Pamela noted that the monitors in the chair reported that Sörli was truly agitated and not just putting on a show. Good. Maybe he'd let something slip.

"You come because I call. You work for me, remember. I want answers."

"You have answers," he snapped. "You even have reports. Against my better judgment. Read them. They have your answers. Otherworld intrusions have increased by four hundred percent. Magic is on the increase. For now, it is mostly manifest in desolate and wild places, but if the trend continues there will soon be fairy beings and monsters haunting the cities. We face a crisis, and it could grow worse quickly."

Damn him! He had taken and twisted things around on her before she'd gotten half started, raising her fears to where she had to ask, "What do you mean?"

"The incident at the Woodman Museum was only the first part of a two-part shift in the balance. The first part you know, the awakening of a man long held in magical bondage in the otherworld. With his release, more of the energy the agents of the otherworld need to operate here has become available. You are seeing the results in the reports you demand so insistently. These strange happenings are only a prelude. As dangerous as these intrusions are, the man himself poses an even greater threat."

"This man! This man!" Damn, she was flustered. "It's been a month since his—what did you call it?—awakening and you still haven't learned who he is."

"Untrue."

Bastard. Always with a trump card. "All right. Who *is* this dangerous man?"

"His name is Artos."

"That's it? Not even a family name? Or is that a family name?"

"Just Artos. Other appellations have been applied, but none was used with a clear preference. He was a warrior once. A ruler, too. Some thought he was very good at what he did. There were songs sung about him."

"How do you know all this?"

"Confidential sources."

Was he baiting her on purpose? "You work for me, you little bastard. You will tell me where you are getting your information."

"For the moment I work for you, Ms. Martinez. Since you have been expressing something less than satisfaction with my work lately, I feel that I need to maintain my independent assets."

"Who else are you working with?"

"You wrong me. You are the only one paying me. But employment isn't what binds us, it is the threat of the otherworld. I suggest that you consider the data I have given rather than worrying about its source. Truth is truth, even when spoken by a habitual liar."

How was it that he got calmer as she lost control? Well, he wouldn't get away with it. She forced herself to sit back and rest her arms on the arms of her chair. Calm, she told herself as she pressed the stud that activated her chair's relaxation routine. It took effect almost immediately, and her voice was down to its normal register when she said, "The problem with habitual liars is that you can never believe anything they say."

"Do you consider me a habitual liar, Ms. Martinez? Is that why you use this chair?"

In the grip of the relaxation routine, she didn't start. Her voice held only curiosity. "You know about the chair?"

"I do. I take no offense from it because it is a sensible precaution. You are wise to take precautions."

"Am I wise to trust you?"

"I am not the one to ask. I have not led you astray."

"Not yet."

"It is not in my interest to do so. We have a common enemy and we need each other. Especially now."

A surge of fear threatened to overwhelm her relaxed state. She forced it away. Information. She needed information to control the situation. "Why now? Something to do with the crisis you mentioned?"

"Yes. The second part. In the past, this Artos has been associated with a magical artifact of significant power. Through close association with this talisman he has become, shall we say, dependent on it. Now that he is free, I believe he will seek it out. Should he do so and successfully retrieve it, there will be a significant increase in the otherworldly energy permeating our world. Such an increase will be enough to cause a radical shift in the balance. Society will fragment and civilization as we know it will devolve into a new dark age."

"So you want to find him and kill him before he gets this talisman."

"No. Ultimately, that will change nothing. The talisman is the key. It must be destroyed."

"And what will happen if the talisman is destroyed?"

"The energies enwrapped in holding it will be forever bound. Having curtailed further disruption, we may be able to deal with the current effects and minimize the damage."

"Return the balance to where it was."

"Possibly. I can make no promises."

"Can I trust you, Sörli?"

"We are working for the same goal here, Ms. Martinez. I no more want to see my world controlled by the beings that rule the otherworld than you do."

Truth, the monitor said. Rock-solid truth.

Pamela would not let her world be destroyed by magic.

"All right, Mr. Sörli, do whatever you have to. Destroy this talisman thing."

Astrid was relieved to see the wan light illuminating the emergency phone box. She knew she hadn't been walking for more than a quarter mile, but the dark made it seem forever. Her heels didn't help either; the gravel by the roadbed was safer than the slush-covered ice on the road, but too unstable for comfortable walking. Not for the first time she chided herself for not taking reasonable boots. She'd heard the forecast; she knew better.

But the car wasn't supposed to get a flat tire and she wasn't supposed to be here slogging along a deserted highway at eleven-oh-bleeping-thirty at night.

There was a dark, shadowy lump by the phone box. Her first thought upon seeing it was that it was some derelict or wino huddled against the cold. Silly girl, she told herself. Too much city living. It was probably just a pile of debris collected from along the highway, put here by the cleanup crews for easier spotting by the truck that would haul it away.

It stirred, and she thought her first impression was right. Then she saw the pale, curled fingers on the ground. Dead man's fingers. The dark lump rose up, resolving itself into the shape of a hulking Sumo refugee. She froze in place, chilled deeper than the cutting wind could account for.

The killer held something in his hands, something soft and yielding in the grip, something that dripped. A dark-red watch cap. The killer pulled on the cap, drawing her attention to his face. That face would have been at home in a horror vid. He grinned crookedly at her, showing teeth out of a dentist's nightmare.

"Good night it is. Two for Old Shaggs tonight."

She screamed, but the wind tore away the sound.

Turning, she immediately lurched off balance as one of her damned heels slid off a rock and snapped. She fell hard. Before she could scramble up, she felt a presence looming over her. The heat of his body washed over her, as did his fetid breath. The smells of decaying organic matter and fresh blood clogged her nose.

A huge hand came down on her shoulder, half engulfing her neck. Sharp nails dug into her flesh. She screamed again and started her hopeless struggle.

The bastard strangling her actually laughed.

Holger saw the thing that had taken to living in the alley behind Rezcom 3 every night during the stakeout. He didn't know what it was, but he knew it for something from that other place, the place where the monsters came from. Out of habit he noted its patterns, the way it moved, its hunting grounds, and soon had it pegged as a scavenger living off the bountiful refuse of the rezcom. But he didn't do anything about it. Not even when it took the addict that stumbled into its territory. Scavengers kill live prey when they can get away with it; it was the way of nature. Watching with professional interest, he noted that nature's way applied to the unnatural as well. He didn't interfere. It wasn't his business.

He knew about the other watchers too, but he stayed out of their way, especially once he spotted a familiar silhouette spending time parked next to one of the watchers' cars: Vadama. Staying out of *his* way was usually the safer course. Holger did his best to keep his own surveillance less visible.

But two weeks of physical and electronic watch on the rezcom brought him nothing. Even tailing Marianne Reddy unearthed no sign of the missing John Reddy. Holger wasn't really surprised; the kid hadn't even shown up for his own funeral. Tailing the mother had seemed a good tack; since John wasn't dead, it seemed likely that he would try to contact his mother once things calmed down. It had been a bad guess.

The trail was cold; he left it to the Mitsutomo boys.

Abandoning his watch on the boy's mother, Holger retraced his steps, looking for something he had missed, anything that might be out of place. He looked again at the murder that had happened a few days before John's disappearance. The victim, one Emilio Winston, had been missing for several days before turning up dead in a drug-related crime. Winston had been a student at John's university. A connection?

Holger hacked his way into the university computer net.

Winston, the victim, had been on the freshman basketball team with John. That was a connection, but what kind? Another kid, a freshman named Trahn, had disappeared from the university about the same time as Winston. Holger ran a few files and discovered that Trahn's psych profile didn't look like your typical runaway's. Trahn had been enrolled in one of John's classes. Holger set a couple of search routines loose on the files and waited for results. The expert systems didn't live up to their name; they turned up nothing.

Maybe it was the fact that John himself had disappeared now that made Holger want to connect the two previous disappearances. Maybe he was just grasping at straws. In any case, he took a look through the university records for himself.

He started with campus security, since they had checked into both disappearances. Trahn had last been seen on the day before Winston's last appearance. Close, but not close enough. Lots of witnesses, John included, had seen Trahn in an Enviro lab, but nobody after that. The kid had been there after most of them had left, but John's account said that Trahn left before he did. Sometime after Trahn left the lab, then; and before supper, since his roommate reported that Trahn had failed to show up for their supper date. A window of only an hour or so.

Winston's disappearance was more problematic. In fact, he seemed to be almost nonexistent for most of the day before he was listed as missing; only his roommate had seen him that day. Odd, since the psych profile showed him to be a gregarious sort. But then, the profile didn't show him as a drug abuser, either.

Why hadn't the police followed up on that? Even if they had, what would they have turned up? There didn't seem to be any connections between the two disappearances. But nearness of the timing still bothered Holger; that, and the fact that they were both too uncharacteristic for the people involved.

He cast his net wider, using one of the Department's cover idents to put a general request into the police computer. Scanning the missing-persons list for a month on either side of the museum incident, he found another university connection in among the list of names. Four days after the museum incident one Harold Black, a custodian at the university, was listed as missing. Holger called up the report. Black had checked out of work on time the Friday before the incident and failed to report to work the following Monday. Coincidence? Maybe. The investigating officer noted that Black had checked out the previous Friday, citing illness, and had been absent from work for the first three days of the following week. No one had seen the guy during that period. Interesting time frame. Black's whereabouts were unknown for a period almost exactly matching Winston's period of being the invisible man.

Holger added Black into his mixing bowl and stirred, waiting for something to stick together. Black popped up as the source of Winston's reported connection with unsavory characters on the day before the boy disappeared. Very interesting. Holger called for Black's file. The datapic was unfamiliar, and Holger was sure he would have remembered such an ugly face; he had never seen the guy before. The file was sparse; the guy was a work-relief type and had been with the university for only a little over a year. The university computer didn't have anything but the basics on him before that. Holger ran down the references and learned they were fakes. Not unusual in itself, but suggestive in the current circumstances.

Not expecting any results, he placed a call to the last address in Black's file. To his surprise, a gruff voice answered.

"Hello?"

"Am I speaking to Mr. Harold Black?" Holger asked in his best phone-solicitor voice.

"Yeah," the voice responded suspiciously.

"Mr. Black, you have been selected by our computer to receive a wonderful prize. All you have to do to receive this prize is to verify a few bits of information. Would you be willing to do that?"

"Don't want no prize. Good-bye."

The connection went dead, but Holger's console displayed confirmation that the phone line had connected to the address in Black's file. It was in the Providence district of the Northeast sprawl. Not a nice place by all accounts—but by implication, Mr. Harold Black was not a nice man.

Holger had a few questions for Mr. Harold Black.

Jessie didn't want to wake up, in fact she dreaded the idea, but the alarm across the room shrilled at her insistently. She'd made sure it was across the room when she'd crawled into bed—what? She squinted across at the clamoring clock—four hours ago. If she had left it within reach of the bed she would have destroyed the blasted thing.

And her chance for making the deadline, as well.

Summoning a gigantic effort of will, she flung back the covers and dragged herself up, crossing the room in quick, chilled strides.

Silence, blessed silence.

But not relief. For that she'd have to make the pour. Greyshelda Prototypes would be unhappy if she didn't deliver the model today, so unhappy that they'd invoke the failed-delivery clause in her contract. She knew they would; they'd always done so before. But this time she couldn't afford it; she needed every one of the dollars credited to her account. She tugged on her robe. If she made the pour right away, the model would be cured—barely—by the time she got to their offices.

The light in her workroom was on. She didn't remember leaving it on, but then, she hadn't been thinking very straight when she'd collapsed last night. Two days without sleep did that for you. Waking up with her head on her worktable, next to the food she'd just fixed, had been a clue that she'd needed sleep more than sustenance. Now that she'd had some of the former, the latter sounded good, even if it was to be the Zapper Instameal™ she had 'waved before crashing.

She was annoyed when she saw that the Paperform™ tray was empty, its compartments as clean as if they had been licked. The ultrasonic vermin guard had to be on the blink again if the rats had gotten in. Then she noticed the pyramidal pile of peas next to the tray. Rats didn't do that.

Beyond the peas was something that made Jessie's knees weak. She sat down to avoid falling down, and stared. Sitting on the table next to the plate was the mold, open, and next to it a casting, all clean and polished.

Rats didn't do that, either.

Pamela swiveled the secondary monitor around to where McAlister could see the image.

"Can you tell me what it is?"

He gave the screen a quick glance. "One of Sörli's toys."

"He built it under your nose and with Mitsutomo money, and you're telling me that you don't know what it is?"

"No idea." He seemed undisturbed by his lack of understanding. "Technics isn't my specialty."

"Can you get it to one of our research teams?"

"Sure, but he'll know." The monitor registered agitation in McAlister. "He won't like it."

"I don't care if he likes it."

"He'll jump ship."

Pamela didn't think so. "By his own admission, he can't afford to just now."

"He won't like having his toy might taken away."

"He hasn't got time for a temper tantrum."

"You don't know him very well."

Who did know Sörli? McAlister had worked with him more closely than anyone Pamela knew of. Had she pegged Sörli right on this one?

Mike Powers clucked his tongue as he listened to the announcer. God above, what was the world coming to? Used to be that you only heard that sort of trash on the tabloid channels. Dragon men from outer space! Who believed that crap?

He hit the remote and called up the Astrology Channel. Shelli Crystal was breezing and jiggling her way through Virgo, so he wouldn't have long to wait for his horoscope. Shelli didn't do the 'scopes herself, she had a staff for that; but Mike didn't mind, Shelli put on a good show.

Something thumped on the balcony. With the windows blanked Mike couldn't see what it was, but he figured it was Ms. Colomo's cat knocking over his flowerpots again. Stirring himself, he hauled his mass out of the chair. If he caught the damned beast he'd pitch it off the balcony. That'd teach Ms. Colomo to let her animal intrude on people's God-given privacy.

He slid open the door and saw the broken pot immediately. But he didn't see the cat. All he saw was the sharp, sharp teeth in the snout that thrust at him.

"There's no one there," Spae said as they pulled up.

Holger shut off the engine. He didn't like this car as much as the one they'd had in Worcester. That seemed appropriate; he didn't like being in the sprawl proper as much as he'd liked its exurb satellite—and he hadn't liked Mitsutomo's version of Worcester much at all.

"Wait here anyway," he told her.

"I thought you always wanted backup."

"This is just reconnaissance."

"Oh, that makes all the difference."

But she folded her arms and stayed put.

The area wasn't quiet, but Holger didn't see or hear anything that didn't fit. It looked and sounded—and smelled— like a run-down neighborhood full of run-down tenements. Nothing he hadn't seen before. His trench coat was out of place here; made him look like cops. Useful at the moment. The street people eased out of his way and watched him with wary eyes.

The door to the building he sought was open. He entered the hallway and paused by the bottom of the staircase. A naked bulb halfway up the stairs to the next floor was the only light working to push back the gloom of the windowless hall. He went up the creaky stairs, headed for the third floor.

Two teenagers squatted on the second landing. They wore gang colors but they didn't posture or threaten when Holger reached the landing. For all the attention they paid him, he might not have existed. Holger noted the syringe one of them held in her dirty, limp hand. The sudden, harsh smell of fresh urine and the puddle spreading from beneath her companion said that these two pieces of urban trash were the real thing.

Holger passed them by and walked down the dark hall. Black's apartment was the next to last on the left. Holger slid a card into the frame and encountered a resistant bolt. Locked. He listened but heard nothing from the other side. One of the junkies on the landing sniggered when he rapped on the door.

There was no response.

After a minute, Holger took his lock opener from one of his trench coat's inner pockets. Standing to one side, he inserted the opener's rod into the keyhole, triggering the enzyme that would expand the plastic of the rod to match the tumblers. When the expanding plastic had nowhere to go but back into the opener, a second enzyme was released to halt expansion and stiffen the rod's new shape into a custom-fit key. Holger turned the opener and felt the bolt retract. Firmly gripping the Glock concealed in his pocket, he entered.

The room was empty.

The debris suggested that more than one person had been living in the apartment, possibly as many as three or four. Nothing suggesting that any of them were female. No doubt there were things here that a good lab could tie the people who had lived here to anyone he found—once he found them—but right now a full scraping search of the place was a waste of time; a hair was anonymous unless you had other hairs or something else with the same DNA structure to compare it with.

His search gained him one significant item to confirm that he was on the right track. Gummed to the inside of a trash can by some noxious black substance was an embroidered patch. Pried free and turned over, it revealed the likeness of a small dog in armor, a symbol of the Woodman Armory. Such patches were worn by the security guards at the museum. Examination of the patch showed that it had been carefully cut from a garment, probably by someone who had wanted to keep the shirt wearable. Someone who had left Worcester wearing only the clothes on his back might want to keep such a shirt wearable even if he wanted to rid himself of any visible association with the museum. Someone like John Reddy maybe?

Circumstantial evidence, but suggestive.

He heard familiar footfalls in the hall. He wasn't surprised when Spae spoke from the doorway.

"I told you there was no one here."

"And you were correct, Doctor. I've satisfied myself here for now. We may as well leave."

He had seen enough. Black's return to this place showed him to be unimaginative and, frankly, fairly stupid. But the runaway custodian was not so stupid as to stay here once he had a hint—as Holger's call had been—that someone was onto him. Black and his companions had abandoned this place, but they were still out there somewhere, probably gone to ground. Their coming here in the first place suggested that Black was their leader, or at the least their native guide. That was fine by Holger, for Black had already demonstrated his skill level in hide-and-seek. Holger would find them. It was just going to be a matter of time.

At least he and Spae were ahead of the Mitsutomo team. Those corporate slugs were still working Worcester.

CHAPTER
12

It was the first truly sunny day in weeks, and John couldn't pass up the chance to take in some of the warm radiance. His fears of being recognized had been laid to rest long ago, so lounging on the porch of MaxMix Manor didn't seem dangerous in the least. This was his neighborhood now—more or less; he knew the people who lived here and could spot a stranger as far as he could see along twisty River Street.

But for all that, he didn't really belong here.

Still, the day was too fine to let old anxieties nag him into a foul mood. He sat down on the railing and swung up his feet; the balcony support at his back allowed him to maintain his balance on the narrow seat. The sun washed over him, warm and soothing, seeming even to mute the music blaring from the Ramirez house down the street. It was still weeks before the real spring weather would arrive, and the heat felt good. He felt calmer than he had in some time, mellowed.

Was this how cats felt when they stretched out in a sunbeam?

Like a cat, he slitted his eyes and watched the street without seeming to. River Street didn't get a lot of traffic, mostly just locals on foot or bicycle going about their business. Not too many cars; the road was full of untended potholes. It *was* a bad part of town, don't you know.

Feeling relaxed, John just watched the kids playing in the street, racing between the old multistory houses and across yards, sidewalks, and street as if there were no distinction. Once in a while a car would negotiate the road, dodging pits and kids as necessary. Slick Dick put in an appearance in the lot by Rosamund's Haircuttery and set up shop early; Slick must have been touched by the fineness of the day as well, because John saw him actually accept trade goods for the junk he was pushing. The day was almost ruined when Mr. Talisano's thunderous old Chevy fumer rumbled past in blue clouds of foul-smelling exhaust. Mr. Talisano was a good mechanic, which was the only way he could keep that old antique running, but he wasn't a sensible guy; gas guzzlers like the Chevy were just too anti-green.

A twin pair of black leather jackets turned the corner from Pickett, a guy and a girl with arms wrapped around each other. He recognized the male's silhouette at once; such a tall, rail-thin scarecrow had to be Hector. Since the guy was Hector, the girl had to be Carla, his woman. John didn't need to see the backs of their jackets to know they were painted with the flaming-rapier emblem of the Downtown Dons. Though the pair were both several years younger than John, their emblems were older and more worn than the one on the back of John's jacket.

Hector disengaged himself from Carla and bounced up the steps. Spinning, he kicked out and knocked John's feet from the railing. John nearly followed them, but not quite. He'd anticipated Hector's move and had taken a restraining grip on the railing. Hector grinned at John while he swung his feet back up onto the railing. Once John was settled, Hector's face went all solemn.

"Watch them rays, okay, Compadre Jack? They make you pale boys look like the main course at Red Lobster house. Don't you be thinking you can go cancerboy on us and darken up to a real color."

Life with the Dons wasn't the same as living on the street alone, nor was it like having a corporate family, but it was a way of getting by. If getting by was all you wanted. Three months hadn't reconciled John to thinking of Hector as any kind of family, even if he was friendlier than many of the gangers. Nor had those months gotten him used to the physical liberties Hector took. But those months *had* taught him how to play the game.

"Making like a lizard, Compadre. Rays is warm." He stretched out a hand and inspected it ostentatiously. "Girls like me well enough pale like this."

Carla giggled.

Hector looked at her sideways. "Girls get strange sometimes. Who can figure?"

Carla tilted her head down and gave Hector a wicked grin. "I thought you *liked* strange."

"Time and place, babe." He grinned. "Time and place."

They welded themselves back together. When they came up for air, Hector turned to John.

"Say and hey, where's the warlord?"

"Why? Trouble brewing?"

Hector shrugged. "Who can say? Nothing the Dons can't handle, hey? Don't got all day to look." He squeezed Carla and she squeaked. "So, where's he be?"

MaxMix Manor had once been a beautiful private home with a big bay window that punched out the front of the building on the first two floors. John pointed with his head toward the second story, where an open window leaked something that sounded like a documentary on helicopters.

"Bear's facing again," he said, using the slang the loose way most of the folks around here did. The warlord wasn't actually in direct machine interface, just using the vid set. He didn't even have a virtual receptor headset, but any interaction with tech was "facing" around here.

"Don't seem right, ya know?"

No, John didn't know. Artos was doing what he'd been doing since he woke up, learning. Learning about anything and everything about the strange world he found himself in.

There was nothing wrong with that, but around here, learning anything not directly related to survival was considered a waste of time. *That's* what didn't seem right to John. Life in the Northeast sprawl, and the people here, were very different from what he knew. He didn't feel at home at all; too much was different, and it made him unhappy.

Hector looked up at the window, uncertainty on his face. "You been hanging with him longer than me, Compadre Jack. He gonna get squeaky if this ain't important?"

"Depends on how stupid your news is."

"I dunno. Maybe I should come back."

"He'll squeak for sure if it's important and you don't tell him. Only one way to find out."

Hector looked dubious. Apparently, intruding on the warlord was a very serious business.

"No balls, no fun," John taunted. Hector's interruption of his lazing, then the hesitancy to follow through, made John testy. "He does have *cojones,* doesn't he, Carla?"

"More than you, *blanco,*" Hector bristled before his woman could answer. "Maybe I'll cut yours off and add them to my collection."

"And maybe I'll eat yours for lunch."

"Anytime, *blanco.*"

"That's what Chico said."

"This ain't no dark alley and you ain't got no allies."

"You said 'anytime.' But it ain't gonna be now, 'cause I ain't starting a cut and slash under the warlord's nose. I can wait. I've waited before."

It was low and a little stupid, but that was the way John felt most of the time around these people. Low, and a little stupid. If he didn't come to grips with it, it'd get him in real trouble. To judge by Hector's scowl, he might be in real trouble already. And Hector was one of the friendlier gangers. Making sexual slurs in front of the guy's squeeze might not have been the brightest idea, but it was beat by bringing up that business with Chico. *More* than a little stupid. But the code said you never backed down unless you wanted to get torn down.

The only way out was sliding around the problem. Later would be, well, later.

"You want to see Bear or not?"

"Yes," Carla answered quickly.

Hector accepted the out. With an elaborate shrug he resettled his jacket and dropped the tension out of his shoulders.

"Compadre Bear's the man we came to see."

"Let's go, then." John led them upstairs to Bear's room, rapping twice on the door before opening it. The warlord of the Downtown Dons spun his rickety old office chair around and stood. The Don of Dons wasn't a tall man, but his breadth of shoulders was impressive. He looked a lot more commanding in black leathers and studs than he had in a ratty velvet robe.

"Hector, my man," said Artos, whom the Dons knew as Compadre Bear, their warlord.

Compadre Bear was a different man from "Ar-tos, not Ar-tur." A lot had changed since John and Artos had abandoned Trashcan Harry's apartment and hit the streets, and Artos had come a long way from the confused and confusing refugee who'd followed John's lead since that night of magic at the museum. Together with Trashcan Harry they'd gone from homeless wanderers to members of this urban gang. Artos had even made himself leader of the gang. He was a quick learner; his command of street idiom was only one proof of that.

Uncharacteristically hesitant, Hector started, "I don't wanna bother . . . "

"No bother, Compadre. Always time for a warrior." Hector grinned at the implied compliment. He even flashed his teeth at John, as if to cement his worth and superiority over John. John had yet to fight in one of the gang's wars. Bear ignored the byplay. "Jack, get the lady a seat."

While John did as he was told, Hector, obviously impressed by his reception, just babbled out his thoughts. "You're not like Compadre Ferd."

"Ferddy was a booter," Bear said admiringly as he rubbed at his rib cage where the previous warlord had cracked it in their first encounter. The demonstration of scars was good etiquette here. It served as a form of history, a way of remembering what had happened to you. It also served to show you belonged, a way of demonstrating you had earned your place. John's scars weren't so demonstrable.

"Yeah, a real booter," John agreed. "All fist, no brain."

"But Ferddy's gone," Bear said firmly. "I do things differently." Hector nodded and Carla looked expectant, almost hopeful. "Why have you come to see me?"

Carla and Hector exchanged glances. She nodded almost imperceptibly. He spoke.

"Trashcan Harry ain't come into Louie's last night."

"He doesn't go every night," John pointed out.

"He does when Ledo's singing," Hector informed him.

Bear ran fingers through his beard, thinking for a moment before stating, "Ledo sent you."

Carla nodded. "She got a soft spot for strays. Thinks the old dode's sweet, not that she'd want him to know. God help her, the dode trails after her too much already. But she's, you know, worried that, like, something might have happened to him. We're just doing a favor for her, you know."

"Compassion for others is nothing to be ashamed about." Bear didn't specify anyone's compassion in particular, but John took it as a condemnation of his attitude. Bear wasn't looking at him, though. "Anyone seen him around today?"

Trashcan Harry rarely passed up a meal, and John realized the old custodian had done so today. "He wasn't in the kitchen this morning."

He was surprised to find himself worried about the guy. Strange as it was—strange as Trashcan Harry was—Harry was John's only link to the life he used to lead. Well, not only. Faye was still around. Occasionally. Very occasionally.

His memories swept him back to the night his old life had died. He remembered the terror and the confusion, the wonder of what he had seen. Trashcan Harry had shown up and offered a way out, and John had grabbed it, running away from what he couldn't deal with. At the time, the custodian had seemed a godsend, someone who knew what to do, which John had found comforting. The next morning, John had learned that he was supposed to be dead; Trashcan Harry had shown him the net story.

In shock, he'd listened to Trashcan's plan, listened and agreed. Trashcan Harry had told him that there were people out there who knew that John was involved in what had happened at the museum, and who knew that he was not dead. They had to avoid those people. John had listened. That was how he'd found himself at the train station, telling himself over and over that the old guy had experience and that he was older than John, that he had some idea of what was going on. The only part of Trashcan Harry's plan John had balked at was the suggestion that they leave Artos behind. John insisted; it had been obvious that the guy needed someone to look after him. More than obvious when it came time to get Artos on the train. Artos had been pretty passive until he saw the train pull into the station, but one look at the train had set him to backing up and quivering. Only continual assurances from John that it was safe had persuaded him to board. Artos had been nearly catatonic the whole way to Boston, but it had been easier to get him onto the next train and, by the end of that ride, Artos had been almost back to his nervous, paranoid self.

It wasn't until they had been holed up in Trashcan Harry's Providence apartment for a couple of days that John realized the old guy was as clueless as Artos about what to do next. But before John's trust was totally undermined, the phone rang. The call had immediately put Trashcan Harry on edge. He'd insisted that they bail out of the apartment. They'd hit the streets, directionless. With winter coming on, it had been . . . unpleasant, with even worse prospects. Then they had their run-in with the Downtown Dons and life had changed again. If it hadn't been for Artos . . .

They'd joined the gang, and now even John could see that the gang was better off. Artos had restructured the Dons, bringing his brand of law and justice. Even the gang's neighborhood had prospered; though most of its inhabitants still lived in the twilight world of shadows cast by the corporate mainstream and neglectful governmental monoliths, they were better off than they had been. But while living in MaxMix Manor wasn't like living in a rezcom, life in the Manor wasn't as bad as it used to be. If it hadn't been for Artos . . .

Yeah, if it hadn't been for Artos.

Was his mother still living in their apartment in Rezcom 3?

"Jack?"

Bear's voice. Time had passed; Hector and Carla were gone. The warlord's interruption wasn't exactly welcome.

"What?"

"You're thinking about going back again."

It wasn't a question. It also wasn't a wrong guess. When John had followed Trashcan Harry into the night, he hadn't realized that all of his previous life was being left behind. If he had, he might not have followed Trashcan.

"Is it that obvious?"

"To some." John felt Bear's eyes on him, but the man didn't say anything else until John looked up and met his gaze. "You can't, you know."

"With all the weirdness that's been coming down in the world, who says the dead can't rise?"

"You're not dead."

"My mom doesn't know that. I shouldn't have let her believe that."

"What's done is done. You thought it wise at the time."

"So I was stupid, all right?"

"Perhaps not. It may not yet be safe to let her know you live."

"What do you mean?" John felt suddenly anxious. What had he missed?

"Don't worry unduly. I only meant to suggest caution. Trashcan Harry's disappearance may mean nothing; or it may mean that someone who was seeking him, or us, has found him. We should be cautious for a while."

"I'm tired of looking over my shoulder."

"Even were you to go back, it wouldn't stop. Willingly or not, you've been involved in significant events. Events, or their creators, will involve you again. Willingly or not."

"You making some kind of occult prediction?"

"You know I don't do that. I'm just speaking from past experience."

"How far past?"

"You're deliberately being difficult. I'm just trying to point out something that will improve your chances of making something of what has been handed to you. Your old life is gone and you can't have it back. You have to deal with what you *do* have, with the here and now. Failing to learn from what is happening around you is asking to be handed your head. The serpent lies in wait for the unwary."

"Dump the aphorisms. This isn't one of your lectures to the Dons."

"You make it sound like aphorisms are worthless and boring. That's a cheap shot. There is accumulated wisdom in such sayings. Hard-earned wisdom. To dismiss something just because it's old is to throw away wisdom. The Dons are learning that. They've learned a lot since we've been here."

"And we haven't?"

Bear laughed. "Yes, we've learned, too. But I think they've come further. We're just learning the outside of the way they live here. Haven't you been watching them? They're changing *inside* and learning how wrong they were to follow a serpent-lover like Ferd. They're beginning to see the inherent weakness of the rule of simple might. They're learning important things. You're helping me teach them."

"You don't need me."

"No, I don't."

Blunt, but not very reassuring. John was surprised to feel that he wanted Bear to say that he *did* need John. Hadn't this guy's entry into his life *trashed* his life? "You want to teach a lesson so much? What are you wasting your time here for? The whole *world* needs the lesson you say you're trying to teach these people."

Bear sighed tiredly. "Some things never change."

"So what if you get what you want here? What difference will one educated gang make to the world?"

"As much difference as anyone can make. Haven't I made a difference with these folks?"

"Yeah, I guess so."

"I'm just one man."

"So?"

"So. One man can make a difference."

John didn't want to hear it. He folded his arms. "One man can shoot you dead."

"And one man can save you. Under the right circumstances." Bear gave John a chance to respond, but when it was clear that he wouldn't, the warlord went on. "When I said that I didn't need you, I was telling the truth. But it was a simple, incomplete truth. Other people could have taught me what you have. Other people could continue the job; the Good Lord knows I still need teaching about this concrete and plastic world of yours. There's so much about the way people live here that is familiar to me, but there is even more that is totally strange. I've never liked strangeness much, Jack. You've helped me with the strangeness more than anyone, and I am grateful. I want to do something for you."

"There's nothing you can do for me." That you haven't already done *to* me, that is.

"I could take you on as my *comes*."

"Say what?"

Bear's brow furrowed as he sought a way to explain himself. "The word that comes to my mind is 'man,' but that doesn't explain it right. Not with the way I've heard the word used recently. Companion of my house, maybe?"

"You mean like a squire?" An unaccountable thrill electrified him. King Arthur's squire? Even if this guy wasn't Mallory's Arthur, he was still a legend maker. His squire! John reined in his enthusiasm, fought it back. This guy was a gang warlord, not a king. Who needed, even wanted, to be his squire?

"Squire?" Bear was saying. "Don't know the word. What does it mean?"

Without thinking, John answered, "A squire is sort of a student to a knight, learning how to be a knight himself, but it's more than that. They have a sort of deal where the squire does things for the knight, going where he goes and fighting whoever he fights. The knight is supposed to teach the squire how to fight and how to behave in polite society."

Nodding, Bear ran his fingers through his beard.

"The exchange of obligations sounds familiar, but I don't understand that polite-society part. Most of the warriors I knew had their own society. It was polite in its own way, though, I guess.

"As for teaching you how to fight, you already seem to have a grasp of that, and much of what I know is very outdated. For what it's worth, I can teach you what I know.

"Behavior, now. That's different. There are still ways of thinking, ways of dealing with people, that seem to have applications today. I've had some success in those areas. I'll teach you what I know of that, if you like.

"And you talked about a squire fighting for his knight, but you didn't say anything about the other side of that coin. A lord must care for his men. That I will do for you by all means in my power. Being warlord of the Dons is a position of no small local authority. Further, I can offer you my own roof and give you of my wealth. These are all things I can do for you."

Some roof. As a member of the Dons, John was already assured of a place in MaxMix Manor. He looked around at the dingy walls and the battered furnishings. Some wealth. Bear watched him and smiled.

"Things will get better," he said.

"There are a lot of people around here who would as soon see me gone. I'm not useful to your position here among the Dons. Why are you making this offer?"

Bear was quiet for a moment. "I don't always operate simply for advantage."

"Don't you?"

"Jack, you stood by me when you didn't have to. I came into your world almost like a child. Here in the sprawl, we've sort of grown up together. Certainly we've shared trouble together. I've started to put together something here, but there's a long way to go, and I need reliable people around me, people I can count on. You've been steadfast all along. Now that I have position, I want to reward that steadfastness. Becoming a *comes* used to be considered an honor."

"Yeah? Well, I'm honored."

Patiently, Bear said, "You don't have to decide right now."

"I won't. Let me think about it."

CHAPTER
13

Trashcan Harry came sneaking back to MaxMix Manor about an hour after dark. Things had been quiet in the 'hood so there wasn't a formal guard posted, but John was watching. Taking Faye's advice, he'd selected a place to the north side of the porch where he could keep an eye on the back door as well as the front. It was a good spot for lurking; River Street's currently operating lights threw shadows that wrapped the position in darkness. From those shadows, John could watch and remain mostly hidden.

Eyeing the darkened building suspiciously, Trashcan Harry deliberately bypassed the front door and cut around toward the back.

"What's wrong with the front door, Trashcan?"

The ugly little man jumped. "Shit, Jack! Don't do that."

"You're nervous tonight." But not nervous enough to go for a weapon. Things couldn't be too bad.

"*Hell,* anybody'd be nervous with you popping out like that. Just like—well, never mind. I was wanting to talk to you, Jack."

"About where you've been?"

"Kinda." Trashcan Harry hesitated for a bit, as if he wasn't sure what he ought to say.

"Jack, are you happy here?"

That wasn't what John was expecting. Caught off guard, John answered with a question of his own. "What kind of a question is that?"

"It don't mean nothing. Just asking."

John's happiness was a strange sort of thing for Trashcan Harry to be thinking about. Wondering where it might lead, John fed him a line that was true but didn't commit John to anything. "I have to admit I never really saw myself spending my life as a lieutenant to a gang boss."

"Yeah, you were made for better." Trashcan Harry looked around, apparently to see if anyone else was in listening distance. He didn't find anyone. "I been hearing things, Jack. Not good things, either. There's trouble coming."

"The Jackals?" The east-side gang had a long-term enmity with the Dons.

"Not exactly."

"Cops cracking down again?" They'd tried a sweep to pick up indigents a month ago. It hadn't made them popular in a neighborhood where most of the people fit the cops' definition of indigent.

"It's Art—I mean Bear. He's gonna get us all in trouble."

Us? "Is he now?"

"Uh-huh. But we don't gotta let him."

We? "We don't?"

"We can get out of here before he drags us down with him."

Wasn't this down enough? "Getting out" had gotten John here. "Running is easy. Getting somewhere is hard. Where would we go?"

"There's this guy, Jack." Reacting to John's raised eyebrow, Trashcan Harry eagerly added, "He's a good guy, Jack. He can help us."

"Why would he want to?"

"I, uh, I done some work for him before. He, uh, he owes me a favor. I'd call it in for you, Jack. Don't wanna see anything bad happen to you."

Why was Trashcan so worried about John? "I don't want to see anything bad happen to me either."

"Then you'll come talk to him?"

"Who said anything about talking to anybody?"

"Didn't—oh, shit—I was supposed to. Didn't I?"

"You know, Trashcan Harry, I think you just did. But you still haven't told me who this guy is."

"He, uh, he said I shouldn't. It could get him in trouble around here. But he's a good guy. Really!"

"A mysterious benefactor, huh? Do we have to meet him in a bar? Will he be wearing a hooded cloak? Speak in an obviously disguised voice?" Harry looked increasingly confused by the questions, so John cut out the teasing. "I suppose he wants to see me tonight."

Harry nodded. "That'd be good."

"Alone?"

"I'll be there."

"How comforting."

"Then you'll come?"

The whole deal sounded suspicious, but John didn't really like life in the sprawl's underbelly. If this was a legitimate offer of a way out, he'd be a fool to ignore it. And if it was some kind of plot to get an angle on Bear or the Dons, John would have a chance to uncover it. He could be a hero. He could be a dead hero, if things went sour. But then, he already had a gravestone.

"Sure, why not?"

The Friary was up Division Street and situated in the neutral zone between Don, Jackal, and Ferals territories. It had once been a church, deconsecrated after the economic slump had pushed its parishioners into penury and out of the neighborhood. In the last throes of an attempt to revitalize the area, an entrepreneur had remodeled it into a classy restaurant. He'd lost his shirt.

The current owner still ran it as a restaurant, and though the bar far outgrossed the restaurant part, the place still had enough pretensions that it maintained a few private dining rooms. Those rooms were made up to look like monks' cells, but the people who spent time in those rooms would have been more at home in other kinds of cells; a lot of the Friary's clientele didn't do business that was sanctified, or even legal.

The flickering electric torch on the wall outside the cell didn't shed much light, but it illuminated the long coat hung on the hook by the door. There was something familiar about the cut of the coat, but John didn't get time to dredge up the memory, because Trashcan Harry opened the door and ushered him into the small room. One person was seated at the table that filled most of the space. Electric candlelight flickered off his silver hair and chased shadows across his fine-boned face.

It was Bennett.

John halted in the doorway, ignoring Trashcan Harry's urging. Smiling, Bennett indicated the empty space opposite him with a wave of his long-fingered hand.

John hesitated. Well, if Bennett wanted to do something other than talk, they'd already be into it. Leaving Trashcan standing by the door, John sat.

"So you're the mysterious benefactor."

Bennett was silent for a beat, then said, "So I could be termed."

"Why the sudden interest? Or is it only that you just found out where we were?"

"Actually, John, the interest is not sudden at all. I wanted this meeting because I thought it was high time for us to have a serious talk about your future."

"If you're going to make a pitch for a career with the feds, forget it. I already know you're a fake."

"And did you reach such a conclusion by intuition or deduction? Or did someone tell you?" Bennett smiled disarmingly. "It doesn't matter. It's true, I am not a federal officer."

"They why'd you tell me you were?"

"I didn't. I merely let you draw your own conclusions from some general statements. At the time, I thought that the situation would be best served if you thought me connected with some agency in which you had faith. I did not think that you would have faith in a mere stranger off the street. I hope you will forgive such a small deception; it was well-intentioned. Surely you have seen that the woman against whom I warned you has proven dangerous, at least insofar as your life and lifestyle."

"Things haven't been what they used to be," John admitted.

"Nor shall they ever be again." An earnest look replaced Bennett's affable smile. "You watch the news? Of course you do. So you have seen that a lot of strange things, unbelievable things, are being reported these days. Most people think these stories are just that, unbelievable strangeness. Some find a reasonable explanation in mass hysteria, some sort of anti-technological psychosis. Others suggest special effects for some unspecified media campaign, or any one of a number of apparently plausible explanations. Whatever explanation they embrace, most people don't really believe that what they are hearing about is real. But it is, John.

"I don't have to tell you that, though. You know that the magic is real, that magic is becoming more prevalent. You've had personal experience with it."

"I saw you casting spells in the museum."

Bennett shrugged. "A minor thing. The issue is vastly greater than mere sorcery. Have you realized yet that there is another whole realm intruding on this mundane dimension?"

John's wide eyes and open mouth seemed to answer Bennett's question.

"It's true, John. The otherworld, the place where magic dwells, is no longer as isolated as it has been for many centuries. It is once again connected to this world in which you have grown up."

"You're crazy. There's no such thing."

"But there is. Can you explain what you've seen without recourse to magic?"

"Of course," John said. But did he really believe it?

"Then go ahead." Bennett sat back and allowed John to sit silently for far too long. "I thought not."

"Look, I'm just a college kid. Or was, anyway. I'm no scientist, but I know that there's got to be a reasonable explanation to what's happening. There's a scientific explanation for everything."

"Such as your friend Faye?"

"How do you know about her?"

"Dr. Bloch has a scientific explanation for her, an explanation that you don't find reasonable because you know better. You know that Faye is real. And you are correct. She is real, very real. She's from the otherworld, John."

"I asked you how you know about her."

"No need to get hostile, John. I'm not your enemy. I know quite a bit about you. More than you know yourself. For example, I know that you yourself were born of the otherworld."

"No way!"

"Most definitely the way. Haven't you ever had feelings of displacement, feelings that you belong somewhere else? Of course you have, and rightly so. You were born in the otherworld, John. You are what folk of this realm call an elf."

"You're crazy. There aren't any elves outside of books."

"You're not being very accepting of your heritage, John."

"I'm a man. So are you."

Bennett smiled indulgently and shook his head. He held his hand up, palm outward and fingers spread. Passing his hand downward across his face, he rotated his wrist and raised his hand with a flourish.

And he no longer looked as he had. His hair was finer, and of a softer silver. His skull was narrower and more sharply boned. His eyes were more elongate and slightly slanted, their irises the pale unearthly blue of deep ice. His ears were more prominent and, yes, pointed. John had no doubt that this—man?—was still Bennett, but there was no way he could mistake him for *Homo sapiens*.

"This is how I really look, John. The other is just illusion, to allow me to walk more freely in this realm."

Stunned, John heard himself say, "I don't look like that."

"You are a changeling, John. An elven child left in place of a human one. You look like a human because when you were left in this realm, there were spells placed upon you. The spells slant your appearance, rather than changing it entirely. No greater effect was possible while there was so little ambient magic in this realm." Bennett snapped his fingers and his "human" appearance was restored. "You can easily see how closely we resemble each other when I appear as a human."

John remembered imagining when they first met that Bennett might be a long-lost cousin. Could it be true? "If I really am an elf under a disguise spell, show me. Take the spell off."

Bennett looked saddened. "I would love for you to see yourself as you truly are. I would love to see your true appearance myself, but for the moment we are both denied that pleasure. The spells that have let you pass here are locked until you return to the otherworld. Once in the realm of your birth, you will take up your true appearance. You can take up other things then as well, most especially the life that is your true destiny."

"True destiny?"

Bennett leaned forward slightly, his eyes pinning John with an intense stare. "You are a royal prince of Faery, John."

John felt his mouth hanging open again.

"This is too weird."

"It's true, John."

"How do you know?"

"Because I am a prince of Faery as well." Bennett paused. At first John thought it was just to let him react, but there was a difference to Bennett's hesitancy this time. When the guy—the elf—spoke again, his words came out slowly. "And because I am your true father."

John's mind reeled. Elf? Prince? Father? One part of him wanted to believe it. Who wouldn't want to be a prince of Faery? But it was too much. He'd grown up in a rational world; there just weren't fairy princes outside of books and vids. It was too incredible.

But he'd seen a man called out of the air, seen spell-tossing sorcerers, seen Bennett change before his eyes. He'd seen magic. Was an otherworld so farfetched? And what about Faye? As Bennett said, he knew that she was real. Could Bennett be telling him the truth about these other things?

If he was, nothing was as John had believed it to be. It was numbing. But beyond the whats, there were whys. Not the least of which was "why now?" Where was this father years ago? A flash of *Stellar Wars* ran through his head.

"Aren't you supposed to be telling me to trust my feelings or something and know that what you're saying is true?"

"Emotions can be powerful, John, more powerful than reason. Magic and magical thinking do not displace reason; they augment it. I expect you to use your reason and see the truth for the truth. I understand that the truth will take some getting used to, but I can help you, John. I can guide you to a true understanding of your place in life."

Guide me, huh? "If you're really my father, who was Zach Reddy? And my mom, is she really my mom?"

"Marianne Reddy has nurtured you as if you were her own, but she is not your biological mother."

"Who is?" John shouted.

"Her name would mean nothing to you," Bennett replied calmly. "In any case, she is . . . no longer among us. But I am here."

"And just where the hell were you while I was growing up?"

"Your anger is understandable. I was locked in the other-world."

"Why didn't you just magic yourself out?"

"The bridge is not always open, John. I would have been there for you had I been able. Even though I missed your childhood, I did not totally abandon you."

"What do you mean?"

"Fearing that I would be cut off from you, I arranged safeguards for you. The being you call Trashcan Harry is an agent of mine. When it began to appear that I might be unable to stay in this world, I brought him here to watch over you and to protect you. Though you have only recently had direct contact with him, he has always been nearby."

Trashcan Harry had been standing silently near the door through all of this. When John looked at him, he nodded in confirmation.

"He has kept trouble from you," Bennett said. "Eliminated problems where he could."

"Winston?" John asked, still looking at Harry.

Trashcan nodded again.

Had the old guy killed Winston just to keep John out of trouble? Or had he just taken away the body? Eliminated problems. What a cold turn of phrase.

"You cannot afford to dwell on the past," Bennett said in a commanding tone that brought John's head around. "You are an elf. You will come to understand that elves have long pasts. The years of a human's life can be but an eyeblink to one of our kind. All that has happened in your life among the humans is over and done with. You must think about the future.

"And what a future you have, John! All the strange things that this world has been experiencing are only the faintest taste of what is to come. As a royal prince of Elfland, you will come into your full heritage only after the magic is freed to blossom as it did so long ago. Then you and I can explore our relationship, get to know each other. We can banish those lost years as we live our proper lives as elven royalty."

Bennett smiled warmly at him, and John found himself smiling back.

The offer was tempting. How could it not be? To be a prince in a magic kingdom. To live like a king. Wasn't being an elven prince even better than being a knight?

Even if it meant acknowledging a father who had abandoned you? John's smile faltered.

"You abandoned me."

"I can't deny that. But it was not my choice. Sometimes a prince of Faery is not free to make the choices his heart would like. Circumstances have changed now, John. Now we can be together."

"Are you going to take me to Faery?"

"I can. But there is a problem preventing you from claiming your heritage."

"Always a catch, huh?"

"Always." Bennett gave him the sort of smile you give a friend you've just let in on a secret. "But nothing a clever elf cannot overcome."

"Like me?"

"Exactly like you."

John remembered the last time he'd seen Bennett. "This wouldn't have something to do with Artos?"

"As I said, clever."

"So tell me."

"Has Artos spoken yet of Caliburn?"

John knew the name. He'd read about it. Most of the stories used a different name, Excalibur, for King Arthur's magic sword. "The sword?"

"It has taken that shape. Has he spoken of it?"

"No, he hasn't," he answered before he realized that Bennett had said something odd. "If Caliburn's not a sword, what is it?"

"An artifact of significant power," Bennett said matter-of-factly. "It has been hidden away and the spells binding it require enormous energy, energy that is locked away as firmly and completely as the talisman itself. The magic must be freed if you are to enjoy the fruits of your heritage."

"You want me to help Artos get Caliburn."

"I want to see Caliburn freed. However, having it in Artos's possession is not a desirable end."

"Why not?"

"Artos has a history of opposition to Faery. You will find that he has little love for elves like us."

Like us. Why did that sound so right? John forced his mind back to the situation at hand, trying to guess what Bennett wanted of him. "So you want me to help him get it and then steal it from him."

"He threw it away. It's hardly stealing to take what a man throws away as trash."

John wasn't convinced. Arthur and Excalibur were inseparable in the legends. "I don't know."

"John, if you have not already, you are going to find that this Artos is not the legendary King Arthur. He's far less than the myths have made him out to be."

"You called him a murderer once."

"He is that, and more besides. Not much good about him, really. And he hates elves, you know. Ask him about our kind. You won't like what you hear."

"I'd still feel like I was betraying him."

"Betray? He'd *kill* you if he knew your heritage."

"But he—" John thought about Bear's offer to squire him. Somehow the idea of being a murderer's squire didn't seem bright. If he was a murderer. "He's not like that."

"The man is a master of blending in and making people see what they want to see in him. It is the cornerstone of his successes. Don't tell me that he has dazzled your eyes as well?"

"He's been a good friend to me."

"Speak to your good friend Artos about elves. Then you will see where your path lies."

"I don't know."

"Think about it, John. Test him. If he's the man you think he is, you've nothing to fear. But if he is as I have told you, you have everything to fear."

CHAPTER
14

Things in the 'hood were busy after John's meeting with
Bennett, what with the latest phase of Bear's peace negotia-
tions going on. It was almost a week before John found a
chance to get a private talk with Bear. John sat impatiently
through Thursday night's council meeting, but fortunately,
nothing needed immediate attention and the meeting broke
up sooner than usual. Usually a lot of folks hung around
MaxMix Manor after the meeting, but John had put the word
in a few choice ears. Lots of gangers, even some John hadn't
talked to, seemed to have other places to be. That was fine
with John; it meant fewer people to get rid of. Soon he,
Trashcan Harry, and Artos were the only ones left in the big
common room of MaxMix Manor. He could hear the last
bunch making their good-byes in the front room. A nod to
Trashcan set him to fumbling his way through an excuse for
his own departure. Absorbed in listening to the mid-evening
news vid, Artos barely noticed. John pulled a chair over and
sat beside Bear.

"How come you never talk much about the past or the
people you knew back in the old days?"

"They're gone." Pointing a finger at the vid, he said, "The world's changed. Doesn't seem much point in talking about them."

"There was magic back then, wasn't there?"

Bear looked at him, eyes full of a guarded *something*. "Too much."

"And all kinds of weird beings from the otherworld."

"Too many kinds. Where are you heading with this, Jack?"

Bear hadn't blinked at his mention of the otherworld. He knew about it. What else did he know about? "Did you ever meet any elves?"

"Don't get me going."

"No, really, I'm curious. You know, everybody these days has got a picture of elves as keeblers or some kind of half-naked cosmic tree worshipers. What were they really like? Were they really different from people?"

"They're different, all right. Elves are lazy, lying good-for-nothings that would sooner stab you in the back than say hello."

"Don't pull your punches!"

"If you think I was, then you don't want to hear what I really think. Most of the best words aren't in the language anymore."

"So you're saying you have met some?"

"To my sorrow. But let me tell you, boy. If you should meet one, kill it before it starts talking. You'll be better off."

"Kill him in cold blood?"

"They don't have any other kind."

"I don't think I could kill anybody in cold blood." Hot blood, maybe. Winston's face, beaten and bruised, swam before his eyes. According to Bear, elves were cold-blooded, not hot.

"Killing's something you can learn. It's something you *ought* to learn, with regard to those pointy-eared snake-lovers."

"Something *you've* learned?"

Bear—no, that name didn't fit him now. This was Artos, the man John had seen attack Trashcan Harry with a sword. Artos stared at him.

John had to ask. "Do you kill elves on sight?"

"Why? Have you seen one?"

"I—" He was afraid that if he told Artos about Bennett, he'd have to tell him that Bennett had said he was John's father. Was Artos's attitude toward changelings any different than toward ordinary elves? If Artos knew John was an elf, would he hate John? Hell, would he kill John? John didn't want to find out. For the moment, Artos was accepting John as human; and that was something John wasn't ready to chance giving up. "How would I know?"

"How's a good question." Bear seemed to relax a little. "They're masters of deception. They can make themselves look like someone else, blind all your senses so you act like a fool and never know it until they have you in their snare."

It sounded personal. "Did they do that to you?"

"I don't want to talk about it," Bear said firmly.

So they didn't talk. Bear watched the news, and John sat there watching him watch the news. Bennett was right that Bear didn't care for elves. Referring to them as "its"—how cold could you get? Bear didn't treat John as an "it." Would that change if John revealed his elven heritage? He didn't want to think so, but how could he be sure?

There was a clatter from outside, followed by a muffled cry.

"What's that?" Bear asked, tense. He seemed poised to explode from the chair.

"I don't know," John replied. It didn't sound normal, though.

In eerie silence, Bear got up and went to the weapons cabinet. Unlocking it, he took out something long that glinted of metal. Not a sword, a rifle. He tossed it to John. It was a shotgun. Bear took one for himself, pumping it once to chamber a shell.

The front door crashed open. Bear shifted to clear John out of his line of fire into the front room and brought his weapon to bear on the doorway, but it was just Trashcan Harry, breathless, sweating, and bleeding from a cut on his cheek. He shoved the door closed behind him and slammed down the locking bar. Stumbling into the common room, Harry stared at the shotguns with wide eyes.

"John, we gotta get outta here!"

Footsteps pounded on the porch. Out in the back, someone coughed heavily.

"There's half a dozen at least," Trashcan Harry said. "Serious guns."

Bear kicked shut the door to the kitchen and upended the weapons cabinet across it. Metal crashed as the contents jammed together and tumbled free, to spill in a jumble of guns. The ammunition drawer canted out and dumped a pile of boxes and loose shells. As Bear bent to grab a box from the heap, something crashed against the door he had barricaded. The barrier held. Something else hit the door in the front room. The wood groaned, but the bar held. Bear ordered, "Upstairs."

They crossed the front room and started up the stairs, Bear trying to watch both doors at once. Scraping sounds came from the room they had just vacated. Worried and fearful of what he might see, John looked back. Bear's attention must have been on the front door, because he didn't immediately react to the figure in black John glimpsed moving through the common room.

"Behind you!" John shouted.

Bear whirled, shotgun held low. Without hesitation, he fired. The flash was bright and the sound deafening. The black-clothed figure spun and fell back.

Someone on the front porch pounded uselessly on the scarred and pockmarked Perspex™ panels. The panels held. With surprisingly little noise, the lock blew off the door in a cloud of smoke and splinters. The bar kept the door closed. The pounding started on the door again.

Carla was waiting for them at the top of the stairs, wide-eyed.

"What's happening? Where's Hector?"

"Shut up and get out of the way," Trashcan Harry ordered.

She kept repeating her screamed questions until Bear seconded Harry's order. John was afraid the wild-eyed Bear was going to shoot her, but he just used his gun crossways to herd her away from the landing.

"Who else is still in the house?" Bear asked from where he watched the stairs, but he was only half listening for the answer to his question. His attention was focused on the lower level.

"Most everybody's out tonight," John said, thinking about how he had contributed to that.

"Shanta was in the kitchen," Carla said. "Hector was out in the backyard. Where is he? Is he all right?"

"Gillie was on the porch," Trashcan said. "They already got him."

"You said six," Bear said.

"Yeah." Trashcan Harry was breathing heavily. "Two teams of three. Might be more."

"Damn! Back to Gillie's room," Bear said urgently. "Go!"

There was a second stairway there. Someone might be coming up behind them. They ran. John could hear footbeats on the stairs. Bear's shotgun roared again, and somebody screamed. Then the only footfalls John heard behind him were from Bear's heavy feet.

Carla was the first to reach Gillie's room. She opened the door, then jerked back to the sound of the same rapid coughing John had heard from the back of the house. She kept jerking as slugs tore into her. John crashed into Trashcan, who had stopped abruptly. Carla's blood splattered them.

Bear shouldered John aside roughly and dove across the opening, firing as he went past the doorway. There was a thud inside the room. Rolling back to the frame, Bear fired again.

There was no more firing from the room.

"Separate. Hide. Try and get outside. I'll keep them busy in here."

He disappeared into Gillie's room.

With uncharacteristic alacrity, Trashcan Harry ran to the window at the end of the hall. Unlike most of the downstairs windows, those on the upper stories weren't sealed. A creak from down the hall warned of someone climbing the stairs. There wasn't time to join Harry at the window.

In here.

A door opened beside him and, without thinking, John followed Faye's advice.

It was Carla's and Hector's room. Absurdly, he thought that Hector would have a fit seeing him there. But Hector wouldn't have any more cause for jealousy.

John found himself in a corner of the room, panting. It was quiet now, and he was scared. Feeling the cracked, brittle wallpaper under his palms made him realize that he no longer had the shotgun Bear had thrown him. He couldn't remember dropping it. He was unarmed while armed men crept stealthily toward him.

The unlatched door shivered slightly; there was someone outside in the hall.

John felt exposed. His eyes flicked to the closet, the only place large enough to hide.

Don't move, John. Pretend you're not here.

But, Faye . . .

Quiet.

The first thing John saw was the muzzle of a weapon, made fat by a sound suppressor. The weapon was held in black-gloved hands, and those hands belonged to a man clad completely in black.

He looked like something out of a thriller vid as he moved cautiously into the room. His torso was clothed in something bulky like a fencing jacket. Odd-shaped packages hung festooned in various places. His head was sheathed in a black hood that even covered his face below the bulbous goggles he wore. Everything about him was the matte black of night. Not an inch of flesh showed to indicate his humanity.

John could see Carla's contorted right hand on the floor outside the doorway. They had shown no human virtues; maybe there was no humanity to see.

A second figure appeared in the doorway, covering the advance of his fellow. This one was much shorter, though just as broad in the shoulders; he didn't look the part of a classic hunter-killer like his companion, though he was clad the same. And he had just as evil-looking a weapon.

The first moved to the closet, easing the door open. Poking among the clothes, he satisfied himself that no one hid there. He passed John, and though his head swept across the corner, he gave no sign that he saw him. The man crossed the room, suddenly stopping as his head snapped toward the window.

"It's Black," the prowler said softly, pointing out the window with the muzzle of his weapon. John could see Trashcan Harry running away from the house. The gunman raised his weapon and took aim.

"Nix," said the figure by the door.

The gun came down.

"First we find the sleeper," the shorter one said. "Then we sweep up the mess."

The gunman nodded.

Tilting his head down, the short one whispered, "Who's got the sleeper?"

He received no audible reply, but he stepped back into the hallway, motioning the taller one to follow.

Bear's shotgun fired again, and John heard the two men rush into Gillie's room. The house was quiet for a long time after that. John remained where he was, too frightened to move. His mind raced.

The "sleeper" would be Artos, but who the hell were these people? John remembered the men with guns who had broken into the museum during Bennett's magical duel with Nym. Were these the same guys? If so, presumably they had intended to kill Artos then. Hadn't Nym told John and Artos to run away? She must have known about these guys.

Could these be the same guys? One of the men he'd seen at the museum had earlier represented himself as a federal agent, and while breaking into the museum didn't seem like a typical FBI kind of thing, those guys hadn't masked their faces. These men in black were pure terrorist stuff. Or maybe secret agents. They might as well be alien invaders for all the sense their presence made.

Why had they come here with death on their minds? Why did they want to kill Artos?

John caught the scrape of a stealthy footfall in the hall. Had they taken care of their sleeper and come back to "sweep up the mess"?

The new hunter moved into the room in as cautious and predatory a manner as the black-clad gunman, but he was dressed differently. He wore a long coat like some outlaw of the Old West. He carried a pistol like one, too, but not some massive hogleg, a smooth, efficient-looking automatic. He wore a hood like the others but his goggles were different, barely more than wraparound sunglasses. All in all he looked less like a soldier than the others, but no less dangerous.

Their leader? Come to view the dirty handiwork of his henchmen?

The man in the coat scanned the room once before his gaze settled in John's direction.

"Reddy?" His voice was a whisper.

I'm sorry, John. He's not like the others.

Yeah. Unlike the others, this guy could see him.

"Easy, Reddy. I'm here to help."

There didn't seem to be any more point in pretending he was invisible. "Who are you?"

Bear's shotgun sounded again.

"Stay here," the stranger ordered. And he was gone.

John roused himself, reluctantly abandoning the corner. If he could find the shotgun he'd lost, he could help Bear.

He found it, all right. It was lying in the hall, in a pool of Carla's blood. He couldn't bring himself to touch it.

Downstairs he could hear more gunfire: Bear's shotgun, the black-clad men's coughing weapons, and a sharper crack that had to be the stranger's small pistol. He heard the stranger shout orders to something called "Bravo Team." More firing. A flash of light lit up the walls of the landing and acrid smoke was soon drifting up the stairs. There was one last blast from Bear's shotgun, and everything was quiet.

John crept to the top of the stairs. Still quiet. The front door was open to the street, half off its hinges, its restraining bar lying shattered on the floor. There were no sirens, no shouts of alarm. This was the sprawl; there wouldn't be any police to investigate until well after everything was resolved, if even then. The neighbors knew enough to keep their heads down and stay out of trouble.

Two men entered the front room from the common room. Bear had his shotgun sloped over his shoulder. The other man wore a long coat, but he now had his shades off and his hood pulled back. He was a sandy-haired guy who would have looked more at home behind a desk than helping Bear check on the body lying sprawled at the base of the stairs.

"Who are you, friend?" Bear was saying.

"Name's Holger Kun. I'm pleased to meet you, sir."

"I'm pleased to be around to be met. Lot of people seem to want to make my acquaintance today, but not all of them are as polite as you, Mr. Kun." Bear kicked the body. "These folks, for example. You wouldn't happen to know who they are, would you?"

"I've got an idea."

"Then you're ahead of me. Maybe you're far enough ahead to know if there might be more of them around? Or can we leave them for your Bravo Team to take care of?"

"Bravo Team's a fiction, sir. Did its job, though. Made them think there were more of us and bought us some breathing room."

"You think they'll be back?"

"They didn't get what they wanted," John said, coming down the stairs. "They said they wanted the sleeper."

Bear looked up at him and gave him a nod. "Jack, glad to see you're all right. Where's Trashcan Harry?"

"Here," came a voice from the kitchen. He came through the doorway, half carrying a semiconscious Hector. "They're gone."

"But Reddy's right," Kun said. "You're still here, sir. They'll be back."

"You think they wanted to capture me?" Bear snorted. "Weren't enough of them for that."

"Capture you. Or kill you," Kun said. "They might have been satisfied with either."

"What did I do to them? I don't even know who they are." Bear tugged the hood off the corpse. "I've never seen any of them before."

"I have," John said, staring at the face so revealed. It was Surimato, the supposed federal agent. Everyone turned to look at him, but John faced Bear. "I met him before . . . before the night in the museum. He said he was FBI. Showed me a picture of the sorceress who woke you."

"He's not FBI," Kun said. If the mention of a sorceress was odd to him, he gave no sign. "This man's name is Vadama. He was a special agent for Mitsutomo Keiretsu."

John wasn't sure that he had heard correctly. "Mitsutomo?"

Kun nodded. "Not a public branch, mind you."

"Still want to go home, Jack?" Bear asked.

"It must be a mistake," John protested.

"No mistake," Trashcan said.

"How would you know?" John snapped. "This must be some kind of fraud. Somebody is trying to make Mitsutomo look like the villains."

"It wouldn't be hard," Trashcan said. "Don't matter if you don't believe, Jack. We got to get out of here."

"Jack?"

John looked up into Bear's questioning face. Some squire. He hadn't done anything but cower during the fight. Did Bear think he was a coward? "I won't run out on you."

"Good lad."

"This is crazy, Jack," Trashcan Harry said.

Bear looked at Trashcan disdainfully. "Where do you think you're going to go?"

"Anywhere, long as it ain't here. They know we're here."

"Running blind won't help," Kun said.

"I don't like the idea of running away," Bear said.

"You don't have to," Trashcan Harry told him. "It's Jack they want."

"Reddy said they wanted the sleeper," Kun said.

"They shot at all of us. They'll kill us all if we stay here," Trashcan said.

"They didn't do so well this time," Bear said.

"They killed Carla." John was surprised that his voice was so calm.

"And Gillie," Trashcan added. "And Shanta. And Tara, she was with Gillie. They nearly killed Hector."

Tara wasn't even a member of the Dons.

"We know about them now." Bear sounded determined. His face took on the expression John was used to seeing when he was putting together a plan. "We'll just have to be ready for them next time."

"You can't fight a corporation like Mitsutomo without help," Kun said.

"I know." Bear nodded heavily, as though he'd reached an unpalatable conclusion. His expression soured. "I had hoped that the world had changed enough to do without it."

John thought he knew what Bear was talking about, but he had to ask. "Without what?"

"Caliburn. I could use it, if I could get my hands on it."

Kun looked surprised and puzzled, but Trashcan Harry just looked nervous. John felt a little sick to his stomach; Bennett had said Bear would go after the sword. What if Bennett was right about other things as well?

"What's a caliburn?" Kun asked.

"Something that used to belong to me," Bear said. "Something powerful."

"It'll have to be *very* powerful to help you stand up to Mitsutomo," Kun said.

"It's powerful, all right. And if it's not strong enough, I'll go down fighting." Bear shrugged. "It won't be the first time."

"I'll bet you don't even know where it is," Trashcan Harry said.

The sort of probe Bennett would want.

Bear nodded. "Of course I do. It lay by my side for a thousand years."

"Was it one of the swords at the museum?" John asked. If it was, Mitsutomo already controlled it. Did they know they had it?

"No."

"Then it's still in England." Going to England would get them away from here, and Mitsutomo didn't have as much influence there as they did here in the States. They might be safe there. Maybe having Bear go after the sword wouldn't be so bad after all.

"No."

"Then where?"

Bear gave each of them an evaluating look, as if he wasn't sure he could trust them. John felt hurt, then a little guilty. Hadn't he been keeping things from Bear? Didn't Bear have a right to his own secrets?

"It's hard to explain," Bear said. "I may not be able to get to it, but I think I've got to try."

May not? Try? Very tentative words, despite Bear's confident tone. John was confused. So what else was new?

"I'd like to offer my help," Kun said.

"Why?" Bear asked.

John wondered the same thing himself. Was this Kun another of Bennett's agents? If he wasn't, who was he? Should John tell Bennett about this guy, or could he rely on Trashcan Harry to take care of that?

"We're on the same side, sir." Kun sounded sincere. "I work with other people who have backgrounds similar to yours, people who would be very pleased to have you by their sides. We understand your special circumstances."

"You seem to know a lot more about me than I do about you."

"If you will come with me and talk to my associates, that will change. You can do much better than this for yourself."

"I like it here," Bear said. That seemed to surprise Kun. "Besides, I've got people here to take care of."

Kun recovered quickly. "Considering what happened tonight, I think you might want to consider what will happen to the people around here if you remain visible, a magnet for further violence."

"Maybe we should listen to him, Bear," John said.

"I can offer you a place to lie low for a while," Kun said.

Bear looked unhappy. "Sounds like running away."

Which, John thought, was a good idea. He tried to put it in a way Bear would accept. "Consider it a strategic withdrawal, a chance to rally for another battle." At the very least it would buy them some time. John had a lot to sort out.

Bear nodded slowly. "I do need some time to think."

Turning to Kun, he asked, "Where did you say your associates were?"

CHAPTER
15

The place Holger took them to looked like an ordinary townhouse in an ordinary development, but that was the way it was supposed to be. Safe houses were not supposed to look out of the ordinary.

The neighborhood was one of those oases of suburbia contained within the desert of the Northeast sprawl, an island of fin-de-siècle living sitting in the waters of concrete blight. Here rising stars of the corporate world lived side by side with solid middle managers and long-term government employees. Children played in streets made safe by regular patrols of community-approved rent-a-cops. Homeowners tended lawns and gardens. Pet owners exercised their animals. Joggers jogged, runners ran, and walkers walked. A pleasant neighborhood, safe and quiet, a perfect place to hide the unusual.

Headquarters had chosen well.

The safe house was better protected than most of the neighboring townhouses, with security and alarm systems an order of magnitude more effective, but true safety relied on anonymity. So he decided to unload his vehicle within the walls of the garage, unlocking the passenger doors only after the door had rolled down to shield them from the outside world.

Holger watched them as they stretched muscles cramped after the confinement of the GM Runner™. Just looking at them made him wonder if headquarters wasn't right to treat this whole operation like a bastard stepchild.

What a crew.

Harry Black, the man whose trail had enabled Holger to find the sleeper, was a smelly old guy who looked as if he'd lost a few too many bar fights. Reddy called him Trashcan Harry, a good name since the old guy smelled like one and had manners to match. Holger doubted the cleaning crew would ever get the smell out of the upholstery. Holger would have rather left him behind, but the kid seemed to assume that Black was part of the deal. There hadn't been a lot of time to argue, so Holger hadn't argued, planning on cutting Black out here; the prole had too many unanswered questions hanging around him to be trusted.

The guy who was supposed to be the sleeper was a hulking brute of a fellow who fit the name Bear. The man's eyes were always moving, watching Holger suspiciously while simultaneously scoping out his surroundings. He had wary eyes, a warrior's eyes. It was the only thing about him that made him credible. Still, Holger found it hard to believe that this leather-wearing gang boss could be King Arthur.

Then there was Reddy, a gangly college kid who looked out of place in his gang colors the way an English tea lady would at a gathering of an Angolan insurgent cell. But Holger knew there was more to him than that; he had read the psychological reports, including the ones someone at Mitsutomo who didn't know enough about computer files had wanted to suppress. Still, Reddy didn't look to be the sort prone to violent outbursts, and in that he was a lot like Holger. The kid might have potential, but just now he was playing out of his depth.

Holger led them inside, taking them upstairs to the kitchen and offering them refreshment. He'd noticed Spae wasn't in the living room; she'd be upstairs, either busy with her researches or on the line berating headquarters again. He surreptitiously tapped her intercom call button while he was pouring Bear a beer.

"Nice place," Black said, slurping his own beer. "Who pays the rent?"

"Would you believe me if I said the UN?"

Bear turned to Reddy, who whispered "United Nations" to him while Black said, "I don't believe it."

"How about the European Community?" Holger asked, skipping his usual abbreviation for Bear's benefit. "The Secret Service, to be exact."

"I knew you was a spook," Black said.

"European Secret Service?" Reddy said in a puzzled tone. "What are you doing in the States?"

"And what do we want with you? That was your next question, wasn't it? You can relax, Reddy. As far as I know, you and Black are only coincidentally involved in this. We're really interested in Bear here, because he's what you heard the Mitsutomo people call a sleeper." Bear glared suspiciously at Holger, a look Holger found politic to ignore. Procedure required that an alleged sleeper be treated deferentially at all times. "Bear appears to have something to do with a rather famous sleeper. He may even be the man himself. Either way, we're very interested in him."

"What sort of interest, Mr. Kun?" Bear's growling voice made it clear that he didn't like unspecified *interest* in himself.

Holger put on his best "we're-all-in-this-together" face. Spae was the one who should be handling this part; she was the one who liked talking about it. But an agent had to do what he had to do. If Bear was Arthur, he had to be kept friendly.

"You've all had firsthand experience with the way the world's been changing of late. You know these aren't ordinary changes. Phenomena that have no rational explanation are occurring, and things which appear supernatural are being encountered. It is most distressing. We believe that, somehow, the awakening of sleepers is connected to these . . . anomalies."

"It is not my doing," said Bear.

"No, sir, not directly." At least, not intentionally. If it were . . . "Have you heard the phrase 'once and future king'?"

"White's nonsense?"

"Then you've read some of the legends?"

"I think the phrase is 'don't believe everything you read.' "

A cautious and inconclusive answer. Best to continue friendly. "And yet it seems that there is a kernel of truth at the heart of the legends. Many of the myths about King Arthur say that he isn't dead, but only sleeping; lying adream until such time as his people need him again. There are many other legends about other men, other heroes, which say that they, too, lie sleeping until there is dire need for them. Such legends may be found all over the world. Like you, some of those other heroes are awake now, displaced like you from their own times."

Bear looked thoughtful, Reddy stunned; but Black, curiously enough, didn't look as though Holger's words were news. That would bear investigating.

"Who are these others?" Bear asked.

"In time, you'll meet them." One way or another. "But for the moment there are some important questions to which we need answers. Can you tell me who called you forth and, more important, why?"

"She called herself Nym," Reddy volunteered.

"She was the woman the Mitsutomo people showed you the picture of?" Reddy nodded. Holger didn't like the implications of that. If the corporates knew more about this woman than the Department did . . . "Bear, what did she tell you?"

"I didn't get a chance to speak to her."

"So you don't know anything about her, or her reasons for waking you?"

Bear hesitated for a moment, then said firmly, "No."

The hesitation made Bear's assertion play like honest truth; a plant trying to mislead them wouldn't have wanted them to suspect that he was concealing knowledge. Perhaps Bear was a real sleeper; ignorance of the reason for their awakening was characteristic among the sleepers. Some thought they knew, but their reasoning rarely held water in the here and now; old enemies and older ways of thinking had no relevance in the modern world. Bear might be one of those deluded ones or he might be one who knew more than he thought he knew; that kind took a lot of careful questioning before anything useful came out.

"What do *you* know about her?" Bear asked.

"Not knowing her identity for sure, I can't say. If you'd be willing to try to identify her from some pictures, I might be able to tell you something." Both Bear and Reddy nodded in agreement. Cooperative. Good. Best not to lead them to expect too much; bait-and-switch might satisfy the kid, but it would lose the warrior. Policy said tell sleepers nothing till the experts were there, but Holger knew he needed to win this one's confidence. "But even then, I probably won't be able to tell you much. We are still in the dark as to how sleepers are woken, but we know it's happening. Most of the legends connected with these sleepers say that they will wake to face some great danger. Although my superiors do not agree on the nature of the danger, it is clear from the facts of the awakenings we know about that there is a widespread danger. If the legends are true."

Bear stared at him. "Do you have any idea what this danger is?"

"Yes, I do," was all Holger was willing to say, especially since he could hear Spae coming down the stairs. She might not be a policy slave, but she was the local "expert" and she didn't like people stepping on her prerogatives. As she came into the kitchen, he said, "Gentlemen, this is Dr. Spae, my associate. Dr. Spae is a specialist, which is a euphemism in my department for someone who deals in anomalies."

Spae ran her gaze over Holger's acquisitions. Her expression made it clear that she didn't like what she saw.

"So where's Arthur?"

Bear snorted. "I don't think this is going to work out, Kun."

"Give her a chance. You don't exactly match your PR." To Spae, he said, "Be nice, Doctor. I've told this gentleman that you can help him get to something he has mislaid."

"What's pea are?" Bear asked.

It was Spae's turn to snort. Bear didn't take it kindly. "I did not come here to be the object of your derision, woman."

To Holger's surprise, Spae didn't bristle. Instead she dropped into scientist mode. "By which reaction I assume you are supposed to be the sleeper."

"That's what they tell me," Bear said in a surprisingly tolerant tone.

"You don't remember much about it?"

"I have a very good memory."

"Good. Can you tell me about the transition?"

"Yes. But why should I?"

"Hostility is understandable. Culture shock. But we're all your friends here, and we want to help you." Spae's reassurances sounded automatic to Holger, and from Bear's expression he wasn't impressed either. "But in order to help you, I need to know some things. For example, have you been vaccinated for anthrax?"

"Explain what you're talking about, and maybe I can answer your question; though why I should be bothered escapes me."

"Where did you go to school?"

"To what?"

"Who trained you?"

With a slight smile, he said, "The books say Merlin the Magician."

"You can read?"

"These days."

"Good," Spae murmured to herself. "Very good. Given the time since transition, the mix of language acclimatization and ignorance is credible. But the Mitsutomo people could know enough to fake that. A few tests should clear it up."

"I did not come here to take tests," Bear said, obviously having heard Spae as clearly as Holger had.

"Yes, yes. We've established the attitude." She dismissed the concept with a wave of her hand. "Anybody could guess that as a likely attribute. What's your name?"

"They call me Bear."

"No, not your street name. What did they call you when you last walked the earth?"

"Same thing, different language." Annoyance had crept back into Bear's voice.

"What language?"

"I don't know what you call it."

"What name, then?"

"Artos."

"Artos."

Spae was quiet for a moment.

"It correlates with the time frame of the artifacts. A good detail." Something uncertain crept into her manner. "Could you actually be him?"

Bear said nothing.

Faced with his silence, Spae seemed taken aback, even a little awed. Quietly she asked, "Did you know Meliadus? Who were your *comites*?"

"What does it matter?" Bear frowned. "I'm me, not the man you think you know about. This King Arthur legend you all are so wild about is nonsense."

"Not completely, or you wouldn't be here," Holger pointed out.

"I'm not involved in whatever this is," Bear said.

"The choice has been made for you," Holger told him.

Bear gave him a long look. "You remind me of someone I used to know." His tone didn't suggest a flattering memory.

Holger smiled at him.

Spae said, "I still need to do some tests."

"Tests can wait, Doctor," Holger told her.

"A very long time, Doctor," Bear said. "Mr. Kun promised me help. I don't consider making me submit to your tests to be help."

Eyeing Holger distrustfully, Spae asked, "What sort of help?"

"A matter of finding something called Caliburn," Holger said.

"Oh, my G—" She blinked rapidly several times. "Caliburn is real?"

"As real as I am, Doctor." Bear seemed to be enjoying Spae's shocked reaction. "Mr. Kun told me that you'd be able to help me recover it."

"I— Why—I—"

"Articulate, ain't she?" Black said.

"Shall I inform headquarters that we will be—"

She cut Holger off by grabbing his arm.

"You do and I'll shrivel your balls." To herself she said, "Cut me off, will they? Backwater, eh?" She smiled broadly at Bear. "There are some things I'll need to know in order to help you."

"I'll just bet," he said.

But they talked long into the night.

CHAPTER 16

With Kun and Spae paying almost all their attention to Bear, there wasn't a lot for John and Trashcan Harry to do. The townhouse was well supplied with a library of vidbooks and games, but Trashcan wasn't very interested in games and when John finally convinced him to play, he was a poor opponent. After the second match John gave up, and Harry occupied the television with some of the more violent selections among the movies, leaving John to himself. John tried reading, but nothing seemed to hold his interest. Maybe it was the company, maybe it was just being inside the townhouse for two solid days and Holger's regular pronouncement that it was best if they not go outside.

John got very bored.

But fugitives hiding out at safe houses need food, and the place apparently hadn't been stocked with people of Bear and Harry's appetites in mind. The stocks of fresh stuff started to run low. John suggested that he make a food run. To his surprise, Kun consented. The EC agent even suggested that Trashcan Harry go along. John was in such a rush to get outside that he almost left without the debit card that Kun offered him to pay for the groceries.

Within ten minutes of the asking, they were out and headed for the store that Kun's directions said was about half a mile away. The spring sun was warm, taking the chill out of the breeze. John was happy to be out in it, even though the coat Kun had given him to replace his leather jacket was a little heavy for the afternoon's temperature.

Before they'd gone a block, Faye reported that Kun was following. John didn't care; he was just happy to be out of the house. He was even happier to be in a neighborhood where he didn't always have to look over his shoulder to make sure no one was sneaking up on him to mug him. Let Kun follow them. If there were any muggers, he could deal with them.

Shopping the supermarket reminded him of hitting the grocer in the old rezcom.

Which reminded him of his mom.

The charm of the expedition evaporated and John's mood went dark. Trashcan Harry looked hurt when John snapped at him, but John wasn't about to explain or apologize. By the time they finished shopping, John had forced his mind back to the present and had begun to enjoy being outside again.

He felt the sting on his neck about the same time he heard Faye's warning, but by then it was too late. He turned and saw Trashcan Harry slap at his neck. The bag Harry was carrying crashed to the ground.

Run, John!

John didn't feel like running. He felt like sleeping. Odd thing to do in the middle of the street. Still, he really felt like sleeping.

No, John. You've got to run!

"Go away, Faye."

He was amused by the rhyme. Sleepily amused. He was too detached to do more than smile. He was drifting off, oddly comfortable on the concrete. Too tired to even wonder why Trashcan Harry was standing over him and growling at somebody.

* * *

As soon as the policeman left, Holger saw that the tracers were dead. He crumpled the citation for an allegedly inoperable turn signal and ran back the monitor record. The blips last showed at a location a couple of blocks away, so he checked it out on foot. The location was at the intersection of a street running behind the market and a service road that ran into an industrial park, a low-traffic area with few people about.

There was nothing unusual to be seen.

The wind was picking up, plucking at his jacket. Holger stepped into the lee of the industrial park's sign. No, nothing. They might have just disappeared into thin air. He shuddered.

The wind was still tugging at him, which annoyed him; the sign should be protecting him. He put annoyance aside and scanned the area. His eyes fell on a scrap of grocery bag. While he watched, the flimsy plastic fluttered up and away, heading toward a line of trees with uncanny directness. The scrap hit one of the trees and hung there.

Holger looked around. He was still the only one around. Nervously, he walked to the tree. The bag scrap was hanging from something that protruded from the tree. Lifting the plastic, he saw that a crystalline dart had embedded itself in the trunk. Gripping it in the scrap of plastic, he pulled it free, only to see it dissolve from the heat of his hand.

This was a technology he knew, and it meant that Reddy and Black's disappearance was not magical. He felt better, despite the way in which his attention had been drawn to the dart. Careful to retain the tiny drop of liquid that was all that remained of the crystalline sliver, he folded the plastic up. With luck, he'd have a lead after it was analyzed.

John heard voices talking softly as he came again to awareness.

Faye?

. . .

No, not Faye.

He couldn't catch most of what was said, but one thing that came through was a male voice warning sternly about abreaction. He heard the name Pentatell™ and recalled that Pentatell was some kind of truth serum. There was a soft, distant argument and John heard a female voice. That was what had made him think of Faye.

He opened his eyes. Like a slow-warming video tube, images brightened to something approaching clarity. His stomach didn't like the shift, and rebelled. Heaves racked his body and he felt strong hands on him, steadying him, while a voice spoke nonsense words in reassuring tones. The hands eased him back into the bed once he'd stopped retching. Exhausted, he shut his eyes and let the hands prod and scour him clean.

"Feeling better?" a deep male voice asked.

Than what? A dead rat? He opened his eyes and looked at his questioner. The voice belonged to a husky man in a white uniform. He smelled of antiseptic and spice.

"The doctor says you should be up to talking, but that you shouldn't overdo it."

The man retreated and a woman stepped into John's line of sight. She might have been a vid actress playing the role of a corporate bigwig, except she wasn't quite beautiful enough. Which was not to say she wasn't pretty, if you liked well-preserved, middle-aged Latin types. An affiliation button gleamed in the lapel of her impeccable business suit, but John's eyes wouldn't focus on it.

She was accompanied by a bearded guy in a similar suit who was practically a dwarf; he barely topped the woman's shoulder. The man's sour expression contrasted sharply with the friendly smile the woman was offering.

"John, do you know who I am?" she asked.

"No," he croaked. "Should I?"

"My name is Pamela Martinez. I am an executive in the Mitsutomo Keiretsu. This is Mr. Sörli. We've been worried about you, John."

"Mitsutomo?" Hadn't they tried to kill him? He wished his brain hadn't been exchanged for oatmeal.

"You've been keeping bad company, John." There was a tinge of admonition in her voice. "But we've brought you home now."

"Home?" This antiseptic-smelling white room with its chrome and enamel trim didn't look like anybody's home. "Where am I?"

"At one of our Boston facilities."

"Boston? But I was in Rhode Island. I don't remember. How did I get here?"

Sörli started to answer him. "We tracked you down—"

"Unfortunately, you were in the company of Harold Black. In an attempt to separate you from him, you were inadvertently hit with a drugged dart that was intended to immobilize him. I'm afraid you had a bad reaction to the drug."

"Black? Trashcan Harry? What happened to him?"

"Don't worry about him, kid," Sörli said. "We took care of him."

"You killed him?"

"No, he's not dead, John. But Mr. Sörli's right, you shouldn't be worried about him. He's not your friend. He is a subversive and a killer, who has been deliberately misleading you as to his intentions. You are lucky we were able to rescue you from him and his associates."

"I didn't need rescuing."

"I told you he was contaminated," Sörli said to Martinez.

"He is confused, that's all," she replied. To John she said, "We know you've been misled. We are going to help you understand what is really happening, because we need the help of strong, honest men like you."

John didn't feel very strong. In fact, with his limbs all doing an imitation of wet rags, he felt like shit. But he knew flattery when he heard it, even if he didn't know why they thought him worth the effort.

"What do you want with me?"

"We are fighting against the chaos that is trying to destroy our world. It is a threat that no rational person can ignore. We want you to help us."

"I don't understand. I don't know anything about any chaos."

"You understand better than you think you do. We know that you were at the Woodman Museum on the night when agents of chaos achieved one of their breakthroughs. You have seen what they can do. You must know that they have to be stopped, before they rip society apart."

Martinez sounded sincere. Almost too sincere. She might have been a preacher looking for converts. John had never liked pushy preachers much.

"Mitsutomo protected you while you grew up, John. Is it too much to ask that you help protect Mitsutomo now?"

It sounded so reasonable.

"Your mother depends on us. You've spent some time on the streets. You've seen how people who don't have the benefit of corporate affiliation live. Can you see your mother living like that? She will have to, if the agents of chaos have their way. You can do something to prevent such a catastrophe, John. Your mother would never survive on the street. She's depending on you, John."

"She thinks I'm dead."

"That can change. You can go back home to her. It will be difficult at first; she didn't take your 'death' well at all, but our psychologists helped her adjust. We'll be there to help again."

"I want to see her."

"You can't just now, John. It wouldn't be wise."

"Why not?"

"There are things that have to be done. The agents of chaos are unscrupulous; should they learn that you are helping us, they could threaten her. I believe that it is safer for her if you remain 'dead' for a while longer. Once you think about it, you'll agree. When things are settled, we will do everything in our power to see that you and your mother have a happy reunion."

"What do you want from me?"

"Artos," Sörli said.

Martinez gave the man a stern glance. "We need your co-operation in our fight against the chaos. This Artos is one of the enemy's agents. He and those who help him are destabilizing our world. Like Black, he is not your friend, John. What has he done for you, after all?"

What indeed?

"He's taken your life away," she continued. "You don't owe him anything."

Visions of thirty silver pieces swam before John's eyes. "You want me to betray him."

"You can't betray someone to whom you owe no loyalty," Sörli said. "You've seen him kill. People who get in his way die. How long before you get in his way?"

"He's dangerous, John," Martinez reiterated. "You know that."

Too well.

The intensity of these two was frightening. Just like Bear sometimes. Everybody wanted John on their side; everybody told him how dangerous everyone else was. Whom was he supposed to believe?

"We need your help, John. Your mother needs you."

John's vision went blurry as tears welled up in his eyes.

"When this is all over, you can come home, John. You and your mother will have the best Mitsutomo can offer."

Could he believe her? He was so confused, and it was so hard to think.

"I need some time to think about this."

She patted his arm sympathetically. At her nod Sörli left; the male nurse, too. When they were alone, she said, "Don't think too long, John. The chaos grows continually. Time is against us."

Then she left. John caught the sound of a snick when the door closed behind her. He didn't need to get out of bed to know that it was locked, but he checked it out anyway. It was locked. He tottered back to the bed, trying to force his muzzy head into thinking.

CHAPTER
17

It was four in the morning, and Advanced Concepts Engineering was quiet. Nothing Holger and Bear had done so far had disturbed that peace, but they were getting to the sticky part now. Bear moved almost silently as he crept toward the ACE guard. Clearly the man's hearing was not as sharp as Holger's, for he didn't react to the dark shadow approaching him. Watching over the sights of the Hammer-Schoenfeld tranq pistol, Holger waited until Bear was within three meters before squeezing off his shot.

The dart penetrated the guard's neck just below and behind his right ear. The man slapped at his neck, the usual reaction. The drug was fast-acting, and he started to slump, staring stupidly at his clean hand. They usually thought an insect had stung them. Bear moved, grabbing the man before he fell forward onto his console. It was well done.

Holger joined him at the desk. "You move well. Very quiet."

"Ever raid a Welsh camp?"

"No."

"I have. You have to be quiet or you don't get to tell the tale."

"Good sensor net?"

Bear looked at him oddly. "Big ears."

"Right."

Holger scanned the console, noting the layout, and made a few changes to the program on his perscomp.

Bear draped the guard on the desk, arranging him to look as though he had fallen asleep naturally. "Fitting touch, using their own alchemy against them."

"It'll do."

It was chemistry rather than alchemy, but the distinction seemed unimportant.

Analysis on the crystal needle Holger had recovered from the kidnapping site had revealed that two of the three major components of the chemical cocktail were typical constituents in the sort of tranquilizer drugs used in veterinary medicine. Chemogenics product. The lab had been unable to identify the third component's function, although they had spotted a signature section of the molecular chain that was the mark of a Chemogenics designer drug. The first two components could have been bought, but the third wasn't a commercial product. Since Chemogenics was a Mitsutomo Keiretsu affiliate, the evidence almost cinched the certainty that the kidnapping operation had been one of Mitsutomo's. Using a commercial Chemogenics tranq drug for their own operation was appropriate in a way.

Holger popped the prepared chip from his perscomp and slotted it into the console. He ran the trial routine and got a "go" signal. Now, whenever he flashed his laser transmitter at a vid camera, the chip would read the coded light and activate the penetration program. The ACE computer would duplicate the previous two minutes of video and record it again as current input with a time tag starting ten seconds before the coded signal. It could get them in and out without being recorded, as long as they were brisk. An expert could detect the modification when reviewing the tapes, but by then, if all went well, Mitsutomo would have better reason to know they'd been hit.

Holger finished well before the lobby camera's panning swing brought it back around to the console desk. He and Bear retreated to the unmonitored hall from which he'd shot the guard. The camera panned past and recorded the sleeping guard. Holger waited until it finished the pan and went back across the desk. The camera had the footage now to portray an undisturbed sleeping guard each time it scanned the area. They returned to the desk. After showing Bear how to flash the camera, Holger set to work running the ACE computer, looking for something to confirm what Spae's mumbo-jumbo suggested.

Association and Contagion were the authorities she had cited when she had emerged from her ritual circle and handed him a marked map of north Boston, saying that was where Reddy was. Bear had seemed satisfied with her pronouncement, but Holger had needed to run his own check on the map location. Magic was unreliable. After checking each address in the area, his sources revealed one of them as Advanced Concept Engineering, a member of the Mitsutomo Keiretsu. It might have been just a coincidence that Spae had circled a block containing the offices of a Mitsutomo affiliate; but it was the best bet they had.

Holger learned that it was a good bet when his unauthorized prowling in their system turned up the admission logs. Coincidence could be stretched only so far. The log showed the unscheduled arrival of several persons employed by Medinet Corporation within an hour of Reddy's disappearance. There was no record of on-site injury, so they hadn't come in response to an accident. Could it be only more coincidence that Medinet, another member of the Keiretsu, was the primary consumer of ACE's tranquilizer drugs? Not as far as Holger could see; he felt confident enough to continue the penetration.

Checking inventory records, Holger found that there had been a draw on medical supplies within minutes of the Medinet team's arrival. He felt sure that if he knew more about medicine the names of the drugs scrolling by would have told him something significant. The entry did tell him that the Medinet team had a patient, or patients.

But where? Reddy might not even be here anymore. A further check of the admission records showed an irregular pattern of the members of the Medinet team logging in and out. Several were still on the premises, which suggested that their patient or patients were as well. The biological labs were the obvious place to hold a prisoner needing medical attention, and they had the tightest security in the facility. If Reddy was there, it wouldn't be easy getting him out. Much more trouble than Holger wanted to deal with.

But what if Reddy wasn't there?

Direct access to the medical files was beyond Holger; he didn't have the time or skill to hack past the security. He needed a more oblique method to confirm the target. He checked the building facility records. Yes, the labs showed increased power draw at about the right time. So did a number of other sections, including the executive suite, which wasn't surprising. If Mitsutomo's commitment was great enough to send a hit team, they'd have a honcho riding herd on the operation. What was surprising was the continuing power draw from one of the guest suites. Holger ran a cross-match, searching what files he could for something that related to the guest suite. He found a delivery receipt for medical equipment, signed by one of the Medinet team.

He'd found the patient.

Now, if only it *was* Reddy.

Thinking it the best shot they had, he decided to take it. Getting to the room was relatively easy; ACE didn't have high-security protection on the living areas of the facility. Maybe they thought their perimeter measures were sufficient; maybe they expected the boss suits to bring their own security. Holger didn't know and just now he didn't care; he was content to take it the way it was.

The corridor connecting the guest suites did have a camera on watch, so he flashed it with his laser transmitter and moved to the door they sought. Bear slipped along behind him, watching for anyone who might interfere.

The door was locked and operable only from the outside. That was actually a good sign. Only certain kinds of "guests" would be locked in.

Holger took out his magnetic pick and slipped the probe into the lock's slot. There wasn't a lot of time. He hated having to pick a lock under a time limit. Fiddling with the tuner, he got the general pattern in thirty seconds. With a minute and twenty seconds left, he let the expert system take over.

One minute left: the readout gave a 50% probability of match.

Forty-five seconds. The probability had risen only eleven percent.

Thirty seconds. The readout clicked over to 79%.

Too slow. He tapped in a guess at the frequency. 78%. Again. 77%. Damn! Again. 85%.

Fifteen seconds. 92%.

Ten seconds. No more time.

He hit engage with only a 95% probability.

The lock disengaged.

He opened the door and was through instantly, Bear sticking to him like a shadow. He got the door closed with two seconds to spare.

The room was sparsely furnished, more like a hospital suite than a guest suite. The console monitor station at the side of the bed that dominated the room furthered the impression. That bed held a single figure, long and thin. Holger noted the silvery hair. In the low light, the profile looked like Reddy's. The boy lay very still, but all the lights on the monitor station were green. The traces on the screen suggested normal sleep.

"Reddy?"

He didn't stir.

With unspoken coordination, Holger moved to one side of the bed while Bear went to the other. They each took an arm while Holger put his hand over Reddy's mouth to forestall any exclamations. The boy jerked at their touch. Finding himself held, he strained under their grip. They held on. Reddy tried to bite Holger's hand.

"It's all right, Jack," Bear said urgently. "It's Bear and Kun. Friends, Jack. Friends."

Shit! Didn't this guy know about bugged rooms? No, he probably didn't. At least the kid had stopped fighting them. To minimize the damage done, Holger whispered, "Keep quiet, Reddy. We don't know who's listening. No more names, okay?"

Reddy nodded agreement, and Holger removed his hand. To Holger's amusement, Bear looked around, searching for listeners or their hiding places. Sorry, old man, no arrases to hide behind, but then today's lurkers don't need them.

"You used *my* name," Reddy complained.

"They already know who you are. Can you walk?"

"Yeah," he replied.

"Run?"

"I can try."

"Good boy." Holger handed him a bag. "Get dressed. We're going to get you out of here."

Reddy stripped out of the hospital-style gown and drew on the clothes they'd brought for him. Bear paced the room. Still looking for listeners? Reddy's voice was muffled by the turtleneck sweater he was pulling on.

"What about Trashcan Harry? They've got him, too."

"He'll have to look out for himself," Bear said without stopping his prowling.

"We can't leave without him," Reddy said.

"We're going to have to," Holger said. "We haven't got more than twenty minutes left before they find out we've penetrated their security, and we have no idea where they're keeping him. There's no time to go looking for him. He might not even be here."

"How did you know I was here?"

"Spae had some luck locating you. She couldn't find him. Said everything around him was a jumble."

"Forget him, Jack," Bear said.

Reddy shook his head. "I don't think we should leave him."

"You want to stay here?" Holger asked.

"No."

"Then we go now."

Kun went through the door first, pointing a gun at something down the corridor. He looked to be aiming at the vid camera, but nothing happened that John could see. Kun waved Bear and John on out.

A frantic, familiar presence engulfed him when he stepped into the corridor. Faye!

John, I'm so glad you're safe! I couldn't get in there. They had something that kept me out. When they took you, I was so worried! They had something then, too. That's why I didn't know they were there until it was too late. I'm so sorry! I helped Holger, though. I showed him what they used on you. And I helped Dr. Spae find you. She said you were all right. You are all right, aren't you? I couldn't get near you!

Whoa, slow down. You can tell me about it later, when we really *are* safe. We've still got to get out of here.

Bear gave John a push to get him moving after Kun. John stumbled into motion.

Are you going to leave Trashcan Harry?

John stopped. He's here?

Downstairs. He's hurt.

"Reddy, stop talking to yourself." Kun sounded annoyed with him. Too bad.

"I'm not ta— Never mind. Harry's here. He's downstairs."

Bear looked at John suspiciously. "How do you know that?"

"Does it matter? I know. We've got to get him before they do worse to him."

"We're leaving," Kun said.

"I'm not. Not without Harry."

"I can drug you and have Bear carry you out."

"Some rescue." John looked beseechingly at Bear. "How can you abandon him? I mean, I know you don't like him, but he helped us when we were in trouble."

"We're wasting time," Kun said impatiently.

Bear stared into John's eyes. His expression was hard, closed. Finally he asked, "Is he guarded?"

No.

"No."

Bear turned to Kun. "Much as I hate to say it, we should try."

Kun looked as if he wanted to kill something.

It wasn't in the plan. It wasn't in the schedule. But they were doing it anyway. He could hear Spae's voice insisting that they had to keep the sleeper's goodwill. It was the reason for the whole expedition to ACE. For goodwill, Holger told himself over and over. For goodwill.

It would take more than goodwill to get them out of the facility if they didn't find the old bastard and get him out soon.

Following Reddy's directions, they avoided two guard posts and a roving patrol. The room Reddy said held Black was locked, as his had been. But having opened Reddy's lock, this one was easier. The lock snicked back and they entered.

The room stank of sweat and excrement and fear. And chemicals. Familiar chemicals. From behind a perspex barrier, a single bulb burned mercilessly down on the huddled lump in the corner. No bed here, no bedside monitor. Nothing but a lump, lying in a puddle of his own waste.

"*Harry?*" Reddy sounded appalled.

The lump stirred at the sound of the kid's voice. A bloodshot eye appeared among the twisted swathes of the threadbare blanket. Groaning, Trashcan Harry uncoiled and sat up. The man looked as though he'd gone four rounds with a heavyweight trash compactor.

"Jack?"

"And B— And friends. You okay?"

"Didn't tell," Black mumbled. "Didn't tell 'em nothing, Jack."

Unlikely. But Holger didn't think this was the time to make an issue of it.

"Come on, Harry." Reddy helped the man to his wobbly feet. "We're getting you out of here."

To Holger's surprise, they were as good as their word.

They'd been on the road for half an hour, but it wasn't until they took the long curving exit from Route 128 to I-95 South that John had any idea where they were going. It hadn't bothered him until then; he had been happy to be away from that place, where he had apparently spent several days that he couldn't remember. Bad enough what they'd done to *him*; that still might have had a rational, reasonable explanation. Certainly Martinez had sounded rational and reasonable. But seeing what they had done to Trashcan Harry made John question everything they had told him. How could people do what had been done to Harry?

"We going back to the safe house?"

Without taking his eyes from the road, Kun shook his head. "Couldn't take the chance that it had been compromised. We've moved."

"Another safe house?"

Kun nodded. "One of the advantages to working for a big organization."

Wherever this new haven was, it was in the general direction of the last one, since they were headed south. Direction didn't really matter as long as they were headed away from Boston and the Mitsutomo torturers.

Of course, they were headed away from Worcester, too, away from where his mother was. According to Bennett, though, she was just the woman who had raised him. But wasn't that what a mother was? Certainly he didn't know any other mother.

She was still under Mitsutomo's coldhearted shadow.

But he didn't see what he could do about it. They'd be watching her, waiting for him to try to reach her. He didn't have any illusions that he could sneak by the sort of net they could cast. Kun could do it; he'd proven that by getting John and Harry out of Mitsutomo's clutches. But Kun, like everyone else tugging on John, had his own agenda; and rescuing helpless people didn't seem to be part of it.

Maybe he could be tricked into helping?

Worth a try. Got any ideas how?

Not yet.

Me neither. Let's think on it.

John thought all the way down to Providence without success. He just didn't know enough about Kun and his organization to guess at their real motives. They headed east on I-195, cutting off almost immediately onto Route 44. Still, John couldn't think of a handle to use. Their surroundings began to shift from concrete and brick to clapboard and trees. It seemed that this safe house was going to rely more on isolation than on camouflage.

Kun headed down a side road that had no name John could see. Several turns later, he pulled off to the side of the road, stopping just before a gravel track that led into the trees.

"Why are we stopping here?" John asked.

"I'm not getting a handshake from the security system." Kun sounded worried.

"What's that mean?"

"Someone has disabled it."

"Mitsutomo?"

"How could they have beaten us here?" Bear asked.

"Any number of ways," Kun replied. "Let's hope it's not them. It may just be a glitch in the system. Sit tight while I try something."

He punched a number into the car phone. The number he reached rang five times before someone picked up.

"Hello?"

"Is this the Jones household?" Kun asked in a voice that didn't sound much like him at all.

"No, it's—" The person on the other end paused. "Kun, is this you?"

Kun sighed. "Yes, Doctor."

Spae's voice was recognizable more by tone and content than by sound as she snapped, "What do you want? Did everything go all right?"

"I'm fine, Doctor. How about you?"

"Are you feeling all right, Kun? You don't usually worry about my health."

"Have you checked the security system recently, Doctor?"

"Didn't I get it back on?"

"You turned it off?" Kun sounded more exasperated than surprised.

"Of course. How else do I let someone in?"

Kun's head snapped up. "You have someone with you?"

"Yes. A very interesting gentleman, but I don't think you'll like him."

"Why is that, Doctor?" he asked warily.

"You'll see."

"Did you put out the cat, Doctor?"

"Put out the— Kun, you know what I think about your foolish word games. I'm a mage, not a spy. I'm telling you, I'm fine. The house is fine. Everything's fine. Better than fine, actually. We're going to make Magnus eat our shorts."

"What's going on, Doctor?"

"You'll see when you get here."

"I'll be there in about an hour," he said, cutting the connection.

An hour? "But we're only a half block away."

"A hedge. You'll note that I didn't mention you or Bear."

"Wise," Bear said.

"Or Trashcan Harry," John said.

"He's in no shape to be useful," Kun said.

"Agreed," Bear said.

They both sounded grim enough to be going off to war. They brought out pistols from holsters under their coats and started checking them.

"But Dr. Spae said she was fine," John protested.

"She might have been coerced," Kun said.

"She didn't sound coerced."

"It's best we don't take chances." To Bear, Kun said, "Cover me, like I showed you?"

Bear nodded.

They opened their doors simultaneously and got out of the car.

"Stay here with Black," Holger ordered.

He and Bear headed down the road.

Like hell.

"You going to be okay, Harry?"

John took the mumbled reply for a yes. Getting out of the car, he followed the other two.

John, is this wise?

No.

Bear and Kun made their cover-and-sprint approach to the house that lay beyond the trees. John waited until they got through the front door before running across the unkempt lawn to join them. They spun on him, weapons pointed, and for a second he thought they might actually shoot him. They didn't; they lowered their weapons, although Kun's eyes suggested that he did indeed want to kill John. Those eyes were cold enough to make John shiver.

It wasn't as though he had disrupted some vital tactical maneuver. The room was empty of evil nasty villains and nothing looked disturbed. He could hear Dr. Spae speaking conversationally in the next room. Shifting, he tried to see whom she was talking to. Before he succeeded, the two men entered the next room. Since they had abandoned the stealthy approach, he did too, bustling in behind them.

Doctor Spae and a tall, rail-thin figure sat at the table. Spae's visitor was facing her. His silver hair lay close against his head, making his pointed ears prominent. As John entered the room, the man turned, revealing his face.

John gasped.

It was Bennett.

"You!" Bear snarled.

"And a pleasant good morning to you, too, Artos."

Bear started to bring up his weapon. John and Spae both shouted, but Kun acted. He got a hand on the barrel and pushed it aside, retaining his grip to keep Bear from firing. Bear and Kun stared at each other until Bear shrugged and let go of the gun.

"I take it you two know each other," Spae said.

"We've had dealings," Bennett said lightly. "We did not part on the best of terms. A misunderstanding."

"He's a liar," Bear said.

Bennett turned to Spae. "You see, I told you he would accuse me of that. He's almost pathological that way."

"Deal with him at the peril of your soul," Bear said. He stomped out of the room. John heard the front door slam behind him.

John looked around to see how Bear's pronouncement was being taken. Spae was shaking her head, a bemused look on her face. Kun was staring at Bennett, wide-eyed and ashenfaced, as though he were scared of the elf. The man's reaction made John uneasy. Did everyone hate elves? Bennett was looking at John and smiling.

"Ah, John, I'm glad to see you well. Sit down. We have a lot of catching up to do. Things have changed since last we talked."

John sat, feeling Kun's burning gaze on him. A glance showed the man's expression had closed up, locking away whatever emotion he felt.

"You too, Kun," Spae said.

Kun shook his head slightly and made no move.

"Suit yourself," Spae said. Smiling, she turned to the elf. "Now, Mr. Bennett, where were we?"

CHAPTER
18

John stood on the back porch of the safe house, staring out at woods. The trees were dark, entwined shapes, their leaves patches of night prematurely stolen from the deep-blue sky. It was quiet out here, which was okay by him; he could hear Faye just fine, and no one complained about him talking to himself. In a way it was like old times, just Faye and him, talking quietly like they used to. They speculated on what might hide among the boles of those mighty trees, and made guesses as to what strange creatures ran along the ancient branches. In the midst of an elaborate description of the courtship rituals of the Pear-Chested Wallagarber, Faye suddenly stopped and went away.

The back door of the house whined open and the boards of the porch creaked ever so slightly as someone joined John. He knew without looking that it had to be Bennett; no one else walked so softly on the old boards.

Bennett stopped beside John and looked where he was looking. He stared at the trees for a few moments before speaking.

"The woods have a strong lure."

In full daylight you could see the next house over. Even now, you could hear the sound of traffic moving along the road to the west beyond the trees. "It's not like it's the primeval forest."

"Those woods are deeper than you think, if you know the path."

"Which you do, of course."

"Don't sound so bitter. You can learn to walk the path. Soon, I think, you will have an opportunity."

John turned to look at him. "You going to teach me?"

"I am not the best of teachers. There are others from whom you could learn more quickly."

"Other elves?"

"Of course."

John turned back to stare at the trees. "Haven't seen too many around."

"Nor will you. Not yet, anyway."

They stood in silence for a while longer. Clearly Bennett had come out to talk to John, but he seemed in no hurry. John decided to let the elf start things, but the minutes dragged on and Bennett's patience proved greater than John's.

"You want I should start calling you Dad?"

"Without your heart in it, there is no point. Until you find a form of address that is comfortable for you, Bennett will do."

John inclined his head toward the house. "You tell them that you're my father?"

"No. Beyond the fact that it is none of their business, I would not presume to force an end to your relationship with Artos by doing so."

"He calls himself Bear."

"So he does. And he calls you Jack. Do you prefer that name?"

"It's fine."

"Then I shall use it from now on, Jack."

"Suit yourself."

Who was being called what certainly wasn't what Bennett had come to talk about, and they lapsed into silence again. The air felt full of unseen ice, poking and scratching. John really wanted to be elsewhere. He resented Bennett's intrusion, but felt guilty at the same time. The guy was his father. Wasn't a kid supposed to be comfortable around his father?

Irritated at his discomfort, he snapped, "So, what brought you here? You get tired waiting for me to rat on Bear?"

"Not at all," Bennett replied calmly. John thought they were headed for another bout of lockjaw, but Bennett surprised him by speaking again after only a short pause. "Circumstances have changed. As you know from your recent adventure, there are other players in the game now. We no longer have the luxury of time."

Grateful that there was something impersonal to talk about, John asked, "Are you saying Mitsutomo wants Caliburn too?"

"I think it likely, and frankly, I would rather see it in the hands of Artos."

"I thought you didn't want him to get it. I thought you hated him."

"Hate is a strong word, Jack, and not one that I would use. He has not told you much of his previous life, has he?"

"No."

"He won't. He is a very mistrustful man. For all the good you have done him, he still doesn't trust you. I don't think he trusts anyone anymore. But he's probably not to blame; he's had a difficult life, and been betrayed by more than one person to whom he had given his trust. For now, let me just say that he and I are not friends. It is because of our history that Dr. Spae thought it best that I not be present while she explained my offer to him."

"What offer?"

"I told the doctor that I will assist her in opening a way to the otherworld, so that Artos may recover Caliburn. If he agrees, we will be leaving shortly."

"Leaving? Who?"

"All of us here. Doctor Spae desperately wants to see the otherworld, whether we recover Caliburn or not, and Mr. Kun will find his duty compelling him to go along as well. Harry will perforce be part of our entourage."

"Our?"

"You sound surprised. Did you think I would return to the otherworld and leave you behind, now that it is possible for you to make the trip?"

Well, yes, actually, John thought, but he didn't say so.

"Or are you just surprised that Harry would be a part of *our* entourage? Though of a base race, he *is* a faithful servant. By serving you well, he has served me well, and he should be honored."

"What about—"

"Your companion Faye? She will join us too, if she wills."

Who wouldn't? The otherworld! Bennett had said that John would take on his true appearance there. It would mean the end of doubts, if it was true. He would see if he really was an elf. He would know if Bennett was just leading him on or was really telling the truth about John's parentage. It was something he needed to know. But—

"I can't go. It wouldn't be right."

Bennett gave him a curious look. "And why is that?"

"I've got to go back to Worcester."

"No, you don't."

"Look, I know you told me she isn't my mother, and maybe she isn't. But she raised me. I owe her, and I'm not as coldhearted as some people; I can't just leave her to the mercy of those Mitsutomo goons."

"I am not blind to your sentiments, Jack. In fact, I find them very noble, and worthy of the prince you are. What I meant was that she is no longer under the control of the Mitsutomo villains. I have arranged for her to be taken to a place of safety."

"In the otherworld?" Could he get to go to the otherworld *and* see his mother safe?

"No. That would not be appropriate."

Maybe Bear was right about elves. "Then where is she?"

Bennett waited a moment before slowly saying, "I think it best that you not know at this time."

Had his mother been rescued, or had she simply changed wardens? "You're as bad as they are. You want to use her too."

"Not at all. And I must say that I am somewhat disappointed that you would think that. Bear has poisoned you a bit, I think. Not telling you her whereabouts is as much for her safety as for your own. You've already spent time in the hands of those corporate monsters and know what they can do. You saw what they did to Harry. Should you be captured again by their agents, they could easily extract her location from you, because your concern for her brings thoughts of her forward in your mind. They can strip those thoughts from you with ease. Once they know her hiding place, they will capture her and use threats against her well-being to force cooperation from you."

It sounded reasonable. Kun had told him that the Mitsutomo people had lied when they told him about his drug abreaction; Kun had said they'd used truth drugs on him. He'd seen for himself what they had done to Trashcan Harry. They *were* monsters. He didn't want to think of his mother in their hands. But was she any better off in Bennett's hands?

But how could he think that his father would be a monster like those people who had captured him?

Too many questions without answers. He tried asking one.

"Why are you doing this?"

"I told you that."

"Let's try that again. Why you?"

"I'm your father, Jack."

"But you didn't rescue me. Bear and Kun did."

"An act worthy of reward."

"You don't want to reward Bear. I heard what you said about being too late to prevent him from waking. The sorceress Nym woke him and you tried to kill her for it."

"You were overwrought at the time, Jack. I think you mis-understood what was happening. I tell you truthfully that I didn't kill her."

"But you tried."

"I concede that it appeared that way. But you should know that she is a mistress of illusion and has made a career of causing men to see almost anything other than the truth. And it is truth that Artos is a dangerous man."

"He says the same about you, only he doesn't use the word 'man.'"

Bennett shook his head ruefully. "He wouldn't. He has a memory that finds it easier to hold the bad than the good. He will probably have even less kind things to say about Nym when he learns who she is."

"And who is she?"

"Someone who has done you and me a great service. The magic released by Artos's awakening has changed the bal-ance of energies between the realms. For that, I am grateful to her. This new balance allows me to bring you home."

"You didn't look grateful when you were tossing spells at her."

"As I said, appearances can be deceiving. She took no harm."

Could he believe that? Kun had told him that the police had found only one body, a male, the poor guy the police thought was John. But if Bennett hadn't killed Nym, what had happened to her? "So where is she? She must have woken Bear for a reason. Where is she now? Why hasn't she contacted him again? Why isn't she helping him find Cal-iburn?"

"I can't answer your questions, Jack. Nym's mind is not mine to know. She has been a little . . . strange for some years now. I must assume that she has gone about her busi-ness, whatever she conceives that to be."

"Speaking of being about one's business," Dr. Spae said from the door. The open, sunny look on her face didn't look at all at home, but it was undoubtedly genuine. "Pack your bags, Jack. I've finally got those two boneheads to agree to Mr. Bennett's plan.

"We'll leave as soon as you're ready, Mr. Bennett."

"Perhaps now you understand my insistence that we needed to treat the captives less lightly."

Pamela tried to ignore the superior attitude Sörli was taking, but it was damn hard. He'd been right and she'd been wrong. Still, she didn't like the way the little man said "captives." It made it sound as though they were engaged in a clandestine war. Which, she had to admit, they were. So what was it about the way he used the word that bothered her? The two individuals he had kidnapped and brought to Advanced Concepts Engineering *were* captives, prisoners of this undeclared war. They were also prisoners that Mitsutomo had no legal authority to hold. Lack of legal authority was why she had denied his request to use one of the Keiretsu's legitimate holding facilities.

Now, looking at the empty bed in the empty room, she saw she had been wrong. She had placed too much reliance on Sörli's word that the acquisition operation had gone smoothly. Somewhere there had been a slipup; otherwise no one would have known that Reddy and his companion had been brought to the ACE facility. But crying over it wasn't going to help; they had to pick up the pieces and move on.

"What results on tracing the names mentioned on the audiotape?" she asked.

"Bear is the name the sleeper is using, and so we need look no further."

"And Kun?"

"As yet unknown. Since the sleeper could not be versed in penetrating modern security systems, Kun must have led the breakout attempt. From the traces of tampering in the facility's computer system, we know that he is highly trained or has access to very sophisticated expert software, which means that he has backing. We must assume that he is an agent of an unidentified faction. A powerful one."

"Not an otherworld faction?"

"I do not believe so."

"Are we looking at an ally or an opponent?"

"He stole our captive," Sörli said with a tone that made her feel mocked. "He is no ally."

Sörli's opinion was clear, but Pamela preferred a wider, more optimistic view. If this unknown faction was simply protecting the sleeper and his friends, they might actually oppose the rulers of the otherworld. If so, they were allies of sorts, no matter how opposed to Mitsutomo they might be in other, lesser matters.

Still, she could not ignore Sörli's fears of an opposition faction. If Kun was part of an organization, and that organization was seeking to shift the balance toward chaos, they had to be identified. Immediately. An unknown enemy was the most powerful kind. A known enemy could be watched and steps could be taken to neutralize them. If Kun's organization favored the chaos, they would have to be neutralized.

Sörli's conviction that this mystery organization had no connections to the otherworld was encouraging. Mitsutomo had the resources to deal with a real-world threat, even a rival megacorporation. Pamela knew how those resources could be brought to bear; she had plenty of experience in dealing with the real world. She knew how to pressure organizations, knew how to break them if necessary. A real-world rival was something she knew how to handle.

The idea of taking a direct hand against the chaos was appealing, far more appealing than relying on Sörli and his arcane expertise. She was sure that more direct supervision would get better results from Sörli and his team. She'd be taking a more direct hand now. She would add other teams to the operation as well, separate from and operating independent of Sörli. *She* would get results.

Dismissing Sörli with an admonition to get something onto her screen within the day, she headed for the office the ACE president had arranged for her. She had planning to do.

CHAPTER
19

The journeyers began to gather on the back porch of the safe house about an hour after sunset. The air was chilling fast, the way it did in the late spring, when the land still held the cold of winter too closely for the sun to warm it away during the day. The clothes that had seemed overly warm to John in the house didn't seem out of place in the light evening breeze.

Bear and Kun were already there. Like John, they were wearing dark sweatshirts and cargo pants tucked into high-top hiking boots, outfits that had come from the storeroom of the safe house. Kun's fit perfectly, and Bear's sweater stretched tight across his shoulders but was otherwise a good fit. John's pants barely covered the top of his boots and the sweater's sleeves ended a good two inches short of his wrist. Kun was explaining to an attentive Bear about the fine points of handling an H & K 5mm Viper™ machine pistol. John felt the heavy weight of the gun Kun had issued him hanging at his shoulder; even though he had collapsed the stock and removed the suppressor so that the weapon was barely a foot long, the Viper seemed awkwardly long.

"You ought to listen to this too, Jack," Bear said.

John nodded, but he didn't really listen. The weapons made it seem as if they were getting ready for a war, and that wasn't what they were supposed to be doing. Was it?

No, John.

Ah, Faye. Just what are we supposed to be doing?

You're trying to help Artos. I'm just trying to help you.

Is it that simple? Why does it feel so complicated?

I don't know, John. It doesn't feel complicated to me.

Trashcan Harry arrived, maneuvering himself and his crutch through the door with some difficulty. He was looking better and gave John a snaggle-toothed smile; he was clearly weak, worn down by his ordeal in the halls of the Mitsutomo monsters. John thought again about suggesting that Harry stay behind, but the determined way the man clumped across the porch to hear Kun's lecture said that he would be as adamant as ever about going along. John couldn't understand why Kun, who was obviously viewing this adventure as some kind of testosterone-powered fast strike, had backed Trashcan Harry's intent to go along. The battered Harry couldn't possibly match Kun's ideal of a soldier or even a spy. All you had to do was look at the old guy to see he should stay home; even the stealthy aspect of Harry's dark clothes was undermined by the bright white bandages wrapping his hands and head. Kun obviously didn't think Harry was too useful, because he hadn't bothered to give him a weapon—although from the pistol butt sticking out from under Harry's sweater, he had found one of his own.

Bennett and Spae were the last to arrive. He wore the same street clothes and trench coat he had been wearing when John had first met him, while she was dressed like a hiker in flannel shirt and jeans. To complete the image, she wore a multipocketed backpack and carried a metal-shod walking stick. They looked as if they had completely different travel plans from each other, let alone the rest of the crew. Neither of them looked weighed down with the gravity Kun, Bear, and Harry were showing.

Kun acknowledged Spae's arrival with a nod. Putting down his weapon, he strapped on a ballistic vest studded with rings and snaps and straps. Bulging pockets and attached packets made it look lumpy. Once he had his vest seated to his satisfaction, he handed similar but unequipped vests to everyone.

"Ballistic armor," he said.

Bear took his and started to play with the Velcro fasteners, opening and reclosing them clumsily. John stepped over to help him. Like a good squire, he helped Bear slip into the vest and fastened it securely on him.

"It doesn't feel much like armor," Bear said. "And there's no protection for the shoulders or the arms."

"Most shots are aimed at the body," Kun said. "Arm's too difficult a target in a firefight."

Bear made a sweeping motion with his arm. "The arm is exposed when a blow is made."

"He's talking about guns, Bear," John said. "Not swords."

Looking down at his vest, Bear fingered the thickness of the garment. "This protects against guns?"

"Most," Kun said. "You'll still feel like you've been kicked by a mule."

Giving Kun a disbelieving look, Bear didn't say anything more. He headed back into the house. John helped Trashcan Harry into his vest before donning his own. Spae refused the vest that Kun offered her.

"For the record, Doctor?"

"Yes, Mr. Kun. For the record."

Sour-faced, he opened the door and started to toss the vest inside. Bennett, watching the proceedings with an amused air, stopped Kun's motion by asking, "None for me, Mr. Kun?"

Without looking at him, Kun replied, "You can have the doctor's, since she doesn't want it."

"How kind of you." But when Kun held it out to him, he said, "No, thank you. I believe the doctor has a more realistic view of our excursion."

"Suit yourself." Kun dropped the vest at Bennett's feet and went back to his weapon.

Bear came back, wearing his leather jacket. He held John's out to him. "You might be wanting this. It's not much, but it's better than cloth. Not a lot of guns in Faery last I heard."

"Thanks," John said, taking it from him. But he didn't put it on, just slung it over his shoulder. It flopped down, concealing the Viper.

"Well," said Bennett. "Now that we're all here and suitably accoutered, shall we be off?"

Spae was the only one to give an unambiguous assent, and Kun said nothing at all. Oblivious to the varied level of enthusiasm, Bennett led them toward the woods behind the house.

"Stay close to me or you might go astray," he said as they passed through the brush at the tree line. Bear and Kun followed close on Bennett's heels, the three of them moving far more quietly than Dr. Spae, who seemed to stumble over a root or bumble into a bush with every other step. Trashcan Harry had trouble negotiating the terrain with his crutch. John lagged behind with him to help him out over the rougher bits. They hadn't gone more than a dozen yards when Bennett halted and turned to Dr. Spae.

"Are you ready, Doctor?"

"Lord, I hope so," she replied nervously.

"Then we shall proceed."

Bennett held his hand out, palm up, and closed his eyes. In a moment, John smelled ozone; and then faint green light began to flicker around Bennett's fingers with the fitful energy of an alcohol fire. Kun sucked in a breath. Bennett opened his eyes and, reaching out with his luminous hand, grasped the metal tip of Spae's walking stick.

"I don't feel anything," she said.

"Concentrate, Doctor."

For almost a minute nothing happened. The ozone scent increased, and the green light extended its fugitive brilliance down onto the metal ferule. The shifting flashes encompassed both hand and staff. Bennett took his hand away, trailing silvery streamers that stretched and sagged like half-dried paint before vanishing utterly. He smiled a satisfied smile at the lambent light wreathing the tip of the doctor's staff.

"We may proceed," he said as he turned to lead them on.

They walked on, the light from Spae's staff casting strange shadows on the undersides of the leaves above them. Kun spent as much time casting slit-eyed glances at the doctor's light as he did scanning the woods around them. He carried his weapon ready, which made John nervous. Bear, for all his earlier arguments against trusting Bennett, followed the elf more complacently; his Viper was slung and he appeared almost relaxed, as if the woods were more comfortable for him than urban surroundings. But then, they probably were to him; John tended to forget that Bear came from a more primitive time. In Bear's time they didn't have cars and roads and skyscrapers and electric lights . . .

Electric lights.

By now they should be seeing the lights of the house on the neighboring property, but all John could see was trees. He looked back the way they had come. Trees. To the left, trees; to the right, trees. For all he could see, they might have been in a forest that stretched around the world. He looked up, searching for a patch of sky through the canopy. He found one, and in it more stars than he remembered from the cloudy sky under which they'd entered the woods.

Something gave a low, moaning call. John looked around, but he couldn't see what it might be. The call came again; it wasn't a sound that John had ever heard on a nature vid.

The edges of the leaves around them glistened; light reflecting from them shone in pure colors as though it were bent through a prism. Such a rainbow effect shouldn't be visible at night, but John saw it anyway. The air seemed charged, and his skin tingled. Ahead, Kun seemed to glance around with more frantic intensity. Spae turned her head in wider, more regular sweeps, taking in all around her with an expression of wonder on her face. She didn't even notice when the flickering light of her staff faded and died. Bear marched on, neither nervously fidgeting like Trashcan Harry nor rapt in awe like the doctor. He was taking it all in stride, and John tried to emulate his casual acceptance of the oddness around them.

After they'd walked for a half an hour or so, the trees thinned, opening into glades and finally meadows. Above them a silver moon shed light that somehow did not diminish the multitude of stars studding the clear sky. Occasionally, John glimpsed something pale moving among distant copses. Once he spotted dark shapes moving in the sky, occluding stars with their swift passage.

Bennett led them on, in more or less a straight line, until they came to a river; John recognized the curves, especially an odd, muddy oxbow he had seen from the highway while they were driving to the safe house. But it wasn't the same river. It couldn't be. There were no houses here, neither the battered shacks that had stood by the riverside for a hundred years, nor the more modern getaway cottages favored by well-off corporates. There were no piers, no weathered skiffs or gleaming pleasure boats, no strip mall at the roadside, no road, even. Bennett headed upriver to a wooden bridge carved with strange shapes. They crossed.

The countryside on the other side of the river was open, rolling hills. It might have been an idyllic pastureland, but no flocks grazed the moonlit slopes. It seemed to John that he couldn't see as far as he should have been able to on such a clear night; it was as though the haze of distance started sooner here. Off to the left, at the edge of visibility, he spotted the dark shape of a tower. A blue light gleamed from slits halfway up its height. The scene was at once strange and familiar. With a shock John realized that he had seen this landscape before. In dreams.

Bennett took a sharp turn, taking them up a slope rather than along it as he had been doing. Ahead, where their course would have taken them, John could see a pool of darkness that seethed and bubbled like a pit of pitch. A waft of air from that direction was filled with the stench of decaying matter and a harsh chemical stink.

"What's that?" he asked.

"A gift from the realm of man," Bennett answered. "Do you recall the Carenelli plant? It is situated about a mile from where Route 44 crosses Sefton Road."

"Vaguely."

"This is what it looks like here."

"How can that be?" Spae asked.

"It is part of the nature of the realms, Doctor. If you have been observing carefully, you will have noted that the land-forms here are almost identical to those in your realm. The ground cover and the living things are perforce different, but there are correspondences which arise from use of a place. For example, your dead buildings cast a depressive shadow into this realm, making some places less than pleasant for my sort. There are, however, things that are even more obtrusive. More offensive.

"The foulness that mankind spews and dumps injures the land simultaneously in both the realms. Surely you've seen the effects in your own realm. Sometimes your kind even does something about it, though you are so deadly slow to notice and slower to react. Here we must accept the damage you cause. Sometimes we can lessen the effects, but only rarely since we cannot attack the cause. The foulness you see below us is a wasteland which corresponds to the toxic dump site that is called the Carenelli facility in your realm. The beauty of our realm is blasted and corrupted by thoughtless-ness in yours."

Spae looked unhappy with Bennett's indictment. "Do you have proof of a connection?"

"You see it below you."

"I see a blight. I don't see a cause."

"In your realm you are accounted a mage. Here you are a child. Were you better versed in the Way you would see." Bennett sat down, legs folded. "We will rest here for a while. You can contemplate what you have seen so far."

He closed his eyes, ignoring them all.

Bear gave Bennett a venomous glare, but said nothing to the elf. Instead he looked at John and shrugged. "Elves," he said conspiratorially, as if it explained everything.

Which didn't explain anything, but did make John think.

They were well into the otherworld, and here was Bear reacting to John as he always had. Something was supposed to happen in the otherworld that should have changed Bear's attitude. Stealthily, he reached up and felt his ears. Round, as they always had been. Bennett had said that the spells making him look like a human would go away in the otherworld.

So much for being an elf.

But if he wasn't an elf, why did this place seem so right? If Bennett was lying about John's being an elf, how could this place feel right? Or was there something wrong with the spells? Maybe too many years in the real world had made the spells permanent. Or something had gone wrong due to pollution like the morass down the hill. Maybe he had mutated or something.

Kun and Spae wandered off a ways and soon began a heated but quiet argument. Trashcan Harry limped down to poke at the edges of the corruption. Bear stayed on the slope and watched Harry with a wary eye. Left alone, John sat with his back to the darkness down the hill and stared out toward where he had seen the tower. He couldn't see it now—the haze of distance, maybe—but somehow he knew it was still there; it was almost as though he heard someone calling him. Was this his home? How could it be, if he wasn't an elf?

"Put away your doubts, Jack. The spells will not fall apart by themselves."

He hadn't heard Bennett sit down beside him.

"You said—"

"I said the spells could only be lifted here. It is an operation that will take some effort."

"But you *can* do it?"

"In the proper place."

"Which, of course, is not here."

"The proximity of the blight makes this a most inauspicious place for magic." Bennett looked over at Bear. "Also, I think you will agree that this is not the best time."

"Will it ever be?" John mumbled.

"If you will not put away your doubt at my word, will you trust your eyes?"

"What do you mean?"

"Down in the vale, among the trees, there is a pond. The surface will serve as a mirror. Go look at yourself."

"And what will I see?"

"A true reflection."

"All right." John would give Bennett another chance. The otherworld was real enough; maybe Bennett's other assertions were true too. Besides, being an elven prince was too good a deal to pass up just because it didn't happen all at once. But when he stood up, Bennett remained seated.

"Aren't you going to come along?"

"I should remain here. The others might become alarmed if we wandered off. You will be safe enough."

"More secret protectors?"

"No more than usual."

John didn't think Bennett's protectors had done all that good a job so far, but the countryside seemed quiet enough. And he had the Viper, if there was trouble. He left Bennett sitting on the hilltop.

He found the pond easily enough; he seemed to be able to . . . smell it. The surface of the water was still, shiny as a mirror in the moonlight, and thin wisps of fog drifted across its surface. Somewhere something broke the surface and reentered the water with a plop; whatever it was, it was too far away for the ripples it caused to disturb the reflective waters near his feet.

The brink of the pond seemed more than just the boundary between earth and water. He found himself reluctant to approach it. What was he afraid of? As soon as he did, one of the questions that so troubled his mind would be answered. All he had to do was look into the water.

Knowing he should be eager, he felt frightened instead. He could go back to Bennett and say he'd looked. No one would know he hadn't. No one but himself. But Arthur had known when Bedivere hadn't thrown Excalibur into the sea, because Arthur had known what Bedivere would see. Did Bennett know what John would see? What if he asked him questions about it, as Arthur had asked of Bedivere?

Ultimately, there was only one thing to do. Like Bedivere, he had to do what he was told.

Selecting a spot where the bank projected out a bit over the water, he took a few steps closer. Keeping his eyes on a distant part of the pond, he moved closer to the edge. He stood for a moment, steeling himself; then, slowly, he looked down.

There was an image in the dark mirrored waters: a tall, thin figure in dark clothes whose feet vanished into the earth of the pond's verge. The clothes made the person almost invisible in the water, save for his head and hands. Those hands might have been human, for all they were slender and had long, tapering fingers. Tall people often had hands like that. But the head—there was no mistaking the head for human. A long, gaunt face dominated by wide, slightly slanting pale eyes. Ears with finely pointed tips, easily visible where they poked through silver hair as delicate as moonbeams. The features were at once familiar and alien. John's heart beat faster. That familiarity did not come just from the bit of Bennett's features that he saw there. He knew that face very well, even though he'd never seen it quite this way before.

It was him.

Wasn't it?

Wondering, he stared into the face of the elf that stared at him from the surface of the pond. What had become of the John Reddy who had lived in Rezcom Cluster 3? Dead, they said.

What of Marianne Reddy's child? Who was *he*? Here before him was evidence that John was not that child, never had been. Marianne Reddy was human, not elf. The mother he missed was not his.

He wished he were home, safe in his bed, and waking from a bad dream.

But nothing changed. He stood beneath the moon of Faery and looked down at an elf with his face. How could his life ever again be what it had been?

Now the boy without a father had one, an elf. He had a father who said that John was a prince, and the son of a prince. He didn't feel like a prince; but then, he didn't know what a prince should feel like. The closest he'd ever come to royalty was in books, songs, and vids, and nothing he'd encountered in those seemed to fit the here and now.

But was it real? If only he could know whether this was a true reflection, as Bennett had told him it would be. Was this elf before him really himself?

"Yes, John."

John started at the familiar voice, realizing that for the first time he was hearing it with his ears.

A new image appeared in the pool beside the familiar-strange elf. She was tall, though not so tall as he, and slender, moving with a lithe fluidity as she walked up beside him. He couldn't see her ears beneath her flowing mane of spun-silver hair, but she had the fine-boned, attenuated features John had learned were elven.

"Faye?"

"Yes, John?"

Afraid she would vanish, he turned away from the pool. But she was still there. More *there* than ever, being no longer a disembodied voice in his head. He drank her in. Her eyes were sparkling silver, the irises of a shade that rendered them almost invisible. Her skin was as fair and pale as starshine.

And she was . . . beautiful.

John was surprised at the heat in his loins; he had always thought of his companion Faye as a friend, sometimes even as a sibling. Sexual matters had been irrelevant. He realized with a shock that he had never considered her gender seriously at all. Now she stood before him, more beautiful, more desirable than any girl he'd ever wanted to date.

Did she find him attractive as well?

She smiled as if she read his thoughts, and his knees felt weak. She stepped closer and he retreated a step. His foot slipped at the edge of the verge and he started to lose his balance. She reached out and pulled him back from the edge into the safety of her arms. She laughed at him. No, with him. Then they both stopped laughing and their lips met.

Not like kissing your sister at all.

A shadow rose up inside him. Since he was an elf, she might actually be his sister. Or at least a relative.

Awkwardly, he broke their embrace.

"What's wrong, John?"

"Nothing," he lied. "We, ah, we really ought to get back to the others. We've been away for a while. They'll be worried."

Her slight frown spoiled the perfection of her face and tore at him. Unable to bear it, he didn't look at her face when he took her hand and tugged her away from the pond. She resisted for a brief moment before following along.

John wrestled with his troubled thoughts all the way back to the others, without managing to find something to say to her.

CHAPTER
20

When they cleared the tree, the first thing John noticed was the pair of horses standing silhouetted against the sky. At least they *looked* like horses, at first. As he and Faye got closer, John could see that the black beasts were longer legged and slimmer than any horse he'd ever seen pictured. Their long, narrow heads were crowned with tall, tapering ears that might be considered an equine version of an elf's pointed ears. They stood so still that they might have been statues; but they hadn't been there when John had gone off to the pool, and no one could have moved statues there in the short time he'd been gone.

Were they the elven steeds of legend? If so, to whom did they belong?

His answer came as he saw the stranger. The stranger's tall, slim silhouette couldn't belong to anyone but an elf. And his clothes! They might have been out of a fantasy vid, the way they glimmered and flowed. The effect of the dagged sleeves and lace and decorative embroidery would have been comic on someone without the elf's air of restrained menace. He was the first to notice John's return and stared at him with cold eyes of silver.

John couldn't match that glare and looked away. Only then did he notice the tense stances of the humans on the hill. Bennett stood at ease, turning to follow his fellow elf's diverted attention. He smiled when he saw John.

"Ah, Jack. I'm glad you're back," he said. "Something has come up and I must leave you all on your own for a while. Certain affairs of my estate here require my attention, but I was hesitant to leave before you returned. It is so easy for newcomers to get lost here." He turned his smile to Faye. "I see my fears were groundless."

"There are two horses," John said, wondering where his was. If his father was going to his estate, shouldn't he be taking his son along?

"Yes. Shahotain was foresightful enough to bring an extra for me."

"What about me?"

"What *about* you?"

"Aren't I going with you?"

Bennett paused for a beat before saying, "I'm afraid not, Jack. It would not be . . . appropriate."

So much for being elven royalty together. "Well, you don't have to hang around anymore; I'm back."

"There will be other times, Jack. Better times."

"Yeah, sure."

Bennett clasped John's shoulder in farewell, whispering, "Watch Bear. You've said too much about our relationship already." Louder, he said, "I will return as soon as I may."

The other elf was already astride his mount. With practiced ease, Bennett mounted. Without further comment, the two of them rode off and soon disappeared into the odd distant haze of the otherworld. John wasn't sure whether he was happy or sad to see Bennett's back. He *was* sure that he was confused. Normally a talk with Faye would be in order, but a look at her told him that he wouldn't get an answer there; she was a large part of his confusion and uncertainty. Bear wouldn't be any help—explaining his troubles would require talking about his elven heritage, and that was something else

John didn't want to face just now. Maybe if he put his mind to less personal matters . . .

"What's going on?" Selecting Dr. Spae as the safest person to talk to, John directed his question to her, but Kun answered him.

"That other elf—Shahotain, was it?—came galloping up on a horse—a *horse*, for God's sake—and went into conference with Bennett. Our native guide didn't deign to tell us what the private chat was about, beyond some vague stuff about duties."

"I'm sure it was important," Spae said.

"Who's your friend?" Bear asked.

It took John a moment to realize that none of the others had even acknowledged Faye's existence, let alone seen her. "She's an old friend of mine."

"She's fey," Bear said.

His tone was suspicious, but John was too busy wondering how he knew Faye's name to do more than nod and say, "That's right."

"The invisible friend?" Kun asked.

Did everyone already know about her? If they did, they should have better manners. "You're acting like she was still invisible."

"You haven't been much better," Spae said. "Are you going to introduce us?"

Spae was smiling as though she knew some secret John didn't. His cheeks burned as he went through the introductions, stumbling to a conclusion with, "Faye is an old friend of mine."

"Sorry, Jack," Bear said. He nodded to Faye. "John's friends are my friends. Until they prove themselves other than friends. Well met, girl."

"So we trade one elf for another," Kun said unhappily.

"I am not an elf," Faye said. To the disbelieving faces that turned to her, she added, "Of the prince's kind, anyway."

"Prince?" Kun and Spae said simultaneously.

"So he *is* a prince," John said. He thought he'd spoken to himself, but Kun at least had heard him.

"You knew Bennett was some kind of royalty?"

"He'd said he was, but who could be sure he was telling the truth?" John's response sounded lame even to him.

"You were wise not to trust him," Bear said.

"And bloody stupid not to mention it to us," Spae said.

"What else haven't you told us?" Kun asked. He didn't look at all happy with John.

"Nothing much."

Bear spoke. "I think Jack was wise not to tell us that the elf had said he was a prince. Look at how you react. You allow this Bennett too much power over your thoughts already. How much more under his sway would you be if you thought him royalty? Weren't you listening when I told you how easily elves lie?"

"But Faye has confirmed that he is a prince," Spae said.

"You have seen no proof," Bear said.

"You've got Faye's word," John protested.

Bear looked at John thoughtfully. "So we have."

"Are you saying she's lying?" John asked angrily.

"Do you believe her?"

"Yes!"

"You know her better than I," Bear said. "But Bennett's rank isn't the issue. We haven't come here to visit his court. We gain nothing by remaining here. We should push on."

"Bennett said to wait for him," Spae said.

"All the more reason to move on."

"You heard him. We could easily get lost in this dimension. It's not like our own. Bennett's our only guide."

"Not true. John's friend is a native." Bear pointed at Trashcan Harry. "The goblin belongs here too. He knows this realm."

Trashcan Harry looked nervously back and forth at the others. Bear was calling him a goblin again, and for the first time John thought he could see why. Bennett had said that Harry was one of his agents, brought from the otherworld to watch over John. Here under the starry skies of the otherworld he looked the part of an otherworld denizen; it was a difference akin to the transformation Bennett had undergone when he revealed himself as an elf, but less pleasant. Harry looked even uglier than usual now, less human. His skin had a pallor that John somehow knew was not related to his injuries. Harry's teeth looked sharper, his ears more pointed, his skin scabrous. The change must have occurred when they crossed the boundary between the dimensions, but everyone had been so intent on their surroundings that no one had noticed. But then, everyone pretty much avoided looking at Harry unless they had to.

"Shit, another one!" Kun exclaimed.

"Behave yourself, Mr. Kun," Spae said. To Harry: "Why didn't you tell us sooner, Mr. Black? I have a lot of questions—"

"They can wait, Doctor," Bear said. "We waste time here."

"Bennett said to wait," she shot back.

Trashcan nodded vigorously. "Yeah. We gotta wait. We need his protection."

'Protection?" Kun took a step toward Harry. "From what?"

"Things," Harry said timorously.

Spae stepped between them. "Don't let him intimidate you, Mr. Black. What sort of things? Come, now. You're not going to be as uninformative as Mr. Bennett, are you?"

"You *are* supposed to help, aren't you?" John asked.

"Uh-huh." Harry looked miserable.

"Then talk to us," Kun snapped. "What sort of things?"

"There's all kinds of things," Harry said.

"He's not trying to be difficult, Mr. Kun," Faye said in a placating tone. "It is hard to be specific about these things. You wouldn't know the names we use for dangers that we know, and there are dangers for which even we have no names."

"We should go back. Get reinforcements," Kun said to Spae.

"Better to push on. We have no guarantee that we will get another chance," Bear said. "Bennett is only trustworthy as long as his goals are the same as ours. I mislike the way he abandoned us; I fear that he plans some treachery."

"You're being paranoid," Spae said. "Bennett said to wait for him."

The argument went on without reaching a conclusion. Finally, Spae made the suggestion that they take a vote.

"But the creatures get no say," Kun amended.

"They are as much a part of this expedition as you are," Spae said.

"They are creatures of Faery," Bear said.

"And can't be trusted," Kun finished. They both nodded solemnly at Spae.

"All right. All right. Just humans vote," Spae agreed. She mumbled something under her breath, but John didn't catch it. "I say we wait for Mr. Bennett."

"We go on," Bear said.

"We go back," Kun said.

John quailed when they turned to him; he didn't want to make the decision for himself, let alone the rest of them. He felt a strong urge to do anything contrary to what Bennett wanted. What did he owe the guy, after all? Bennett had ridden off to his Faery princedom alone, despite all his speeches about parental concern and the importance of John's elven heritage. Right now, John would be happy to see *him* disappointed big time. The best way to do that would be to go with Kun's plan and go home. That'd throw all of Bennett's plans into the trash. But going home might mean leaving Faye behind. Or the corporeal Faye, anyway. That thought was very bothersome.

"Jack?" Bear prompted.

Bear was the only one of the three who really cared about John. Maybe if John went with him, it'd be easier for Bear to take it when he learned John was an elf. He could prove to Bear that all elves weren't bad. John didn't feel like the sort of guy Bear seemed to think that all elves had to be. Bear needed to know that, and John could prove it to him. He'd start by helping him here. Still, John was a little bothered that Bear seemed to be expecting John to side with him just because of the *comes* thing. If Bear had such expectations, they'd straighten that out later. Bear would be a lot easier to deal with once he got what he was looking for.

"I don't think we should sit here," John said. "The point of this whole trip was to help Bear get Caliburn. Let's do it."

Bear slapped him on the back, staggering him. "Well said."

The decision made, the group set out again with Bear leading, striding confidently down the knoll. Dr. Spae did not give up her position gracefully and grumbled as they marched along. "How will Mr. Bennett know where we've gone?" she asked Bear's back. He ignored her question, but Faye assured her, "He will be able to follow us." The doctor grumbled some more, and Kun looked decidedly upset. The agent began to check his weapon with a compulsive regularity.

Although he had stood with Bear, John didn't understand how Bear intended to find what he sought. He stretched his legs to catch up with their leader, who was striding confidently across the countryside. Bear acknowledged him with a nod and they walked along quietly for a quarter mile or so before John worked up his nerve to question Bear.

"You sounded pretty confident that you knew how to find Caliburn, but how are you going to do it? Neither Faye nor Trashcan Harry knows where it is, so we really haven't got a guide. Maybe if we had a map."

"We need neither map nor guide. We have what we need. You must have faith, Jack."

Faith made a lousy compass and a worse map. From what John had learned of the otherworld, they had some serious obstacles in front of them. "Didn't you go to sleep in England?"

"Yes."

Bear's blunt answer suggested he didn't see the problem. "Bennett said that Faery reflects the real world. Won't there be an ocean between us and England?"

"I expect so."

"You don't know?"

"No."

"You don't know! How in hell are you going to find *anything* when you don't even know if there's an ocean between us and England?"

Bear seemed unperturbed by John's strident tone, but he stopped and stared dreamily into the distance. "Have you ever touched Caliburn, Jack?"

"What kind of a question is that? Of course I haven't."

"I have."

"But—"

"Don't question me," Bear ordered. More kindly he added, "Have faith."

Bear started on again, leaving John staring after him.

CHAPTER
21

Holger knew the decision to press on was wrong. He knew it. He thought again about heading back to where they'd crossed over into this place; but even if he found it again, he wasn't sure he'd be able to make the crossing without either Spae or Bennett. More important, if he made it back he'd have to explain why he had abandoned Spae. Headquarters wouldn't like any answer he gave them.

Artos was leading them across a countryside that the foolish might think placid and innocent. Placid it might be, for the moment, but Holger had heard the alien sounds and seen the furtive motions of the things that followed them from time to time, and he knew that their surroundings were anything but innocent.

He had to be vigilant.

The fog was rising, closing the night in around them and cutting down the already poor visibility. He didn't bother pulling on the Nightshades™; he'd tried them earlier and they hadn't made any difference against the strange night of this otherworld. It was like trying to see through a fog. Back in the real world the shades were not much help in fog except on the thermal setting; not a viable option here. None of

253

the shapes he'd seen flitting through the trees during that first test had registered on the electronics.

The lack of visibility made him itchy.

At least the Viper was in working order. He checked again to be sure.

The Viper's 5mm rounds weren't much individually, but the weapon had a rate of fire that could cut a man in half like an angry buzz saw. Very useful in a short-range fight. He slapped the pouches that held his reserve ammo. Still there.

So were his other hedges against trouble. They were a small selection, chosen for a broad spectrum of applications. He hoped he wouldn't need any of them, and that if he did he had what he would need. There was only so much he could carry. If he'd been working with a reliable team, they could have carried more, been better prepared for anything that might jump them.

But this crew ... This crew was something less than he would have chosen for any operation.

Spae was ... what Spae was, so she could only be trusted so far. She had her own load anyway, and he could guess what she'd say about what he would have wanted her to carry. Even if she had agreed to be prudent, it wouldn't have done much good; she was too ready to believe anything she was told by the creatures that belonged to this place.

Dealing with these otherworld creatures would only get them into trouble.

At least Bennett was gone. As little as Holger liked being abandoned in this place, he liked traveling with Bennett less. He especially didn't like the way Spae hung on the elf's words. Like his every comment was the word of God. The devil, more likely.

The whole place was populated by devils.

He hadn't liked finding out that Black was another godforsaken Faery thing. At least he hadn't armed it. Not that he'd trusted Black before his true nature was revealed. Holger's instincts had been sound there.

Distrusting Black was something he shared with Bear; the sleeper would be watching the goblin too. But that watchfulness was a small reminder of the hopes he'd begun to nurture about the sleeper. Bear had begun to seem okay on the raid that freed Reddy; he'd shown himself competent in the basic tactics anyway, even if he didn't have an appreciation for modern tech. That sort of thing would come with time. If he ever got that time. Now he was leading them on this walkabout mystic quest in never-never land. Naturally, as a sleeper, the man had been touched by magic, but such contamination didn't have to mean that his brain had gone soft. By his dogged insistence on this trip, it was apparent that he'd been corrupted beyond redemption.

Of them all, Reddy was the one who should have been most trustworthy. No agenda, no magic. Just an innocent kid swept up in this mess. But Reddy had insisted on rescuing Black. Loyalty to a comrade was commendable, though in this case, ill placed and ill timed. Now he had to look at the kid in a new light, especially since Reddy had shown up with another elf. Holger had read Mitsutomo's psychological reports on Reddy. Read all about the childhood friend who persisted past the usual age for such things. Read all about how Reddy was "reconciled" on the issue. Now Holger had seen the "invisible friend" for himself, something *he* was not in the least reconciled with. This clustering of inhuman creatures around Reddy made the kid suspect, but it would be too awkward now to disarm him. Holger would just have to keep a close watch.

On all of them.

With no one to whom he could trust his back.

He checked the Viper again.

And Spae had called him paranoid!

The woman had no appreciation for reality. Paranoia was a survival trait in his business, a tool of the trade, the way you made it through to tomorrow.

The fog was rising higher now, shrouding them almost as completely as a smoke screen. Military operations used smoke screens to mask attacks, as a way to get closer to the enemy without revealing yourself. Were they going to be attacked?

Watching for an attack was what a paranoid would do, wasn't it?

This was fairyland, the wondrous place, all green and natural. Who could have enemies here? The very thought was paranoid. The eminent Dr. Spae didn't think that this was a suitable place for paranoia.

The eminent Dr. Spae didn't think clearly enough.

Holger caught sight of a dark shape in the fog, moving parallel to their path. He took a step in its direction, trying to get a better look. When he reached the point at which he had seen it, there was nothing there.

He must have scared it off, which was good. As long as the things out there were scared of them, they had a chance.

The thickening fog made it harder and harder for John to see where they were going. Bear, in the lead, became an indistinct dark shape, then disappeared from sight altogether. The thickening murkiness swallowed Kun soon after.

When Dr. Spae started to become indistinct, he thought about taking Faye's hand. He told himself that he wanted to do it to reassure her, but when he looked at her she didn't seem worried at all. He kept his hands to himself, unwilling to look like a wuss.

With each step the mist became thicker. Trashcan Harry, limping along behind, disappeared into its hazy embrace, though John could still hear the irregular rustle-clump of his passage. For a moment he and Faye were alone in the vaporous nothing, then his foot snagged a root, slowing him, and she was gone as well.

With them all out of sight, the only thing John knew of his companions was the sound of their passage. He quickened his pace, intending to close up the distance between him and Faye, but after a few yards he hadn't caught up and he slowed again. He must have walked at an angle to her path. Fearful of getting lost in the dimness, he followed the sounds. The ghostly tendrils of fog grew together overhead, hiding even the stars from his eyes. The sounds of the others' passage grew fainter until they were swallowed altogether by the mist.

At first, John didn't notice. The silence made it easier for him to think about where he was and what he was doing. Or rather, to worry. Faye's face kept forcing its way into his thoughts, and that worried him too. How was he supposed to deal with the change in their relationship, in her *presence*?

When he finally realized that he could no longer hear the others, he stopped. Silence. The noise of his passage wasn't masking anything. There were no sounds around him, no hint of the whereabouts of the others. He might have been the only living thing in the chill gray world of slowly swirling mist.

He shouted out Bear's name, calling for a halt.

No response disturbed the silence.

He called for Dr. Spae and Kun.

No answer.

Faye.

No reply.

Even Trashcan Harry.

Nothing.

He was alone. Lost. Abandoned, or just mislaid? Most likely it was his own fault for having strayed from the line of march. He'd been straying for some time if they were out of earshot. Had they noticed yet that he was gone? And if they had, what would they do about it? An effective search was impossible in the fog.

The ground upon which he stood was uneven, a hillside, so John headed upslope in the vague hope that a higher elevation might allow him to see over the fog and get his bearings. His companions might try a similar approach. Maybe they'd all find hilltops and spot each other across the mist. He began to think he'd made the right choice when he noticed the mist thinning as he climbed. He changed his mind when he emerged from the fog bank as though he'd walked through a wall, and saw what stood before him.

It was a tower, a slender spire of dark stone. Its shape was similar to the one he had seen earlier, and for all he knew, it might even be the same one; he could have easily gotten turned around in the fog bank. John searched for an entrance but found none on ground level; the only door he could see had a threshold a good ten feet above his head. He stepped back from the tower's base, pondering the smoothness of the walls and wondering if he could climb up to the door. Just as he was concluding that there were not enough hand- and footholds, the door opened. As it gaped wide a stone stairway came into being, step after step appearing in a curve along the wall from the door to the ground. John didn't need to feel the tingle that prickled his skin to know he was seeing magic in action.

A shape appeared in the doorway. The figure might have been a demon clattering forth from hell, as it stepped out onto the landing that had not been there before. The being's shoulders were broad and humped, ridged with spines, and its head was crested, its face drawn out in a snout. Wan moonlight glinted from steel and John realized that it was a man in ornate armor, armor formed and fluted into curious shapes that disguised the human silhouette. The fantastic, bestial face was simply the helm's visor wrought by art into an inhuman visage.

A gauntleted hand rose and lifted the visor, revealing an elven face with skin so brown as to be almost black. The pale eyes stood out starkly, seeming to burn with a white light as they turned on John. The elf did not speak loudly, but John heard his voice quite clearly despite the distance between them.

"Who stands before my door?"

John had heard the songs and read the stories, and decided not to give his name. "A traveler," he said.

"What brings you to my keep?"

"I was lost. I climbed the hill thinking I might find a place to see over the fog, or at least someplace to wait until it lifted."

"You did not come here deliberately?"

"By chance only."

"Chance?" The elven knight didn't sound as if he believed it. "You did not come seeking me?"

"I was hoping to find my friends."

The elf's head lifted slightly. "You are traveling with others?"

"I'm supposed to be."

"Humans?"

Something in the elven knight's tone made John suddenly cautious. Certain that complete honesty was not the best policy in this circumstance, John tried to be vague, saying, "Some of them."

"I see."

"Please, sir knight. I didn't mean to disturb you." John had no desire to enter the chill fog again, but he wasn't sure he wanted the elf's company either. "If I could just wait out here. I'll be gone as soon as the fog clears."

"Come inside."

It was as much an order as an offer. Having given the order, or made the offer, the elf turned and reentered the tower without waiting to see whether John would comply. Lower down the slope, hidden in the fog, something moaned low and long. It sounded hungry.

John found himself on the stairs; and once he had started, it seemed only reasonable to continue. Shortly he found himself standing on the landing where the knight had stood, short of breath and sweating lightly, though less from the climb than from nervousness.

The knight awaited him inside the tower. Though the elf was no longer wearing his armor, he was no less fantastically dressed. His principal garment was a robe with voluminous folds and glittering silver spangles, and he wore a torse of feathery fronds about his head. The fall of silver curls flowing down the back of his neck stood out starkly against his dark skin. It was a decadent effect, but he seemed no less menacing than he had in the armor.

But the hall looked warm and inviting, especially the fire roaring in the great stone fireplace. The chill of the fog had seeped into John's bones; his clothing was damp, his skin clammy with the mist.

"Enter," the elven knight said. "If you will."

John hesitated, looking back over his shoulder. The keep might have been an island in nothingness, for the fog stretched from the ground below into the sky, making a bowl of fog to enclose the structure. The mist seemed somewhat closer to the tower's base than it had been. The thing in the fog moaned again.

What did he have to lose?

He stepped over the threshold. Trying to be polite, he turned to close the door and found it already shut behind him. For a moment he was puzzled; the massive wooden door would have had to have swung through where he stood. Magic, of course, was the answer. It was still a little unnerving to have it happening around him.

"Tell me, young sir. What has brought you to my home?"

John fed him a line about wandering travelers, so heavily edited as to be more of a blipvert than a story; it didn't have a plot or any motivation, and John was the only definite character in the sparse cast, but the elf seemed not to notice.

"Your story is most interesting," he said. "You say you became separated from your companions in the fog and found your way here by yourself?"

"Yeah. I was thinking about some stuff and kind of lost track of them. I called when I figured out we were separated, but I didn't get any answers. I guess I wandered pretty far."

"Far afield, of a certainty. Few come here uninvited. Fewer still with peaceful intent."

"I mean you no harm." It seemed the right thing to say, though John had no idea how he could harm such an obvious master of magic. When the knight pointed to what was slung over his shoulder—the Viper—he thought of a possible way.

"Yet you carry a weapon from the human realm."

"Would you wander this realm unarmed?"

The elf smiled. "No, I would not."

John shifted the weapon sling so that it hung more on his back. The weight of it felt heavy and awkward, but he was reluctant to part with it. Fortunately, the elf didn't suggest that he should.

"But I am being a poor host," the knight said. "Your ordeal has clearly tired you, and you must be hungry."

John realized that the knight was right. He was so hungry that he couldn't understand why he hadn't noticed until now the savory smells permeating the room. Already he could feel his mouth water in anticipation. When he turned, and saw the table laid to overflowing with plates and platters and bowls heaped with food, his saliva production went into overdrive. There was far more food than two people could eat. Were there more elves about?

"Please," the knight said, handing John a golden plate. "Help yourself."

John was reluctant at first; there were songs about people who accepted an elf's invitation to dinner. But this wasn't an elf hill and he already was in Faery. How bad could it be?

As if to alleviate John's fears, his host stepped up to the table, his own golden plate in hand, and heaped mounds of meat and vegetables onto it. He waited until John had selected enough from the table to feed the entire fencing team, then led him to a pair of ornately carved chairs with arms wide enough to set the plates upon. A jeweled golden goblet already sat on the right armrest of each chair. The knight seated himself, motioning John to do the same. Without benefit of eating utensils, the elf started in on his food. John was still a little uneasy as he selected his first morsel, the drumstick of some small bird. But the taste won him over at once, for it was smokily flavorful and the meat was cooked to a perfect blend of juiciness and tenderness. He started tucking away the rest of his selections like a football jock after the big game. Having devastated the contents of his plate, he laid it on the chair's arm and leaned back.

"There is more if you wish it," the elf said.

Burping embarrassingly, John said, "I think I've had more than enough."

"Forgive my lack of decorum, young sir, but I find it most curious that you travel in disguise."

"Disguise?" Sure, he wasn't wearing what he usually did, but— It dawned on John what the elf meant. "You can tell I'm an elf?"

The elven knight took a sip of his wine and nodded. "Of course. Your disguise is built of such simple spells, and ones clearly designed to operate in the earthly realm, at that. But even there I would be able to see through them. Here in Faery, they are the merest flicker of light, a trivial hindrance to the rankest novice on the Way."

"If they're so bad, what's the point? Why are they still working?"

"Am I to understand that they are not your spells?" The knight actually sounded surprised.

"A present from my father." Whom he didn't want to discuss. "You think I was a mage or something?"

"That is ob—" The knight put down his goblet. "Is it you who wish to test me, or do you do so under the command of another?"

The elf sounded offended. Which didn't make sense. As the visitor here, wasn't John the one who was supposed to be tested? And what was this "command of another" business? "I don't know what you're talking about."

The elf seemed puzzled by John's response. "You speak sincerely. Could it be that you are truly ignorant?"

John's anger flared with sudden heat; he'd never liked being called ignorant. He knew he didn't understand a lot about the otherworld. He couldn't help not knowing. It wasn't as though he'd grown up in Faery. This elven "better than thou" attitude was really starting to be prehistoric. "Yeah, I'm a real jerk. I don't know nothing. Okay?"

Slamming his fist down on the chair's arm, he upset his plate. The knight stayed him from fumbling after it, with a light touch on his arm. Jaw set, John looked away, finding the corbel supporting one of the room beams utterly absorbing; it was a cold deep place he could pour his frustrations.

"Let it go and calm yourself. I meant no offense." The elf waited until John had relaxed a little and released his death stare at the corbel before he spoke again. "I must admit to fault in myself; I was misled by how you found my keep. Now I think I begin to understand. I believe I would be correct to name you a changeling."

"Yeah, so?" The anger hadn't all drained away. "You got a problem with that?"

"It does explain certain things."

"Maybe you'd like to explain these certain things to me."

"Given the right circumstances, I would. But first, let us try something in the nature of an experiment."

John didn't like the sound of that. "What have you got in mind?"

"Nothing dangerous, I assure you. If you have not already learned it, our society is to a large degree based on merit and accomplishment. Here, little is accomplished without magic."

"I told you, I'm not a mage."

"Say rather that you have had no training."

What? The last shards of anger popped and vanished. "Are you saying I *am* a mage?"

"Mage is a word I would reserve for one who has considerable experience in the Way."

"What's this 'Way' stuff?"

"The Way is magic and magic is the Way. It is a path of art and craft and science by which one touches the stuff of the universe and binds it to one's will."

"I suppose it's got a light side and a dark side?"

"That sounds like a quote," the elf said.

"Maybe you should just tell me what you've got in mind."

"Very well. Now is not the time for philosophy. Now is the time for a demonstration. You must believe before you can take your first step along the Way." He gestured, and the dozen candles of the candelabra between their chairs went out. "You will relight one of them."

Right. "I haven't got a match."

"Without a match."

"You're gonna have a long wait, sir knight."

"I think not. Your temperament would seem to indicate an affinity for fire." The knight reached out and touched the central candle with his finger. "Take a good look at this, then close your eyes."

John closed his eyes and gave it a try.

"Clear your mind of all but the image of the candle. See it white against the black. Do you see it?"

He saw a candle, anyway. He wasn't sure that it was the one the knight had touched.

"It is incomplete, isn't it? What is the point of a candle that gives off no light? Concentrate on the image. See it as it should be. See the flame. Feel the heat. Smell the burning wick, the hot wax. Know it." The knight's voice was compelling, but John was having trouble conjuring the image. He felt hands on his temples, rubbing, and tension eased from him. More relaxed, he found it easier to picture the flame.

"See it as real," the knight coaxed.

John saw the flame in his mind's eye. The heat, the light, the smell, even the tiny, tiny sound of it. It began to seem real.

"Make it real."

That was exactly what he wanted to do. He wished the reality of the flame. He wished it hard. Something gave, and he felt heat rushing through him.

"By the Dark!" the knight exclaimed, shocking John out of his concentration.

John opened his eyes and saw that all twelve candles burned.

He'd done it. Not just one, but twelve little flames, all of his creation. It was wonderful. He'd called fire into being. If he could do this, what more was he capable of?

"Show me more."

The knight held up a cautionary finger. "Before we go further, I must know how you came to this realm. You did not make the crossing yourself, did you?"

"No." What did this have to do with learning magic?

"An elf came to you and helped you make the crossing."

"Are you guessing, or do you know?"

"It seems the most likely circumstance. Is it so?"

"Yeah."

"Did he tell you that he was your father?"

"Yeah."

"And do you believe him?"

John started to answer, to say yes, but a sudden surge of caution urged him to be circumspect. "Don't see that it's any of your business."

"You know very little of this realm." The knight turned his head slightly, to regard John from the corner of his eyes. With a gesture of his hand he conjured an image of Bennett. "Is this the elf who brought you to the realm?"

So much for withholding information; the knight already knew. "Yeah. Calls himself Bennett."

"Bennett," the elf said thoughtfully. "Very well, then, Bennett is what we shall call him."

Meaning it's not his real name. "You know him?"

"He and I are not of the same estate."

"You didn't answer my question."

"And you are very blunt and impolite, but I do not hold it against you. Doubtless you have had a deficient education."

"I had a very good education," John protested.

"Perhaps for the earthly realm. There is much you have to learn of your birthright, and of what is open to you because of your blood. Such things were closed to you in the other realm. They need not remain closed. For example, I can teach you to touch the magic in your soul."

Having had the taste of it, John wanted more. "Okay. I'm ready."

"Swear to me as apprentice and I will. I can open your heritage to you. With my guidance, you can reach your true potential."

John had always heard that an education wasn't free, but he'd never had to face the payments. "And what do I have to do for you?"

"For me? No more than any apprentice. A good student is reward enough for the teacher."

"There's a catch, isn't there? There's always a catch."

The knight laughed lightly. "You have been listening to too many stories told by humans. They harbor a most unkind prejudice. Would you like to try another spell?"

John nodded.

"There is very little that an untrained mind can initiate, but by the strength you have shown, I judge that you might be able to hold a spell that another casts. Would you like to try that?"

"What kind of spell?"

"An imaging."

"Okay."

"Good. Close your eyes again, and think of someone you would like to see. Think of someone you know well. Someone for whom you have strong feelings. Your best friend, perhaps. I will draw the image from your mind."

John thought of several people, but his thoughts kept flitting back to Faye. Whom else did he know so well?

"Ah, there. I have it."

The knight took John's right hand in both of his and turned it palm up. The elf's hands felt as though they were studded with a billion tiny needles.

"Do you feel the energy?"

How could he not? "Yeah," he whispered.

"Let emotion guide you as I release the spell to you; the strength of your feelings will aid what we do."

The knight took his hands away, but the prickly feeling remained.

"Open your eyes and see what we have conjured," he said.

John looked. Without a doubt it was Faye's image, but unlike the knight's earlier image of Bennett, this one was full figure. A tiny Faye stood stark naked on John's palm. John gaped at what his imagination had supplied. The image rippled and was gone as the magic fled his shattered concentration.

But for all the embarrassment the image caused him, it had brought wonder and joy as well. *He* had done magic. It was like a dream come true, and he wanted to shout with delight.

He was an elf, and he could *do* magic! The knight seemed pleased by John's foolish grin.

"This is but the faintest shadow of what is yours by birthright. You have but to claim it."

"How do I do that?"

"First, you must put away all that you have known. Now is the time for you to think of your future. You must come to your life in this realm with open arms, forgetting your life in the earthly realm."

Suddenly the dream seemed a little tarnished. "What about my friends?"

"They must go on without you. You came here without them; you have shown that you do not need them anymore. Soon you will understand that you never needed them. Ephemeral humans can lay no claim to an elf."

"Ephemeral?"

"You will see them wither and die while you enjoy the eternal moment of your own nature. Forget them. Ultimately they can mean nothing to an elf. Put your hands between mine and swear."

John looked at the narrow hands, the long tapering fingers. They were hands like his, fingers like his. Like the knight, he was an elf. Who better to teach him than another elf? But—

"What about my mother?"

"She is dead."

"That's what he said. But I meant my earthly mother."

"She is nothing."

Something in John couldn't accept that. Sure, John was an elf; but he was John Reddy, too. He wasn't ready to abandon his past. "I don't think I ought to sign on with you just now."

"You reject me?" the knight asked with a chill of winter in his voice.

"I just don't think the time's right. Maybe we could work something out later."

"You are a fool! Unworthy of my teaching." The knight sneered at him. "If you leave this place, you will never know true magic."

John felt his own anger rise. "How do *you* kno—"

Something flashed behind John's eyes, and for a moment he was blind. He panicked, flinging his arms up as though to ward off a blow. To his surprise, nothing came at him. Then he realized that he should have struck his goblet from the chair in his flailing. His sight cleared and he saw that he was no longer in the knight's hall. He sat alone on a rock in an empty field.

Of the knight and his tower there was no sign.

CHAPTER
22

Don't panic! Panic gets you dead.

Holger listened again.

Nothing. Try as he might, he could hear nothing and no one moving in the fog. The only noise, the soft rustle of cloth, came from Spae fidgeting annoyingly by his side. She was only willing to put up for so long with his demand for silence.

"Well?" she demanded.

"I don't hear any of them."

"We already knew that."

"Doctor, I think it would be wise to use a tether."

"I know you don't like being a watchdog; I would have thought you'd have even less liking for a leash."

"I am concerned for your safety, Doctor."

"We should have waited for Bennett."

"A moot point now. We should try to find some shelter before this chill saps our strength too far. Are you ready to start walking again?"

"All right," she agreed grumpily. "But no tether."

They set out again. The fog-bound world remained eerily quiet, the silence broken only by the sounds they made themselves. It was unnatural, disquieting, but strangely appropriate; the impenetrable fog made a fine metaphor for this magical place of nightmare. Fog was something you couldn't fight.

Holger desperately wanted to be somewhere else.

After an indeterminate period of time—he'd stopped relying on his chronometer when it told him it was noon while he could still see the moon in the star-filled night sky—they found a wall of stone. In the wall was a dark doorway offering access to some respite from the clammy mist. Holger flashed in a light and saw nothing extraordinary or dangerous, just a bare chamber where the fog was less dense. Another door across the room offered passage deeper into the structure. The curling tendrils of vapor that wafted in from the archway in which they stood did not seem to reach so far in. The room beyond might actually be free of the clinging mist.

He crossed the chamber to check it out. The space through the second doorway was a corridor rather than a room, its length sufficient to swallow Holger's light without revealing anything of note, including its other end. Not wise to stop here without knowing what was at the other end.

"We'd better give a look about before we rest, Doctor."

"Expecting an ambush?"

"I'm not *expecting* anything. I'm just being cautious."

The corridor went on for some distance, far enough that the doorway through which they'd come disappeared into the gloom. It was quiet here too, but at least there were proper echoes.

Still, there was something about this place.

He craned his head around, looking for some clue as to why this place should feel familiar. He got his answer as he turned and saw Spae reaching for a meter-long, greenish crystal cylinder that sat on a half-meter plinth of bloodstone. He knew this place now. He'd seen that cylinder before, seen the dark shape embedded in it, seen hands reaching for it.

Panic swelled in his throat, binding his limbs. It was almost too late. He fought it down, trying to warn her.

"Freeze, Doctor. Don't—"

It was too late.

Spae's fingers touched the crystal and virulent green light bloomed around her, encompassing her as the crystal surrounded its dark heart. Like that heart, she was still as stone.

Holger felt panic gnawing at his spine. Spae was frozen, as O'Connor had been. It was just like before, except it wasn't. He knew it couldn't be like before because Mannheim was dead, had been dead for three years now. And the damned crystal was smashed. Thoroughly, utterly destroyed. He'd made sure of that. "Destruction of a unique treasure," the *specialists* had said. And they meant *unique*, not simply rare, of that they had assured him. "Deplorable," they'd said.

But they hadn't been here—no! *there*—and the damned crystal shouldn't be *here*. But it *was* here. And Spae was trapped as thoroughly as O'Connor had been.

His nerves felt jagged, rubbed raw with broken glass. Everything around him stood in stark relief, like video effects without adequate dimensional compensation. The light from the faceted crystal threw Spae's lean shadow against walls and floor in sharp-edged, multiple images of his inadequacy.

But one of those shadows was neither acute nor thin. Nor was it rigid. Holger's eyes tracked the motion as he calculated angles. Locating the apparent position of whatever cast the shadow, Holger turned toward it, machine pistol ready.

There was something there. A *presence* of some sort.

He almost tightened his finger on the trigger, but stopped himself. Whatever this was, it hadn't been there before. Maybe it could help Spae.

"You are unusually perceptive, for a creature of the dirt," said a disembodied voice.

No, not disembodied, for as his eyes adapted to the gloom away from Spae's glowing prison, Holger began to perceive a form. It was transparent as glass, its outline easier to see than any details; it was roughly man-sized and man-shaped, but it was no man, transparent or otherwise. Its shoulders were humped and its lupine head thrust forward from the mass where the hulking shoulders met the mass of its neck. It was furred, and he could not tell if it wore any clothes. Despite its speech, he could think of it only as a beast.

Beast or not, the tint of green he perceived in the translucent creature matched that in the crystal, suggesting that it was somehow connected to Spae's entrapment.

"Release her," Holger demanded.

"You assume me capable of things beyond my power," the beast said. "For this moment, she must remain as she is."

Holger raised the Viper to his shoulder and snapped on the laser sight. The red targeting dot appeared on the wall behind the beast, but he put that from his mind and aimed as best he could. "I said, let her go."

"Threatening me will change nothing. Besides, if I were the key to her release, as you seem to believe, hurting me would not help her." Sharp teeth glinted in the gloom. "Time is the issue here, and time holds us all prisoner. An individual may only contrive escape for himself. You would do well to consider your own situation, for this locus is far more yours than hers." The beast shifted, but its motion was not threatening, so Holger didn't fire. "Time flows strangely here in the otherworld; and with time fluid, space must perforce follow. Moving in one is moving in the other. All is connected, though the paths may not be obvious. Do you remember this place?"

"Gibraltar." Hearing the truth in his own voice, he lowered the weapon from his shoulder. Sweat forming on his brow, he switched off the targeter. "The tunnel the workers found beneath the old armory."

"You remember it very clearly," the beast said.

Holger heard the soft pad of footfalls approaching from the darkened end of the corridor. His hands itched where flesh touched the warm plastic grips of the Viper. He knew what he would see if he turned around. He didn't want to look, but knew that he had to. Pivoting slightly, he kept his weapon pointed toward the beast while he turned his head to get a view of the corridor behind him. He saw what he had feared he would see: himself, moving cautiously along the corridor. O'Connor was right behind, gawking around like a tourist. Though Holger's image was as insubstantial as the beast's, O'Connor looked real and solid.

Had Holger come back to that time?

O'Connor and the ghostly Kun stopped next to where Holger stood. For the first time they saw the plinth and its deadly, deceptive burden. Apparently they couldn't see Spae pinned in the lambent light. The transparent Kun kept watch while O'Connor circled the waiting trap, examining it.

O'Connor was a specialist like Spae; he was the one supposed to deal with the weird stuff. Knowing about things like the crystal was his business. Holger's job was the physical security; and true to his training, the ghostly Kun steadfastly stood guard. Finally, inevitably, O'Connor stepped to where Spae stood and his hand reached out.

"No!" Holger wanted to shout, but the warning stuck in his throat. How could you change what was?

Hand overlaying Spae's hand, O'Connor's fingers contacted the crystal. Light flared, as it had. As it had. The floor shook, and deep rumblings growled through the surrounding stone. The floor around the plinth dropped away, making a moat of dust-filled darkness around the double-imaged, trapped mages.

"You know what's happening now, don't you?" the beast asked.

The words shocked into Holger's brain. He knew. He knew all too well.

Mannheim.

Mannheim always said you couldn't change anything you didn't try to change.

He hadn't been standing here watching himself stand in shocked paralysis before. That, at least, was difference. Maybe more could be different. Since Holger was here, maybe he *could* change it. How could he not try? Holger turned and ran down the corridor. Behind him, he knew his image would still be staring in shock at the changes in the chamber.

Too slow, Kun. Too stupid.

Ahead of him the stone barriers were closing to block the archway; one falling from above, one rising from below. The shifting flanges ground to a halt as he reached them. Last time they had already been jammed when he reached them. The granite teeth of the upper and lower panels, fangs in a closing mouth, gaped open less than half a meter from full closure. He skidded to a bruising halt against them.

He stuck his head through to look down the corridor that had been there the first time, not the room through which he and Spae had passed. Mannheim lay where he and O'Connor had left him, wrapped in the thermal sheet, shocky but still alive. Mannheim's blood spattered the stone redly where the trap had caught him. The *thing* hadn't arrived yet. There was still time. Holger tossed his Viper through and started to squirm between the teeth. The pouches of his vest snagged, but he shoved harder until something gave with a rip, allowing him to force his way through.

He was untangling his feet when the *thing* arrived, its twisted visage as clear before his eyes as it was in his memory. It looked a mockery of a man, made by a sculptor with little skill and too much redfire in his veins. The *thing* rotated its head, scanning past Holger and turning the dark pits of its eyes on Mannheim's helpless form. Its lipless mouth cracked open in a grin that showed dark flinty teeth.

Holger popped a pouch and felt the grenade drop into his hand. If he was quick enough, there was still a margin of safety. Slipping his thumb into the ring, he popped it and threw. The explosion erupted just behind the *thing*, where its mass would help shield Mannheim. Holger might have done nothing, for all the effect it had on the *thing*. The *thing* stalked forward, intent on Mannheim's supine form.

Holger snatched up the Viper. He knew better, but there wasn't anything else to do. He fired, emptying the magazine.

No effect.

The *thing* leaned over Mannheim, reaching out a blunt-fingered hand to touch his forehead. Mannheim screamed. And screamed.

Beyond the screams Holger heard the running footfalls. He was coming. Too late. Too late.

His insubstantial self stuck his head through the opening and perceived the danger. Too late. There was no time to get through, only time enough for—

His image opened fire. The 5mm slugs ripped into the *thing*, tearing away chunks, but no wounds showed. For long, anyway. The surface of the *thing* shifted, flowing into and filling the craters. His image's bullets had no more effect on it than they'd had that day.

Mannheim's screams died away to a throaty gurgle. The *thing* was finished with its feeding. It turned cold, dark pits of eyes on the insubstantial Kun and smiled its dark smile.

Holger sat down hard. It had been hopeless. Tears he had thought long banished returned to wet his cheeks.

He heard himself crying and cursing as, a few meters away, his image tried to squeeze past the teeth. The ghostly Kun struggled until cloth tore. Like last time. He ran to Mannheim, but Holger knew what he'd find. He had found it before. The transparent Kun stood next to Holger, staring down at Mannheim's husk. Though the body was still breathing, and would go on breathing for almost a year, Mannheim was gone.

Deader than dead.

Again.

His image slumped to the floor, tears coursing down his cheeks. Holger felt a brief shock when the image overlaid him; then he was alone, staring at an empty stretch of corridor.

"So tragic. It need not be that way," the beast said.

Mannheim, Holger, and O'Connor came through the door at the end of the corridor. The cycle was starting again.

Another chance?

Holger forced himself to his feet. His image was the only one that did not look real. His own hand held before his face looked as solid and substantial as his former companions. He remembered the shock he'd felt when his image had collapsed in grief and touched him.

He walked up behind his image. A tentative touch brought a tingle. He stepped forward, standing where the image stood, and his whole body tingled as Holger blended with Kun. He went through the same motions. So easy, so familiar.

If he could direct the actions differently, he could take the trap, so Mannheim wouldn't be injured. Things would have to be different after that.

Holger walked beside Mannheim as he had that day. As they neared the trigger, he stepped forward directly onto the false stone in the floor, while his image turned away as he had that day. The tingle of separation rippled through him.

Moving through the space Holger occupied, Mannheim took the fatal step.

"You can't do it that way," the beast told him. "You are not in phase with them, for time still flows past you. You need the doctor's staff."

The rumble began. The stone balls shot from their tubes. The same one caught Mannheim in the same shoulder; it smashed muscle and bone again, just as it had before. The other balls smashed against the far wall, shattering into deadly splinters that ripped and tore. Mannheim went down in a welter of blood.

Helplessness draining him of all motivation, Holger watched as O'Connor and the ghostly Kun tended the injured Mannheim. He listened to their assurances and knew them false.

The beast spoke from behind him. "You know what will happen."

Holger spun to face it, screaming, "Why are you doing this to me?"

"You can do something about it. Change it."

"What can I do? I've tried! I can't change anything!"

They were back in the crystal's chamber. Spae was still locked in ice, but O'Connor's shape no longer overlay hers. The beast spoke.

"Take the staff. Accept the magic."

He hated magic. Magic had killed Mannheim. "No. No magic. It's not natural. It doesn't belong."

"But it does belong. It's the only solution. *His* only hope."

A ghostlike Holger Kun was just entering the chamber. Right behind him came O'Connor.

"Take Spae's magic," the beast said. "You can save Mannheim with it."

"You can go back to hell."

Holger pointed the Viper's muzzle at the beast and triggered a burst. The bullets went right through it to chip flakes from the stone of the wall. The beast laughed, while the ghostly Kun and O'Connor discovered the plinth and the cylinder.

Again.

O'Connor touched the crystal cylinder.

Again.

Holger emptied his magazine into the beast, screaming, "Stop it! Stop it! Stop it! Stop it!" until his throat was raw.

His shouting couldn't drown out the screams from the exterior chamber. Kun's image ran back into the blackness of the corridor as the Viper clicked empty. There was no noise now to mask Mannheim's screams.

He had failed. Again. Holger hung his head, eyes blinded with fresh tears. When he looked up, he and O'Connor were entering the chamber again.

"The staff," the beast prompted.

Holger looked at it longingly. Mannheim always said you can't unmake your decisions. What if he was wrong?

But whom was a man to believe in? A thing of magic or the mentor who had taught you how to make life livable? Mannheim had known the answer to that and had taught it to Holger.

There was no choice to be made, because a man could only make one choice.

Holger threw himself on the beast. Through it, actually. He bounced from the hard gritty stone. The beast snarled at him, baring its teeth. But instead of leaping on him, it recoiled. For a moment it seemed more substantial. Holger seized that moment, making it his as Mannheim had always counseled. He drew his boot knife and flung it. His aim was poor—a transparent beast was a difficult target—but the thing howled as steel embedded itself in its shoulder.

It took a step back, then staggered as a bolt of energy hit it.

Spae lowered her staff, looking to see what her magic had done. She was no longer trapped within the column of light. Holger didn't know how she had done it, but he was glad she had. Face knotted with rage and determination, Spae raised her staff, pointing it at the beast. Another bolt leapt from its tip, crackling into the beast and raising a smell like burning fur.

The beast howled. It stepped sideways and was—gone.

As if it had never been.

Spae took a deep breath and let it out in a sigh that sounded as though it had come from her feet.

"I'm glad it's gone. I don't think I have enough left to hit it again," Spae said. Her knees buckled, but she retained a strong enough grip on her staff that Holger was able to reach her in time to ease her to the floor.

"Thanks," she said.

"Are you all right, Doctor?"

"Me? You're the one that thing was slavering over."

"I don't seem to have been quite what it wanted." He rubbed at a spot on his cheek that was stinging; his hand came away bloody. He didn't remember receiving the wound. "How did you escape the crystal's trap?"

Spae shook her head. "I haven't got that completely sorted out. You're right, though, the crystal *was* a trap; it sent me somewhere else, a place outside the otherworld, yet not back to our own world. I don't think I can explain it. No, I *know* I can't explain it. At least not to you, because you're not open to magic; you couldn't go there, so you won't be able to understand."

Holger was not sure he wanted to understand, but he was glad she was back. Spae went on, trying to explain the unexplainable.

"I—I learned something there. A lot of things, actually. It was a bit humbling. I think the beast expected me to be helpless there, but I learned some things and used some of what I learned to find my way back to this locus."

"The magic told you how to escape the trap?"

"Well, that, and the tug on my staff."

Was there an accusation in her tone? "I never touched your staff."

She nodded. "But the beast wanted you to take it, didn't it?"

And he had almost succumbed to the temptation. He felt a need to confess. "It told me I could use your staff to—to help someone."

"It lied. If you'd touched the staff I would have been lost forever, and you wouldn't have been any better off. You're a mundane; you wouldn't be able to use the staff. You couldn't have helped anyone with it."

So it had been a false temptation, had it? Or had it? "How do you know that?"

"It's something I learned in that other place. I'll tell you more if you want, but I have to warn you that it's magic, and fairly esoteric magic at that. I don't think you'll want to hear it."

"You're right. I don't want to hear it." He'd take her word for it.

"You don't look like you're in very good shape," she said sympathetically. The concern didn't fit his image of her, but he found he liked it.

"I'll survive." He'd gotten this far, hadn't he?

"I expect you will," she said thoughtfully. "But I must tell you, Mr. Kun, I think we're *both* lucky that my return disrupted the beast's spells."

"I was told never to believe in luck, Doctor."

"Times change, Mr. Kun."

"No, they don't, Doctor." She started to speak, but he cut her off. "Doctor, the walls! They're dissolving!"

It did appear that they were, but Spae made no move; she just squinted and said, "I'd wager they were never really there."

Holger wouldn't have taken that bet on his life.

They were in a field. It was still night, but the fog was gone, and the star-dusted sky of the otherworld sparkled above their heads. Holger immediately snapped alert, slapping a new magazine into the Viper.

"I hear something."

"It sounds like someone chopping wood," Spae said.

The sound seemed to come from beyond a rise to their left. Together they crept up the slope. Holger motioned the doctor to remain below the crest, and to his surprise she did so without complaint. He dropped to a crouch, then to all fours as he approached the crest. Finally on his belly, he raised his head to where he could see down into the next vale.

There he saw Bear, looking haggard and battered, determinedly hacking down a sapling with a belt knife. Holger called Spae forward and started over the hill himself. Bear looked up and waved as Holger stood. The first thing Bear said was, "Got any ammo? I've about used mine up."

Holger didn't ask how or why, he just tossed a fresh magazine to Bear. It was better not to know. Bear tossed away the sapling. "Don't need this now." Picking up his machine pistol, he slapped home the magazine. "You didn't tell me how fast this stuff is used up."

"Shorter bursts or single shots."

"Yeah. I should've remembered."

Maybe later Holger would ask. Later, under a real sky, in a real world.

CHAPTER
23

"He's over here!"

It was Faye's voice.

John looked around to see Faye running down the slope toward him. The sight of her, long silver hair streaming behind and white dress flapping in the breeze of her rush, banished his worries.

Behind her, Trashcan Harry came over the crest. The goblin had lost his crutch somewhere and replaced it with a crooked tree limb. Harry was making better speed than he had been making and appeared to be in better health; the otherworld seemed to have a restorative effect on him. Maybe the air was better for goblins here, maybe they needed magic to heal.

But questions didn't seem important with Faye running toward him, a happy smile on her face. A few feet from him she launched herself into the air, arms outstretched. John caught her, but the impact staggered him back and half spun him around. It was fortunate that she was so light; otherwise they would both have been sprawled on the grass. Her arms encircled his neck and she hugged him fiercely. He hugged her back, immensely pleased to see her safe.

They broke their clinch only when Trashcan Harry arrived. John became acutely aware of many things at once: the warmth of Faye's body, his own rather, uh, strong reaction to it, the goblin's watching eyes. He put Faye down. She still clung to his arm, taking both John and Harry into the radiance of her smile.

"John, you don't know how worried we were."

We were, not *I was.* Maybe she wasn't as personally interested in him as he'd thought—hoped—that she was. He caught Trashcan Harry leering at him and flushed. He rubbed at his cheeks to hide the redness, hoping his gesture would be taken as thoughtful. To complete the illusion, he asked a question.

"Where are the others?"

Faye looked confused. "They're not with you?"

"No."

"Maybe they gave up and went home," Harry suggested.

"Bear wouldn't give up," John said.

"Too stupid," Harry groused.

John put Trashcan Harry's remark down to the old animosity toward Bear, and ignored it. "We'll have to find them. Faye, you can fly. Could you do an aerial search?"

She looked away. "It's different here, John. I can't do everything that I could in the sunlit world."

Just looking at her made it obvious that there were things she could do here that weren't possible back home. Be seen, for one. For another— John cut off that line of thought. They were in the otherworld, not a park in the Benjamin Harrison Town Project; the others could be in danger or hurt or . . .

"We should start looking for them." He pointed at the nearest and tallest hill. "We'll head over there. We should be able to see quite a ways from there."

Trashcan Harry turned his head to look at the hill, but stayed leaning on his crutch. He swung his head back and looked at John from under his dark brows. "Do you think that's a good idea, Jack? I mean, if they're looking for us too, we could wander around missing each other. Maybe we should stay here and wait for them to find us."

"That might work if there were just Kun and Dr. Spae to consider, but Bear will push on. You know he will, Harry."

"Yeah," Harry admitted reluctantly.

"Well, come on, then."

The hill gave them the view John wanted; they spotted the others marching in a line directly away from their position. Bear was in the lead, striding determinedly, and Spae was moving briskly as well. Kun was bringing up the rear; he was the only one looking around, but somehow John didn't think it was for him, or Faye, or Trashcan Harry.

John ran on ahead, leaving Faye to help Harry make his best speed. He shouted when he thought he'd gotten within earshot, but Kun didn't look in his direction. It seemed that the air of the otherworld dampened noise, shortening the distance sound carried, much as it scattered light to cut the range of clear vision. John kept going, closing a third of the distance before trying again. This time Kun did hear, spinning and pointing his weapon. He put it up when he recognized John and shouted for Bear to hold up.

The reunion involved a lot of earnest questions about people's conditions, but all involved seemed curiously reluctant to provide details of what had happened to them while they were separated. John knew he didn't want to talk about his visit with the elven knight; the whole episode seemed somehow best kept private.

While they waited for Faye and Trashcan Harry to join them, John saw that he had caught the others just in time. Beyond the hill on which they stood lay a forest of dark, towering trees that went on in an unbroken ocean of leaves as far as he could see in the twilight. It was awe-inspiring in its primeval beauty. This, he thought, was what the land might have looked like before the European colonists came.

Faye and Harry had barely reached the crest of the hill when Bear headed off, saying, "Come on." He walked straight toward the forest.

And into it.

The open country and its occasional woods had been strange to a city boy like John, but this shadowed stand of massive trees was as different from any woods he had been in as a rezcom was from a trash-district shanty. The most noticeable difference was that it was much darker in the shade of the forest giants, darker than anywhere he'd yet seen in the otherworld. There wasn't much in the way of underbrush between the huge boles, which seemed strange until he considered how little light penetrated the canopy of leaves high above their heads. Their feet scuffed through a deep carpet of brown leaves, and though their passage sounded loud to John's ears, the silent trees seemed not to mind. There was a deep peacefulness here within the forest that soothed him, and urged him to forget that he had ever dwelt among the concrete barrens of the earthly realm. Had it not been for the brisk pace that Bear set, John might have lingered to listen to the silent songs of the trees; they were so old, and they must have seen so much.

But even the forest doesn't last forever, and soon John noticed a curious lightening in the direction Bear led them. Not long after, they encountered brush and saplings, and finally emerged from the embrace of the great trees onto a shoreline.

Mist hung over the water, obscuring everything beyond about ten yards. The farther shore was invisible. It might have been a river or a lake, or even an ocean. It didn't smell of salt and there didn't seem to be a current, so John decided it had to be a lake. No lake had been visible from the hill. A small body of water might be hidden under the cover of the leaves, but judging from how the shoreline stretched out of sight in either direction, this was no small body of water.

With sudden certainty, John knew it was no ordinary body of water, either.

Kun looked out across the water, his index finger twitching slightly where it lay along the trigger guard of his machine pistol.

"I don't like the fog," he complained.

"There's magic here," John said.

"He's right," Spae agreed.

"This is not news," Kun pointed out sourly.

Bear ignored the byplay, staring fixedly out over the water. Finally he turned to them with a strange glint in his eye and said quietly, "She is here."

"She? Who's she?" Bear ignored Kun's question, setting out along the shoreline at a brisk pace. Kun hollered after him. "Who is she?"

Bear kept moving, disappearing around a finger of the forest that thrust out the shoreline.

"He will go on without us if we don't follow," Spae said.

Kun shot her a dark look and strode after Bear.

John understood Kun's frustration; he wanted to know too. But Bear was being Bear, talking only when he wanted to. John followed too.

They caught up with Bear at a narrow spit of sand, where he was inspecting a small rowboat.

"This is the way we must go," he said when they had gathered around his find.

"I don't like the fog," Kun said again.

Laying a hand on his arm, Spae said, "I think it will be all right this time."

He didn't look reassured.

"Boat doesn't look like it'll hold all of us," Trashcan Harry said.

"Nonsense," Bear said. "She could carry ten men in full war harness."

"Looks leaky," Harry said.

"Goblin courage." Bear shook his head. "Stay here, then. You can stay if you want too, Kun. Jack and I can handle her. Jack, help the others on, then we'll shove her out."

While John was still nodding yes, Kun stepped aboard, saying, "Hard to get separated in a boat."

John helped Dr. Spae first, steadying her as she climbed aboard. Turning to help Faye, he found her whispering to Trashcan Harry. Their conversation stopped as John faced them. Whatever they were talking about, they didn't want to share it with him. She might just have been trying to convince Harry to come along; her expression was unreadable, but the distinctly unhappy look the goblin was giving the boat said he hadn't changed his opinion.

Faye took John's outstretched hand and climbed aboard the boat with superb grace. Trashcan Harry stood fidgeting on the shore. Bear gave him only a brief look before bending to put his shoulder to the bow of the boat. After his own brief glance, John bent to help Bear.

The boat seemed reluctant to leave its berth on the sand. They leaned into it and slowly got the boat moving. The pushing got easier as the water took more and more of the weight.

"Hop in, Jack," Bear ordered.

John scrambled aboard, feeling the keel grate as his weight was added to the craft's load. Bear gave another shove and the boat wallowed free. In an instant he was aboard as well.

"Wait!" Harry shouted as he waded into the water. "Wait for me!"

Bear scowled at the goblin splashing toward them, but he stopped his preparation of the oars and waited for Harry to awkwardly haul himself aboard. Setting the oars into the locks, Bear explained to John how to hold an oar and how to use his legs and back for the power, demonstrating the stroke in the air so John could see. The water's resistance to John's first stroke surprised him, but he bent to with a will. It still took a while before John got the hang of it, but Bear was good enough at it to compensate for John's poor efforts. He probably could have done the job alone.

The rowing put John and Bear with their backs to the boat's bow and the direction of travel. John kept trying to turn around to see where they were going, until Bear told him not to worry about their heading, he was taking care of that. John didn't know how Bear was managing it, but he put his trust in Bear's competence. To his surprise, the job of rowing got easier when he stopped trying to see. Facing the back of the boat, he could see only Trashcan Harry. The goblin looked miserable as he sat in the stern, intermittently dipping his tree limb into the water. When Bear noticed, he snapped at Harry.

"Drop it, or pull it in and keep it in! Otherwise you'll be using it as a raft."

Harry winced and pulled his crutch back aboard. No one said much of anything; the creak of the oarlocks, the splash of the oars in the water, and the rowers' grunts of effort were the only sounds. All around them the mist grew ever heavier, until they could see nothing beyond an oar's length from the boat.

The sense of *something* that John had felt earlier returned, redoubled. He could feel magic all around him. He hadn't felt anything in the fog that had separated all the companions. So why was he feeling it now? Was the magic stronger here? Or had his experience with the knight sensitized him?

The air grew clammier as the fog enwrapped them more closely.

John looked up, searching for the moon. He found it, a faint, pale disk in the misty sky. Something moved across that silver orb, something shadowy. John strained to see what sort of bird flew the night skies of the otherworld. He lost his stroke when he saw that it was not a bird, but a fish.

"Steady, Jack," Bear said. "Keep your mind on the rowing."

He tried, but he couldn't help stealing glances at the sky— if that was what was above them. There weren't a lot of fish in the sky, but schools of them swam—flew?—above the boat. He wondered what would happen if they had to abandon ship. Would they splash down into water, or could they swim away toward the moon?

After a time, Bear threw a glance over his shoulder and grunted with satisfaction. John couldn't resist; he looked for himself. The fog had cleared enough that he could see they were headed for a rocky shored island. A low wall seemed to rise directly from the rocks, and beyond it was greenery. Two concentric walls lay beyond that, ringing a tall, slender tower at what John presumed was the center. John could see the roofs of lesser buildings scattered within the rings. A gate of wrought metal was set in the outer wall, just above a broad set of steps that led to a dressed stone jetty.

Bear pulled hard on his oar, turning them toward the landing place.

"Pull, Jack. We're almost there."

John pulled. He didn't turn his head to look again until the boat's bow bumped against the stone. When he did look, he saw that someone awaited them, an elven lady in a long gown of shimmering silver fabric. Unlike all the elves John had seen, she had golden hair, but there was no doubt that she was an elf; her fine-boned features were of surpassing delicacy and configured in a beauty beyond any he had seen. A belt of intricately wrought gold links girdled her hips and vied for attention with the tall, pointed circlet of gold on her head. The crown said that she was royalty, but John suspected that even without it she would have had the air of a queen.

"I have been expecting you, Artos," she said in a voice as melodious as bells.

Bear sprang to the jetty, leaving the boat rocking behind him. "I don't intend to stay this time, Lady."

"I understand."

As he helped John to maneuver the boat alongside the stone landing, Kun whispered to John, "I thought he hated all elves."

"So did I."

Bear waited until they had all come ashore before making introductions.

"This lady is Viviane, *Domina Lacorum*. Until recently she was my hostess."

"The Lady of the Lakes," Spae whispered.

The elven queen turned her blue-green eyes to Dr. Spae and smiled, inclining her head slightly.

"Come inside," she said. "If you will."

Holger had read about the Lady of the Lake in the briefing folder about Arthur; or, more correctly, the Ladies of the Lake. The legends as they had come down suggested that it was more an order of priestesses than a single noble entitlement. "Viviane" had been one of the names in the folder, but Holger couldn't remember whether that name had gone with the bad witch or the good witch. This Viviane might not be the same person in any case. Still, she bore watching.

He didn't want to be here at this odd palace, but Spae was here and so he was here, like it or not. Protecting Spae was more than business now. The thought of forever reliving the day Mannheim had died chilled him beyond all reason, and she was responsible for their escape from the beast. He owed her.

The gates that opened as they approached didn't make him feel any better about the place. He couldn't spot any proximity sensors. So what had been used to open them? He supposed there might be a servant concealed somewhere watching the gate, opening it, then scurrying away. Somehow he didn't think that such an explanation, however rational, was the right one. He didn't want to admit magic was involved, but he was sure he was getting deeper and deeper into places where magic replaced logic.

The grip of the Viper was hard and reassuring under his hand.

The Lady led them to a building within the second wall that looked to John like some sort of Greek revival temple on the outside. The inside was totally different; the best description he could think of was a cross between an airport lounge and a museum gallery. The interior was subdivided into areas of varying levels separated by no more than a half-dozen shallow steps. Railings and room dividers of stone separated some of the areas, while plants and glass cases demarcated others. Exquisite paintings hung on the walls, and sculptures in many sizes and materials were scattered about. Antiquities of various sorts occupied some of the cabinet shelves or stood in the open, on pedestals or, in the case of what looked like a Roman chariot, directly on the floor. The decorator's fee for the place would have beggared a major corporation; the cost of acquiring the contents would have done in a megacorp.

"Feel free to look about. There are refreshments by the reflecting pool. Please indulge yourselves."

Spae was the first to oblige, taking the two steps down into a carpeted area. The doctor stopped at the first case with an exclamation of surprise. She bent over to study whatever had caught her attention, blocking John from seeing it. Trashcan Harry went past her, heading for the reflecting pool. John was torn between seeing what treasures were here and heading for the food; it seemed that rowing had worked up an appetite. He'd just about made up his mind to follow Harry when he noticed that Bear was standing still, arms folded, and staring at Lady Viviane. Bear cleared his throat to attract her attention.

"Lady?"

She favored him with a smile. "Still no patience, Artos."

"When necessary, Lady."

"And you do not find it necessary to indulge me?"

"I came with a purpose. I know that you have it near."

"And so I do."

A shaft of light appeared in one of the darker areas halfway across the chamber. Impaled within the beam stood a block of what looked like ice. A sword hilt protruded from the block.

Caliburn.

John moved toward the sword almost unconsciously, noting the details of its appearance as he drew nearer. The long, tapering blade was visible through its crystalline sheath; it was pitted and corroded, stained dark with rust. It looked like one of the older blades in the Woodman Museum's collection, one that had been in the ground for a dozen centuries. The hilt was in better shape, its grip wrapped with dark leather above the simple crossguard. The best-preserved part was the disk-shaped pommel decorated with an engraving of a dragon coiled about itself.

It didn't look like a legendary blade, but . . .

"That's Caliburn?"

"It is," Bear said solemnly.

The sword was a puzzle, leaving John both awed and distressed. He could feel the power residing in it, lying dormant like the sleeping dragon on the pommel, but the sword looked so . . . battered. How could this tarnished relic be the fabled sword?

He looked to Bear for an answer, but couldn't ask when he saw the anguish on the man's face.

"Caliburn is a mirror of the land," the Lady said.

Artos nodded sadly. "This, then, is the peril for which I was awakened?"

"The land must be healed," replied the Lady.

Bear bowed his head, and it seemed to John that his shoulders bent under an invisible burden. But only for a moment. Bear raised his head and stepped forward, hand reaching for the hilt.

His fingers never touched it.

A thunderous sound shattered the peace of the chamber. Bear's hand jerked away from Caliburn as some force spun him around. Arms flailing, he slammed into the glassy column. Man and block crashed to the floor.

CHAPTER 24

John stood stunned as Kun launched himself into the air, firing his machine pistol. He slammed into Dr. Spae and the two of them tumbled to the floor behind one of the couches. Automatic-weapon fire ripped into their shelter, sending puffs of upholstery and splinters of wood flying.

John couldn't see who was shooting, and realized that they must not be able to see him either. That was all that had saved him while he stood there like an idiot, looking down at Bear's sprawled form and the red stain spreading across his shoulder and onto his upper chest. Belatedly he moved, grabbing Faye and pulling her down behind one of the cabinets. She squawked when they landed and he was afraid he'd hurt her, but as soon as he rolled off she was up and peering through the glass. He joined her, trying to see what was going on.

From his new angle he could see a hole hanging in the space between two of the columns of the north colonnade. A *hole*? What else could you call a circle, bounded by an eye-searing rainbow of colors, whose center seemed to be somewhere else? Though where that someplace else might be, the swirling, pearly white of the hole gave no clue.

Men leapt over the lower bound of the rainbow. Most carried automatic weapons. Most were short and broad figures. All wore black clothes, combat vests, and helmets with dark, featureless visors. One of the short figures stood to one side of the hole, shouting orders and pointing his shotgun toward the fallen Bear. To the crack of his voice, the invaders landed on the floor of the Lady's house, rolling to take the shock. One after another they bounced up and scrambled away in random directions to seek cover among the Lady's furnishings.

John had seen outfits such as they wore before, on the night Mitsutomo had raided MaxMix Manor. He'd heard that voice as well, ordering the other murderers to concentrate on "the sleeper."

From somewhere behind the nearby chariot, Trashcan Harry started shouting.

"I'm sorry! I couldn't help it. They made me do it!"

One of the dark figures popped up from behind a planter overgrown with rhododendron. His weapon burped. Trashcan Harry began jerking as slugs slammed into his body and sent him sprawling over a low railing into the area in which John and Faye cowered.

The goblin was exposed where he lay, so John grabbed Harry's hand and tugged hard. Harry moaned with pain, but slid a foot closer to cover. John was able to get a second hand on Harry's arm and start pulling him to safety behind the case. Some of the Mitsutomo raiders opened fire. Glass rained down on John as he tugged on the limp goblin. Harry's body slid suddenly and the motion forced John almost upright. Something buzzed past his ear. He dove for the floor. Unfortunately, Harry's smelly body was between him and the cool stone. The goblin whoofed when John landed on him.

"Lay down some fire, Reddy!" Kun shouted.

"Harry's hurt," John told him.

"Damn the goblin. We're all dead if you don't do something."

Kun knew about these sorts of things; he was probably right. In an awkward rush, John unslung the Viper and clicked the selector to full autofire. Without looking, he poked it around the case and pulled the trigger. The recoil nearly pulled the weapon out of his hand. The black-clad men fired back, forcing John to huddle behind the case.

"I'm sorry, Jack," Trashcan Harry moaned. "I didn't want to do it, but they hurt me. They made me do it."

"Do what?" Faye sounded infuriated. John knew instantly he never wanted her to use that tone of voice on him.

"Open the door," Harry whined. "They put a tracker under my skin."

Faye slapped the goblin across the face, and he whimpered.

With a shout, a knot of the raiders burst from their hiding places, running forward under covering fire from their fellows. Something small and black arced out from Kun's position to meet them.

A grenade.

The explosion broke the charge, scattering men like tenpins. One of the attackers, a man much taller than the rest, was lifted off his feet by the explosion and tossed back through the hole. In his flight, he struck the short one with the shotgun, knocking him backward. The man flung out an arm to regain his balance and his flailing hand struck the rainbow fringes of the opening. Screaming, he was sucked into the rainbow.

The survivors crawled for cover, but Kun showed them no mercy, firing at anything that moved. John joined in, sticking his head up enough to see what he was shooting at. His fire caught one of the raiders dashing between a couch and a cabinet. The man fell without a sound. But instead of lying there bleeding, he turned black, not the cloth black of his clothes, but a total, utter, light-swallowing black.

And then he was gone.

Only a few drops of blood remained to show that he had ever been there.

The firing died down. There was furtive movement on the other side of the chamber, but none of the attackers showed themselves. John thought he heard voices and guessed that the raiders were conferring. Kun took the opportunity for a conference of their own.

"Bear dead?"

"Can't tell," John replied. "Don't see much blood, but he's not moving."

"Anybody else hurt?"

Faye shook her head, her tousled hair and hard-eyed expression making her look feral. She held a knife she'd gotten from somewhere.

"Just Harry," John said.

"Fuck him. You see the elf lady anywhere?"

The Lady of the Lakes seemed to have disappeared.

"Not since the shooting started. She was standing right next to Bear."

"Elves don't seem to be much for hanging around when it drops into the pot."

John couldn't deny that.

"How's the doctor?"

"Bumped her head. She's too dizzy to be helpful."

Faye laid her hand on his arm. "John, they're surrounding us."

"Better shift over here, Reddy. I'll cover you."

"What about Harry?"

"Leave him."

"But I can't—"

"John, they're coming. Let's go." Faye ran toward Kun's position.

John followed. Miraculously, they made it to where Kun and Spae were waiting without getting hit.

"Only two firing on overwatch," Kun said. "That would make a half-dozen unaccounted for."

"Over by Caliburn's place," Faye said.

"Flankers," Kun pronounced them.

John looked and caught a glimpse of a black figure disappearing behind a cabinet. Another flashed between a dividing wall and one of the couches. Kun ordered them to shift around to a position where they would have cover from both the overwatchers and the flankers. By the time he was satisfied, they were under fire again and the flanking raiders were advancing across the area where Bear had gone down.

Looking like a bloody spirit of vengeance, Bear rose up behind the flankers. He held Caliburn in his hand. He raised the sword high, adding his free hand on the pommel to take a two-handed grip as he advanced. Their overwatchers spotted him, but with partners between them and Bear, they shouted a warning instead of firing. The raider nearest Bear tried to turn and face the threat, but he didn't get halfway around. Bear swept the sword down, burying it in the man's shoulder. The raider fell with a strangled cry, blackening as Bear pulled the sword free. Bear stepped through the space the man had occupied and was in among the rest of the flanking party, sword swinging.

Kun's elbow jogged John out of his openmouthed inactivity. The agent popped up to fire at the raiders on overwatch. John rolled to the edge of the cover to add his weapon fire to Kun's effort. Just then, the raiders around Bear broke, scrambling away. Two more of them had gone down to Bear's sword work. The two survivors fired as they ran, but Bear was too fast, ducking to safety behind one of the low walls.

The failure of the flanking maneuver seemed to sap the raiders' will. They started retreating toward the hole in the air, firing as they went.

"Let them go," Kun shouted.

The black-clad forms leapt over the rainbow line into the nacreous white and vanished one by one. The polychromatic circle contracted into a ball and winked out. Whoever they were, they were gone, gone back to wherever they came from.

"And good riddance to them."

John and Kun, weapons ready, spun at the sound of the voice, but Bennett didn't look at all impressed.

CHAPTER 25

With a ripple of air, the Lady of the Lakes appeared at Bennett's side; and that, John supposed, was what saved him. At least John was sure that was why he hadn't tightened his finger on the trigger of his machine pistol; no one seemed interested in hurting the Lady. Not that he wanted to shoot Bennett, but the fight with the raiders had left him ready to fire at any unexpected thing and Bennett's appearance was certainly unexpected. With a sigh of released tension, John lowered the weapon.

"You can come out now, Artos," Bennett called. "I know you have Caliburn, so you're not going to surprise me with it."

Bear emerged from behind a cabinet. Blood streamed from his wounded shoulder and he was shaky on his feet. "You're late again, Bennett."

Bennett chuckled. "As usual, you misunderstand. I wanted Caliburn free."

"You'll never take it from me."

"I don't intend to. You've already accomplished what I sought. Caliburn unbound is what I sought. That, and my son."

"What?"

Bennett laughed at Bear's confusion. "I thought it most amusing that you took him as your 'man.' "

"Jack, what's he talking about?"

"See for yourself," Bennett said.

John felt a blast of hot air. Bear's eyes went wide, as though he were seeing John for the first time. In a way, he was; John didn't need a mirror to know that his true face and form had been revealed at last. Bear's gaze passed from John to Bennett and back, his expression darkening into a scowl.

"I've been blind. You've been a serpent in my camp all along."

"Bear, I—"

"Speak no more to me, traitor."

Bear moved over to Kun and Spae, but kept his face turned from John. In a way it made it easier. The expressions on the faces of the other two were hard enough to bear. Too hard. John turned away to avoid seeing their betrayed looks.

"Behind you, Jack," Bennett called, gesturing over John's shoulder as he spoke.

To the tolling of a great iron bell, John turned to see Kun and Spae standing unnaturally still. Kun's weapon was half raised and a faint light flickered around the tip of Spae's staff. It died even as John saw it. Bear was stepping forward, Caliburn ringing in his hand. Bear took another step toward John and Bennett. At John's side, the elf gestured again. The sword tolled as the spell struck, but the tone cut off as Caliburn slipped from Bear's grip. The blade clattered as it hit the floor, not like a bell at all. Bear came on and Bennett gestured yet again. Bear, shorn of the sword's protection, stilled into immobility.

"You see, Jack? He is not so great and powerful, after all. Just another lumbering human who is ready to kill an elf without asking questions first."

"Questions like, what do you think you're doing?"

"Exactly like that. I took action only to ensure your safety."

"They wouldn't hurt me."

"You trust them far too much." Bennett held out a slim-bladed dagger of dark metal. "Take this, Jack."

John took it; it was lighter than he expected.

"The blade is ensorcelled and will pass through the stasis."

"You want me to kill him," John said, not really believing it.

"Now that he knows who and what you are, he will try to kill you. You heard what he called you. In his time, a traitor to the king was killed out of hand. Act now, and save yourself trouble in the future."

John looked into Bear's face. Could he hear what was being said? Was what Bennett was saying true? Bear's lips remained frozen, and his still, staring eyes held no answer.

John was on his own.

Savagely he thrust the dagger back at Bennett. "If you want him dead so badly, why don't you do it yourself? He's helpless. He can't hurt you."

"I could kill him. Perhaps I will yet. I thought, however, that you deserved the chance."

"To commit murder?"

"One cannot murder lesser life-forms."

"He's a human being!"

Bennett raised an eyebrow. "I will say one thing in his favor; for all that he was only a human, Artos understood the value and importance of symbols. He became a rather powerful one himself to his fellows. Don't you think it fitting that he be a symbol one last time?"

"What do you mean?"

"Show me you know your blood, Jack. There before you is the symbol of mankind, of the life you knew: a king of the earthly realm. Throw off that mundane yoke. Strike off your fetters, by striking down the tie that binds you to the dross of their realm. Kill him, and be free to take up your heritage."

Was this the price of being an elven prince?

"I can't."

"Of course you can. If you don't want to use the dagger, use your gun. Or—yes, I think he would understand that the best—use the sword. I can free it from the spell. Having lived by it, Artos would surely appreciate dying by it. An honorable death, by his lights."

"No!"

"I told you he wouldn't," said the Lady to Bennett.

Bennett frowned. "Jack, there is no more time for foolishness."

"If being an elf means being a murderer, I want no part of it. I'd rather be human."

"There is no place for humans here."

"Then I'll go home."

"And be used against me?"

"I don't want anything to do with you."

"You cannot change who you are."

"Look, just let me go home. Let us all go home. We'll stay out of your way."

"I think not."

Bennett called fire to his hand as he had that night in the museum. John looked fearfully at the growing flames. He was not a mage like Nym; he had no defenses against those deadly energies.

Faye threw herself between Bennett and John, taking the brunt of the spell. She screamed and bent over at the waist as though she'd been gut-punched when the fire hit her, but the flames died out. She straightened, trembling, and faced Bennett.

"Your job is done," Bennett told her.

"Come away, little one," the Lady said.

Still trembling, Faye shook her head. She held her knife out, pointed at Bennett.

A contemptuous sneer on his face, he called the fire again and cast it at her. It wreathed her, clinging as she crumpled to the floor. Her screams tore at John's heart, but the sight of her pain paralyzed him. What could he do against such magic? Faye's screams shuddered down into whimpers, then into silence. The flames flickered and died.

Trashcan Harry threw himself at Bennett, but the wounded goblin's attack was crushed by a downward flick of the elf's hand. Harry collapsed in a heap at Bennett's feet. Bennett bent down and lifted the goblin by the throat. With a twist of his wrist he snapped Harry's neck.

"Your part is over, too, pathetic creature," he said as he tossed the lifeless body away.

Trashcan Harry had never had a chance, but he'd shown a courage beyond his strength. Could John do less? He stepped forward and snatched up Caliburn, sweeping the sword up into *en garde*.

Bennett frowned. "What good do you think that will do? It is not yours. It will not protect you."

"No? But then, maybe I've had enough defending."

John's lunge caught Bennett off guard, but still the elf managed to twist lithely away from the attack. The blade did nothing more than slice through his coat. Bennett backed away rapidly, opening space between him and John.

Instead of pursuing, John turned back to Bear. Bear knew the sword, he knew how to use it best. Jamming the sword's grip into Bear's palm, he folded the man's stiff fingers around it and hoped he was doing the right thing.

"Stupid wretch," Bennett shouted.

Fire ate at John's back. He screamed as the pain dug iron spikes into him. He smelled the stench of his leather jacket burning; then another, more awful smell penetrated his agony. He collapsed to his knees, the world blackening around him. Somewhere, very far off, a bell began to toll.

Everything went dark.

After a sensationless interval of unknown duration, John found himself looking up at Bear standing astride him. Bear was brandishing Caliburn—not at John, at Bennett—and shouting.

"Face me alone, elf! We'll settle matters once and for all."

Bennett laughed.

"Another day, Artos. For today, I am content with how the game has played." With that Bennett vanished from sight, winking out like a terminated holoprojection. But like the Cheshire cat's smile, his voice remained for a last echoing comment. "The reign of magic is begun again."

"He is right," said the Lady of the Lakes solemnly.

Bear turned on her and demanded, "What part did you have in this, Lady?"

"I was only an observer."

"You could have defended us."

"The cost would have been too high."

"I had dared think you a friend, Lady. I see I was wrong."

"Wrong is what you are now, Artos. You have more friends than you know. When you arrived, you told me that you did not intend to stay long. Now I think the time has come for parting."

"I have questions," Bear said.

"There will always be questions," the Lady said. "Now, you must go. I give you all health as a parting gift. Return to your earthly realm."

And with that, John stood on a grassy knoll in what appeared to be a small park tucked in the midst of office buildings. His back no longer hurt, and he shivered a little in the cool breeze blowing over his exposed skin. Little remained of his jacket save charred sleeves, and the H & K Viper was gone, left on the Lady's floor to be placed in one of her cabinets, no doubt.

He turned in place for a quick survey of the area. He didn't recognize his surroundings, and none of the others was in sight. Where had the Lady sent them? Wherever it was, he hoped that they had received her healing gift as well. Especially Faye.

He intended to find out what had happened to all of them. Especially Faye. It might not be easy, but he had reason for optimism, for there was something different now.

Very different.

He could smell the magic in the air.

The story will continue in . . .

A King
Beneath
The Mountain

Here is an excerpt from the second book in Robert N. Charrette's exciting trilogy of the clash between magic and high technology. Look for it, available in April 1995, wherever Warner Aspect books are sold.

"Legends are unsubstantiated fantasy," Pamela Martinez said. "Very dangerous in the modern world."

"Unsubstantiated? Not at all." Ryota Nakaguchi was a *kansayaku*, an auditor, of Mitsutomo Keiretsu. His position gave him great power, and he wore that power arrogantly. He had a tendency to pedantic speeches.

"Have you never wondered why there are certain myths that have analogs all over the world? The very persistence and pervasiveness of such myths give weight to their truth. At the heart of such persevering stories there must be a foundation of reality, something true and concrete upon which the stories are built. Consider the legends from all over the world about heroes who lie asleep, awaiting the time that they will walk the earth again."

"The age of heroes is over," Pamela told him.

"Is it? The myths say that the time for heroes will come again. Look at the state of the world today. Could we not use a hero or two? Say, an Arthur with his dream of Camelot, or a Charlemagne to stand against the hordes seeking to tear down civilization. Or a Siegfried, slayer of giants and dragons. Consider what such a man could do today."

"There is not much call for dragon slayers today. A knight in shining armor can't do much against an automatic weapon."

"Your view is excessively narrow. Such a man was not a hero because of mere physical capabilities. A man nearly deified in the memory of his fellows had to be more than a simple warrior. He would have had attributes and skills necessary to make him a great man, a leader. At their core such skills are as applicable today as they were then; people are still people. Such a man would be capable of changing any world he was a part of." Nakaguchi's tone became conspiratorial. "But such a man will need guidance to understand the changes since they last walked the earth, guidance that we must stand ready to provide."

Stand ready to provide? Despite the sun's heat, Pamela felt a chill. "You have found a sleeper."

"Very good, Ms. Martinez. Yes, we found a sleeper, a man who has been in suspended animation through the power of magic. I believe that he is a man who can change the balance of power in the strange new world we face."

"For the good of Mitsutomo?"

With only the slightest hesitation, he responded, "Of course."

"And who is this sleeper?"

Instead of answering, Nakaguchi directed his gaze over her shoulder. She turned to see a heavy-set man approaching. The man wore soiled fatigues and a battered hat and looked more than a little disreputable. He spoke, loudly, before he reached a normal conversation distance.

"It's good you're here." The man spoke Mexican, but his accent wasn't that of the city. His dark skin and hooked nose said he had some of the old blood, so she guessed he was from the southeast part of the country. He gave her a quick, leering glance and spoke to Nakaguchi. "Traveling with amenities, Patrón Nakaguchi?"

Did he know she understood him? Did he care?

3

"Ms. Martinez is an officer of Mitsutomo," Nakaguchi said.

"Sorry, señora. We see few company officers out here." He didn't sound sorry at all.

"Ms. Martinez, this is Joaquín Azaña. Joaquín is the head of the discovery team. He is very well known in certain antiquities circles."

A polite way of saying he was a tomb robber. He certainly had the manners of one. He gave Pamela only the slightest of nods and focused his attention entirely on Nakaguchi.

"You want to see the site today, we must climb now, patrón. There is little time to reach it before dark."

"Surely you have lights up there."

"Ai, yeah. Battery lamps only. Not enough for all night."

"Then we will bring more with us."

Azaña shifted his footing. "There's not a lot of room up there. Best we come back down to the camp before dark."

"Afraid of the dark, Mr. Azaña?" Pamela asked.

"No," Azaña said rather quickly. "It is just the desk people. They will not fare well on the mountain in the dark."

Pamela tucked her hair up under her climbing helmet and tightened the strap. "Then we'd best be going, hadn't we?"

Azaña looked from her to Nakaguchi.

"Ms. Martinez is right."

"Yes, patrón."

They left the camp, walking in a disorganized clump until the path forced a more linear arrangement. Azaña took the lead, with Nakaguchi second. There was a moment of tension when Hagen moved to follow on the heels of his boss, and Duncan stepped in his way. The little man glared, but subsided after a glance at Pamela. She took the third position and Duncan stepped in immediately behind her, leaving Hagen standing there. When Pamela looked back the little man was still standing there, glowering; the rest of Nakaguchi's people had filed past him.

Azaña swarmed up the mountain like a llama, and his previous concern for the "desk people" didn't seem to extend to making allowances for their slower speed. Nakaguchi followed close behind the Mexican and, not to be outdone, Pamela pushed herself to keep up. The Breathe-EZ™ acclimatization tablet she'd taken was improving her oxygen uptake, making the climb less dangerous than it would have been, but the headache starting to pound behind her eyes almost made her long for the altitude sickness she could have otherwise expected. At least then she could have passed out and taken a rest without losing face. As it was, she pushed herself, feeding the headache with her exertion. She wasn't overheating though; the HiClimber™ suit was doing its job and keeping her body temperature comfortable.

The path, where there was a path, grew narrower and more treacherous. The climb became steeper, and their pace slowed. Each time she looked back, Duncan's red-and-white HiClimber was farther and farther behind. One by one, Nakaguchi's drones in their matching blue Rocker™ climbing suits passed him. An hour into the climb, he was trailing the entire group. Hagen, on the other hand, proved to be a superb climber, passing the other aides easily. He slowed his pace as he came up behind her.

"Nice suit," he said. He wore one of the Rocker suits, but she noted that his harness held some nonstandard accessories. "How'd you find out?"

"I've played these sorts of games before."

"I'll remember." He dropped back to leave her climbing room.

The Mexican angled around to the shadowed side of the mountain, leading the troop away from the warming sun. Almost immediately after she stepped out of the sun's direct rays, Pamela felt a warmth spreading from her fanny pack as the HiClimber's heater kicked in. It was cold up here, and only the HiClimber was keeping her from noticing just how cold.

The slope here was gentler, easier to take, but they still climbed for another half hour. If the trip down took as long as going up, she doubted they'd be back to the camp until well after dark.

Ahead she could see Azaña sauntering across a high meadow. By the time she reached it, the Mexican was assaying an almost vertical climb past an old rock fall. Nakaguchi was close on his tail. Azaña reached the top of the sheer stretch, clambered over a mound of small, loose rocks, and seemed to disappear into the mountain side. Nakaguchi dodged a couple of fragments that the Mexican had dislodged and followed, disappearing as well. Pamela trotted across the meadow and scanned the rock above her. No sign of them. She started up. As she neared the top of the old fall, she saw how the pile of small stones had kept her from seeing a small dark opening in the rockface. There was a cave.

She managed to get over the piled rocks without kicking any down on Hagen, who had just reached the base of the fall. Nakaguchi hadn't shown such consideration for her.

The cave entrance was barely a meter high. Piled stones stood in the corners of the opening, suggesting a breached wall. She guessed that the cairn over which she clambered had been made from stones that had once walled over the opening. She crawled into the darkness to join Azaña and Nakaguchi. There was more room inside, enough to stand up. She did, brushing dust from the knees of her Hi-Climber™. Azaña was just turning on a battery lantern.

The light reflected from the walls in thousands of tiny sparkles from the minerals embedded in the stone, revealing a cramped space, barely bigger than a public washroom. It smelled of dust. Scattered about the floor were more stones, many encrusted with what looked like hardened mud. Adobe? More stones still embedded in an earthen matrix were part of a second wall partially closing a narrow cleft in the far wall; there was enough debris to have completely filled the gap. The lantern's light didn't reveal anything beyond the partial wall; she could only see deep darkness through the narrow slit.

"This is where the offerings were?" Nakaguchi asked.

Azaña nodded.

Nakaguchi examined a mud-encrusted rock. "The second wall was intact?"

6

"As I told you, patrón. Solid and undisturbed. Only the ritual holes."

Stone grated outside the chamber, and Azaña jumped. Hagen's short, broad shape appeared in the entrance. He stepped inside, further crowding them, and swept the chamber with his eyes, a disapproving frown on his face. He picked up one of the encrusted stones and poked at the hardened mud. His frown grew deeper.

"Well, Mr. Hagen?" Nakaguchi asked.

"Looks plausible," he declared. "Been inside?"

"Not yet."

"It'll be a while before the others get up here."

Nakaguchi nodded. "Show me the inner chamber," he ordered Azaña.

Azaña edged past him, the lantern throwing strange shadows on the rough walls of the chamber. They had to squeeze sideways to move through the opening into the mountain. Azaña led them through the darkness, his lantern the sole feeble source of light. Pamela didn't like the idea of following Nakaguchi into the darkness, but it was preferable to staying behind and waiting for him to come back and tell her secondhand what he found; he was not exactly a reliable source. Pamela slid down the goggles of her helmet and dialed up the light amplification circuits. It helped some. The lantern now provided enough illumination for her to see where she was going. She was careful not to look directly at the lantern.

When the sounds of Azaña's passage began to echo, she knew they'd come to a less closed-in area. She was relieved. New light blossomed as the Mexican turned on a second lantern. Pamela quickly slipped off the goggles; there was no need to be blinded.

Azaña had led them to a nearly circular chamber almost ten meters across. The walls had been smoothed by human hands and plastered over. They were covered in paintings and glyphs that looked a lot like some of the decorations she'd seen in Mexico City. The paintings were old; a glasslike sheen of calcite lay over some of them where mineral-bearing water had seeped from the rock. It was clear from the tools lying about that some work had recently been done to uncover one of the more obscured paintings.

"They look Aztec," she said.

"They are," Nakaguchi answered absently. He seemed absorbed in examining a particularly convoluted glyph. Hagen took up a lantern and stood by his shoulder, grumbling.

Pamela didn't understand what Aztec paintings were doing here. "Wasn't this Inca territory?"

"As much as it was any tribe's," Hagen said.

"What do you mean by that?" she asked him, but the little man ignored her.

Nakaguchi abandoned the glyph and moved to a door-sized patch of almost undecorated wall. A dark circle was centered in it about ninety centimeters from the floor and there were three smaller dark circles at the bottom, touching the floor. Nakaguchi ran his fingers along the wall's surface and then across—no, into—the central dark circle, revealing it to be a hollow.

"It is intact," he said dreamily. "The oracle hole. The paths of the lesser life. Everything."

"As I told you, patrón. The workers will not break the wall. Oliváres has told them this is a bad place, great magic."

"What would this Oliváres know about it?"

"The workers, they say he is a sorcerer."

"A what?" Pamela asked. She didn't believe she had heard correctly.

"A sorcerer," Azaña repeated.

Two years ago she would have laughed in the man's face. Now, she held her tongue.

"And is he a sorcerer?" Nakaguchi asked.

"I would not know, patrón."

Hagen looked up from the glyph he'd been studying. "Dynamite the cave," he said abruptly.

Nakaguchi snorted. "Don't be ridiculous."

Pointing at the glyphs, Hagen asked, "Can't you read it?"

"Well enough."

Pamela was surprised. "What does it say?"

"It says that this is the place where the feathered serpent awaits death," Nakaguchi replied.

"Dynamite the cave," Hagen repeated, this time more insistently.

"No," Nakaguchi snapped.

Pamela found the split between the two interesting.

In a more reasonable tone, Nakaguchi continued. "If it hadn't been for your help, we would never have found this cave. Now you want to destroy it?"

Hagen glared for a moment, jaw working beneath his beard. "I thought you understood the danger that the sleepers pose."

"I understand the power they offer."

"You're a fool."

"And you're in danger of losing your job."

Perhaps with you, Nakaguchi. Pamela was beginning to see Hagen as a potential ally. But she needed a lot more information. "I asked once before, Nakaguchi. Are you ready yet to tell me who you think this sleeper is?"

"I thought I knew before. Now I am sure."

"And he is?"

"The Mayans called him Kukulcan. The Guatemalans called him Gugumatz. I suppose he is best known by his Aztec name, Quetzoucoatl. Their languages were different, but to all of them, he was the feathered serpent."

"Quetzoucoatl?" Pamela couldn't quite believe it. These sleepers were supposed to be men. Wasn't Quetzoucoatl a god?

"Surely you've had some contact with the legend?"

She had heard stories, but it had been a long time ago. Legends about gods were things of her childhood, long abandoned.

Nakaguchi didn't wait for her response.

"Quetzoucoatl was quite influential in the Central American region, though he wasn't a native. He and his companions arrived by ship from a place far to the east. Since he was black skinned, you should have a good idea of where he actually came from, in a continental way, at least. He was a being with godlike powers who brought an age of peace and plenty. The primitives were saddened when he announced that he could not remain among them, but they were cheered when he said that he would return. They waited for him, making his doings into myth and always remembering his promise to return. When the Spaniards came, the Aztec coast watchers mistook the shining armor of the soon-to-be conquistadors as his sign, their coming a fulfillment of the prophecy of his return. They were wrong, of course."

Pamela knew how wrong the Aztecs had been. Mexico still groaned under the legacy of that fatal error.

Nakaguchi shrugged. "And, of course, he is not a god. Godhood, for him, was merely the inspired awe of a primitive people who had no true understanding of his nature."

Had Pamela heard correctly? "You said *is. Is* not a god."

"Of course I used the present tense, Ms. Martinez." Nakaguchi turned back to the undecorated wall and ran his fingers along the edge of the hollow. "Quetzoucoatl is not dead. He merely sleeps, awaiting the time of his return."

Nakaguchi detached a climbing hammer from his belt. Hagen stepped up to him and, disregarding all corporate etiquette, laid a hand on Nakaguchi's arm.

"If you won't destroy it, at least leave it be."

"Take your hand away," Nakaguchi said coldly.

Nakaguchi's voice was hard as steel and sharp as broken glass. Hagen removed his hand and took a step back. Hefting the hammer in his hand, Nakaguchi stared at Hagen until the small man took another step backward.

Nakaguchi turned back to the wall. Thrusting tool and hand into the darkness of the central aperture, he twisted his wrist to set the alloy spike against some unseen resistance. He tugged. A spidery crack ran from the edge of the hole. Nakaguchi tugged again. Powdery adobe exploded out as a stone shifted in the wall. Nakaguchi wrenched until he ripped the stone free from the wall to fall behind him. Attacking the wall again, he jerked and yanked until he tore another stone free, and another, until he had opened a half-meter hole. He peered through.

"Azaña, the lantern!"

The Mexican stepped up. Pamela crowded closer as well. She had come this far to be in on the uncovering; she wanted to see. Azaña shoved the lantern partially into Nakaguchi's opening. Light speared into the space beyond, to be reflected in a dazzle of ruddy glints from something within the darkness. Pamela gasped when she realized she was seeing a golden face, serene and perfectly composed. Turquoise and emerald studded a headband from which a riot of plumage emerged. The regal face did not so much as twitch or lift an eyelid.

"Quetzoucoatl!" Azaña gasped.

The Mexican jerked back and dropped the lantern, but Hagen caught it before it struck the floor.

Nakaguchi attacked the wall with a will, ripping and tearing until he had removed enough of the stones to squeeze through. Pamela and Hagen exchanged worried glances. Nakaguchi's hand thrust back from the other side.

"The lantern!" he shouted. "The lantern!"

Hagen handed it to him, then squeezed through the gap himself. Pamela had no desire to meet a god, but neither did she want to remain behind with the cowering Azaña. Wondering what sort of fool she was being, she slipped through the opening.

ABOUT THE AUTHOR

Robert N. Charrette was born, raised, and educated in the State of Rhode Island and Providence Plantations. Upon graduating from Brown University with a cross-departmental degree in biology and geology, he promptly moved to the Washington, D.C. area and entered a career as a graphic artist. He worked as a game designer, art director, and commercial sculptor before taking up the word processor to write novels. He has contributed three novels to the BattleTech™ universe and four to the Shadowrun™ universe, the latter of which he had a hand in creating, and is now developing other settings for fictional exploration.

He currently resides in Springfield, Virginia with his wife, Elizabeth, who must listen to his constant complaints of insufficient time while he continues to write as well as to sculpt gaming miniatures and the occasional piece of collector's pewter or fine art bronze. He also has a strong interest in medieval living history, being a longtime knight of the Society for Creative Anachronism and a principal in La Belle Compagnie, a reenactment group portraying English life in the late fourteenth century. In between, he tries to keep current on a variety of eclectic interests including dinosaurian paleontology and pre-Tokugawa Japanese history.